ZERO ROGUE

THE AWAKENED BOOK 5

MATTHEW S. COX

DIVISION ZERO PRESS

Zero Rogue
The Awakened Book 5
© 2014 - Matthew S. Cox
All Rights Reserved

DIVERGENT FATES
—NOVEL—

ISBN (ebook): 978-1-949174-32-8

ISBN (print): 978-1-949174-33-5

The Awakened Series

CONTENTS

THE MORNING AFTER THE NIGHT BEFORE

Broken from a fitful sleep, Aaron's mind struggled to impose order on the chaotic inrush of ambient information. A blur of echoing voices, stomach-churning stink, and cursed bright light coalesced into a single, horrid intruder pounding on the front door of his brain. Soothing cold spread across his cheeks, a herald of consciousness seeping into his being. With it came the stench of hours-old vomit and urine mixed with some unidentifiable chemical that left the taste of walnuts in his mouth. It struck him as strange to taste anything at all, save for the occasional reminiscence of scotch whenever he let out a small burp. He struggled to regain control of his arm, forgetting for several crucial seconds how it worked. As he stared at his hand, a shoe appeared and vanished. The pain of a man's weight on his fingers took a distant, muted back seat to the metaphorical one-ton cargo box balancing on his skull.

A voice sounding as if on the other end of a long, glass pipe came from somewhere far above him. "Sorry, man. Didn't see ya."

Aaron gathered his hand against his face, smiling like an idiot at the smell of whatever-her-name-was. Fleeting images of a grinning young woman peeling a bra off over her head flashed in his mind, followed by snapshots of a stumbling walk to the terminal. He forced himself upright, shifting to put his back to the wall. Light stabbed his brain with the sharp subtlety of an icepick when he opened his eyes.

The man who'd stepped on his hand backed up and stooped over him.

"Want me to call someone?"

Aaron waved with an aimless gesture. "Naw, mate. I'm fine. Morning snuck up on me from behind, is all."

"Whatever, man." The hand-stepper walked away.

For several minutes, he sat, dangling his head between his knees while attempting to massage away the headache and forget the taste of synthetic alcohol mixed with bile.

Blurriness of vision cleared, and he found himself seated on the floor of a PubTran maglev station. The commotion of a crowd congealed in an echoing warp, distorted by the pneumatic *whoosh* of a departing tram drawing air into the tunnel behind it. His brittle mind recoiled from the noise of everyone hurrying. He clamped his hands over his face, fingers kneading skin that felt like a putty mask. A cold spot where his cheek had been in contact with the plastisteel ground throbbed with a paradoxical burning.

A woman's laughter punched him in the back of the brain seconds before the shrill squeal of a small child smashed into his headache with the force of a sledge. The crowd wasn't getting any quieter. Breathing seemed as loud as if a maglev shot down a tunnel between his ears, a deafening roar of air in… air out… excruciating to hear as well as feel.

Right, maybe I overdid it a bit last night.

Aaron cracked one eye open again. Even bracing for it, the harsh light hurt and brought last night's absence of food up to tickle the back of his throat. He blocked off the evil radiance with one hand, too stunned to close the eye. A shield of spreading fingers helped him acclimate to the daylight; moving, disorienting smears of color sharpened into distinct people walking by. Anyone close enough to notice him flashed expressions of concern, disdain, or mirth.

Aaron glanced from person to person, making sarcastic faces at those who still lived humdrum normal. His gaze didn't linger on anyone long enough to perceive a recognizable face, only vague suggestions of age and gender.

A mocha-skinned child, a girl about six, hovered at her father's side over by the platform, watching Aaron watch the crowd. The moment their stares met, she grinned and waved. Aaron offered an unenthused smile, managing to coax a few fingers of one hand to return the greeting. He leaned back, adoring the frigid wall against the top of his head.

The faint hiss of moving air grew in prominence over the din of a few hundred conversations.

"Attention PubTran passengers." A pleasant female voice emanated from everywhere. "The approaching nine-thirty-three is an express to Sector 510 commerce district. For your own safety, please move at least ten paces—"

Wind blasted out of the left tunnel, stealing hats and knocking a few elders and toddlers to the ground. Two hundred feet of gleaming white PubTran maglev, five cars in all, shot out of the tube, blurred across the station, and vanished into the far end, dragging debris in its wake. Despite the horrible sound, the chilly air brought a wave of euphoria. Aaron smiled an idiot smile for the few seconds he could enjoy the breeze, letting the rush of wind and noise lift him out of the PubTran station.

"—not responsible for injury or death resulting from passengers disregarding the yellow safety line. Thank you for choosing PubTran."

He found himself daydreaming of the old days in the stadium, playing for Arsenal. Aaron sprinted after a nine-inch silver frictionless orb skimming inches above a surface of artificial grass. Interlocking panels of alternating pentagons and hexagons covered the outer surface; the five-sided spots opened and closed as the orb spun, creating the illusion that the same three small hover thrusters supported it. He chased the little bot in his daydream, weaving around six defending players in bright red suits bearing the logo of Kurotai Electronics Corporation; the spinning sphere reacted to the prodding of his armored boot like it could read his mind.

Erratic jinking got him past the first four, before he kicked it over the heads of the last two while sliding low. He swung his leg up from the ground early, as if he knew where the orb would go before it went there. The kick was true; the tumbling bot went right where he expected it would. With a loud *clank*, the orb met the tip of his boot and zoomed in an arc.

Only one man remained between it and the goal.

Adoration poured off the crowd.

The defenders had fallen for his wild rush to the side, trying to corner him. Aaron skidded to a halt on his ass, leg in the air, eyes locked upon the silver sphere rocketing off in a graceful arc. The goalie dove, reaching with armor-plated gloves for the easy save, but the orb dipped without warning an instant before contact, striking the turf and bouncing right over him.

Goal—Arsenal.

Game—Arsenal 3-2 in overtime.

The crowd went crazy. Hands grabbed Aaron, hoisting him up over a

4 | ZERO ROGUE

mass of yellow-suited bodies. Flashing lights, orbiting cam-bots, and the dull roar of cheering spectators diminished into the discontented grumblings of two hundred soon-to-be-late commuters and harsh, naked LED bulbs overhead. Someone had shot out the lights years ago and no one had bothered replacing the covers. A weaker rush of air blew the stink of city over him as another maglev pulled in and stopped.

Two men in suits, walking abreast, passed him while muttering about indirium ore shipping rates. A distant woman, only a voice in the sea of bodies, yelled about 'having a deal' and someone 'just couldn't do this to her.' The shrieking drilled at his headache, making him wince. He patted down his severely-in-need-of-laundry formerly nice suit, ignoring the splash of bright red in his breast pocket and thrusting his hand under the jacket. Even the sheen from the blue-black fabric burned his retinas, much less what's-her-name's smalls.

Probing fingertips found metal at the base of the inside pocket, and he withdrew a strip of non-glossy black three inches long and half-an-inch tall. He set his elbows on his knees and held the nameplate in both hands, tracing his thumb over the curved face and the engraved letters PRYCE. Beneath the larger name, the tiny word Allison appeared grey, having collected lint. To the left, an engraved 0 with a sword speared through it as tall as both names, and on the right, a Corporal's rank insignia.

Aaron stared into the flat black surface, puffing on it to clear the dust. Distant feminine laughter echoed in his memories, calling his name.

"Aaron, what are you doing?" She laughed.

A vision of his hands pulling red panties down over caramel thighs.

"Aaron? What are you doing!" She squealed.

He remembered carrying her nude onto the patio, to their tiny hot tub.

"Aaron!" she screamed, "What are you doing!"

Color drained from his face. The nameplate in his fingers shifted away and up, perched on the chest of Division 0 Psi armor. He stared into his wife's terrified brown eyes past the fog layering the inside of her visor—and over the blue ring-dot sight of his E-90 laser pistol. Wisps of blonde framed her face, and tears ran down her cheeks. His arm trembled. Pain racked his head as if an army of tiny creatures scraped knives on the inside of his skull, stripping his brain from the walls of its prison.

"Aaron?" she whispered. "You can fight it. Please..."

His horrified scream drowned out the electric thrum of the laser core.

A split second was all it took for his wife to die on her feet. The laser had left a finger-wide hole at the center of the forehead; her brain boiled away to steam like a blown egg, leaving her skull an empty cavity.

The look of shock and horror in those beautiful brown eyes had haunted him every morning since. Helpless to stop himself, he'd stood paralyzed as she fell to her knees, teetered for a second, and continued face first onto the floor at his feet.

Another woman's laughter broke through the rage and pain. Tall, prominent cheekbones gleaming upon dark brown skin, her pale grey suit shimmering, she threw her head back with a haughty laugh. Thin dreadlock strands of dye-blonde hair hung down to her waist. In his daymare, the braids writhed in a mass of ropey, Medusine serpents, hissing and snapping.

That woman had compelled him to murder his wife, his partner. Burning started at the tip of his brain and crept back; his world vanished, engulfed by searing white light. Aaron muttered, unsure if he spoke for real or only in his head. In the blankness, the scent of a sterile conference room hung, tinted with a hint of hibiscus perfume.

"There was a scream. My head felt like it was going to explode. The building just... vanished."

"Why did you attack six of our own people?" asked the voice of an older female, far away yet loud.

"I... didn't even see—"

A young woman broke the silence. "Aaron?"

"Alli?" Aaron's head shot up.

Glare faded to a destroyed store. The bodies of three salespeople and a handful of customers lay strewn about under slabs of wall studded with thin reinforcing wires. His wife emerged from a cloud of pale dust that hung over the destruction like a mass of angry spirits. He didn't find it the least bit odd that her uniform had become a barely-there pink nightshirt. Short blonde hair framed her angelic face. Allison Pryce, née Dominguez. She advanced, barefoot over jagged fragments of thermacrete, both arms raised, unaffected by the devastation upon which she walked.

His dream-self collapsed to his knees, again in the throes of the pain that tore apart his mind the instant he'd failed to resist the horrible command.

Agony like a red-hot lance impaled his head; his right eye felt as though it had swelled to the size of a frictionless orb before someone lit it on fire.

"Aaron?" She beckoned him with an inward motion from both hands.

"I'm so sorry, Alli..." He broke down in sobs, struggling to reach for her.

He cried out in his mind, begging the dream not to end. Despite the horrendous pain, he wanted to be with Allison, even a nightmare of her.

"Aaron?" The voice changed to that of a man.

His eyes snapped open. No longer did he stand in that awful place, seconds before blacking out from the building pain. Once again, Aaron Pryce sat on the floor of a PubTran maglev station, two feet away from a puddle of semi-dry vomit—probably his. The sharp scent of clove surrounded the man hovering over him. Aaron struggled to raise his ponderous head.

A thin wisp of flavored Nicohaler vapor trailed out of a broad nose, conjuring the image of a dragon pondering fire. Air from another departing tram flapped the man's long green coat and baggy pants, which might once have been camouflage. Aaron lost the battle to keep his head up; in the corner of his eye, police-issue boots from ten years ago tapped. A dark hand squeezed Aaron's shoulder.

"Damn, man. You look like shit."

The deep voice provided the final bit of familiarity his brain needed to understand why this man spoke to him as if they knew each other: his 'roomie,' Darwin.

"Was on the piss last night. This is the morning after the night before."

"Whatever the shit that means..."

Aaron frowned at the tear collected in the engraved letters of his wife's name. He grabbed for the red handkerchief, discovering it not such an item at all when he snapped his hand to unfurl it. Scarlet panties. What's-her-name's smalls.

Darwin laughed, deep and baritone. "At least it looks like you had a good time. Tell me you at least got this one's name? Was it worth it?"

His lips formed a noncommittal smile. "Ugh. It ain't worth it since I's too bevvied up to remember." Aaron squinted at the man's face, surrounded by cruel overhead lights. "Bollocks. What the devil time's it?"

Some inexplicable force pulled him upright. It took him a few seconds to notice Darwin's grip on his shoulders.

"Time to get you cleaned up. In case you forgot after whatever you did t'yerself last night, we got a job to do." He patted him on the chest. "You asked for Shim's help, so you gotta do this."

"Aye." Aaron stuffed the panties in his pants pocket. "Lead on."

2

WORST LAID PLANS

Aaron cringed in anticipation of the last mouthful of synthetic beer, knowing the innocent-looking suds were more than they appeared to be. That last bit would tear out his tongue and beat him with it. A mixture of weakness and misery lingered at the bottom of the metal canister, laced with the paint-stripping flavor of whatever chemical allowed it to go from room temperature to ice cold the instant it opened. He decided against doing that to himself again. Taking the dreaded *final swig* was the act of a desperate man. Aaron would buy a fresh one. He held it at arm's length and saluted it.

"The Crown thanks you for your sacrifice, soldier."

He lowered the empty canister to the table with a *klonk*.

Darwin had squeezed himself up to the bar some minutes ago. When the woman on his right got bored with him, he struck up an easy conversation with an Asian man on his left. Even Darwin couldn't tell if he flirted or simply tried to be friendly. Unlike most of the bars his roommate of circumstance dragged him to when the pale grey cinder blocks got too boring, this one didn't have music that smashed his brain. Usually, these places felt like an experiment on the effects of sonic pressure waves upon gelatinous tissue enclosed in bone.

His gaze settled on a slender woman dancing on a raised platform at the deepest part of the building, flanked by holographic doubles mirroring every move. Her costume consisted of scraps of black fabric cut in leaf shapes, adhered to the critical points as well as a few decorative ones. NanoLED tattoos created the effect of moving fireflies on her arms and torso. She moved with practiced ease, undulating through a routine she'd no doubt done a thousand times. Her intangible backup dancers broke sync, and three forms interlaced in a mesmerizing ballet. Clever holo-projector work made the fireflies appear to leave her skin and circle the performance.

A clatter on the tiny table preceded the fragrance of something fishy mixed with pepper. The plate in front of him contained an inch-thick slab of greyish-pink matter covered in black specks on a bun, next to a mass of fries. Darwin sat opposite him, wiggling his fingers over a huge basket of bright orange wings in some manner of anticipatory ritual. Enough sauce covered them to water Aaron's eyes from three feet away.

"What the devil is this?"

"They didn't have fish and chips, closest they could get."

"Hilarious." Aaron lifted the top bun. "Is this disaster supposed to be a tuna steak, or dare I try to call this thing salmon?"

Darwin stuck a tiny drumstick in his mouth whole. Seconds later, he pulled out a bare bone, which he pointed at Aaron. "It's fish." He wagged the bone at the fries. "Those are chips."

"Not even close, but I've had worse." Aaron resigned himself to the OmniSoy horror. "Flavor is but an illusion."

"Yeah, yeah," said Darwin. "OmniSoy food is like politics. Looks good on the outside, but it's all the same slime inside. No matter how many times you see it, you don't realize it 'til you bite, and then it's too late. I got these wings 'cause they real."

Aaron finished chewing. "Real?"

"Well, as real as they kin get growin' shit in a tank. You know—" Darwin's eyes tracked a peppershaker floating up from the table and gliding into Aaron's hand. "Shit, this would be one freaky chicken if it ever lived… wings bigger than its legs. Don't think I'm ever gonna get used to the Omni."

"Don't feel bad, mate. Neither am I." Aaron forced a cheesy smile and dumped more pepper on the 'fish.'

Darwin shook his head, chuckling while working on a few more wings. "I never in a billion years would'a thought I'd be splittin' rent with a cop."

Aaron scowled at a fry before biting it. "Ex-cop, and you don't pay rent."

"Don't mean it right you just walk inta my place and stake a claim."

"It's not your place. It's no one's place." Aaron smiled. "Besides, it looked empty."

"The fuck you think the point of hidin' in the side room was? I don't want no wrong people getting' no wrong ideas 'bout takin' what ain't theirs."

"Christ." Aaron waved a hand past his watering eyes. "How can you even eat that? Did they spray it with violence inhibitor?"

"A what?"

"Chemical pacification agent." He waved a hand around his face. "Gets in your eyes and throat, burns like bloody hell."

Darwin shrugged. "Whatever it is, it's perfect. Tuna man ain't got no room bitchin' on my wings."

"You know, contrary to popular belief, people from London do eat things other than fish and chips."

"Then why you always whinin' about 'em?"

"This"—Aaron gestured at his half-eaten meal—"is about as far from it as one can get. Besides, I'm grumbling about *good* chips. These sad things are fries, mate. I'd have been happy with a decent steak. Just because I happen to fancy a stereotypical dish does not make me a stereotype."

"Uh huh," said Darwin. "You keep on tellin' yourself that."

Aaron rolled his eyes and took another bite.

"Oh, right." Darwin wiped sauce from his lips, sauce Aaron figured would blister his skin on contact. "Next time we run out to a dive for food, I'll make reservations at the Crystal Swan."

"Now you're just being patronizing." Aaron poked the holo-emitter in the table, calling for another beer.

"Didn't you just drink yourself stupid last night?"

"Aye, but this is witch piss." Aaron plucked the canister from a passing hover tray. "It helps."

"So about that whole rent thing—"

"There is no 'rent thing' as far as I can tell, mate." Aaron took a huge bite, hoping to get it over with as soon as possible. The spongy consistency of the not-fish would only get worse the longer it sat.

Darwin leaned back in his seat. "All right, but I want the master bedroom."

"You chose the small room months before I moved in." He popped the seal on the canister. Frost spread over the can from bottom to top. "It's a bit late for that. There's a dozen apartments on that floor with no one to argue with. You'd have moved out weeks ago if it was an issue."

"That's beside the point." Darwin pointed another bare bone at him. "It was my place before you showed up. Just because you're a cop doesn't—"

"Ex."

"Ex-cop; what-the-fuck-ever, man." Darwin laughed. "You're right about the food. I know this place just past the sector border. Great burritos."

"You've been on me to go there for months." Aaron stared at the roiling froth in his beer. A moment later, he sighed. "Pass."

"Somethin' wrong with Spanish food?"

"No." He took a long swig, trying to force thoughts of his wife away. "Just bad memories."

Darwin gave him a knowing look, one hand on his stomach. "Yeah, man. I hear that. Got a bad batch once myself. Took me awhile to risk it again. Trust me, Sammy's place is clean."

Aaron smirked but said nothing. Explosive diarrhea was as apt a metaphor as anything for what fate had done to his life. His gaze settled on an Asian woman sitting alone at the bar in a short business skirt-suit, gloss white high heels hooked on the lowest ring of her stool. Her expression and body language dared anyone to approach. A small black datapad with a security cover rested on the bar in front of her, bearing a stylized M in a red circle.

"You won't have to worry about rent if things work out."

"Say what?" Darwin looked up from his capsaicin ecstasy.

"If that girl of yours makes good, you can 'ave the lot of it."

"A lot of what?"

"About six hundred grand, give or take whatever I have to spend. It's all I could siphon off the main account when everything went to fuck. Least I can do, mate."

Darwin stared at him long enough for half a wing to fall out of his lips and hit the plate. "You got six hundred grand to throw at me and you're squattin' in the grey? I call bullshit."

Aaron chuckled. "I got a touch more than that, but it's mired up in contracts back in Holloway, not to mention has the government all over it. The six hundred represents the last of my worldly wealth that I can realistically access without anyone noticing."

"What you sayin' man? Sounds like you wantin' ta check out. I thought we settled that bullshit already." Darwin wiped sauce off his hands, unable to suppress a persistent shake of the head. "Nah, man. Feel wrong takin money from a dead man." He cocked an eyebrow. "Almost."

"Oh, I'm not *trying* to snuff-it. I'm just being a realist." He stared over a dollop of ketchup at the tip of a fry, looking past it into the man's eyes. "There's a noticeable difference between *wanting* to die and just not giving a fuck what happens."

Aaron cracked a faint smile as the Asian woman crossed her legs the other way.

Darwin exhaled, deciding to order a beer himself. "Who is this bitch you're after anyway? I saved your ass. You could at least tell me that."

"You shoved me headfirst into perhaps the single most ghastly trash compressor in the city," said Aaron. "I had to burn that suit."

"Yeah, an' those damn cops wanted nothin' to do with searching it, did they?"

Aaron flicked his finger on the side of the synthbeer canister, hesitating as it reached his lips. "Someone I intend to kill." After a long swig, the plain silvery metal dropped out of his vision to reveal Darwin's incredulous stare, forehead bedecked with glistening beads of moisture. "Those wings look hot."

His friend leaned over the table, lowering his voice to a whisper. "This bitch ain't no cop, right?"

That made Aaron smile. "Quite not." Again, he turned his attention to the still-solitary woman. She looked around his age, teasing thirty without making contact with it. Granted, if she had enough money for the Reinventions clinic, she could've been twice his grandmother's age. "So, what's the plan?"

"I need to get the particulars in order. Work out some stuff with Shimmer."

"You do that then." Aaron slugged down the last of his second beer and put the empty canister down as he stood.

"Where the hell are you going?"

"I'm in the mood for sushi."

3

DETARAME

Sleep gave way to idle contentment, basking in a swirl of mild incense and the perfume of the woman at his side; the scent of flowers clung to her hair, battling with the smell wafting from the tray that held their sashimi hours before. Aaron stretched, sliding one arm under his cool satin pillow while staring up at drop ceiling tiles either brown or some bizarre shade of red, of its name a secret known only to artists.

Taking a room at the Alta Pointe Suites had been a risky move. Up until the woman suggested the place, he'd not been inclined to test the skills of Darwin's hacker. He figured she at least verged on competence since his former buddies hadn't yet found him.

Glasses on the nightstand rattled and clinked as a hovercar shot by outside, too close to the building. Aaron tensed at the high-pitched warble of a police siren.

Her breath puffed warm across his chest. She lay on her side with her cheek on one shoulder, hand on the other, curled around him in a posture that said 'this is mine' more than 'protect me.' He traced the contours of her back with his left hand while idly scratching at the pillow with the other. The urge to move, to do anything but enjoy the feeling of silk and woman on his skin, was nonexistent.

Momentary alarm struck him. He glanced left to the nightstand on her side of the bed, and wrapped his mental focus around her sleek, silver

NetMini. Telekinesis lofted it airborne; the device glided without a noise until it hovered over his face. Moving with great care, he extricated his hand from the pillow and keyed in a police override diagnostic sequence. The screen went black and displayed the owner's name, address, place of employment, and several links to her various accounts. Bands of text, cyan on black, scrolled by in alternating Japanese and English.

Kimiko Asada. Right, that would've been embarrassing to forget.

Aaron levitated the device back to where he'd found it and let his head flop to the pillow. She reacted to the motion by emitting a soft, alluring noise. He made it a point not to look at her innocent face; asleep, the woman seemed like an altogether different person than the one he'd brought here. Lost to dreaming, she had the face of a *person*, not a score, not a hard-edged corporate shark in a skirt-suit. Vulnerable, content, feminine—but not Allison.

He looked away from her to the wall where narrow goldenrod curtains shifted in the downdraft from a ceiling vent. The windows, at maximum tint, turned the sky bronze and kept out much of the light of late morning. A few harsh glints flared wherever the sun caught a reflection on a passing chromed advert bot.

Kimiko rolled onto her back and stretched her arms over her head, feet straight out. Aaron shifted onto his side and put a hand on her stomach; her muscles rippled until she went lax.

"*Saido?*" she purred, narrowing her eyes. "*Ima?*"

Aaron cast a helpless glance at his NetMini. Before he could grab it for the translator, she rolled on top of him and raked her nails down his chest.

"*Anata wa akueikyō desu.*"

He chuckled. "Bad influence, right? I've heard that before."

Her hair fell around his head in an ebon curtain as she bent forward to kiss him. His hands went roaming as she gave his lip a playful bite before thrusting her tongue into his mouth. He cradled the back of her head with one hand and they moaned into each other's mouths. Kimiko scratched her blood red nails across his pectorals, leaving raised pink lines. Aaron shifted, rolling on top of her. She tolerated it for a moment before threading her leg between his and twisting him over. As soon as he hit the bed, she pounced. He panted, sweating, clutching the silk sheets in both hands as she reached down between her legs and grabbed his cock, lifting it into position. Aaron gasped, arching his back, waiting for her to lower herself.

The door rattled. *Bang, bang, bang.*

"Shite." He fell flat on the bed. "Forget whoever it is."

Kimiko looked at him as if to ask if he planned to ignore it. He grinned. She eased herself onto him. Aaron moaned. She clutched his shoulders, kissing him as she gyrated.

Bang, bang, bang.

"Aaron, where the hell did you go?" Darwin yelled through the door.

"Bit busy!" shouted Aaron.

Kimiko moved her attention from his lips to the side of his neck.

"Oh, God!" wailed Aaron. He shuddered as she took his hands and placed them on her breasts.

For a minute, they rocked in unison.

A chirp came from security panel by the exit. Kimiko gasped, grabbed the sheet, and spun in an acrobatic whirl that wound up disengaging her from Aaron as well as covering them both up to the neck before the door opened. Darwin, in his tattered glory, stomped in; the door hissed shut behind him. Aaron convulsed, red faced and frozen in mid thrust.

"Christ, man. You're unbelievable." Darwin gestured at them. "Did you forget we have a job to do?"

Aaron, still panting, held up a hand. He tried to speak, but could only wheeze. Kimiko glared at Darwin.

"Don't give me that look." Darwin pointed at Aaron. "You damn well know we had shit to do today. It's almost noon."

Kimiko went pale. She rolled left, grabbing for her NetMini, dragging the sheet away from Aaron.

"Aww, man." Darwin held a hand to his eyes as if exposed to raw sunlight. "I didn't need to see that. Get a goddamn towel."

The moment ruined, Aaron salvaged his dignity and got up. Taking no small delight in Darwin's discomfort, he walked right past him to the bathroom and got into the autoshower tube. Sporting a mischievous grin, he touched the holographic control panel without using his hands, selecting a basic cycle.

"Sorry, mate," he said to his unsatisfied erection. "Couldn't get 'round the goaltender that time."

Hot water, soapy slime, more hot water, and a powerful torrent of warm air left him clean, sober, and disappointed ten minutes later. He plodded into the main room, which seemed much colder than it had before, and recovered the clothes forming a trail from door to bed. Pale light flickered on the walls from the holographic head of an older woman hovering over Kimiko's NetMini.

She sat on the side of the Comforgel pad, wrapped from armpit down in the sheet. He couldn't follow the rapid conversation in Japanese, but her mannerisms seemed deferential. She nodded several times at the ethereal woman. Her apparent superior gave Aaron a sidelong glance as he streaked by and seemed a few degrees less upset with Kimiko. When the call ended, she crept around the room clinging to the sheet while gathering her clothes from the carpet before shuffling into the bathroom.

Darwin moved to the far wall and slid his finger over a silver panel. The windows changed from near opaque to clear in a second, letting in a flood of sunlight.

"Gah!" yelled Aaron. "Little bloody warning please."

"I brought a clean suit." Darwin pointed at a case on a chair.

"You went into my closet?"

"As you so eloquently pointed out yesterday, if it ain't *my* apartment, it ain't *your* closet." Darwin clasped his hands behind his back and pivoted to face him. "You need some sun."

The whirr of the autoshower vibrated in the floor.

"This is tan for London." Aaron removed a dark navy suit from the case and laid it out on the bed. "I'm not so sure about this, Dar."

"What's there not to be sure about?" Darwin paced like Napoleon before his troops. "You need information, which you have no other means of obtaining... Shimmer needs our help. She can get your information, we can help her."

"It's illegal." Aaron, clad only in boxers and one dark sock, felt ridiculous pointing at Darwin as if he had some kind of authority. "It's just..."

"You keep remindin' me you ain't no cop no more. *Ex*-cop, right? What are you glitching on? You sure as hell ain't tryin' to stay clean so they take you back. They don't take back motherfuckers who kill four cops. Get over bein' *the man*, 'cause you ain't *the man* no more."

Aaron glared. He leapt to his feet, waving his other sock at Darwin. "I didn't fuckin' kill her. It was Talis... and"—he slumped, staring down, sock hanging limp from his hand—"Garber brought it on himself. I had no idea it would happen." He scrunched his face up in an open-mouthed gawk. "Wait a minnit. I never told—"

"No, you didn't. I took the liberty of asking Shimmer—"

"Son of a..." Aaron fell on the bed.

Darwin held up his hands. "At least you know she's capable now. If she can get into the police case records, she's gonna be able to do what you need. Get dressed. You look ridiculous."

Aaron slipped into his suit, standing and pulling on the jacket as Kimiko emerged from the bathroom, wearing everything she came in with except for her shoes. She sat on the opposite side of the bed, back facing Aaron. Darwin grabbed his arm and pulled him toward the door. Aaron glanced back at her and pulled his NetMini out.

"How do you say 'I'll call you' in Japanese?"

Kimiko looked up with a sardonic grin. *"Dono yō ni eigo de 'detarame' to iu no desu ka?"*

Aaron's NetMini chirped, displaying the translation. "How do you say 'bullshit' in English?" He tittered a nervous laugh. "You speak English?"

Kimiko made a face as though he'd asked her if she knew how to breathe. "Of course. It is only the people in this country who think it sufficient to know one language."

"Why... what?" Aaron blinked. "You've not said a bloody word in English the whole time."

She slid her feet into her shoes and tapped her heel on the bed. "It was easier to get you to do what I wanted if I acted like a foreigner."

"But..." He looked at Darwin. "But, I—"

Kimiko stood and grabbed her coat. "I know exactly what you were trying to do, but I did it to you first." She winked. "Thanks for a wonderful night."

He feigned a wounded look at Darwin. "I feel so used."

Darwin laughed all the way to the lobby.

Aaron fidgeted in his seat, still not quite rid of the awkwardness of his earlier interruption. He stared off through the haze of Nicohaler vapor hanging in the air, unfocused. Darwin wasted no time attacking his omelet, even the suspiciously symmetrical battered, fried potato nuggets.

"They grow them square," mumbled Darwin over a full mouth.

"What's that?" Aaron snapped out of his fog. "Square?"

Darwin gestured with a fork. "The potato things. This place is high end. Hydroponics." He speared three one-centimeter cubes at the same time and held up his fork. "It's more efficient. Brick-shaped potatoes. Easier to pack."

"Lovely image." Aaron added more black pepper to his. "I thought you were in some kind of mad hurry?"

"Can't pass up an opportunity for real food. Besides, I gotta get you up to speed."

Aaron sectioned off a bit of egg and stabbed it. "This couldn't have waited twenty minutes?"

Darwin flashed an ivory smile. "Had I known before that breakfast was part of the deal, sure."

"Brilliant timing." Aaron washed down his egg with some hot tea. "Nice suit, by the way."

"Rental. Look, you wanna find that bitch, we need Shimmer's help. You want Shimmer's help, we gotta do this thing."

"Yeah, yeah. Infinity Casino."

"I don't get what's up your ass about this, man." Darwin dropped his fork with a *clank* on the empty plate. "We ain't stealing or killing. All we gotta do is plant a Horus on their network so's Shimmer can tap in."

"What do you think is going to happen as a result of that?" Aaron cocked his eyebrow. "Stealing and killing."

"Yeah, but not by us." Darwin drummed his fingers on the table. "Look, Mr. Ex-Cop. How bad do you want this Talis bitch to burn? Yo' ass is plannin' to kill a bitch, and you're freakin' on a little data theifin'?"

Aaron closed his eyes, forcing the image of Allison's last moments out of his mind. "Right." He slugged half a mug of hot coffee and slammed the empty on the table. "Let's get on with it then."

4

CHEATING DARWIN

Aaron leaned against the side of the PubTran taxi as the little car rattled along. In London, ground transport was the norm, yet after two years in the UCF as a Division 0 tactical officer, hovercars had left him spoiled. The thin, plastic bench seat seemed to have a direct link to every bump and pit on the road. Each shock went from tire to frame, to seat, to spine. Adding to the discomfort, the little car smelled like the inside of a well-worn shoe. Ten minutes into their ride, the cloud of clove-scented vapor clinging to his friend became suffocating in the small space.

Darwin, seated to his left, busied himself with his NetMini in the periphery of Aaron's awareness. Gargantuan century towers, hundred-story plus buildings, surrounded them with a canyon of shining glass and plastisteel. His breathing fogged the tiny window. Unconsciously, he squeezed his jacket, clutching the nametag hidden inside the pocket.

"Somethin' interesting in the sky?"

Aaron shifted his weight away from the wall and let his head tilt back. The roof had the same bland grey cloth as the seat, patterned with little teal squares. "Same shite for sale as always."

Darwin swiped onto another screen, highlighting his dark face with orange instead of blue. "You can just say you don' wanna talk about it." His face tinted yellow as the screen changed again. "You with them special cops a while, man. You believe in ghosts?"

"Never really thought much about it." Aaron closed his eyes.

"Hmm," said Darwin. "Ya always hear people sayin' ghosts stick around when they have a bad end."

If ghosts existed, which he doubted, it would mean Allison—or what remained of her—had gotten quite an eyeful of him with other women. What would she think of him now? Drunk more often than sober, on the outs with the law, lost somewhere in a desperate search for revenge. The situation didn't make him *feel* like a criminal, but the brass didn't care. He sighed, finding it more comforting to hope nothing waited on the other side but oblivion.

"'Til death do us part."

"What?" Darwin glanced over. "You mutterin' again."

After Allison, every woman he charmed into bed became another tiny revenge against the gender. He pictured Talis standing half in a doorway, long hay-colored dreadlocks lofting in a casual breeze like some pre-Columbian goddess come to Earth to spite him.

Kill your partner.

Her words echoed in his head, repeating in an endless cycle, alternating loud and soft. The command sped up like a squeaking pixie before plummeting to a demonic timbre. Pain had lanced down his spine as the compulsion warred with his love for his wife. All his strength fought the urge but could not overcome it. His aim changed. Allison only stared at him, pleading with her eyes. She'd had so much faith in his love for her, his ability to resist, she never even tried to move. Right before his finger tensed, a bolt of agony shot from the top of his head down his entire body. Aaron forced himself to picture Talis, to get angry before he turned into a blubbering wreck in front of Darwin.

"We here, man."

Aaron sat up and looked. Bright amethyst light bathed the street in front of the Infinity Casino. The little vehicle whirred past an elaborate entrance bedecked with fountain sprays. Serpents of water leapt between individual pools, flying back and forth over a long stairway split into eight sections between flat areas. Holographic tropical fish danced with Chinese dragons in the air.

The car continued past the edifice, taking a sharp right as it ducked into a sublevel parking area. Pale grey walls slipped by, their monotony broken by the occasional bare metal wire-guide or pipe. Fist-sized floating spheres guided distant patrons to parked cars in a labyrinth of berths stacked three high. Aaron rocked forward as the PubTran braked hard in a yellow-striped patch adjacent to a walk path by the elevators. 'PubTran Lane' repeated in painted letters every six feet, and a flickering holo-panel depicted a smiling cartoon sphere, offering 'car locator assistance' for forty credits.

"Thank you for using PubTran Taxi. Have a pleasant day," said a placid female voice.

A gull-wing hatch, most of the right side of the tiny car, opened. Aaron got out and straightened his suit. He frowned at the Arsenal F.C. pin below the lip of the breast pocket. The act of getting out of a car made him remember the blinding flashes from a legion of news-orbs blaring lights in his face.

"Come back to Earth." Darwin patted him on the shoulder. "Since we're here, I got a idea."

Aaron followed him into the elevator. "Oh, this couldn't possibly go wrong."

"Shimmer's set us up with a dummy account. She hacked in some credits for us to have fun with. We gonna get paid for this little foray."

"If she can just hack money in, what's the point?"

Darwin thrust a gesture at the door, face twisting in an effort to disguise frustration. "She ain't makin' it outta thin air. Skim too much and it gets noticed." He straightened up, waving both hands in front of himself as if showing off an elaborate scene. "We need to diversify our assets."

"I don't think that means what you think." Aaron chuckled. "You want to gamble."

"Naw, man." Darwin gave him a playful punch in the arm. "Gamblin' implies risk. I wanna make money." He leaned in close. "You's a telekinetic, right?"

"I've been called worse."

Darwin grinned. "Ever play roulette?"

Ping.

Aaron greeted the busy casino floor with a beleaguered sigh. Anyone watching at that moment would have assumed his boss just told him he had to work a sixteen-hour shift for the sixth day in a row. He stood still as Darwin surged forth onto the black and maroon squared carpet, basking in light and music, the fragrance of alcohol, and a cacophony of electronic gambling.

"Come on, man." Darwin beckoned with a wave.

"Can't this wait 'til after?" Aaron fidgeted with his jacket as he emerged from the elevator.

"I gotta scope the place out a bit. Schematics only go so far."

Aaron raised an eyebrow. "No virtual tour?"

"No plug." Darwin pointed behind his ear.

They walked astride into the main gambling hall. Aaron pivoted to keep his face away from a woman in a clingy black suit. Flickering light inside her eyes hinted at some manner of scanning cybernetics. Casino Security. If she ran his image in the system, Division 0 would tag him. He followed Darwin past a gauzy violet curtain, which turned out to be a hologram hovering between a pair of ornate columns resembling silver cubes emerging from obsidian. Once he had wall between him and security, he relaxed. Darwin stopped short, causing Aaron to bump into him. He pondered the unmarred skin behind Darwin's ear, hidden under a frizz of greying afro.

"How is it a man in your line of work doesn't have an M3?"

"Do you got one?"

"No, but I'm psionic," muttered Aaron, a response drowned in the ambient noise. *No, I'm a psionic. Cybernetics, especially brain implants, don't play nice.* "It messes with my chi."

Darwin broke out in a sweat at hearing Aaron's voice in his head.

"You forgot already?" Aaron flung an arm around him in a buddy hug, talking into his ear. "You look like you just saw a ghost."

"That's just strange shit." Darwin rubbed his face. "Look, you head over to that table there an' get started. Don't do too well. I'ma check around a bit before I join in. This'll work better if the guy runnin' the thing doesn't know we're together."

Aaron scanned the room. Six security men, all in black suits, stood at regular intervals around the gambling hall. Not one of them had surface thoughts, though they looked like ordinary humans. That meant either synthetics or military-grade dolls. The only way to find out would be to try to kill one, something he had no plans to do. He breathed a sigh of relief. As dangerous as they were, machines had no way to detect a psionic at work.

Darwin wandered off into the crowd. Aaron filled his lungs, gave the flashing maroon-tiled ceiling a contemplative stare, and approached the bar. By the time he had a vodka tonic in hand, Darwin returned and handed him a device resembling a half-sized NetMini displaying the logo of the casino, a silver infinity mark rotating in the center of a one-by-three inch black screen. The device linked to a private account, separate from the InterTrust Commerce Facilitation Corporation, which managed most of Earth's intangible money.

In his hand was anonymity.

"Half hour, maybe forty-five minutes." Darwin headed into the crowd again.

Aaron sipped his drink, astounded at how many people packed a casino at one in the afternoon. *Seems like the only people with money are the ones without jobs. How does that happen?* Wearing a grin halfway between nervous and ironic, he sidled up to the roulette station Darwin had indicated before. People slinging around big credits tended to prefer physical games of chance as opposed to digital ones. Pervasive suspicion regarding rigged program code kept the true high rollers away, but for every body at a table, a hundred more lurked in cyberspace.

A small white ball bounced around the rotating wheel, hopping partitions before settling on a spot.

"Twenty, black," said the croupier.

The players grumbled.

From an interested, but uninvolved distance, Aaron observed several spins before advancing on the table. The uniformed man running the wheel gave him a curt nod and spun it. Others called out bets. Chirps emanated from their tiny devices and holographic chips appeared on the layout. Aaron put two chips on the split 31–32. The attendant flung the ball around the track. Aaron fixed on it but only teased at sensing its weight.

"*Rien ne va plus,*" said the croupier.

Aaron suppressed the urge to roll his eyes. The ball eventually bounced to a halt on three, triggering another series of groans. A holographic dolly appeared floating over the square, near no chips.

He took small sips of his vodka tonic, enough only to get the taste on his tongue. After four more spins, telekinetic fiddling landed the ball on his bet, winning enough to recover what he'd lost plus a tiny gain. A petite woman with deep midnight blue hair down to her knees and chalk white skin tucked up near him two spins later. Her dress, a black ribbon attached to a metal choker, wound about her lithe figure, existed in defiance of gravity. The sight of her reminded him of his earlier interruption with Kimiko.

"Sorry," she whispered after she bumped his drink.

"My fault." Aaron smiled, savoring the fruity scent clinging to her hair. "You know, they say these games favor the house."

She put six chips on a 28-29 split, and two on the top line. "So I've heard."

He tossed one on twenty, inside.

The croupier spun the wheel as a few other holographic chips appeared.

The woman held on to the side of the table, tapping her foot and glaring at the ball. Aaron listened to the tip of her thoughts: simmering anger at a boyfriend who continually belittled her artistic endeavors and exhaustion after a twice-delayed shuttle flight from Mars.

He shifted his attention to the orbiting ball and his weight toward her. "You know, they also say kissing an Englishman is good luck."

"Do they now?" She gave him a sidelong glance, causing a gleam on her azure lipstick. "What makes you think I'm in need of luck?"

The ball settled on 21.

"Oh, just a hunch." He pursed his lips as the losing chips vanished. "Aetheria?"

Her mouth opened a touch as she stared.

"It's quite a beautiful name, but it hardly matches you in person." Aaron winked.

"How...?"

"I thought I saw you at the exhibit," said Aaron. Her eyes widened, more answers flooded to the surface of her thoughts. "Primus City, Mars... what was it, four months ago? Didn't some pompous ass in a Yoshnori suit make a scene about... that piece with the mermaids?"

Chirps signaled the placing of bets.

Faint traces of pink appeared on her face, and her eyes narrowed. She looked away, glaring at the layout.

"Three-dimensional study of the feminine aquatic amid chaotic orbitals." Aaron brushed his chin. "I suppose 'Mermaids in Space' would've have sounded too academic."

Aetheria burst out laughing.

He placed no bets this turn, instead tapping a finger to his lip. "It makes an interesting corollary. Comparing space faring vessels to ancient sailors' legends of sirens luring men to their deaths upon the rocks. That fool missed the symbolism and went straight to complaining about how they'd not be able to breathe."

"I know!" She faced him. "Lancaster's so obsessed with his neo-realist snobbery, anything with a whiff of abstraction is subpar."

"*Rien ne va plus*," said the croupier.

She leaned her hip against the table, staring at the bouncing ball flying over the pockets in the wheel. "My name isn't that pretty. Aetheria is a wide-open field of nothing west of Elysium. A desert."

"I think it's a lovely name. I knew you were an artist. You have expressive eyes and those delicate hands."

Her head dipped forward. Aaron cringed. *Too much.* She flipped up, tossing her hair back and pinning him with a mischievous grin.

"Of all the men that've approached me tonight, you are the most determined." Aetheria stretched, arching her back. "Head implant? Running my face through the GlobeNet looking for facts?"

"Not at all. I will confess to making a clumsy attempt to win your attention." Aaron laced his fingers together and leaned one elbow on the table. "Forgive me; your presence had rather intoxicated me beyond reason. I've not a whiff of cybernetics. I find talented, independent women irresistible."

Aetheria gave him a disbelieving smirk and squeezed her casino mini. Ten chips appeared on 20. "All right, mister…"

"Pryce." He smiled a hopeful little smile.

"Pryce." She slipped her fingers into his jacket and grabbed a fistful, pulling him down to her stature. "Boys aren't the only ones who sometimes need a little stress relief. Let's see about that luck then. Twenty black comes up, and you got yourself an evening."

She stretched up on tiptoe and kissed his cheek like the Blarney Stone. A tentative gesture, but a kiss nonetheless. Aaron tracked the ball out of the corner of his eye, nudging it with the faintest hint of telekinesis. Aetheria pulled away a few inches, her stare hungry, mouth open.

"Twenty black," said the croupier.

Awe, shock, worry, and a trace of regret collided on her face. She gawked at the tiny sphere sitting in the wheel, right on her bet. Aaron patted her hand where she held on to the table.

"Sometimes bluffs get called." He stooped to put his lips at her ear. "Told you, it's good luck to kiss an Englishman."

Aetheria flashed a nervous smile at the croupier as her ten chips multiplied to three hundred and fifty. "Well, I suppose I should quit while I'm ahead."

He took her hand, drawing it up to his face, and kissed her on the back of the fingers. "You weren't expecting that." He winked. "It's fine if you don't want to do anything. Please don't feel uncomfortable on my account."

Tension seemed to flow out of her.

"If you happen to change your mind, meet me at the bar in an hour or so. No obligation."

"Nice meeting you." Aetheria left the table, glancing back over her shoulder at him twice on her way to the elevators leading to the hotel.

"Please clear the table if you're done, sir," said the croupier.

Aaron put a few chips out at random, not caring where the ball went. Once the elevator closed, he looked around the room for Darwin, finding no trace of him. For a while longer, he played, nudging the miniscule white sphere once to get back to breaking even. Around the time he'd almost had enough of studying a tiny ball bouncing around a spinning wheel, Darwin emerged from a doorway marked 'Employees Only' and blended into the crowd.

Handheld minis chirped as bets appeared. Aaron glanced over the sea of faces for any sign of Darwin as he absentmindedly set a four-chip bet on twenty black. The croupier gave him a sympathetic look, but the 'girl that got away' wasn't on his mind.

Darwin stepped between a short, pudgy man in a suit and a wealthy-looking six-foot woman who appeared drunk, stoned, or both. Aaron cocked an eyebrow, unable to follow how the man had gotten across the room without notice.

How'd it go?

His friend jumped at the unexpected telepathic voice. After the subsequent shock wore off, he thought about his exploration and the path to the computer room downstairs. Everything in the man's memory made it seem quite doable. A security guard or two, which shouldn't be much of an issue at all. It didn't take a lot of telekinetic power to jog a brain enough to knock someone out. That he could do even before his... incident. Finesse had always been his forte. Of course, if he had to, he could also fling a bloke out a window with ease. Months ago, lifting a man at all would've been tiring as hell. Satisfied with his reconnaissance, Darwin wanted to make some side money, though his motivation surprised Aaron. He intended to give whatever he won to his twenty-year-old son, Kurtis. A too-little, too-late gesture from an absent father.

Aaron's prepared rationale for talking Darwin out of his idiotic scheme crumbled.

What's the plan?

Darwin didn't jump that time. He locked eyes with Aaron and

concentrated on a series of incremental, but small, wins leading up to a huge single payout.

Right, then. When you want to hit, do something as a signal.

His friend thought about Jesus. While Aaron didn't have much of an opinion on religion at all, his roommate despised it. More than once, he'd been kept up late listening to the man rant—Darwin considered it a conversation—about how the 'two percent' used religion to control people. He had grinned and nodded his way through the diatribe, waiting for the man to run out of steam and wander off scratching his ass. In Darwin's mind, it was his turn to use God to get something for himself.

If there *was* some sort of higher power up there, Aaron figured he better not piss it off. He caught sight of a blonde-haired Latina and shied away; she could've been Allison's distant cousin by appearance. If any supreme being *did* exist, he, she, or it was a fucking bastard for taking her away.

Better not to think about it at all.

They played three rounds, letting fate have their way with them, which wasn't a kind process. Darwin put four chips on 11-14, and flung his arms in the air over the layout.

"Come on, Jesus! Hear me now," he bellowed.

Aaron made sure the ball landed on fourteen. Darwin took his sixty-eight chips, putting ten on 31-33, street. He didn't invoke the Lord, so Aaron let the ball do what it wanted to do. Darwin put on a show of exaggerated disappointment. He threw away another ten chips before dropping ten more on thirty-one black.

"Come on, Jesus. Thirty-one black." Darwin buckled at the knees.

Aaron guided the ball to thirty-one black.

Darwin hit the ground, wailing like the bastard son of a holo-net minister and a faith healer. Aaron glared at his own twelve-chip loss and cursed. When he recovered from his 'presence of God' routine, Darwin put twenty chips on 27-30. Half the table joined him, as did Aaron.

No Jesus, no manipulation. A few other players grumbled and one walked away. A member of the security staff wandered over after the croupier did something at his terminal. A flick of the eyes set the artificial person's attention on Darwin. Even this close, Aaron still couldn't tell if the security man was a synth or a doll. Given the money floating around the Infinity, he assumed doll.

More expensive and more dangerous.

They let several more rounds go by with moderate losses before Darwin put his twenty-one remaining chips inside on zero and invoked Jesus. His eyes rolled back into his head as he pantomimed a seizure of divine influence, while Aaron bet on four black. Everyone gasped as the ball landed in the zero pocket and the pile of tokens bloomed up to 756. The doll had been staring back and forth between the wheel and Darwin. Several more players wandered away to other tables. The doll moved to Darwin's side, whispering.

Seven hundred and fifty-six thousand credits out of thin air. Aaron made an appraising smirk. *I can see why people get addicted to this.*

"No way, man. It's God lookin' out for one of his own." Darwin pointed up. He wagered 700 chips on two.

"Apologies, sir, I'm afraid that exceeds the house maximum bet," said the croupier. Darwin's indignant expression had barely formed before the man reacted to a voice in his ear. "I apologize again, sir. Management has decided to take your bet."

"Don't be an idiot," droned an aristocratic older woman. "They want their money back. Walk away while you can."

Darwin bet anyway, grinning. "Praise Jesus."

The croupier spun the wheel. Four of the six remaining players at the table, including Aaron, put chips on two. As much as he cringed at making his own bet win, it would look suspicious to be the only player not following the sheep.

Darwin looked at Aaron; Aaron watched the ball leave the croupier's hand as he tossed it into the track. Everyone at the table leaned in, afraid to breathe as they stared at the ball racing around the wheel. A tall woman in a painted-on red dress bet on 10-11-12.

"*Rien ne va plus,*" said the croupier.

"Dammit, just say bets are closed," roared a fat man in a cloud of genuine cigar smoke. "We ain't in France."

Aaron forced himself not to smile as he caused the ball to linger on the partition between twenty-one and two for several agonizing seconds. When it fell into the two bucket, Darwin howled praises to God. He fell to the ground kicking, thrashing, and cheering for several seconds. Seven hundred chips, paid out at thirty-five to one odds, became twenty-five thousand two hundred. At a thousand credits per chip, twenty-five million and change.

"Hey, what the fuck?" shouted Darwin.

The noise dragged Aaron's attention away from the tiny white ball. A slender Asian man had taken up position flanking his friend; the doll had grabbed Darwin's arm. After gazing deep into Darwin's eyes, the new arrival looked right at Aaron. One second later, the diaphanous presence of incoming telepathy caressed Aaron's mind—a surface read. As Aaron's chief thought at that moment was eluding detection as a cheat, the man had him dead to rights. The security man dragged Darwin away.

"Come with me," a light flared in the man's eyes.

Energy built up in the forefront of Aaron's mind. A psionic compulsion burrowed deeper into Aaron's thoughts, searching for how many people were involved in the fraud. Before Aaron could scream in warning, a crack of thunder tore through his brain, mixing with an anguished scream. He clamped his arms around his head and collapsed to his knees. A violent release of power lapped at the periphery of his consciousness, fringed with burning as though molten steel poured over his skull.

Aaron rocked back on his heels, screaming at the ceiling. A rush of air and debris came over him and blasted away. Distant sounds of smashing glass and splintering furniture mixed with howls of pain and the buzz of destroyed electronics. Smoke choked off his breath. Other screams pierced the veil of delirium; hot tears ran from the inner corner of both eyes. He swiped his hands at his face; bright red fingers came away.

Swaying on his knees, Aaron opened his stinging eyes and peered at the room around him. Moaning people and smashed furniture had stuck in the walls, hanging out of cracked holes. A severed leg twitched on the carpet in front of him. The energy pulsing out of his head throbbed in time with his pounding heart, lessening with each beat. Shuddering from the effort, he looked up. Bodies and chairs crashed to the floor, some peeling away from bloody splat patterns on the wall. Sparks spurted from the ceiling, falling like comets amid a thick haze of smoke. Warm liquid covered him; blood had sprayed everywhere, running down his cheeks and dripping off his chin. The pattern in the maroon carpet, tiny black diamonds in a regular grid, mesmerized him. Soon, the rug flew up to greet his face.

"What the shit was that?" asked Darwin in a choking wheeze, minutes or maybe hours later.

Aaron moaned. One hand flapped like a beached tuna trying to flop itself back into the ocean. The pressure of Darwin's arms circled his chest, lifting him upright. Chaos exploded around him as the fugue of disorientation churned.

Darwin dragged him across the floor, grabbing at his shirt. "We'z outta here, man."

"Mmmff! Arpfh! Ey!" Aaron raised a pointing finger in a gesture of triumph… and passed out amid the distant wail of sirens.

5

BUTTING HEADS

Aetheria closed her eyes and tilted her head to expose her neck. Aaron kissed his way over her jawline and down to her collarbone as she reclined. Her fingernails raked at his back, building an uncontained need for her. She rolled, letting him get on top. He shuddered as her legs wrapped around his, and they became a single undulating mass.

She pushed up on his chest, staring into his eyes. "I want this to last forever, Aaron. Tell me you love me."

He flashed a weary smile and threw up onto her face.

Or, at least, what he dreamt was her face. One eye popped open, focused on bubbles forming and dying in the pinkish-orange mess painting the pillow he had been kissing. It took close to a full minute to process the state of lying in a puddle of puke. His discontent with his current situation manifested as a "harrumph," which flung some of the vile substance onto the wall.

Aside from being cheek-deep in such a mess, he felt fine. That lasted until he attempted to move. No sooner had he rolled over and sat upright than the room whirled about in a frenetic blur, triggering a bout of dry heaving, cold sweats, and convulsions. A dull ache lingered inside him; his skull and spine had gotten into a bad argument, and he couldn't tell which won.

His eyes focused between the fingers covering his face, recognizing his jacket and pants draped over the back of a chair at a small, bent desk. Between the lack of blood and the layer of thin plastic, it looked like Darwin had sent it off for cleaning. Trust that man to know a laundry that wouldn't ask questions when receiving a blood-drenched seven-thousand-credit suit.

Pea-green walls streaked brown from old condensation trails. Perhaps mercifully, only the presence of his own spew registered to his nose. Visible bloodstains and missing patches on the threadbare carpet coupled with the 'artwork installation' on the ceiling above the bed—about twenty old condoms—made him thankful he couldn't enjoy the aromatic ambiance of his surroundings.

Somewhere outside, two men carried on a shouting argument drifting back and forth from English to Spanish, with a little Russian added from a female. They sounded some distance away, but the noise still tore at the inside of his eyelids.

At least whoever was responsible for his being in this room had left him his boxers. The rest of his clothes: shirt, socks, shoes, sat in a pile on the seat of the chair, also in plastic. He pinched his nose, trying to clear the lingering nasty. Soft orange light below him melted to red as the Comforgel pad increased its heat. He found the lack of a sheet unusual, but the powered sleeping surface compensated.

"Kinn'ell... I didn't drink that much." He pressed on his temples, kneading. When he looked in the direction of the battered nightstand, a small silver bar chirped and displayed holographic numbers. 5:19 a.m. "Shit."

He slid to the edge of the bed, slinging his legs over the side with a belabored moan. Every muscle in his body hurt, as if he'd attempted to go from couch potato to paramilitary specialist overnight. Memory of the casino peeked out from behind the slats of a fence of denial. He hadn't imbibed; his brain had turned traitor.

His toes slipped over rough carpet fibers, clenching for a second before he risked putting weight on his legs. They failed. Aaron slithered to the floor with the kind of moves popular among intoxicated youth attempting to dance. His involuntary mosh left him tasting the rug: foot mixed with a hint of something fruity.

At least it was a woman's foot.

He crawled, gripping fistfuls of hairy carpet, and dragged himself into a tiny bathroom where the floor went from rug to dingy synthetic vinyl, stained and sticky. One hand reached up to the sink, testing its stability.

Satisfied, he grabbed it with the other and hauled himself upright, leaning his hips against it for support. Above the sink, a dust-covered mirror muted the wretch staring back at him.

"Well now," said Aaron to his reflection. "If I was to take a role in a zombie holo, I'd not need much makeup."

He pulled at his eyelids, admiring the shade of crimson before rubbing a handful of cold water over his face. Four more handfuls brought increasing levels of consciousness, until he leaned both hands on the sink again, watching the water drip from his nose and chin. Mirror Aaron glared back at him with a scolding curl of the lip.

"Ripping off a casino? Really, mate? You've done some dodgy shite before, but that's a right schoolboy howler."

"What the hell does that mean?" asked a woman's voice, muffled and with the rasp of a sore throat.

Still holding most of his weight on his arms, Aaron shifted, looking to his right. A girl with frizzy, bright pink hair and protruding ribs slumped in the bottom of an autoshower tube that had seen better days. Glowing azure NanoLED tattoos of stars overlapped each eye, making the rest of her face seem dark. Red furry handcuffs represented the entirety of her clothing. She looked somewhere between sixteen on a small amount of drugs or maybe twenty-five on a shitload.

A sheet covered in frightening stains circled the tube twice, held by a fist-sized knot.

The way his body felt at that moment, he had no reaction to the sight of a naked woman; rather, he found her presence in the shower annoying as she delayed the application of hot water to his hide. Contrary to his libido, the tiny thread of lust rearing up in his mind reminded him of the dream and a vomit-soaked pillow. He gurgled and looked away, managing to get the streamer of bile to land in the sink. Creaky gears struggled to turn in his head; iterating the steps necessary to enter and operate an empty shower tube would've been a challenge.

It took him over a minute to understand the meaning of the tied sheet. Someone wanted her trapped in the autoshower.

"It means I did something right fuckin' spacky."

She kicked the plastic tube. "What?"

"Stupid."

"Why didn't you just say stupid then?"

Aaron looked at himself in the mirror. "I did."

"No, you didn't, you said 'spackle' or whatever the fuck that was about howling schoolboys."

He moaned. "So, what're you then, the shower fairy or the spirit of sarcasm? Did Darwin leave you there as some kind of sex-type hair of the dog arrangement?"

The tube rattled as she struggled to her feet with her arms locked behind her. "Who the hell is Darwin? I'm Strawberry." She banged her knee on the plastic door. "Fucking bastard..."

"The pleasure's all mine, lass." Aaron tested his legs again, deciding to keep trust in his arms for a few minutes more.

"Not you, jackass. The motherfucker from last night." She growled. "I should'a known better than goin' with a damn Driftwraith."

Aaron grimaced. "What the bloody hell is that?"

"Some shithead neotek motherfuckers that operate outta Sector 214. They spend more time in the 'net than out, an' usually only come 'round here for cheap pussy and chems."

"So, that makes you—"

"Fuck you, too." She slammed her knee into the autoshower door again. "Fucker stole all my shit. Talked me into some kink and slipped me something. The cocksucker didn't pay either. Monro's gonna fuck his shit up." She threw her weight at the door twice. "Hey, pretty boy, are you gonna leave me in here?"

"No, you're in my way. I want to shower."

"Oh, I'm *real* done with it. All yours." She kicked the tube again. "What are you waiting for?"

"The ability to stand." He threw another handful of water over his face.

"Don't get any creepy ideas either. Monro will kill you too."

There aren't enough condoms in the world. "No. I'm barely ambulatory."

"Come on dude, speak English. I don't got my 'mini on me to translate."

Aaron's gaze begged his reflection for a reprieve from stupidity. "Only reason I'm on my damn feet now is this sink. Did you happen to notice how I got here?"

"Someone carried you in, I think. I heard someone muttering, but it wasn't you. They were gone before I woke up enough to yell... and you were out. An hour of screaming didn't wake your drunk ass up."

Dammit, Darwin. You picked a right five-star hotel, didn't you? Aaron took a deep breath and let his weight settle into his legs; every muscle from thigh to calf tensed and shuddered. He stared at the two bolts holding the sink to the wall, mentally threatening them with doom if they failed and dropped him. The reek of an unflushed toilet gave him a clue his senses had resumed working. Aaron lost a minute attempting to poke the flush button with his toe.

"Holy shit, you're ruined. What'd you dose?"

"Took a big hit of telepath." He massaged the bridge of his nose, flaking away dried blood from the corner of his eyes.

"That some new shit? Ain't heard of it before."

"Uhh, yeah."

He leaned away from the sink, flailing his arms to steady himself. Once confident he wouldn't fall as soon as he tried to move, he staggered to the tube. The blurry woman on the other side of fogged plastic looked thin and bruised. Despite her situation, she tapped her foot and huffed as though he was the one being rude. She was in *his* room, taking up *his* autoshower tube that he wanted to use.

If not for her being in his way, he'd not have bothered getting himself involved with a prostitute who didn't return from a job. Somewhere, a pimp was on the hunt, and he didn't feel like absorbing assumed blame. Unfortunate happenstance put this woman between him and a shower. That's all women were anymore, problems in his way or something to use for a night. A derisive frown twisted his lip while he picked at the knot in the sheet. He lacked the patience or coordination to untie it, and her impatient bouncing tits didn't help him focus. After a minute of picking and pulling at it, he went caveman and tried to tear it off. Strawberry laughed.

"Look, just be quiet for a tick, eh?" He slapped the tube.

Strawberry gave him a raspberry.

Aaron figured attempting to squat would end up with him on the floor, so he took a knee. Precision had always been his forte with telekinesis. He studied the knot, interpreting the folds of cloth each time the image faded to clarity from the perpetual blur coating his world. A few nudges in the right place loosened the fabric enough to get a finger in and pull it open.

Strawberry shoved her way out, knocking him over backward in a wash of humid fruit-scented air. He lay still amid a blinding dance of flashing lights as she stormed across the bedroom to the door. The migraine faeries fizzled out to faint light spots, which lingered for another moment. Handcuffs clicked when she tried to reach for the doorknob. Strawberry looked down at herself, and sighed.

"Shit." She paced around the bedroom and nudged drawers and cabinets open with her foot. The more she searched, the more she cursed under her breath. "I can't fuckin' go outside like this. Dammit, I think the key was in my purse." A frustrated scream accompanied metallic rattling. "This is the last god damned time I let some asshole talk me into doing kink."

"Not my job anymore." Aaron rolled onto all fours and stood up, again using the sink to keep from falling over. "You should file a police report." He pushed the bathroom door closed.

"Ha, ha," she yelled.

The faint sound of an angry woman stomping continued as he shirked off his boxers. The inside of the autoshower reeked of chemical strawberries and sweat. He managed to get one foot in the tube before she barged in.

"I'll give ya a freebie if you can get these offa me." She shook her wrists at him.

"What, am I supposed to magic a key out of my ass?" He pulled the hatch closed behind him.

"Come on!" She got her toes around the handle, pulling the little door open before he could hit the start button.

"I've seen toms traipsing about with less on than you're wearing. Just go. Cops don't care."

"Less? I'm naked!" she screamed.

"You're wearing those fuzzy things. They weren't, so that's technically less."

Strawberry fumed. "Don't be an asshole. What am I supposed to do?"

He let his forehead rest on the cylinder. Because of her, it wasn't comfortable and cool—it was warm and smelled like hours of screaming. Once again, she delayed his soapy, pleasurable respite. "Oh, I dunno, maybe not be a prostitute?"

She glared, stunned, her face warping into an expression suggesting she might cry. After a couple of stuttering gasps, she turned red and yelled, "You think this is a fucking choice? You think I wanted this life? I never had the money to go to school and all the corporations give all the shitty jobs to dolls they don't have to pay."

"If you put half as much effort into bettering yourself as you do into blaming the world, you'd not be stuck naked in a grotty motel."

Strawberry kicked the tube, causing a sound like a thunderclap to squish his brain. "What the shit am I supposed to be doing then, Mr.

right-here-in-the-same-grotty-motel-with-the-worthless-whore?"   Her lips quivered; her voice faltered to a near-whisper. "What the fuck does grotty mean, anyway?"

He pressed the start button, but got a 'door open' error. "Shitty, poor, dirty... Did you consider military service or signing up for colony settlement? Some companies pay for the transport."

"I don't wanna die for someone else's war... and I'm afraid of space. It would just be my luck I'd never wake up from stasis."

She's going to keep whining at me until she's gone. "Why hasn't he come lookin' for you?" he muttered against the wall.

Her voice changed from antagonistic to pleading and sweet. "Munro doesn't work like that. He waits and gets you when you're not expecting it. Come on, I just need these damn things off."

The cuffs were toys, non-electronic things with a physical lock, far flimsier than police-issue binders. Any time he'd had to defeat a lock, it was electronic and surrendered to a police override code. Old style ones like this were a rarity, though some still practiced the art of picking. Darwin would probably know how or, at least, know someone who did.

"'Ave a seat on the bed. Buddy o' mine'll be able to get it open."

She stared at him. "I can't just wait around here. If he comes looking for me, it'll be my ass even if it ain't my fault."

With an irritated groan leaking from his nose, Aaron stumbled out of the tube and grasped the chain between her wrists. He had been used to his telekinesis having enough power to knock a man over or carry about fifty pounds. An aug could snap the chintzy things with ease. He started to wave her off with a resigned 'not my problem' echoing in his mind, but hesitated. His telekinesis shouldn't be able to fling a roulette table through a wall either. The continued scraping of her high-pitched voice became more painful than any psionic aftershock that might occur if he used his gift.

"It might hurt."

She twisted to peer over her shoulder at his crotch. "Not bad, but I doubt it."

"No..." He massaged the bridge of his nose. "Not sex. I mean breaking them off."

"Breaking? Aren't you gonna like pick em?"

"I'm not a thief, and you don't seem interested in waiting for my friend, who is."

Strawberry faced away. "What, you some kinda aug?"

Aaron focused on the cuff, exerting telekinetic force. Three chain links wobbled and snapped taut. Prior to the day that destroyed his life, he never would have attempted to break such an item. Something had happened to him the moment his mind shattered. Nothing made sense anymore. He concentrated on pulling it apart, sensing the mass and shape of each piece. After a tiny pulse crawled over the top of his skull, the metal around her wrists burst into a spray of shrapnel and pink furry bits. Aaron fell on his ass, as though he'd been punched in the forehead.

"Ow, motherfucker!" She danced around, waving her arms. "What the fuck just happened? The goddamn thing exploded."

Aaron's face twitched. He tried to rub feeling back into his cheeks as he stood up. Using telekinesis again so soon after an 'event' woke up the headache, but at least Strawberry's needles-in-the-eardrums voice would soon cease. The woman looked at him, at his crotch, and at the boxers on the floor.

"You sure you don't wanna—"

"Quite." He held up a hand. "I'm in no shape for a shag. I honestly think I'd get seasick."

And I've no want to learn what sort of nasty little bugs you've got in there.

"'Ave a seat, I'll order you somethin' to wear once I've scrubbed up."

Dozens of women's faces played a slideshow in his memory, an uncountable number of frictionless fans back home. They all wanted one thing. All women wanted one thing, except for Allison—and that *bitch* took her away.

Damn women, nothing but credit siphons. If it isn't sex, it's pity.

He trudged into the tube, gagging on the cloying presence of concentrated fruit-scented perfume. "How the feck long were ya stuck in 'ere?"

"All yesterday since about one." Her voice sounded as though it came from near the floor, rising toward the end. "That Driftwraith better pray Monro finds him before I do. Monro'll just kill him."

"That's half a day. It's not even dawn yet."

"Thanks for lettin' me out."

"Aye." Aaron poked the start button, letting his body bask in the onrush of warm water jets. He wore the same stupid grin for the entire second rinse cycle. By the time hot air swirled around him, he felt like a new man. "A day, eh? Spose you'll be famished. May as well get some food too."

Silence.

He shifted around, wiping fog off the inside of the clear tube to peer into the outer room. No trace remained of the girl—or his boxers.

"Kinn'ell." He let his forehead hit the plastic wall, which sent a ripple of agony bouncing off the inside of his skull. "Ouch. That was stupid."

Once the autoshower cycle stopped, he shoved the tube open and cast a disparaging glance at the sheet responsible for trapping Strawberry in the shower. He'd been distrustful of touching the woman, but that level of disgust paled in comparison to the revulsion caused by the sight of dark spots on the linen. He left it on the floor and trudged into the bedroom. His suit, socks, and shoes were gone—including his NetMini and Allison's nametag.

Aaron ran outside, finding himself on the fifth floor balcony of a cheap hotel, staring down at puffs of fog gliding over a rain-soaked parking lot.

He grabbed the railing with both hands, leaning out and screaming, "Strawberry! Come back. You took her tag!"

His voice echoed against silence, a rare moment when even the distant music of advert bots had stopped. He yelled her name twice more before he slouched, defeated.

The encroaching dawn had brightened enough to render the city in silhouette, except for the neon glow in the skyline of Sector 214. It shone above the decrepit buildings across the street and to the right. A twinge of nausea rumbled in his gut at the prominent Infinity Casino tower aglow in pyramids of purple blue and green. The playground of the rich reflected in neon smears on the wet ground.

Judging by his surroundings, the area looked to be the start of a grey zone. He blinked with disbelief at the still-functional manager's office. At this proximity to an abandoned sector, whoever ran this place had some set of balls to demand people pay to spend the night here.

Winded from shouting, he gasped a mouthful of trash and chemical flavored air. He coughed himself to tears while a slow golf-clap came from his left. A thick, muscular black man in a tank top, dark military style pants, and a red bandanna gave him an appraising look. Small bits of metal studded with tiny blue LEDs protruded from both cheeks, concentrated around the eyes.

"What you seen, man?" He pulled open the top of a backpack, exposing a myriad of autoinjectors ranging from new-in-shrink-wrap to the fortieth refill. "You let Christof know if you be needin' more."

A tongue clucked to his right, where a middle-aged woman with caramel skin shook her head and refused to look at him. She wore a harness with four handguns over a white shirt with the hotel's logo. Her housekeeper's cart had a number of bullet holes.

Anger and loss overwhelmed him, and he let off a blood-curdling scream. The single car in the parking lot wound up embedded in the wall of the fifth floor of the building across the street. Christof the chem dealer un-leaned from the wall and walked away.

"What this city is coming to." The housekeeper blinked at the car-turned-projectile, shook her head again, and went into the adjacent room.

AARON SAT ON THE END OF THE COMFORGEL PAD, ELBOWS ON HIS KNEES and head in his hands. The glowing gel cycled amid red and orange as it tried to keep him warm, bathing the darkened room in the colors of Hades. He didn't look up when the door opened. A figure blocked the light in stunned silence long enough for the scent of char siu ramen to reach him. The room seemed dimmer when the door closed.

"I'm goin' ta guess yo' naked ass has somethin' ta do with the car across the street?" asked Darwin. "And by the way, that's way more of you than I ever wanted to see again. Twice in two days, makes a man start wonderin' if you tryin' ta send a message."

"You didn't check the bathroom when you left me here, did you?"

"I didn't have to go." Darwin put a plastic bowl on the bed before taking a seat at the table. "Why?"

"The tom locked in the tube was a bit pissed off."

"Was some dude—"

"A tom is a prostitute… cretin."

Darwin chuckled. "She give you a discount?"

"You're a right comic, mate." Aaron rubbed his eyes. "I wouldn't touch her with a plastisteel nodder. Besides"—he waved about as if to condemn society as a whole—"she's probably still a minor."

"Did she have tits?"

Aaron glared at him.

"Hey, man. All I'm sayin' is seventeen is still negotiable. Sorry I'm late, it took me awhile to smooth things over with Shimmer. Consider yourself lucky I was able to."

"Oh, that's just grand." Aaron picked up the bowl, twisting it in small, precise motions while flicking at the flimsy plastic cover. "That would be quite the tragedy, if Shimmer was upset with us. I don't know how I'd recover from such a catastrophe."

Chopsticks bounced off Aaron's head. He caught them with a trivial telekinetic effort, and they careened to a midair halt before touching the carpet. He glared at Darwin's still outstretched arm, not moving until the man huddled in a heap of shredded green coat over the table.

"You've got a pair o' brass ones, puttin' any of this on me." Aaron whipped the cover aside, letting it flutter to the rug. Chunks of red-tinted mystery meat floated in a morass of noodles, broth, and unidentifiable green globs. "Was your genius idea to tit about with the roulette table."

"I didn't go nucular on the room." Darwin slurped noodles, making a series of 'oohs' and 'aahs' at the heat. "Or toss a fuckin' car through a window."

"The word is nuclear. Noo-clee-ur." Aaron pinched his fingers at the air as he enunciated it. "You honestly thought you'd… we'd get away with that?" He jammed his chopsticks into the floating mass of pasta. A lump that could've been crabmeat or shrimp bobbed to the surface. "Bugger it. You're right. I used to be a bloody cop dealing with nonsense like this. I shouldn't 'ave let you talk me into doing that at all. I ought to 'ave known they'd 'ave a damn telepath on staff." He pouted into the soup, muttering, "There's a bloody good reason kinetics don't cheat casinos. An' I'm a bit rusty."

"Rusty?" Darwin cocked an eyebrow.

"Never mind. Nothin' to do with casinos."

Both men ate in silence for some minutes. Aaron glanced up twice but decided against speaking.

"Ain't never spent this much time in a room with a naked man before," muttered Darwin. "People gonna get the wrong idea 'bout our relationship."

Tension snapped; Aaron cracked up for over a minute before he gathered himself enough to speak. "I'd order some clothes, but the tom nicked my NetMini."

"Since I've known you… what's it been, four months? I think you've had two or three a week… Law of averages says sooner or later one of 'em's gonna game you."

"She's not *my* tom. Came wit' the room. Didn't even shag that one." Aaron slurped broth. "She'd 'ave had to pay me. The sort of tom I patronize is quite a bit different."

"How so? Payin' for fuckin' is payin' for fuckin', ain't it?"

"Five thousand credits a night compared to fifty or a hundred? That one'd cost me more at a clinic gettin' cleaned out than she charged." He slurped broth. "It's a difference of a woman who enjoys an art form and one who just"—he tapped his fingers on the bowl—"doesn't have a choice."

"The man thinks he is an art form." Darwin raised a hand, as if indicating Aaron to a nonexistent audience.

Aaron bowed.

Darwin gave him a broad grin. "Shimmer said she got to the security feed before the Zeroes arrived. Their cams ain't gonna show a damn thing. No digital evidence, only thing they had ta go on was what people remembered, which wa'n much but a lot of screaming and pants-shitting. Should be safe enough for us to go back in a day or two an' finish off."

"Back? Are you insane? Even if that girl of yours banjaxed the security system, there were dozens of witnesses, plus an entire fecking wall gone. That's the sort of thing people notice." Aaron let his shout hang in the air for a few seconds while gawking. He blinked. "You are serious. You are right fuckin' nutters." He stood, causing Darwin to cringe away. "You bloody well aren't batting on a full wicket. You want to go *back?*"

"Sit down, man." Darwin held his arms up as if to shield himself from the glow of an atomic detonation. "Only the telepath and the dealer got a good look at you, and neither one of 'em made it. Dealer had a roulette wheel where his head shoulda been and they couldn't even find the telepath."

"Fuck."

"No, thanks."

Aaron fell seated again, clutching his head. "Fuck, again."

"Relax, man. Shimmer's got it handled."

"She's got nothing handled." Aaron shouted, head snapping up. "All her talent's a big bag of wank compared to what they're going to send after me." He clenched his fingers into fists in his hair. "Damn."

"Say, man. Why you so upset over a suit? You got a dozen of 'em."

Anger, a sheet of high-polished glass, shattered into a billion flakes of sorrow. All he had left of his wife was her nametag, which he no longer had. He made a squealing noise a step or two closer to a wail of anguish than murderous and clamped his arms around his head. Darwin raised an eyebrow.

"Must've been a damn nice suit."

Aaron glared at him, sitting up. A second of rage passed. Once it no longer seemed like a perfect idea to launch Darwin out the window, he slouched. "I had her nameplate in the pocket."

"Shit, man." Darwin tapped his fingers on the table, looking at the rug. "Sorry. I know some people; maybe we can find her. No one's gonna want a name tag."

"Mmf. She works for some bloke name o' Monro."

"Hmm. I heard that name before. He's a reasonable sorta man, if reasonable sorts of men made a habit of twisting the heads offa people who ran bad on 'em. Can probably work something out."

"Great." Aaron twirled noodles around the chopsticks, trying in vain to summon up the will to eat them.

"Don't worry about it. You ain't need no little bit of metal to remember her." Darwin reached over to pat him on the knee, but thought better of it. "So, about Shimmer's job."

Aaron blinked at him, face frozen in a mask of complete disbelief. "You are—"

The door rattled as though someone tried to walk right in. Both of them looked at it. Aaron reached for a gun he no longer carried. He tensed for the inevitable police voice. Getting taken in by Division 0 would be bad enough, but he'd never live down them dragging him bare-assed from a dive hotel.

A much softer knock than he expected sounded twice.

"Hello? Still in there? It's Strawberry."

Aaron stared at the closed door, unable to move, brain locked to a screeching halt. Darwin got up and opened it, revealing the pink-haired girl with the glowing blue stars over her eyes. She had matching star earrings, also lit up, a barely-there tube top, and a black imitation leather skirt with faux tatters and shreds like she'd walked in five minutes ago from the Badlands. He locked eyes with his suit, a bundle of folded cloth tucked in her arms.

"Sorry for running off before. Monro gets touchy about punctuality. I woulda called him, but your 'mini was locked." She slipped past Darwin and dropped the suit on the bed. "I got lucky. He's more scorched at the Driftwraiths than me. I didn't even get slapped."

"See, I told you the man's reasonable," said Darwin.

Aaron's gaze fell upon pink toenails peeking out from transparent orange plastic sandals. Glitter stars adorned the nails of both big toes.

"I, uhh, can't stay long. If they find out I'm talking to a cop they'd—"

"Ex-cop," said Darwin.

"Oh. That why all you got's a nametag? Zero huh? That's cool. I dated a psionic once. I don't see what the big deal is." She offered a weak smile, but couldn't look at him or hide her faint tremble. "Allison's an odd name for a guy."

"My wife." Aaron pulled the jacket into his lap, grabbing at where the pocket should be. Relief washed over him at the sense of a small metal bar under the fabric. "Thanks."

The luminous tattoos made her eyes seem darker. "I, uhh... Sorry."

Aaron pulled his boxers out of the wad of clothing and put them on.

"'Bout damn time," said Darwin.

Aaron extended a middle finger in his friend's direction while he fished out his NetMini. As soon as it recognized his fingerprint, it warned him of forty-six unauthorized attempts to open it. He disregarded the notice, assuming the suspect stood right in front of him, and flipped through a few screens. He went to the GlobeNet presence of a sporting goods seller and ordered a motorbike helmet and a gym bag.

Strawberry looked around the room, biting her lip.

"What're you waitin' on?" asked Darwin.

"Uhh, nothing."

"I think she's expectin' you to give her the routine 'bout gettin' offa the street, find social services or some shit. Maybe go to a colony adoption." Darwin looked her up and down. "Seventeen. Damn I'm good."

She rolled her eyes. "He already mentioned the colony thing."

Aaron pulled his undershirt on, wilding his hair. "If she wanted to get off the street, she'd get off the street." He snatched his pants up with a telekinetic fling. "She's not goin' to take the word of a wanker like me, and I'm not wastin' my breath on it."

"You said somethin' about food. Offer still there?" She glanced at the door. "Can't get pubsist since I'm not eighteen yet. They'd detain me."

"Military's always hiring," said Darwin.

"He went there already too." She gave him a patronizing glare. "You look homeless. Why don't you join?"

"Too old." He shifted and grumbled. "I'm past thirty."

Aaron mouthed "forty" without lending voice to it as he cinched his belt, making her giggle.

A metallic tap sounded from the door.

"Like I told pasty here... I ain't takin no fuckin' bullets for some corporate ass war." She moved to answer it.

"You're more likely to take a bullet in the city than you are in the military." Aaron slipped his shirt on and buttoned it. "Especially with your line of work. You know a working prostitute is four point two times more likely to get shot than a Division 1 patrol officer?"

"No shit?" asked Darwin.

A delivery bot the size of a footlocker glided into the room, seeking Aaron's NetMini. It chirped a happy tone when it got close and opened a side hatch. Once he unloaded his purchases, it zipped away.

"What the hell is that for?" asked Darwin.

Aaron put on the helmet.

He closed the visor, patted it twice, and went outside where he pivoted on one heel in a military about-face, planted his palms on the metal wall, and drove his head into it as hard as he could. Aaron staggered back, close to falling over the flimsy railing. Darwin and Strawberry emerged, both staring. Aaron recovered his balance and rammed his head into the wall again before removing the helmet and putting it in the bag.

"I s'pose the least I can do for you returnin' my kit is feed ya. Ready to go eat, luv?"

She nodded.

"God damn," said Darwin. "You got some strange fuckety-boo ways of dealin' with anger."

6

A SECOND INFINITY

The nametag remained cold to the touch no matter how long Aaron held it. With Darwin next to him in the back seat of a PubTran taxi, he didn't voice an apology to Allison for nearly losing it, though a mantra of contrition repeated in his mind. In another life, he might've taken Strawberry in on a solicitation pop. *Lettin' 'er spend a night or two in a clean bed with real food and a complimentary med scan seems a right bit of charitable.* If the officers running the holding facility figured out she was only seventeen, she'd be off the streets for a while longer. Maybe it would have scared her into a change of course.

Probably not. Can't save the ones who don't want it.

It wasn't his place to give a shit anymore.

"So what the heck was up with that helmet thing?" asked Darwin.

Aaron tilted the trinket in his fingers, letting light play off the surface. "Like you said, mate. I got strange methods of coping."

"Yeah, but—"

The blare of a NetMini erupted from Darwin's coat pocket. His startled face set Aaron off on a laughing fit. When the device came out, the holographic bust of a young woman with coffee-colored skin and iridescent powder blue hair appeared. Glittery silver-teal paint formed a butterfly shape over her eyes, and a faint set of faerie wings fluttered in the air behind her. Instead of eyes, almond-shaped spots of bright aqua light glowed from within her head. She opened her mouth, but Darwin held up a finger.

"One sec, Shim." He stared at Aaron. "What the hell is so damn funny?"

"It struck me as amusing a fringer's got a NetMini."

"Everyone's got one, man. How's a guy supposed to beg if I ain't got no way ta take in the creds?" Darwin flashed a disaster of a grin at the hologram. "Hello sweetness."

Blur at the bottom of the image hinted at folded arms. "The two of you made one hell of a shitstorm out of a simple plant."

"Don't look at me, sweetness. Talk ta the English Apocalypse here."

The flickering image rotated toward Aaron and frowned. "That's the guy? How'd you wind up sharing a squat with a shafter like that? I feel like I need a shower just from the way he's looking at me."

Aaron squinted. "The fault doesn't all lie on one person's shoulders, 'ere. Ask this tosser about roulette."

"You went gambling?" Shimmer glared at Darwin. "I bet you made him cheat for you." She seethed out a long "ooooh."

Darwin cringed.

Shimmer threw her hands up. "I should just walk away from this clusterfuck right now."

Darwin almost said something twice before she whipped her ire back at Aaron.

"Do you have any idea how much of a pain in the ass it was to erase that little temper tantrum of yours?"

"Temper tantrum?" Aaron tucked his wife's nameplate back in his pocket. "Look here, girl. What happened there wasn't my idea, nor could I have done fuck all to stop it, other than not bloody cheating at fucking roulette." He glared in Darwin's direction for a few seconds. "People died, and you've got the gall to give me lip for creating a 'scene?' Your little electronic tricks won't slow down the people that'll get involved now."

"The only ones who can identify you didn't make it," she said. "They won't know who they're looking for."

"Oh, I'm sure they will." Aaron tapped his temple with two fingers. "Psionics, luv. They'll recognize the effect."

"You've done that before?" Darwin cocked an eyebrow.

"Not by choice. I don't"—he thrust his arms forward—"*Do* it. It just happens when someone tries to get into my brain. Their telepath read you like a bloody wiki article, and knew I was helping you. It went to shite when they tried to burrow into my head."

Shimmer frowned.

"He might be tellin' the truth," said Darwin. "He was pretty well fucked afterwards. I'd never seen him that hung-over."

"You got drunk too?" she shrieked. "Unbelievable."

"No," droned Aaron. "He meant hung-over as a metaphor."

"Look, Shim… I got it all covered. I know that setup we talked about is gonna work." He patted his pocket. "The Horus is fine. We'll get it done for you. We'll be in and out before anyone feels it"—he smiled at Aaron—"without gambling."

Aaron picked his eye with his middle finger.

"You look familiar," said Shimmer.

"I have one of those faces."

"Yeah." She glanced to the side. "Five minutes in the room with me, you'd be trying to talk my pants off. I know the type."

Aaron twirled his hand at the side of his head in a mock formal bow. "Standing offer."

She rolled her eyes. "You couldn't handle this ride." The hologram rotated to Darwin. "I can't believe I'm not hanging up on you two idiots already, but my tits are in a vice. I need that Horus planted at Infinity. Fuck it up this time, and you'll know why they say hell hath no fury."

The car went dark as she killed the call.

"Right bit of cheery, that one." Aaron rubbed his face. "Like getting scolded by a constipated woodchuck."

"She's one of the better deck jockeys this side of the Badlands." Darwin tucked his two-generation-old NetMini into his coat. "Word is Syndicate's been after her for years and still can't find her. Anyone who can stay under *their* radar is good."

"She's lucky. Probably a kid or maybe not even a girl." Aaron undid his collar button. "Have you ever seen her? Might even be an AI. Syndicate couldn't find a person what don't exist."

"No, just on holo-calls. You think? 'Cep for fuck dolls, AIs don't usually refer to themselves as havin' tits. Anyway, I got us a way in. Won't have nothin' ta worry about."

Darwin rummaged in a bag between his feet, pulling out a pair of white smocks. On the breast pocket of each, a smiling cartoon chef with outstretched arms embraced the words "Black Hat Catering."

Aaron stared at him. "You don't seriously…"

"I do." Darwin wagged his eyebrows.

"This is ridiculous."

"You wouldn't be the first frictionless player to get into food service."

Aaron glared.

Darwin shrugged. "Shimmer picked the place. Said the name made her laugh, some kinda inside joke wit' net heads. We even got an 'in' with the outfit; they know we're there and will conveniently fail to notice."

"They're not the blokes I'm worried about."

7

FOLLOW THE FAERIE

"Well, this doesn't look like a casino," said Aaron.

His voice echoed across the back end of a warehouse full of white vans. Four lines of six boxy vehicles queued up behind garage doors. Garlic stood out as the prominent fragrance in the air permeating the building, crushing a hint of chicken or steak; two breaths in, he found himself too hungry to concentrate on much of anything but food.

Sounds of human activity drifted in from beyond the parked trucks. Aaron made a face of distinct unease as he wiped his palms down the front of his white smock.

A crowd of three-foot-diameter orb bots glided overhead in precise flight paths, weaving in a mesmerizing aerial ballet. As each one loaded its cargo of food trays in the back end of a waiting truck and floated out of the way, another came in behind it.

Darwin walked along a row of vans, stopping at the third vehicle in the second line. "Are all cops this slow? Come on, this is our ride."

Aaron ducked under sixty pounds of chicken parmesan on his way to catch up to his friend, who exchanged a few brief words in Spanish with a heavyset driver before climbing into the back seat. The man swiveled around as Aaron took the seat right behind him, wearing a smile so wide his eyes seemed to close. In addition to the same white smock and dark pants, he wore a yellow cloth about his neck, knotted in front. Excess weight lent a circular quality to his face.

Aaron hoped the scent of fish came from the back and not the driver. He leaned to his right, closer to Darwin, whispering, "Why don't we have those yellow things."

"He's like a supervisor or something. Soup chef or some shit."

"Sous chef?" Aaron stifled a chuckle.

"Welcome, Mister Pryce," said the driver. His eyes opened wide, his gesturing became a pointing finger. "Aaron? Aaron Pryce? ¡*Mierda*!" He grabbed Aaron's hand in both of his, shaking it. "It is an honor to meet you! I never missed a match." The driver pulled down the sun visor, revealing an impressive collection of Arsenal F.C. pins before leaning out the window. "Jorge, Mike, Vlad! Get your asses over here!" He fell into his seat, rocking the van. "I'm Arnie, Arnie Hernandez."

Aaron wasn't sure if he should smile or bury his face in his hands. "Hello, Arnie."

"What's that about?" asked Darwin.

Arnie launched into an explanation of Aaron's career as one of the more famous strikers for the Arsenal Frictionless Club.

"Mister Pryce led the league in goals per game for three years running."

Aaron forced a smile. "It's so nice to have fans."

A handful of men ran up on the door, each wanting to shake hands with him. He graciously obliged.

"He was on track to be the best player in the game, 'til he had his leg thing." Arnie shook his head. "Damn shame."

"Thanks." Aaron leaned on the wall wishing they'd get on with their day, but not to the point of wanting to slam the door in the faces of his past life's glory.

"Mister low profile," muttered Darwin.

"I hope your leg is feeling better, Mister Pryce." Arnie whirled to face forward as rapid-fire Spanish erupted from the console. He nodded at no one until it stopped. "*Lo siento, lo siento. Me voy.*"

The vans ahead of them had already left. Aaron didn't need to know Spanish to understand Arnie's boss chewed him out for slacking.

"Leg's got its good days and bad days. Wound up having to get a MyoFiber graft to replace most of my right calf. League rules calls it 'augmented,' so I'm barred from playing in the standard class." Aaron shivered, grateful that his cyberware existed only as a convenient cover story. "I don't *feel* augmented, and I have no interest in getting turned into raspberry jam by those meatheads. What's in the back? All I can smell is garlic and fish."

"That's a pity, Mister Price." Arnie steered them around a gradual turn. "Sushi. The Infinity don't get the usual shit. Fried stuff, chicken parmesan, ziti, all the finger foods, they're big with the corporate meetings. Not for the Infinity though, they like the expensive stuff: sushi, caviar, orbital-grown seafood... the whole nine. That mess of bait back there, hundred grand easy."

Aaron settled into the seat and closed his eyes. "I'm in the wrong damn business. Wake me up when we get there."

A dozen employees of Black Hat Catering swarmed the food prep area in the first basement level of the Infinity Casino. Getting in the service entrance had been as easy as Darwin predicted, no doubt helped along by the other workers treating them as if they belonged. Aaron leaned on the wall by an interior door, scowling at nothing in particular.

Darwin pushed a hovering cart with several plastic cartons of sushi separated into individual meal portions. At the look on Aaron's face, he paused. "Somethin' wrong?"

"Wasn't expecting to run into fans."

"That's a heck of a way to react. You should be grateful. Bastards like you got more credit than you know what to do with, and people love your asses for runnin' around in circles."

Aaron looked off at nothing. "I wasn't as good as he made me out to be."

Darwin blew air through his teeth. "That sounds like guilt." He handed over a pair of thin silver frames with no lenses, two prongs curved inward on each side where glass or plastic ought to be.

"Great. Everything I see will be in parenthetical."

"What?" asked Darwin.

"Forget it." Aaron slipped it on.

Within seconds, an eight-inch faerie with dark skin and blue hair appeared in front of him. Butterfly wings made of silver glitter thrummed behind her, raining pixie dust that ceased existing once it fell past her feet. She seemed nude, but glowing spots brightened enough to obscure vision at the critical points.

Is every hacker a head case? "She wants to nanny us along then?"

The faerie scoffed. "Hardly. It's going to be much faster for me to get the doors for you. Darwin will be busy feeding the admins and the floor security, so he won't be able to work his usual magic. Not that he'd be fast enough anyway."

Darwin grumbled. "I ain't that slow... or that old."

Shimmer continued looking at Aaron, presumably because Darwin saw the same vision of her glaring at him in his glasses. "Can you open six electronic locks simultaneously?"

"Well, I... er, no." Darwin stared at the tray.

"Besides, I can tell you where the patrollers are in case one of them decides to be dutiful and not run for the free, expensive food."

"Won't they find the glasses suspect?" asked Aaron.

Darwin patted him on the shoulder. "If anyone asks, say you're new and using it for a building map."

It was rare for the man to say something both so obvious and that made perfect sense. Aaron raised both eyebrows, feeling a modicum of stupid for not thinking of it himself. "Fair point."

They went through the door and down a red-floored hallway to an elevator. The doors opened without prompting, and the elevator selected one floor down before either of them could touch the controls.

"Just let her drive, man."

Aaron exhaled. A pair of security officers hanging out by an alcove full of vendomats jumped as the elevator arrived. Both had compact rifles and charcoal-grey body armor. The woman tensed and put a hand on her weapon.

Her associate scrunched his eyebrows together. "You boys get lost? Executives are upstairs."

"Miss West sent this down for Andrea's five-year anniversary," squeaked Shimmer.

Aaron put on the smile that shed a thousand panties. "It's an anniversary gift from Miss West, for Andrea."

The man inherited some of the other officer's apprehension. "West wouldn't send us premium toilet paper."

Darwin offered a warm smile. "Officer Lees, do you really think we'd cart two thousand creds worth of raw fish down here without an official go ahead?"

Aaron plucked a thought out of the female guard's head. "Maybe West is thawing out after having a baby?"

"Yeah, maybe." Lees popped open his instant cooling can, some manner of high-octane energy drink with a frothing green troll on the outside. After a sip, he went down the hall. "Come on."

The female officer waited to let them pass. Her body language indicated she meant to walk behind them. Aaron tensed but kept a pleasant face, pushing his cart along behind Darwin.

"I got it," chirped Shimmer.

Not quite ten feet down the hallway, the woman behind them sighed. "Son of a bitch."

"Better go, Santiago," said Lees.

"Little damn convenient." Officer Santiago narrowed her eyes at Aaron. "Something doesn't feel right. Montez wants me upstairs right at the moment we get a special delivery?"

Lees glanced at Darwin. "Now that you mention it, the timing does seem rather convenient."

Aaron clenched his hands on the cart, concentrating, seizing telekinetic hold of both guards' rifles and swinging them up and under their arms into their faces with a loud *crack*. Darwin ducked. Lees' nose burst into a gusher of blood and a distinct *snap* came from Santiago's jaw. Aaron switched his focus to holding them upright. Shimmer squealed incoherencies, wings fluttering into a glitter-spewing haze. Every few seconds, a recognizable word crept out: cameras, security station, reroute.

"Christ, man." Darwin straightened up. "Did you kill them?"

He floated the unconscious security officers together and guided them into the nearest doorway, which turned out to be a small six-person meeting room. Aaron rotated them horizontal and left them on the table. After a moment's consideration, he relocated them under it.

Darwin ran over and checked their gear. "Shit, no cuffs. What kinda cops don't carry cuffs?"

"Private security. The kind of 'cops' that don't take people into custody."

"Oh, damn."

Aaron glared. "Oh, damn. Yeah... that's a right fine way to put it. 'Oh, damn' works perfectly. You just now figured out a fuckup in here is going to translate to bullets and body bags, a whole mess of 'orrible shite." He kicked the wall. "Shimmer, can you do something unseemly to this door?"

"Yeah," said the faerie.

The access panel buzzed, and cast off a puff of dark smoke carrying the scent of burned silicon. Darwin rushed to the food cart and pushed it to the end of the corridor where a T intersection stopped them. He pulled a small, rectangular device about the size of a thumb out of his pocket and held it out. "Take the Horus. I'll go to the break room with the fish. You head to the network room." Darwin pointed left before dragging both hovering carts with him the other way. "Fourth door on the right side."

Aaron pocketed the electronic tap and jogged into the corridor.

Shimmer yelled, "Left, now!" when he'd made it about halfway.

He dove through a door as it opened, surprising a thin Asian woman in a white laboratory-style coat over a black sweater and slacks. Four large shelves held an uncountable number of personal electronics, portable terminals, and desk units. One such terminal lay disassembled in front of her. Aaron had no idea what the sparking wand in her right hand was, except for knowing he didn't want her to poke him with it.

"Who are you? You shouldn't be in here."

"We just brought some food. It's in the main break room." Aaron pointed over his shoulder. Someone heavy walked by in the hall outside.

"How did you even get that door open?" The tech reached for a NetMini. "It shouldn't work for a contractor temp badge."

"Officer Lees had to umm... Call of nature. He gave me temporary access." She squinted. Aaron grabbed onto the thought at the tip of her brain. "Okay, he told me to say that. I think he was just being lazy."

She relaxed.

"Clear," said Shimmer. "Wow, look at all this shit. It's impressive 'cause there's so much of it, but it's all year-old crap. Oooh, four years ago, I would've demanded you steal that Nakamura Kishinoken." She pointed at a long, narrow box, about the size of what a single rose might come in, featureless save for two M3 interface plugs and a holographic emitter.

"Lazy doesn't begin to describe that idiot." The woman made a shooing motion. "Consider his message received; now get out of my lab."

Aaron backed into the corridor and jogged to a dark blue door marked 'Server 03.' It looked armored, or at least reinforced, and had no window.

"Wait," said Shimmer. "There's a security checkpoint and airlock inside. Beyond that, the corridor splits into three zones. I'm going to open every door at once and kill the lights. The headset will give you an approximation of the path. You'll need to haul ass. Ready?"

"No."

The faerie tapped her foot on nothing.

"I mean yes."

"Three... two... one..."

The heavy door slid to the side with such speed it appeared to vanish. Inside, everything went dark except for a green wireframe outline rendered in hologram by his headset. A floating dotted line pointed the way ahead. Shimmer overlaid the floor plan on his vision, which didn't account for movable objects like furniture. Aaron attempted to sprint, but bumped a handful of chairs and one small table, before tripping into an embrace with a standing plant. Spitting out leaves, he swung around to align himself with the digital outline of a corridor and collided with a woman at a full run in the opposite direction.

Their face-to-face meeting was brief, intimate, and left him seeing stars with her unconscious on top of him. Shimmer vanished as the goggles flew from his head and clattered to the floor somewhere in the dark.

Aaron moaned, fingertip testing his lip for blood. "What kind of bloody idiot runs in the dark?"

"You," said Shimmer. The voice emanating from the distant device sounded even more like a Faerie.

He pushed the woman off to the side, patting her on what he hoped was the shoulder, whispering, "Sorry about that."

Heavy pounding, the hands of an immense ticking clock—or his heartbeat—got him scrambling about on all fours and sweeping his hands back and forth in a frantic search for the goggles. His fingers brushed plastic, swatting something farther away. Cursing, Aaron crawled in the direction of the skittering. He cringed at the rapid approach of another person, stifling the urge to grunt as a leg caught him in the gut and a body toppled over him. The man crashed into the side of a desk behind him, metal from the sound of it, and cursed as he fell in a rain of small objects.

A tiny patch of white light came on, highlighting every crevice in the rug six feet ahead. Aaron grabbed the goggles, fumbling to put them on as he leapt to his feet and leaned out of the way of another runner who sounded female. With the headset in place, luminescent green highlights once more created a sense of his environs.

Shimmer's holographic avatar zoomed into his field of vision, pointing. "Go! You've only got two minutes."

Aaron pointed at her, not that she could see, and pondered a series of choice invectives before he let his need to find Talis overwhelm his momentary indignation. He jogged in the direction indicated by the floating dotted line past two turns to a door. Once it closed behind him, the lights came on.

"Gah! Feck, I'm blind!"

"Oh, grow up," chirped Shimmer. She flew among racks of server components, hovering by a panel. "Here. Open this one."

Aaron stared at the tiny, floating apparition, disappointed a creation of mere light could not feel pain. He stormed over to the indicated machine, seething at her for a few seconds. She stomped on nothing and pointed. Grumbling, he lifted a hood-like panel to expose several arm-thick bundles of fiber optic cable, pulsing with a blue and red glow.

She zipped under the cover, indicating a regular M3 socket. "Plug it in here and then hide the box in back as far as the wire will go."

Aaron fished the Horus out of his pocket, extracted an asterisk-shaped prong from the underside, and plugged it in. The cable unwound to a length of two feet. Telekinesis allowed him to levitate the small component deep into the cabinet where even a child's arm couldn't fit.

Shimmer stared at him with her mouth open. "That was... awesome. They'll never find it."

"Is that it then?" He closed the cabinet.

"Not quite."

He glared.

Shimmer pointed with her toe at the exit. "You gotta get outta here."

DARWIN JUMPED AS AARON SLAMMED OPEN THE DOOR TO THE BREAK ROOM. A modest group of security officers, technical personnel, and other casino employees looked up from their sushi at the sudden noise.

Aaron pointed over his shoulder with a thumb. "Arnie's lookin' for you. He wants us upstairs to help with the conference room."

"Oh, damn, sorry all." Darwin offloaded a few pre-pack meals into a mini-fridge. "I'll leave these here in case more show up. Toss 'em if no one eats them in a day."

Aaron slipped into the hall, trying not to look as frustrated, worried, and angry as he was. He grabbed Darwin by the smock as he emerged, spinning him around and putting his back to the wall. Aaron raised his finger, hand shaking, as if he were about to unload some bit of profundity.

Instead, he sighed, and trudged toward the elevator.

"Looks like things went well." Darwin tugged at his catering jacket.

Aaron huffed. "I'm starting rather not to like faeries."

8

LUCKY BREAK

Matte black metal turned in Aaron's fingers. He angled it back and forth, watching the shadows deepen and recede within the engraved letters of his wife's name. The trinket blurred as his focus went past his feet to the bare concrete wall a short distance from the end of his bed. A former living room served as his private space, sectioned off from the rest of the apartment with standing barriers of debris and unwearable clothes hung from cords. He stared between the legs of a pair of moldy pink pants sized for a tween, pondering the source of the flickering light in Darwin's sanctum.

Aaron wondered how he hadn't noticed him there when he'd settled on this apartment. He assumed the presence of a Comforgel pad in the larger area would've attracted a squatter before the glorified closet his friend preferred. He remembered his disappointment at discovering a blown pad; the once gelatinous material inside had dried out into a substance with the consistency of thick, rubbery snot.

It didn't heat up or cool anymore, but he'd come to regard it as comfortable in an unsettling way. Lying on it felt simultaneously relaxing and disgusting. He'd lost almost an hour the first time he'd touched it, watching the indentations of his hand fade back to the shape it had been in when it dried.

Green and grey fungus spread out from daisies embroidered on the shins of the little girl's pants, souring his mood. He dwelled on the somber thought of a girl young enough to fit into them stuck living in this squalor and hoped they had been left behind when her family fled the blight. Twenty years ago, average people lived in this sector. He almost chuckled at the thought the previous owner of those pants might be older than him, then hoped she was.

The creep of decay over such an innocent article brought his mind back to Allison and the last thing she would ever say to him.

"Aaron! What are you doing?"

He closed his eyes, weathering the memory of her scream. Three days had passed since they'd planted the Horus in the casino without word from Shimmer. Talis was out there somewhere, off the radar of Division 0 and out of his reach. Aaron's thumb brushed over the lettering again; he could almost read it by touch. Revenge seemed like an unattainable goal, something he'd gladly sacrifice for a chance to be with her again. The ruined pink jeans stirred in a breeze that scraped plastic sheeting over a window long devoid of glass. His mind tricked him into seeing those pants as belonging to his daughter, once he and Allie had kids. The rot faded, the pink brightened, and he pictured a blurry-faced nine-year-old running around giggling. For a few seconds, Aaron smiled.

Gunfire rang out a few blocks away, but he'd stopped flinching weeks ago.

The pleasant daydream world lost its color. Grass browned and died. Mold crept over the pants, and the little girl stopped laughing. She had no face because he couldn't imagine her. Allison had died before they'd ever even discussed having kids.

Aaron set the nameplate on his chest and reached to his right, rummaging amid a pile of junk until he found the rubberized grip of his E-90. He pulled it from the debris and held the laser weapon with both hands, studying the twisted smears of his reflection along the silver housing. He turned it over, looking at it from all sides, the instrument of her death; the last time it fired, it took his wife from this world.

"You're a cruel bitch, fate," whispered Aaron. "Two years, I carried this miserable, bastarding thing. Only drew it three times when I wasn't on the range."

He gripped it in one hand and held the nameplate in his left as he moved to sit sideways on the bed. The rug had long ago disintegrated; beneath his feet, a giant hole of cold, scratchy concrete. Aaron's gaze focused on the tip of the E-90.

He put his finger on the trigger. "Suppose if there's any truth to the 'ole ghost thing, I could hurry things along a bit. How 'bout it then, Allie? You fancy revenge or a reunion?"

After a moment of perfect silence, he pressed the pistol under his chin. He had stopped caring about this world as soon as the life had left his wife's eyes. Only the need to hunt Talis and put the bitch down kept him clinging, enough not to give up, but how much difference would killing her make? A woman like her would make an enemy worse than Aaron sooner or later. Did it really have to be *him* to end her? All he'd accomplished so far was delaying fate. Chasing her had cost him everything, and the more he stared at the child's pants, the more he couldn't bear not to be with Allison anymore.

Sound faded from his perception, save for the faint howl of wind somewhere distant. Aaron fixed his stare on a smear of dark substance in the corner where wall met ceiling, mold, paint, or something charred, he couldn't tell. The pink pants in his 'bedroom wall' wavered in the moving air. What was the name of the girl who once owned them? Had she escaped the blight, or had it consumed her? Could Allison's ghost be watching him now? Would she be staring at him, eagerly awaiting him to cross over or would she be trying to scream at him not to do it?

"Bollocks."

He let his arm fall into his lap, E-90 dangling from his limp fingers. Allison would never have wanted him to kill himself. She had to have seen the look of abject horror on his face when his arm moved on its own. A sidelong glance at the child's pants inflated a lump in his throat. Something innocent and pure, ruined and forgotten—like Allison. Sorrow deepened at his feelings of impotence at failing to protect her, worsened at his sense of inadequacy at avenging her. During his years as a frictionless player, he had women lining up, but he'd never had the least bit of interest in any of them. They saw a sports star, a giant credit statement, not a man named Aaron Pryce. Allison had no idea who he had been, and she still liked him.

"Fuck!" he screamed, leaping to his feet.

He looked around in a frenetic whirl, searching for something to shoot, but wound up slamming the E-90 down on a shipping crate forced into duty as a nightstand.

A deep, orchestral presence flooded Darwin's room, stalling Aaron in his tracks. The eerie sound would have been the perfect opening to a fascinating documentary about deep space, narrated by someone with a bass voice.

The music cut.

"Hey, babe."

"Don't 'babe' me, Darwin. Is your friend there?"

Shimmer.

"Yeah, one second, babe."

A faerie-sized snarl grew louder as Darwin moved to the loose, indigo curtains hanging in the doorway between his sanctum and Aaron's space.

"Oi, mate." He flicked his NetMini at Aaron as if it were a jai-alai paddle.

Aaron frowned at Darwin's horrible mockery of an English accent.

Shimmer's holographic head leapt from the device, flickering into nothingness about three feet away. Aaron's NetMini emitted a traditional and boring sound—a ringing phone.

"There you are," said Shimmer, smiling. "Is something wrong? You look upset."

Her aqua-colored hair shifted in a breeze existing only to her hologram. A glittering butterfly image spread its wings over her eyes, its body down the ridge of her nose. The digital tattoo cycled among shades of blue into violet. He smirked. Odds were high she looked nothing like this in reality. *Probably an old man.*

"Oh, no, just peachy. I adored sitting around for three days without a damn word. Please tell me you've got something."

"This woman you're trying to find wasn't born on Earth. I think she came from a colony settlement and arrived via RedLink from Mars."

"I don't much care where she came from." Aaron narrowed his eyes and lowered his voice, speaking in neat, clipped words. "I need to know where she is right now."

Shimmer's hologram leaned back, right eyebrow raised. "Well, she's gotta be staying fringe. She's got no 'mini I could find, and she's keeping herself out of the reach of citycams, which puts her in at least a grey zone, possibly under the city."

Aaron's face reddened.

"Before your head explodes, that video data you sent me helped. I did get a hit on one of the others in the background."

Four panels stretched out in midair around her head, each eight by ten inches. The left-most one displayed a still from his Division 0 helmet camera recording, frozen on a man in a bulky, green-camouflage coat. Muzzle flare from a pair of large handguns highlighted his dark brown face with blue; fat dreadlocks coiled into the air behind him like asps.

Shimmer advanced the video frame by frame. The figure sailed left to right in the air, falling while firing both guns in the general direction of the camera. Aaron knew the video well. He paused playback before Allison ran into the scene from the left, returning fire.

The second panel showed the man's citizen ID photo with the name Aston Davis; he looked older when not roaring and firing guns. Division 2 Gang Task Force data on the third panel indicated he went by 'Lucky' among his social circles. Citycam recordings split the fourth panel into seven hexagonal sections, six arranged around a larger middle image. Each showed a view from a different lens, all covering the same white plastisteel tower.

"Are you saying that bloke survived? He dove out a window to get away from Allie's E-90. Laser went right through the wall he chose to hide behind."

"I guess he got, umm... lucky." Shimmer chuckled. "He's staying at the Vittorino."

"Oh, shit," moaned Darwin. "Bad idea."

Aaron fell into a seat on his bed, landing hard enough to make the pillow jump. "What the heck is a Vittorino?"

"A name," said Shimmer, as if the answer was so patently obvious she thought him an idiot for asking. "Probably the guy that owns the hotel."

"You could've said hotel."

"Yes, but you look good in purple." Shimmer winked. "It's frequented by Syndicate associates and contractors."

"Maybe you oughta leave that one alone, man," said Darwin, still protruding from his curtains. "Need I keep remindin' yo' ass, you's an *ex*-cop now. They won't think nothin' of putting you out of their misery."

Aaron stared at him with a blank face.

"S'pose you don't much give a damn anymore." Darwin backed into his room, shaking his head. "Getting yo'self killed ain't gonna bring her back."

Shimmer looked off to the side.

"Right," said Aaron. "Send me a nav pin."

THE DEPARTING PubTran taxi stirred a misty breeze as it pulled away. Aaron glanced down the length of his long, black coat at his old police-issue boots. Allison's faint voice teased at the back of his mind, making fun of him for 'losing' them in his locker for the umpteenth time. He compressed the sorrow into a hard little nugget and filed it away for later. After a moment of silence, he took a pair of thin sunglasses out, put them on, and returned his hand to the coat pocket.

Allison's nametag still felt cold.

Across the street, the Vittorino Hotel stood out against the dingy surroundings. Boundaries of grey zones were inexact things, fluctuating from month to month depending on the prevailing climate of greed and apathy. The hotel represented a rare anchor point; the presence of the Syndicate kept the surroundings in a perpetual teeter between civility and barbarism. A block or so farther east and the city gave way to the Old West—if the old west had psychotic cyber freaks and advert bots.

On the outside, the place struck him as unremarkable, save for a clean coat of white paint and in good repair while surrounded by rot. No men in suits guarded the front door, nor did any 'suspicious black sedans' sit anywhere in sight. Aaron chuckled to himself as he crossed the street, feeling a bit the fool for expecting the Syndicate to be so obvious.

An automatic door made from an inch-thick slab of transparent material slid to the side at his approach. The lobby, decorated in grey and blue, was far less ornate than he expected. He did a double take at the sight of live clerks behind the reception desk rather than dolls. It made sense after he mulled it; real brains can't be hacked from the GlobeNet, and dolls didn't typically have families to threaten into compliance. A small waiting area to the right contained three sofas arranged around a holo-bar projecting a muted Gee-ball match. Aaron scoffed at the game. *Fecking barbarians.*

"Can I help you?" asked the man behind the counter.

His co-worker seemed ready to dart into the office behind them. Her surface thoughts contained a debate between his being a cop or an assassin. Either situation required her to notify someone higher up, but she froze with fear and indecision at the flashing red on her terminal, indicating the silhouette of the E-90 under his coat. She had never been in the same room with an energy weapon before and had no idea what to do.

Aaron walked right past the desk, heading for the elevators. "Not really."

Lime green light danced around his fingers as he swiped at the control pad on a strip of synthetic granite. Plain steel doors parted down the center and opened with a pneumatic *puff*, revealing a chamber lined with waist-high panels of rose marble. A strip of Epoxil faux wood trim, carved with a repeating pattern of olive leaves separated the marble from mirror-polished brass. He stepped in and spun about to face the doors. The woman at the desk ducked past a burgundy curtain into the office, while the man made faces at him as though he'd just farted into a microphone at a ten-thousand-credit-a-plate dinner.

"Keep your hair on, mate." Aaron touched the panel for the sixty-fourth floor. "I'm just visiting a friend."

Closing doors blocked his view of the clerk scrambling to place a vid call. The elevator got underway with a hum at the edge of notice. Aaron opened enough fasteners on the left side of the coat to let him get to the E-90 in a hurry. He counted thirteen seconds before the doors opened.

Aaron tromped out of the elevator, his stride projecting the authorityof the law enforcement officer he no longer was. Bas-reliefs of stylized mermaids adorned the hall on repeating pre-fab panels made to look like plaster. Thin blue rug, identical to that of the lobby, ran the length of it, and a clinging presence of artificial pine scent permeated the air.

A jet-black orb bot, the same size as a frictionless sphere, emerged from an offshoot hallway up ahead and faced him. Aaron disregarded the sentry, as it displayed no evidence of a weapon. The bot pivoted to keep itself oriented at him as he approached and went past it, whereupon it drifted along behind.

He walked to the end and turned left into an outer ring corridor that went around the entire structure. The expensive rooms, the ones with real exterior windows as opposed to holographic fakes, went by on his right. Aaron stopped in front of room 68-44. Pulsing electronic music on the other side of the wall vibrated the air in the hallway. The soundtrack muted, giving way to the floor-shaking thunder like a massive starship passing overhead. Voices shouted, tinted with panic and anger, something about taking too much hull damage to avoid the gravity drawing them to the surface.

Aaron waited.

Silence followed the sound of a long, rumbling crash. Digital noises conjured the image of text appearing on a holo-bar as a soft symphonic accompaniment played under the title card for whatever game or movie Lucky and company had put on.

Since it became quiet enough to knock, Aaron extended his arm and tapped twice.

"Mother…" The clank of a drink canister on a glass table rang out.

"S'like they fuckin' know when we gonna start," said a man's voice. "The fuck I payin' you for?"

"I got it," replied a deeper tone.

The door hissed to the side, putting him eyes-to-pectorals with a bald man in a pale grey tank top. Aaron looked up, but instead of making eye contact, he found himself staring at a flat black metal panel spanning the man's entire face. A triangle of tiny lenses at the center glinted with multicolored light, and scuffmarks gave away where it had deflected bullets. Inhuman contours to the man's chest betrayed the presence of implanted armor weave.

"The fuck?" yelled a familiar voice from inside.

The big man regarded Aaron with an unimpressed frown. "Girl scout."

A chirp preceded silence from the game system. "Cookies?" Lucky leapt up from the couch.

"Nah," said the titan. "This one ain't that tough."

He started to reach for the button to close the door. Aaron made a light shoving gesture at nothing. Telekinetic force swatted the ogre flat on his back and sent him sliding twenty some yards into the room, peeling up carpeting.

"I'm out of choco-mints," said Aaron, stepping past the doorway. "Lucky… We need to have a chat, mate."

Two scrawny men sat on the ends of the couch, the darker of the two still wearing a senshelmet connected to the game system. The other, his face liberally possessed of edged weapon scars, had a helmet in his lap and stared with bugged-out eyes at the prone monster. A battered Nicohaler, no doubt loaded with something it wasn't meant to vaporize, dangled from his lip. Several pistols, synthbeer canisters, and autoinjectors littered a glass coffee table. A hundred-inch holo-panel on the left bathed them in eerie greenish light. The high-res display looked like a hole in reality holding a scene from inside a crashed starship overcome with alien biological growth. Two figures in high-tech armor stood motionless, the game paused. Why game systems still projected screens when most players used helmets or M3 jacks confused him.

"D'that many people stand around watchin' others play these things that they need ta put it on a screen?" asked Aaron.

Lucky's thick mane of dreads shifted, swaying past the back of his thighs as he tilted his head. Eyebrows scrunched together. "You some kinda fuckin' nuts to come in here like that." He reached for a gun.

Aaron smirked. Five pistols slid off the table and floated out of reach before thudding to the thick beige carpet. The big guy howled and lunged upright; his metal knuckles swelled and sprouted spikes. A telekinetic shove tossed him airborne again. His scream of anger turned to surprise as he flipped foot over head and came down hard on his chest, with a groaning exhale. Aaron removed his sunglasses, folded them, and slipped them into the pocket with Allison's nametag.

"Lucky…" He held out his hands. "I'm hurt you don't remember me. I'd love to stay and piddle around, but I need to find someone. Where's Talis?"

"Aww shit." Lucky waved at him. "Kill this motherfucker!"

The goliath got to his feet and charged at the same time Lucky made a break for a bedroom door. Aaron thrust his arm in the raging man's direction, again lifting and holding him in midair. Lucky blurred into a streak of military-green pants, speedware flinging him out of sight faster than Aaron could react.

With a wave, Aaron sent the behemoth headfirst into the wall, shattering a skull-sized hole in the crumbly white material. Groaning, the oaf pushed himself loose, fell the rest of the way to the floor, and cradled his face in both hands.

"Hey man, don't bust the Yume Koujou!" The lighter-skinned guy jumped off the couch to shield the game system with his body. "Shit's bank! Gen eight just came out."

Lucky, now wearing his baggy, olive drab coat, ducked around the archway by the back bedroom. Two large handguns, bristling with after-market modifications and gold plating, chirped. Aaron leapt back out of reflex, telekinetically seizing the huge man and using him as a meat shield before Lucky opened fire. Alternating shots came so fast it sounded like a machine gun going off. He swerved the oaf left and right as Lucky attempted to get a shot around him. The giant body convulsed, groaning and wailing in concert with the fleshy slaps of pistol-caliber rounds failing to pierce dense subdermal armor.

The skinny man gathered the game system from the table, cradling it like a precious infant, and scurried deeper into the apartment.

Aaron dropped the wheezing thug when the pistols ran dry, shifting the focus of his power from levitating a body to the five pistols he'd tossed on the floor. The weapons floated around him in a cloud, pointing at Lucky, who screamed. Aaron would have fired right away, if not for the delicate process of feeling out where the triggers were with his brain. He made the delay look stylish and deliberate, but it gave Lucky the chance to dive for cover before the floating handguns tore up the wall. He fired each one only a few times before letting them fall.

Bullets lodged in the armored weave beneath the giant's skin popped loose from his reddening tank top, like a strawberry shedding its seeds, as he rolled over. More blood leaked between his teeth. Incoherent groans and a tendril of snot ran from his lips as he pushed his weight up on all fours.

"Are you going to play nice?" Aaron raised an eyebrow.

The man bellowed and hurtled himself airborne. Aaron's telekinetic defense reduced a body-crushing tackle to an intimate bear hug pinning him to the wall. He grunted, breaking out in a sweat as he forced the man's augmented arms out to the side.

"You're really not my type, mate."

The monster smashed his forehead into Aaron's face, knocking him loopy. Instinct brought Aaron's hands over his probably-broken nose, exposing his gut to an incoming fist. The punch crushed him into the wall, covering him in flakes of white material and doubling him over. Lucky's associate brought his fist down hard onto Aaron's back, knocking him flat to the floor.

"Ugh…" Wheezed Aaron, seeing stars. "That's a rib."

"I kill you!" bellowed the man, drawing his arm back for a skull-shattering punch.

Lacking the wherewithal to move, Aaron gave himself a telekinetic shove to the side, cringing inwardly at the sight of the enormous metal-knuckled fist crushing a two-inch deep crater in the slab concrete floor. Lucky reappeared, having reloaded while hiding.

Aaron coughed, spitting a bloody glop aside. Allison's voice returned, riding a wave of rage that rippled over his brain and flung the oaf from his feet. He drilled the aug face first into the floor before levitating him upside down. This time Lucky hesitated, trying to aim around the floating giant. He took a few shots, managing to get bullets past the big man, but also missing Aaron.

Equal amounts confusion and anger sounded in the thug's voice as he flailed and kicked. Huge hands swiped at the air by Aaron's shins and pulled at the carpeting, tearing it up in chunks.

"I get the feelin' this one got marked 'does not play well wif others' eh?" Aaron leaned on the wall, fighting to maintain concentration despite the pain in his face. He touched his upper lip and drew back bloody fingertips. "I'm just after a chin-wag, Lucky. Put down the gun, and we can all walk away."

"I ain't goin' down like this!" screamed Lucky, risking a shot that hit the big guy in the back.

The floating man shouted curses in Russian, straining to reach for Aaron as his face turned the color of a fire suppression bot. Veins swelled in his forehead, spit flew from his lips, accompanied by an endless stream of semi-intelligible death threats.

Aaron took a breath and held it, tossing the monster across the apartment into Lucky. Bodies collided with a resounding fleshy *smack*, sweeping Lucky airborne for several meters before they smashed into a wardrobe cabinet. The smaller man remained embedded in the shattered furniture, as if run over by a truck. Aaron advanced, drawing his E-90 from the gap in the coat.

Lost to blind hatred and adrenaline, the aug struggled upright and wobbled about to face him. Surface thoughts contained fantasies of pulling Aaron's internal bits out fistful by fistful. Aaron shook his head and fired.

Two laser streaks appeared one after the next; a brilliant line of deep blue light connected the tip of the pistol to the wall, through the man's chest. Unlike the bullets, the high-intensity energy weapon melted the implanted armor—and the building. Outside, an unfortunate advert bot sputtered into a fireball and spiraled toward the ground.

The giant succumbed, emitting a heavy wheeze as he collapsed in a heap. Aaron stepped over him, coaxing Lucky out of a twisted mess of particleboard, plastic, and clothes. He levitated the screaming mercenary to the side of the bedroom, smashed the patio doors open with his body, and held him off the balcony, sixty-eight stories off the ground. Bits of glass poured out of folds in his coat, sparkling as they fell.

Lucky screamed, and fainted.

Aaron tapped his foot.

A boxy advert bot glided over, hovering at Lucky's side, tilting back and forth as it scanned. He regained consciousness in a few seconds and screamed again. The bot projected several holo-panels selling climbing equipment, life insurance, and underpants. If not for the substantial amount of pain he felt, Aaron might've laughed.

"I had nothing to do with killin' that cop!" screamed Lucky.

"I'm aware of that." Aaron narrowed his eyes. "If I thought you did, we wouldn't be having this conversation. Tell me where I can find Talis. I rather don't think your luck will hold out this time."

"I dunno, man. Bitch just took off after that shit went south."

The advert bot's panels changed to show several variations on parachute systems from standard fabric to implanted ion-assisted cybernetic airfoils.

Aaron smirked. "I'm going about this the wrong way." He pulled Lucky in, close enough to grab on to the outside of the balcony railing. Without having to concentrate on supporting the man's weight, he could read surface thoughts. "Let's try that again. Where's Talis?"

Lucky scrambled to keep a grip on the metal, wailing in a voice three octaves too high for a man his size. "Oh, shit. Oh, shit. Oh, shit. I ain't got no damn idea!"

"While I find it interesting you are re-evaluating your position on atheism, it's completely irrelevant to my question." Aaron concentrated on the sense of Lucky's weight again, flipping the man up and over the railing and dumping him on his back, safe on the patio. "Talis. Where?"

The bot drew closer, changing the displays to wall-repair, furniture and carpeting service.

"No idea..." Lucky panted, closing his eyes. "Look, it wasn't me. That bitch had us all under her thumb. You know what I mean... what she made you do. She did the same shit to us alla time."

Aaron's knuckles creaked as he squeezed his fists. It angered him more to find truth in the man's thoughts.

A *beep* emanated from the huge aug. *Hope that's life support and not a bomb.*

"I ain't got no damn clue where she went off to, nor do I give an intergalactic fuck." Lucky coughed and sat up, picking splinters of wardrobe cabinet out of his coat.

Fleeting glimpses of an Indian woman with gold eyes and vertical-slit pupils appeared in Lucky's consciousness, along with a distinct sense of dislike. Any sense of what happened that day drowned in the immediate fear of dying at the hands of a power against which he had no defense. He cringed as Aaron leaned closer. The advert bot lost interest in its inattentive mark and presented Aaron with a series of offers: tissues, soap, new coats, stimpaks, and medical insurance.

"Who the hell is Rakshasi?" Aaron grumbled as he caved in and ordered a handful of stimpaks. "Annoying buggers... can't say they aren't convenient."

"A tí-zhèn with a bad attitude," wheezed Lucky. "Hates men. I don't think she was"—he twirled his fingers around his head—"brain tampered. She was there 'cause she wanted to be. If anyone knows where the freaky bitch went, it'd be her."

Aaron pinched the bridge of his nose, dreading the idea of having to deal with a woman who had enough neuralware to turn into a blur of speed and death. Out of the distant ambient noise, the faint whirr of a hovering bot grew louder. A spot of light descended from the traffic lane three stories up, coming to a standstill at Aaron's side. The size of a shoebox, it nudged toward him in the manner of a sniffing dog until it found his NetMini signal and emitted a happy chirp. Its front end opened, revealing a trio of small, red autoinjectors shrink-wrapped together.

He held them up as the delivery bot flew away. "Great. Wonderful. What are the odds you can tell me where this Rakshasi is?"

Lucky flashed a weak smile. "She probably wit' that Talis bitch."

Aaron sighed at the ceiling. "Bollocks."

9

ZERO FOR TWO

Elbow propped on the table, Aaron swirled a glass of scotch. About a finger and a half remained of his third helping. The drink dulled his frustration as well as the lingering soreness in his ribs. Syndicate enforcers had met him outside Lucky's apartment, but seemed content with his explanation of personal business not involving them or their interests. Despite that, at least one had tailed him all the way to Mina's.

The man didn't follow him into the bar, the first place Aaron found without brain-smashing music throbbing from the walls. It had a quiet ambiance reminiscent of his old haunts back in London, not that he had been much of a drinker when he had lived there.

Chirps and beeps drifted in from the far left where a handful of people threw credits away with electronic gambling machines. One man wearing an oversized helmet draped with wires kicked a recalcitrant VR unit, which failed to turn on. Aaron chuckled into a sip, grimacing as the burning liquid scorched down his throat.

Damn synthetic shite.

Still, he wasn't quite angry enough to pay 190 credits a cup. Synthetic would have to suffice at least until something catastrophic destroyed all reason. He slumped back in the seat, musing about the status of the pretzel nuggets languishing in a bowl. Large and puffy, they seemed as though they should have been soft and served with fake cheese.

They crunched.

He debated intentional hardness versus staleness while eyeing the room. A girl caught his eye by the bar, as much for her diminutive size as for her stark white hair. For a moment, he wondered how she'd gotten past the guy at the door. A high-necked black shirt ran into a matching skirt, which would have been short to the point of slutty if she hadn't worn it over leggings. His initial estimation of her age, somewhere between fourteen and 'going to jail' changed when she made eye contact.

Aaron relaxed. *Just a petite woman. I wonder what she's cheesed off about. Looks like she's ready to kill someone.* He sipped his scotch, chuckling to himself. *I'm one to talk.* His gaze wandered over a few couples, a number of single men, and settled on a different woman standing by the bar. Her neat business suit and designer purse at her side said she had credits to spare and probably a comfortable job. Aside from the bartender, of all the women in the place without a visible date, she seemed the most approachable, but she had a ring on. A trace of wet on her chocolate-hued cheeks hinted at a recent painful experience he could exploit.

The short, white-haired woman looked fit to be tied, ready to bite the head off anyone who dared speak to her. Something about her made him unwilling to consider her in the running for a one-night toy. At first, he thought her size made her childlike to the point only a nonce could sexualize her, but her eyes spoke a language that his brain missed, connecting deep inside him, a sense that she, too, had suffered a tragedy like the loss of Allison.

He held eye contact with her for a few seconds, sharing the sort of standoffish camaraderie that might've occurred between rival gunslingers in the Old West. He let his gaze move on to a woman who looked about twenty with fluorescent yellow hair. She had the disconnected affect of someone who'd recently taken narcotics, so Aaron passed on her as a possible mark. Two other women sharing a small table struck him as being more than friends. The only other single woman here, sitting alone in the back, had the bearing of a Marine and probably had him by an inch or three in height. *Hoy, she's a tank. If she ain't still active, she just got out.*

Sensing the way he surveyed the crowd, two men sent offering looks. Aaron returned a friendly smile and a polite glance of disinterest.

Scotch could only do so much to make him forget. He needed something more, someone to take his mind away from the all-consuming guilt gnawing on the back of his neck. Aaron put on his practiced half smile and sauntered up to the bar near the well-dressed woman. He opened himself to her thoughts, eavesdropping. Internal grumbling about her too-cautious fiancée twisted around her indecision regarding a seat at the bar or a table. The bar seemed too much like asking to be hit on.

"Good evening, miss." Aaron tilted his drink at her. "You 'ave the look o' someone a bit tired of the doldrums. Care to join me at a table?"

The woman's fatigued expression matched her mental sigh. "Are you speaking to me?"

He couldn't help but smile at her opinion of him as a scoundrel. "Aye." He nodded toward the white-haired woman. "That one looks ready ta rip the lips off anyone ballsy enough to dare approach. Those two seem content wif each other. I figured I'd strike up a conversation with the most sincere woman here." He took a sip. "I'd add 'most beautiful' too, but you probably hear that too much."

She shifted her weight away from him, poised to run like a deer in the eyes of a lion. One glance made her hesitate. While the stimpaks had repaired his skin, the dust up left his clothes in rough shape. His overall presence struck her as several shades of dangerous. Discomfort sparring with intrigue showed as obvious on her face as it resonated in her thoughts.

"A conundrum, innit? Come to a pub, and all you want is a drink, an' some bloke wanders over, you fink lookin' for more than you're offerin?" Aaron sipped his scotch and leaned on his accent. "I reckon we want the same thing, miss. The liberation of a good chat wif a complete non-judgmental stranger, a drink or two, no strings. I've 'ad a bad day meself."

"Is that so?" She tapped her long nails, violet striped with black, on the sides of a bright green drink. A hint of honeydew hovered around her.

"Aye. I bet you're standin' here so as not to look too available. Sittin' alone at the bar would be inviting company you're not of a mind ta 'ave."

She glanced at the surface of her beverage, streams of tiny bubbles racing from deep within to congregate in the shelter of the rim. Lips painted in gloss peach parted as if to speak, but she hesitated. Aaron's confidence grew. There it was—doubt. Her man was too safe, too predictable and, in her phrasing, had to theorize six different approaches to any situation before selecting the one with the least risk. Their imminent wedding, on its third delay, had precipitated the argument that resulted in her standing in this bar.

Aaron kept quiet, a mute, invisible presence watching the fight replay from a corner of her remembered apartment. No matter how loud the woman screamed, Ben remained the perfect picture of valium calm. His lack of passion infuriated her and sent her out the door to cool off.

"What do you say, miss?" Aaron tipped his glass at her. "I assure you I'm quite 'armless, but what's life without a little risk? Livin' safe ain't livin'. I'm Aaron, by the way."

"Denise."

Her inclination shifted. Conversation seemed like a good idea. Stage two.

"My table's right over 'ere." Aaron gestured with his non-drink-holding hand. "With the 'orrible pretzel-like things."

Denise smiled and started to follow him to the table, pausing as two men in dark suits entered and strode straight at Aaron. He faced them with a disingenuous smile, hands to the side as if greeting old friends. They walked right up on him, looming into his personal space. Both were unremarkable in appearance and could have been distant cousins. A sheen of perspiration coated the head of the man on the right, which caused his forehead to glow soft brown.

"Somefin' I can help you blokes with?"

"Alley," said the dry one. "We'd like a word."

Aaron moved toward the back door, flashing a casual smile at Denise as she slipped across his field of view. "I'll just be a minute, luv." Once she was out of sight, his face tightened. *She knows Syndicate when she sees 'em. She's gonna bolt.* He rolled his neck, letting the satisfying creaks ripple down his spine. *These two'll 'ave to let me work off my frustration.*

In his periphery, the white-haired woman eyed the suits with an expression of disdain. Aaron went into the back hallway, past two bathrooms, and stiff-armed the door at the end. A wash of cold trash-scented air came over him as the Epoxil slab slammed into the outside wall. The echoing clatter carried down the alley behind the place.

An enormous, white button-down shirt blocked his path. He looked up into the face of a dark-skinned enforcer whose chin hovered above the level of his eyebrows. The man's wide jawline gave his head a trapezoidal shape and called the presence of a neck into serious doubt. He grinned, flashing a pair of gold metal Fangz, cybernetic implants for the vampire obsessed. Sweaty scalp glinted in the channels between thick cornrows. Both eyes glowed orange behind sunglasses.

"That's a great look for you." Aaron tapped the man on the chest.

Smile fading, the enforcer backed away to let Aaron out of the building. He knew they herded him into a space between an overflowing trash compressor and a rain-soaked wall that had likely not been dry in months. The stink of human waste and trash intensified, drawing an involuntary tear from his eye. Vagrants nesting in the sedimentary deposits of debris along the base of the wall went through a bout of mental rock-paper-scissors. Those who lost got up and scurried away. The rest hunkered down.

Aaron stopped a step away from the wall and whirled to face the three men. He had nowhere to go, but didn't care. "Awright then, what do you tossers want? You just cost me a one night stand, so it'd better be good."

"Word is you're a wanted man, Mr. Pryce," said the sweaty one. "Not on the force anymore."

"That means your ass is ours," said the muscle.

"And who would you be?" Aaron skimmed the trio, catching the instinctual response at the tip of their brains. "Paolo, Charles, and Fernando." Of the lot, Paolo was the only one to see the surveillance footage from the Vittorino. That explained the sweat. "What can I do for you, my Syndicate *friends?*"

Charles' smile exposed his Fangz. "We need to have a word with Shimmer."

"Where is she?" asked Fernando.

"Oh, is that all?" Aaron pulled out his NetMini. Paolo almost fainted. "Here." He tapped it. "I've only ever met her hologram. Not a bloody clue where the bint is hiding... or if she's even a she."

"You expect us to believe that?" Fernando tilted his head at Charles and nodded at Aaron. "Maybe he needs some persuasion."

"Sorry, man. Nothin' personal." Charles stopped smiling.

Aaron glanced up, sighing with exasperation. Motion drew his attention to the fourth floor, where a cat trotted across a narrow pipe connecting the building the bar was in with the one across the street. "Charles. You seem like a reasonable man. I've already killed one muscle-brained dogsbody tonight. I'd rather not make it two."

Charles hesitated.

Aaron drained the last of his beverage and frowned at the empty glass. "You're probably wondering why I'm not shaking in my boots given your obvious size advantage, not to mention it's a three-to-one on me, plus firearms."

Paolo took a step back.

"The thought had crossed my mind," said Charles.

Fernando reached into his coat. "That smart mouth has a few too many teeth."

With a resigned 'sorry, but I gotta do this' shrug, Charles cocked his fist back... and then flew straight up to the level of the pipe.

"I'm going to drop you in two seconds, mate. Better grab on."

The pipe slung low under the man's weight. He kicked and screamed, howling at no one in particular, "Get mah ass down!"

"Down is easy, mate. Just let go," said Aaron.

Fernando pulled a gun, which Aaron telekinetically ripped out of his hand before it came to bear. He glided it closer and caught it.

"Nice. Deutsche Technik Firma. Imported." Aaron gave the man an impressed lip thrust. "You Syndicate boys don't skimp. That had to set you back almost two thousand." He offered the weapon on an outstretched palm.

Before Fernando could touch it, the pistol blurred into a motion streak and punctured the side of the trash crusher, leaving a head-sized hole fringed by jagged metal warped inward. The *clang* made both men duck and grab their heads; the sight of the crusher knocked a foot-and-a-half away set Paolo's hands shaking.

A creak of stressed metal rang out overhead, followed by the hiss of a cat.

"Momma!" yelled Charles. "Uhh, nice kitty. Niiiice kitty."

Hiss.

"Now..." Aaron gathered a sense of both men's weight in his mind, levitating the pair a few feet off the ground. "Will you wankers get it through your thick fecking skulls that I haven't got a clue where this bitch is hiding?"

"I-I d-don't think he's lying," whispered Paolo.

Charles screamed along with the yowls of an angry cat. "Come on, man. Let me down!"

"Nothing personal," said Aaron.

Metal creaked, triggering another "Momma!" from Charles.

"You shouldn't kill him," said Fernando, as calm as if he were still the one with an advantage.

"I've got plenty enough to worry about without having to wipe out the Syndicate on top of it." He flung the two men to the left in a heap, right as the pipe gave out with a *crack* and the terrified wail of a cat.

Aaron lent a telekinetic parachute to the four hundred and some odd pound Charles, guiding him to fall on top of them. He slowed the man enough to prevent serious injury, but the impact left the two normal-sized men stunned. The big man set his hands on the alley surface on either side of his associates and pushed himself up, letting out a startled cry at the sight of a levitating mass of screeching fur and claws inches from his face.

Aaron set the cat down and feigned a cringe. "Oh, that looked unpleasant."

The animal ran off, screeching.

Charles crawled away from the moaning bodies under him and dusted his coat off. He leaned forward, fixing Aaron with a stare equal parts anger and embarrassment.

Don't worry, mate. Aaron flicked something green and leafy from his arm, spatter from the pierced trash crusher. *I doubt your associates will speak much of this.*

"How the fuck did you just talk and your lips"—Charles waved a finger at Aaron—"didn't move."

"Either you just learned to fly and you're having a psychotic break from reality, or I'm psionic." Aaron walked to the bar's back door, patting Charles on the shoulder as he passed. "You decide."

The other two struggled to their knees, nursing broken ribs and various other bruises while the enforcer stared into space.

Aaron paused at the entrance. "I'm not particularly enamored with that one, by the by. Her information wasn't much use. I'd tell ya if I knew... It ain't my lumber to carry."

He pulled the door closed behind him with a telekinetic tug. Aaron stuffed his hands into his coat pockets and fidgeted with Allison's nametag while trudging to the bar room. The bartender seemed surprised to see him and sure enough, Denise had vanished.

"Bollocks," he whispered.

Perhaps the brush with danger sent her running home to Mr. Safe. The white-haired woman remained at the bar and still looked pissed off at the universe. The instant he made eye contact, she scowled and looked away.

Her expression would have been a perfect fit for a child forced to eat Brussels sprouts. He stood in the mouth of the hallway, motionless. She snuck a sideways glance at him, and the distaste solidified in the curl of her lips. Aaron tilted his head. Something went on there that defied the initial contempt for men like him when women gave him that look. No, this transcended simple disinterest or surface-level contempt. She radiated 'you killed my cat in a former life' vitriol, yet it blended with a degree of resignation implying she intended—or was forced—to interact with him.

Her surface thoughts were blank. Nothing but white noise.

Aaron smirked. *She's psionic too, blocking me.* A weasel's grin spread over his face as he wondered how much of his interaction with Denise she'd eavesdropped on. That could explain the contempt. Yes, eavesdropping would account for the face she made. Contempt and disgust. She must have watched him work Denise and knew exactly what sort of man he'd become. He figured that's about the look his wife would've given a man like him.

The sort of man Allison wouldn't have said two words to.

Aaron went to take a sip, finding the glass empty. He tilted it back and forth, heaved a sigh, and trudged for the front exit, leaving the cup on the table next to the horrid pretzels. Perhaps a few hours' walking about would help, as he'd lost all interest in women for a while.

10

SITTING ON A PARK BENCH

A aron eyed a trio of young girls with wild colored hair, indecent clothing, and several visible firearms. As much as his shame at what Allison would think of him now had dampened his urges, he paused to admire the scenery. The bad intentions swirling around in his mind dissipated as soon as their surface thoughts gave away their ages—two sixteen and one fifteen. He rubbed his nose and wandered to the left with no real decision behind it beyond moving away from the bar. Cool breezes followed the intermittent passage of ground cars. Patches of clean air let the scent of distant food sneak between gusts of city foulness.

He coughed and rubbed at his nose when a pungent waft of chemical devoured something his brain had translated into the fragrance of fried fish. *Damn, Darwin.* Aaron found himself smiling. *I suppose I am a cliché after all.*

A random turn brought him down a street bordered on one side by Sanctuary Park, a one-sector reserve of nature amid the steel and glass. It was a wonder how land developers had allowed a five-mile-square of 'not buildings' to exist. He collapsed on an empty bench a few paces away from the sidewalk. It faced in the same direction he'd been walking, allowing equal views of the city to his left and the park to the right. The dark expanse of green held his attention for several minutes with the odd sensation of being watched, though a subtle glance around revealed no one in sight. Some areas felt like that; the occasional flake at Division 0 claimed it meant spirits wandered about.

He'd tried to go nosing around the archives after the incident, looking for any solid information on spirits, ghosts, or an afterlife, but as a wanted ex-cop, using his official ID to log in had to be perhaps the dumbest thing he'd ever done. He hadn't seen anything but thousands of reports that sounded like bullshit. He had located one with some promise, from an I-Ops agent named Wren that detailed a 'wraith' terrorizing a small girl, but he'd only read three lines of it before a tactical squad surrounded the net café. If he somehow wound up surviving the confrontation with Talis, and (more unlikely) wound up no longer a wanted man, he'd have to find that woman and ask her if she could contact Allison.

Chirps and tweets lingered in the dark leaves from birds afraid to show themselves, assuming they existed at all. He smirked at the shifting branches. Minutes' worth of concentrating brought him no closer to knowing if the birds were real, synthetic, or mere sounds played to create 'natural ambiance.' At this hour, the place looked deserted. Anyone here would be deeper in the cover of trees, selling drugs or sex—or stealing them. The park comprised the centerpiece of a local councilwoman's revitalization project and had too many eyes on it for serious criminals to come anywhere close.

Aaron examined his fingernails. *Two enormous, augmented meatheads in one day. What else could happen?*

Hands stuffed in his coat pockets, Aaron fidgeted with the nametag. The metal still felt cold. Touching it reawakened the frustration at Lucky's uselessness. He'd gotten no closer to finding Talis than he had been earlier. Well, perhaps the name Rakshasi was a gain, albeit a tiny one. He debated trying to make contact with some of his old buddies, more specifically Tactical Officer Vernon Ridge. The man had been his first partner after his training officer. If anyone still in Division 0 would believe him, it had to be Ridge. His new partner though… she could be a problem; he didn't know a thing about her.

They might be able to find something about who this Rakshasi person was in the police system, though Division 0 officers looking for an aug with a suspicious background would raise red flags.

Aaron debated if he should ask his old friend to take a risk like that. His wife's nametag slid between his fingers inside the pocket, an absentminded thing to do while thinking. The too-young girls passed by, stopping a short distance away to lean on the side of a Nippy-Nom convenience store. He settled into the bench, observing people pass back and forth on the street, mostly unemployed gang types... or those who looked soon to become such. A group of more well-dressed men he remembered seeing in the bar came stumbling along, drunk and warily avoiding the trio of armed teens. He couldn't help but chuckle at the exchange. The girls were as worried about being attacked by men as the 'norms' were about the 'gang punks' robbing them. A shootout waited one ill-timed sneeze away, but two groups from opposite ends of the economic spectrum passed with slow movements and uneasy stares.

"This seat taken?" A woman's voice came from above and behind, to his left.

Her English accent caught his attention. He glanced back at the white-haired woman who'd given him the death stare an hour ago. She still didn't look happy, but her hostility had faded to resignation.

"Looks open." He returned his gaze to the sparsity of pedestrians.

She glided around the edge with feline grace, gathered her coat, and sat. "Are you awright?"

"Feelin' a bit like a dead duck," he muttered.

An almost-smile formed on her lips. "You poor old sot."

"I'm not that old." He ran his thumb back and forth over metal lettering. "A bit surprised you stopping 'ere after the glare you gave me in the pub."

"'Ave we met?" She squinted. "You look incredibly familiar."

"I have one of those faces." He flashed a cheap smile.

"The kind of face people think they remember or the kind of face people want to punch? Seein' your mug this close, it makes me think I wanted to wring your neck at some point, but I can't figure out why."

"Touché." He shrugged. "I suppose a bit of both. Sorry about the poke."

She straightened for a moment. "What? You haven't touched... Oh... The telepathy."

"Yeah." Aaron slouched. "Figured you were givin' me the look on account of—"

"I've not the least bit of interest in your sex life." She crossed her legs and glanced away.

Aaron shot her a whimsical look. "Yet you chose the one bench out of six that wasn't empty." He offered his hand. "I'm Aaron."

"Pryce, yes, I know." She whipped her head around, squinting. "You've the same name as someone I rather detest."

Aaron couldn't help but grin at finding her frustration cute. "You seem like you'd rather not be here."

She drew a breath to speak, holding it while a pair of inebriated men stumbled past them and went deeper into the park. "Aurora usually handles first meetings. She insisted I be the one to make contact with you. Quite takin' the Mick I bet."

"I didn't realize my fan club had a UCF chapter." He leaned back, arms stretched along the backrest.

She didn't react to the hand creeping along behind her back. "A bit jumped up, are we? No, not your 'fan club.' More like people with similar problems."

He let off a sigh, staring past slouching knees at the grass. Above the wavering blades, a memory of Allison's face seemed to form out of the pattern of street light.

"Not that kind of problem," she whispered. "The government."

"Not what kind of problem?" Hostility replaced the charm in his voice.

The woman showed no outward sign of intimidation. "That face you made looked rather personal. I'm not talking about whatever happened to you. I'm talking about what you are."

He bent forward, elbows on his knees, looking away from her into the park. "What exactly am I?"

"Other than a hard-drinking womanizing sod?"

Aaron chucked. "Yeah, other than that."

"Well, I'm not sure just yet. Let me do something?"

"I thought you said you weren't interested."

She smirked. "I mean mentally. I need to look into your mind."

Color drained out of his cheeks. "I wouldn't do that."

"I'm not going to brain-wank you, Aaron. I just need to check something."

"Really..." He held up his hand. "Don't. I..." He hung his head. "I've a bad reaction to it." He lurched to his feet.

"Hey, don't ya start away uneasy." She grinned. "It's only me."

He cracked up, falling to sit again while making noises halfway between laughter and sobbing. "Who's me?"

"Anna. All right... I really ought to verify things before I say any more, but I know you're at least psionic."

He held up his fingers, as if pinching something.

"Telekinetic?"

"Quite."

"Is that your strongest gift?"

"Mm hmm."

"How much can you lift?"

Aaron held up his arm, fiddling with the bicep. "Upper body was never my strong suit; I'm more leg than arm." Her growing frown made him laugh again. "Oh, right. Of course. Umm. Not sure rightly, I've never measured it since. Last check in was about two hundred pounds or so."

"Aaron." She scooted closer, lowering her voice to a whisper. "We think you might be one of us. Do you find your abilities any sort of unusual? More potent than they ought to be?"

He stared over her shoulder at a group of parked cars on the far side of the street by the Nippy-Nom. With a faint smile, he focused on the sense of their mass and lifted three of them several feet off the road.

"What the fuck?" yelled the youngest of the girls. "Those cars just turned on all by themselves."

"Uhh, Mia, those aren't hovercars," said a girl with a teal strip of cloth for a shirt.

The third girl screamed. Mia took off running without making a sound; her friends followed.

Anna whirled around at the screaming. Once she could see the cars, Aaron moved them about in a shell game for a moment before setting them down. A handful of people emerged from alleys and in windows, drawn by the screaming, but noticed nothing out of the ordinary.

"That's unusual, innit? Used ta put me out to haul a desk around."

"Quite," she said. "Was that tiring?"

"Not so much. Though, I admit those are much lighter than a police patrol craft." He winked. "No armor."

When she looked at him again, she had the eyes of an eager little girl. "You've got to be one of us, Aaron. You're Awakened."

"I'm not sleeping."

She frowned. "No, you spoon. It's what we call people with power like ours."

"Well, I've shown you mine. Are you going to show me yours?" He flashed a rogue's smile.

Anna's answer stalled in her throat as she blushed, coughed, and squinted at him. "Another one like that and I will... and not the way you're hoping."

"Pity." He glanced at the park again, eyes drawn to motion.

A small, rectangular hover bot glided along behind a drunken man, chastising him for littering. The figure stumbled, falling face-first into the grass. Shivering with glee, the brick-shaped machine warned the unconscious man about the fines for unauthorized use of public land.

Anna gestured at it. "That little blighter almost looks happy it's giving someone the business."

"Aye."

"You think it's capable of being happy or just programmed to act that way?"

Aaron rubbed his chin. "Seems like a waste of effort to program it to act like that. Also rather silly to imagine it having any sense of emotion."

She had a far-off look.

"You all right?"

"Yeah. Just remembering a little robot. Damn the CSB."

Aaron cringed. "Aye. Bunch of sodding bastards, the lot."

Anna turned her head toward him. A glimmer of something else flashed across her face, as if a different woman peered out from within a hardened shell. He considered offering his hand, but left it where it draped on the back of the bench. A moment of silent understanding passed between them.

"There are more of us, Aaron. The government doesn't know about us yet. Archon has a plan to save us all. We need you."

"Archon?"

"He's the one pulling us all out of the gutter." She fidgeted with her coat. "At least those of us that want to be. Awakened and plain psionics alike, he's going to give us a new future."

"Sounds awful romantic, doesn't it? Some gallant bloke leading the poor, downtrodden psionics into a new age of prosperity. How could anyone refuse that?"

Anna chuckled, still not looking up. "Only someone incredibly naïve thinks the world won't turn on us once they find out about us."

"That's a bit alarmist." Aaron stood. "Well, that's an awful nice story you've got, but I'm a bit preoccupied at the moment."

"You don't understand the importance..." Anna got up and put a hand on his arm, fear and concern brimming from her wide, sapphire eyes.

Aaron pondered a crass remark, something about listening to her offer after a shag, but the stare she gave him rekindled that sense that he couldn't do that to her. She looked like some manner of Dickensian waif afraid of the beating she'd get for failing to bring him home. He stifled a snarl.

"Look, I'm not saying no. I'm saying not right now." He took a step. "I've got some things I need to take care of."

"How shall I find you?"

His second attempt to walk away stalled. "How'd you find me this time?" Aaron leaned back and sighed at the roiling charcoal smog. "Fine, let's 'ave your PID."

"Is that your usual method of asking a girl for her number?" Anna's expression settled on a spot indiscernible between amusement and annoyance. "Fine, lets 'ave your PID?"

Their NetMinis chirped at the exchange of contact information.

"I don't usually have to ask." He winked and wandered off.

11

SERVED COLD

Thousands of tiny black dots blurred into a mass of pale grey, marred here and there by water stains or patches of mold on the ceiling tiles. Few were intact, most sagged, and a handful had ripped, exposing their yellow foam interior and the bare concrete above. Rats scuttled overhead out of sight, the sound of their claws a single instrument among the symphony of urban decay. Darwin's heavy snoring, distant angry shouts, and the occasional whirr of a hovering bot blended into a constant mechanical thrum permeating the building.

Aaron couldn't tell how long he'd been awake, lying motionless in his excuse for a bed, searching the rot above for answers it couldn't provide. Waking up without a hangover hadn't occurred in so long he'd almost forgotten how it felt. Another twenty some odd minutes of mental drifting did nothing to push him back to sleep. He shivered, finally aware of what had dragged him back to consciousness: a blast of unusual chill rolling over him with the intensity of ice water. It vanished before true awareness set in, leaving him wondering if he'd dreamed it.

Odd. He picked at his blankets, at a loss to explain how such a sensation could have affected him. Both hands covered his face, rubbing away the last vestiges of sleep after he sat up. The room was stagnant, neither warm nor cold. Aaron moaned, cringing in anticipation of a hangover's claws digging into the back of his neck, but no headache came.

He splayed his fingers, peering through the gaps at the wall of hanging clothes defining a 'bedroom' out of the larger space.

The pink flower-print pants still hung at the foot of the bed. They reminded him of how Allison had wanted a daughter. He also thought of Anna for no reason that made sense to him. She was small, but the child-sized garment wouldn't have fit her. With another moan, he pushed aside the melancholy thought of an innocent trying to survive in a grey zone and swung his legs over the edge. Why did his brain keep skipping down the path of dark thoughts? Did it search for something gloomier than his reality to make him feel better?

He sat for a while, trying to clear his mind, but kept circling back to Anna mentioning the CSB. Britain's government established the Clandestine Services Bureau as a psionic task force. Due to some rhetoric about preventing mass panic, they did everything in secret. Some bureaucratic wankshaft in a suit assumed if the citizenry didn't know about people with mental powers, the world would be a better place. The agents in dark coats 'disappeared' psionics in the middle of the night, even children. They would've gotten Aaron too if not for who he had been. Another life, so far off it could've been a dream.

He plucked the nametag from the nightstand and held it in his fingertips, elbows on his knees. "Bugger the frictionless club." Aaron wanted her back. He hated getting caught and having to flee the UK. If he hadn't, he never would have met Allison. If he wasn't a celebrity, he'd be rotting in a hidden military prison likely in the ass end of Wales, but she'd not be dead.

A moment of selfishness gripped him. The idea of her bright eyes and smile directed at another man reddened his cheeks. Jealousy flared, lingered for a few seconds, and waned to acceptance. *At least she'd be alive.* He clutched the sliver of metal in a fist pressed to his cheek and shuddered. A tingle ran under both eyes signaling an onrush of tears that never happened.

Aaron froze, staring at a swath of bright red cloth draped over a broken chair.

He sat up straight, blinking at the Arsenal t-shirt set apart from the rest of the clothes he had rushed to pack when he fled his real home. A rat burst through a crumbling ceiling tile, falling to the gelatinous mess of a Comforgel pad with a dull *plop*, amid a snowfall of foam bits.

"Now where do you think that came from?" Aaron gestured at the shirt.

The rat shook off the disorientation of its unexpected dive and scampered off the far side of the bed.

A lack of response to his question should have come as no surprise, being his conversational partner was a rodent. Aaron felt a twinge of rejection from the little furry beast; it hadn't even given him the courtesy of pondering his inquiry for a perceptible span. He shoved off the bed and stood, paralyzed with confusion for the second time in ten minutes.

On the floor by the chair, and consequently near the shirt, a female footprint caught his eye. Obvious as anything, it occupied a patch of exposed concrete a step's distance from a spilled canister of synthbeer. Another dreaded 'Final Sip' he bequeathed to the slow grave of evaporation rather than drink. He crept up to the spot and crouched to touch it. The scent of perfume hung weak in the air where the shape of a bare foot appeared in dark, dried beer upon naked floor.

Fancy that's a bit too big for Anna. He glanced at the bed. *Did I bring a woman home last night?* A forced swallow found his throat dry but not cottony. *I didn't drink that much.*

"Bugger."

He trudged to the miraculously functional autoshower and spent the next ten minutes trying to remember if he had been with a woman last night. At the cessation of the whirr from the dry cycle, he came to the only conclusion possible: the footprint was old, and he'd not noticed it before that morning.

It amused him to think of the shirt's prominence as some manner of omen. Without a second thought as to how it had made it from the duffel bag against the wall to the back of a chair, he put it on. The same feminine scent clung to the fabric, but he refused to let it reignite the debate. He managed an easy explanation for that as well: a female guest had borrowed it at some point. Allison might have, but she didn't wear that perfume. Any woman who he'd share a bed with would run screaming at the sight of this place. Despite his current situation, he still had standards.

"It's got to be the stress."

He moved to sit on nothing; the broken chair swiveled and slid into place in time to catch him. Aaron paused, not even realizing he'd used telekinesis as a reflex until his ass hit the battered leather.

"Hmm. How about that then." He held out a hand, awaiting the NetMini floating over from his nightstand, which slid into his grasp.

"Hey." Shimmer answered on the fourth attempt to call her; the voice sounded far sleepier than the smiling faerie looked. "I haven't found anything more."

"I met some of your associates the other day. They seemed pretty keen on finding you."

She crossed her arms, glaring. At eight inches tall, her avatar was a perfect fit for the limit of the NetMini's emitter, though the top of her head and her toes blurred. A tiny foot tapped. "They're not my associates. What did you tell them?"

Aaron smiled. "Oh, not much. Just gave them a lesson on applied gravity. Alas, they didn't seem the scholarly type."

"I should hang up on you right now." She tossed her glare to the left with an audible "*Hmmf!*"

"That Lucky chap wasn't terribly useful; about all he could give me was the name Rakshasi."

Shimmer looked at him, glowing blue antenna drifting together with a furrow of her brow. "Level 54 evil extraplanar, typically masters of necromancy, illusion, and/or enchantment. I didn't know you played."

"What in the name of heck are you prattling on about?" His face scrunched up.

"Oh, I thought you were talking about the Monwyn MMO. Rakshasa are creatures in the game."

Fantasy obsessed twit. "No... This isn't a damn game. Some Tí-zhèn who worked with Talis goes by the name Rakshasi. I need you to find her."

"I've never heard of a 'tee gen.' Is that a new creature?"

Aaron squinted. "Do you ever go outside?"

Shimmer pouted.

"A Tí-zhèn is an aug with a lot of speedware. Boosted agility, boosted reflexes, run on walls, that sort of thing."

The holographic faerie's eyes turned to white video snow. "Urban slang term coined somewhere around 2210, often carrying a feminine connotation."

"Yes, thank you GlobeNet," muttered Aaron.

Shimmer curtsied. "Rakshasi is the feminine form of Rakshasa. Oh, apparently it's some Hindu thing. Something about a man eater."

"Spare me the encyclopedia electronica." Aaron picked crumbs from the corners of his eyes. "Can you help me find this woman or not?"

"Maybe." A burst of yellow energy fell from her wings. "You have to do me a favor in return."

He closed his eyes and droned, "What."

The faerie held out her arm with an upturned palm, above which a man's holographic head appeared. Expensive suit, later thirties, black hair pulled back into a ponytail. "I want you to kill Julian Cray."

"I'm not a hired thug. That's hardly a fair exchange for information."

She threw the head over her shoulder and leaned closer. Her entire face filled the projection. "You have to do this if you want my help."

Her attempt to sound demanding seemed more desperate.

"I'm not going to kill some random tosser because you ask me to."

Black seeped like ink down her bright wings, darkening from her back toward the tip. "How's it okay for *you* to kill for revenge but not me? I can't confront the son of a bitch myself. I don't have the kind of skills you have. I'm just a..."

"Just a what?"

Shimmer turned her back on him, her tiny virtual body shaking.

"I knew it," he muttered. "You're a little kid, aren't you?"

"No!" she shouted, whirling around.

Balled up fists and a midair stomp did little to convince him otherwise. He smirked.

"I'm nineteen, but I... don't go out much."

"Oh, that's so much better. You're still a bit young to be calling hits."

A cough came from Darwin's room, followed by the wet gurgling of phlegm doing acrobatics in his throat. Aaron cringed.

"Julian Cray ordered my brother killed. I've been trying to get revenge on the Syndicate ever since, but there's only so much I can do over the net, and it's impossible for me to get to someone as high up as him."

"Oh, fuck me." Aaron sprang to his feet and paced in an erratic figure eight. "You want me to kill some muckety muck in the Syndicate? Are you daft?" He let all the air from his lungs in a long moaning sigh. "Explains why they're after you."

"Cory was a cop. He'd infiltrated them, but got found out. He was only twenty-three. You used to be a cop."

"Yeah... *Used to* being the operative fact. Besides, cops don't do contract killings."

"It's not a contract killing when cops kill a cop-killer. He's a criminal!" she shrieked.

The image of an eight-inch woman turning red from rage got him chuckling.

She glared, shaking her finger at him. "You wanna kill the bitch that murdered your wife." Her shrill diatribe fell to a near-whisper. "The way you feel about her is how I feel about the asshole who killed my brother."

Aaron sneered at nothing in particular. Darwin emerged from his curtained enclave, muttered an incoherent greeting, and stumbled into the bathroom with one hand inside his underwear, scratching his ass. Shimmer worked a series of expressions from pleading to demanding to about to cry.

"Getting into a pissing contest with the Syndicate isn't going to do anything more than add another layer of complexity to finding Talis. I'll have ten times the ball ache trying to track her down with thugs coming after me at every turn."

"I'll help you set it up to look casual. Please… I'll do everything I can to help you get revenge for your wife. Please help me. You want to find Talis, you have to do this."

He flicked at the nametag in his pocket pondering what Allison would think of this. She wouldn't approve at all, even if this Julian Cray was eyeballs deep in organized crime. The Syndicate traded in drugs, illegal weapons, military hardware, and girls.

"All right, but I am going to set a condition."

"What?" She sniffled.

"If he didn't actually order it, I'm not going to kill him."

"I know he did it! I have files, video, recordings… what do you want?"

"What's your last name?"

Suspicion hardened her tiny face. "Why?"

"I'm going to mention it and see what he thinks."

The faerie kicked at the ground, fidgeting for a minute or so. Darwin emerged from the bathroom, hand still buried, scratching. He smelled less like Nicohaler vapor and more like cheap soap. He muttered an incomprehensible series of syllables, waved, and disappeared into his room.

"Braddon," she whispered. "My brother was Cory Braddon. How will that help?"

Aaron flashed the smile that brought women home. "I'm psychic."

RIVALS

Regret walked beside Aaron on the three-block journey from his squat to the beginning of civilization. Nervous stuttering came from a thin blonde man in a too-large trench coat, who leaned against the wall a short distance away from the apartment. He'd gotten a pistol handle out of his pocket before he seemed to remember the first time he'd tried to mug Aaron. The hole in the third floor safety glass window still had the profile of a body. He lost composure and ran off, whimpering. Aaron wasn't sure how to feel about inspiring such terror after spending several years with Division 0 trying to convince the world that people like him weren't monsters. Of course, out in the grey zones *everyone* was a monster to a degree—or became monsters' playthings.

Aaron much preferred the former.

The nearest functioning coffee shop sat at the center of a cluster of corporate buildings, behind a wall of private peace officers in plain green armor who maintained a show of force along the edge of where the grey zone 'officially' stopped. A silhouette of a gladius adorned each shoulder, above the words Spartan Security.

They were paid to stand there and hold weapons, responding to any attempted aggression with the finely-crafted overkill reserved for those who enjoyed having power over others. Any crime happening even ten steps outside the corporation property went on uninterrupted. Most struck him as police washouts, bullies, or imbalanced individuals not quite off the cracker enough for Spartan's laughable evaluation process to flag them. At least their presence was sufficient to make the less organized gangs leave the place alone.

'Morning Bean' had become a favorite stop for Aaron in the months since he'd gone off the grid. Tucked into the corner of an office tower's ground floor, it was always busy but never to the point of an arduous wait. For whatever reason, the ubiquitous delivery bots had never gotten into the business of offering genuine coffee, or food that hadn't come from OmniSoy. Walking into a place was the only way to get 'real' food, though only twenty or so percent of the citizenry could afford to do that.

Half the people inside worked for Spartan, vigilant in their protection of cheap plastic chairs and scones. Aaron ignored them, even the ones who made an obvious show of holding their armbands up while scanning him. The E-90 waited under his pillow back home; by all appearances, he was unarmed. A coffee or two mysteriously toppled into laps as he made his way to the ordering station, grinning at the howls of frustration behind him.

The kid behind the counter looked about sixteen, with short, pink hair and a smirk somewhere between boredom and forced cheer. He tapped his fingers on the counter while Aaron looked over the board above his head. A palm-sized white button on his shirt announced he was a living teen and not a doll, because The Bean cares about people.

"Welcome to Morning Bean," droned the boy. "How may I caffeinate you?"

"Cheesy Fiesta omwich, non-soy," replied Aaron, managing a tone even more bored than the clerk. The boy poked at a terminal, which beeped. "With mushrooms. Also, an extra-large genuine tea. English Breakfast or whatever your strongest leaf is."

More beeping. "Uhh, you mean Grande?"

"Extra-large," said Aaron.

"We don't have that size." The kid sighed. "Minuto, Medio, Grande, or Grosso."

Aaron fixed him with a stare, a thin strip of teeth showing between tense lips. "Whatever the largest bloody size you've got is."

"That would be grosso." The boy waited with an expectant look.

Aaron glowered.

"Did you want a gro—"

"What I want"—Aaron glanced at the clerk's nametag—"Josh, is a cup of bloody tea without a bloody lesson in bloody foreign languages. Does it sodding matter what language I say fecking huge in? Tea, now! *Sehr grosse. Ogromnyy. Bahut bada.* Fecking grande! I'm not orderin' tea to look trendy. I'm ordering tea because I am fecking English!"

Somewhere out of sight in the back, a girl giggled.

Josh gawked. He prodded the holo-terminal, which beeped. "Uhh, seventy-nine credits, sir."

Aaron swiped his NetMini over the reader hard enough to make the clerk flinch. A scrape of plasticized armor came from the left. Two Sentinel Security officers eased out of their chairs. Aaron glared at them with a wild flare of 'please do something' in his eyes. The man on the left glanced at his armband and shook his head. They walked out.

"Thanks. Your order will be out in a minute"—he pointed to his left—"at the end of the counter."

Aaron took two steps to his right. "You know, Josh. You've seen me come in here every damn day for at least two months. You'd think I know the routine by now."

Josh blinked, his face a mask of utter confusion.

"He's just following a script," said Anna from behind.

His anger melted away. Enough sunlight fought past the cheap tint film on the windows to make her snow-white hair seem to glow in a frizzy puffball. She clung to a tall cup, clutched to her chest. Steam lofted the scent of Earl Grey from a tiny hole in its plastic dome lid. Pink fingerless gloves lent a splash of color to her otherwise monochromatic outfit of black: long coat, shirt, leggings, and boots.

Her amused grin fell to a flat line when she looked at his chest. "What's that?"

"What's what?" Aaron looked down. "Couldn't have spilled anything, I've not gotten my food yet."

"That." She pointed at his chest.

"It's a shirt, luv."

"Obviously." She squinted, muttering, "twit."

"You looked almost chipper a moment ago." Motion made him glance left. A violet-haired girl with coffee-colored skin forced herself not to look at him as she set his order on the corner pick up space. She scurried away, giggling. Josh made a petulant face at her. Aaron snatched his egg sandwich and tea. "Just poppin' in for a bite. Care to join me?"

Anna picked at the lid of her cup. She took a sip as he walked around her and sat at window table. He took a long sniff of the sandwich before lifting it with both hands to his face. Eyes closed, he inhaled back and forth, adoring the fragrance of egg not made from protein slime.

"Are you going to eat that or snog it?"

He popped one eye open. "Shh. You'll ruin the moment."

"Now it makes sense." She plopped into the chair opposite him, crossed her legs, and let off a long-suffering sigh.

Aaron tuned his environs out as he took a bite—not too much at once—and chewed.

"You keep making faces like that, people will wonder what I'm doing under the table."

"At least do me the courtesy of allowing me to do something crass *before* you get cross with me." He stared over his sandwich at her. "What's that? Makes sense?"

"Aurora. No wonder she insisted I find you. She's usually the one to make first contact. Bitch." Anna popped the lid off her cup and took a swig.

"Mind that." Aaron fanned the air. "All I can taste now is Earl."

"Don't fancy it?" She exhaled over the cup at him.

"It's all right. Just doesn't mix with eggs." He set the food down and grasped his cup. "What did this Aurora person do to you?"

"She's probably watching us right now, laughing her tits off that I'm sharing a table with an Arsenal wanker."

Between the unexpected heat of his drink and her comment, he almost choked. "That? That's what's got you in a tizzy? Fecking frictionless? You looked almost chipper before." He took another bite, mumbling over the food. "Tragic."

"I had hoped having the night to think it over would've made you more inclined to help us out, but I'm not honestly sure an Arsenal wanker would fit in."

"Jealousy doesn't suit you, lass."

Her face reddened.

"Besides, I'm not exactly playing for them anymore."

Her jaw dropped. "What? Did you say *playing*?"

"You said I looked familiar, right?" He held his arms, and the precious sandwich, out to the side. "Lose the scruff, about fifteen pounds, and four years."

Anna's expression went from shock to the bastard child of fear and loathing. "You..."

"Yep. I'm *that* Aaron Pryce." He put on a voice as though narrating a documentary. "A former striker for the Arsenal F.C., Pryce was considered the leading scorer for the last three years of his impressive, but tragically short career."

"You bastard." She leaned toward him, her voice a raspy whisper. "You don't know how many times you made me throw beer across a room. God!" She fumed. "You're the reason I dabbled in abandoning atheism."

"How's that?" He grinned.

"Well..." Her anger receded to guilt. "I... sort of prayed for you to get injured."

Aaron frowned at the crumbs, all that remained of his wondrous breakfast. "You and most of the tools that favor Manchester."

"Yeah, well... Around the time I asked the man upstairs to get rid of you, you had your injury. You'll 'ave to forgive me, I was in a rough patch." She tried to hide behind her tea. "Sorry. Hope it didn't hurt too much."

"I'm over it." He made thoughtful eyebrows while taking a long swig. "Most peculiar thing. When I woke up this morning, this shirt had been set out."

Anna's scowl seemed as playful as it was angry. "Lauren."

"Who's that then?"

"Aurora."

He tilted his head. "Who's Lauren?"

"Aurora."

His face went blank.

"Stupid Arsenal wanker. Aurora and Lauren are the same person."

"You've got a funny way of endearing people to your cause." He stood.

"So, you'll meet Archon?"

"Archon again. What is it with you people and funny names? Do you have a funny name too?"

She blushed. It didn't seem like a cute blush either, more like a crawl-into-a-dark-pit blush.

"Let's hear it."

Anna stared at her tea. "I..."

"Right. I've got things to do." He rendered a salute and walked out.

The scrape of her chair didn't surprise him. She caught up a block later, walking astride until they reached the decaying building where his sorry excuse for an apartment waited. On the outside, the place seemed in better repair than its surroundings. Perhaps why vagrants and spent pneumatic autoinjectors hadn't yet packed the stairwells, they assumed the place still had owners. Perhaps it did, in some bureaucratic on-the-books-but-not-for-real way.

Smoke carried the acrid stench of burned electronics in the ground floor landing. Aaron jogged through the cloud, still blinking water out of his eyes when he stopped at the sixth floor. He held the door for Anna who had her coat up over her face.

"Bloody hell," she muttered.

"Max... Mark... Mike... something like that." Aaron waved at the stairwell. "Lives in the basement, always mucking around with technology. Seems he's the reason this flat's got power."

After passing five apartments, he turned left and went in the second door on the right. A hushed conversation murmured out of Darwin's sanctum. Aaron flung his coat on the bed and collected a nice suit from the one intact closet in the place.

Anna hovered a step inside the door, wearing an expression as though she'd wandered thigh deep in sewage. She shrugged out of her coat and rolled it into a wad around her arms. Aaron didn't bother being subtle about staring at her black leggings.

"Sorry it's not up to standard." He forced a smile and kicked off his shoes.

"It's about right for an Arse—"

He gestured at her with both hands. "Must you?"

"—nal wanker." She advanced another step. "Yes, I must."

Aaron turned his back to her and dropped his pants.

"You didn't strike me as a powder blue boxer sort of man."

"Oh, really now." He lifted the pants into his grip with a leg. "What did I strike you as? Tightie whities?"

"Commando, actually." She glanced at the wall of clothes curtaining the bed. "Maybe butt floss."

Aaron coughed.

"Hey man, you fuckin'?" croaked Darwin from behind the curtain.

Aaron glanced over his shoulder with an inquisitive eyebrow lift before shifting his gaze to the bed.

She squinted, looking less than pleased.

He peeled off the Arsenal shirt, lobbing it into his duffel with a perfect toss. "No, just a guest."

"Excellent." Darwin poked his head out from behind his curtains, giving Anna an up-and-down visual check. "Nice ass. Hair makes 'er look like a little boy though. She should grow it out."

Anna scowled at him. "Aaron, there's a troll in your other closet."

Darwin flung the curtains aside, revealing his scrawny glory, covered only by dark socks and a pair of briefs with an alarming number of holes, some plugged by puffs of black hair. Anna scooted away, as if being near the leering man or deeper into the apartment were equally loathsome options.

Half in his suit, Aaron spared a two second peek. "Oh, that's Darwin. I suppose it could be argued this is his place, even though neither one of us pays any rent."

Darwin picked his eye with his middle finger, still ogling her.

Aaron buttoned up a dress shirt and slipped into expensive-looking pants. "He thinks he's charming."

As if on cue, Darwin patted her butt. She squeaked in surprise, clamping both hands over the spot where his hand had touched. Shock gave way to rage. Darwin instinctively covered his crotch, but she grabbed his face. He had all of a second to look confused before he flew off his feet, back through the curtain in a wash of smoke and the smell of ozone. His body hit the ground, twitching, convulsing, and frothing at the mouth.

Aaron blinked.

Anna scowled. "Darwin was wrong."

Still scowling, Anna thrust her arm out. Scintillating lightning connected her palm to the floor, snaking toward Darwin's crotch. He managed to force a pathetic squeak past his paralyzed jaw as he scooted away. The bolt dissipated before it touched him, leaving a jagged burn on the floor.

Aaron ran to his side, exhaling with relief at seeing his friend still breathing. "What the hell was that?"

"You wanted to see 'mine.'" She crossed her arms and looked up at him. "There it was, and if he touches me again, I'll do more than knock him senseless."

"Electrokinetic?" He levitated the suit jacket from the bed and slipped into it while it floated. "I've never seen one able to create lightning before... not without a conduit."

"I've never known a Tele that could run a shell game with three cars either." She stared up at him; the dark blue of her eyes glimmered in a dusty sunbeam. "We are Awakened, Aaron. The world hasn't seen what we can do. Now do you understand why we need to help each other?" She stared down, muttering, "Even if you are an Arsenal wanker."

He gave her a beleaguered smirk and went for the door. "There's something I need to take care of first. You're welcome to toddle along if you like."

"Small errand?"

"Something like that." He tugged his jacket up on his shoulders. "Probably going to ruin someone's day."

COMING UNGLUED

Aaron clutched the nameplate, safe within the confines of his jacket pocket. The PubTran taxi whirred along The Highway, two hundred meters above the ground, though with so many high-rises, he couldn't see any farther than had he been driving down below. Leaving the grey zone behind, dark alleys and glowering pedestrians gave way to open spaces between the endless forest of silver and glass whizzing by. The thin plastic seats hummed with ass-numbing vibration, and the air vent forced the cologne of the last rider into Aaron's face. On the long straightaway, the little self-driving car made it up to a speed close to ninety miles per hour.

They might as well have been doing nine, or been at a standstill, given how blurry the cars passing on the left were. Few bothered to honk, recognizing the ubiquity of the small silver/teal box with the flashing yellow light on top. The AI driving it, unlike the passengers, ignored the close calls and blaring noises from the ones that did. Private cars routinely attempted 200 miles per hour, despite the limit of 120. Few police precincts bothered with ticketing land cars; the money lay in hovercar fines, easily ten times as severe.

He stared at the passing monoliths, seeing them not as buildings full of people, but as looming black shapes devoid of meaning. In time with his finger tracing her name, Aaron ran the question around his mind over and over again. *Is this what you would want me to do, Allie?* His breath fogged the transparent panel, obscuring the lower part of his reflected face.

"What are you thinking?"

Anna's voice sliced the silence. The tight confines of the modest vehicle concentrated her scent. Aaron closed his eyes, trying to remember Allison's fragrance. His throat tightened at the realization he couldn't. Only the stink of sweaty police armor, locker room, and the awful stench of laser-burned flesh came to mind.

He sank away from the window, staring at the flickering console surrounding the pathetic little emergency steering stick. Sensing his focus in that direction, a smiling cartoon-faced car appeared in hologram over the dashboard. A moment after he didn't speak to it, the image vanished.

"I can't remember—" *How she smelled.* "I..."

"Aaron?"

He pushed the thought away. Now was not the time to get sentimental, especially not with Anna watching. Something about her set him on edge. The way she'd come so close to killing Darwin as blithely as if she'd brushed away a housefly had not settled well. *I'm one to criticize. I've focused the whole of my life these past few months on murdering someone.*

"I'm fine, I'm just thinking."

For the next mile or four, she remained quiet, instead staring out the window on the left side, smaller due to the passenger control console in the middle of the wall. Aaron found himself caught up by the glow of sunlight highlighting the contour of her cheek and neck. A contrast in absolutes, her face seemed as childlike as she did deadly. In that moment, he felt like they were both stuck in a car going somewhere they didn't want to go.

"Pixie," she muttered.

"What's that?" He glanced away so she wouldn't catch him looking at her.

"My other name." She kept her eyes on the window. "I'm not fond of it."

"Pixies are cute... if not a bit small."

"It's not a height remark." She fidgeted with her coat, rolling it between thumb and forefinger and letting it fall flat before doing it again. "It's... just something I'd rather forget."

A momentary earnest glance exposed vulnerability he hadn't expected. He shifted his weight, feeling a sense of distinct discomfort from a peek into some past trauma. His first thought was something the CSB had done to her back in Britain. It didn't matter anyway. The concept of getting this one in the sack for one night seemed demeaning at best, and fatal at worst—if the last he'd seen of Darwin was any indication. Some tragedy had marked this woman in the past; it shone as clear in her eyes as their sapphire hue. That they shared similar emotional wounds put her off limits to his self-destruction. He could no more think of her as an object for the taking than he could've considered Allison in that light. The realization stunned him into staring at her for a few miles.

When she risked eye contact for a mere second, the glimmering fuzz of white hair surrounding her head made her seem innocent, untarnished. A shriveled remnant of Officer Aaron Pryce woke up, wanting to protect her.

"Are you sure you're up for this?" Aaron put on his cocky grin. "I hear Manchester fans aren't terribly good under pressure."

The comment seemed to tear the rug out from under her melancholia. She glared. "We've been doing just fine lately, thank you."

Aaron tapped his chin, studying the ceiling. "Last game I remember was a bit of a drubbing... Nine to two." He glanced at her. "If I recall, we won something like ninety percent of the time against Manchester."

"It's not so one-sided anymore," she said in a threatening, low voice. "Been mostly in our favor for..."

"About three years?"

"Yes... about that." She crossed her arms and stared front for a moment before furrowing her brows with a gaping mouth. "Are you insinuating that it was *your* absence that sank Arsenal?"

He smiled, offering an innocent shrug. "Well you did pray for my injury, didn't you?"

A number of tiny sparks crept over the dashboard. The cartoon car reappeared, screaming.

"Oh, bugger. Looks like we got the clapped out one."

Anna closed her eyes and breathed as if preparing to give birth. A few seconds later, the taxi recovered.

"What was that all about?" He peeked over the edge of The Highway, feeling less than reassured by the elevation.

She took another deep intake of air. "Most Awakened have little oddities about them. Even Archon doesn't fully understand why. I tend to break technological things when I get upset."

He chuckled. "You must've gone through a lot of holo-bars three years ago."

She whipped her head about, fixing him with a glare.

"That's the same look you gave Darwin before nearly roasting his jubblies." He attempted a suave expression. "Not that he didn't deserve it."

"I'm not sleeping with you, Aaron. I'm taken." She sighed. "Except for your irritating tendency to think with your todger, you seem fairly normal. Have you noticed anything unusual about your abilities? Any odd changes to your body, strange effects you can't control?"

He scratched at his chin with one finger. "Aside from a significant uptick in the amount of force I can generate, not that I can say."

"Hmm. Interesting. That would be why Archon's so keen on meeting you. Perhaps you're like him and weren't born with it; t'would also explain why Aurora didn't notice you until recently."

"T'would," he said, raising an eyebrow.

"Twat," she muttered.

An unexpected swerve tossed her against him. The PubTran cut from the center lane across two others to get into the far left. She righted herself. Flashing yellow lights ahead flanked a sign reading 'PubTran Only' over an exit tunnel in the channel between opposing sides of the elevated road. With a *ka-clunk ka-clunk,* the taxi entered a tube barely large enough for it and descended at such a sharp angle Anna had to brace her hands against the roof to avoid banging her head. The ambient sound of traffic became an eerie pneumatic whoosh, accompanied by faint whirring overhead from unpowered roof wheels against the pipe.

Aaron's NetMini rang, filling the cabin with harsh techno-punk music that made him cringe. Anna shot him a confused look as he fished it out.

"Random. Got bored of plain ringers, but I couldn't think of what to use." He shrugged and swiped his thumb over the screen. "'Allo?"

Shimmer's faerie avatar phased into view, sitting cross-legged in midair with a steady rain of white energy particles from both wings.

"She's adorable!" Anna leaned closer.

The tiny woman gave her a middle finger.

"You chose the sprite," said Aaron. "We're almost there, by the way."

"I've rearranged Julian's schedule today." Shimmer beamed. "He's meeting with you, or should I say Ian Galbraith, at one in the afternoon. He's the CMO for Halcyon Logistics Interstellar, a shipping conglomerate with established routes to several dozen colony settlements... on both sides."

"Sounds lovely."

The faerie glowered. "I don't even want to think about what giving the

Syndicate access to something like that could mean for people. The real Ian Galbraith is arriving tomorrow. As far as he knows, nothing's changed. I made it look like the appointment got rescheduled. Aaron, it's really important you kill this piece of shit. Not just for my brother."

At the word 'Syndicate,' Anna scowled.

With an audible *foomp*, the PubTran car shot out of the dedicated off ramp tube and onto an approach lane shrouded in clear paneled walls. Onyx-windowed corporate buildings dominated the view in all directions from their isolated track.

Anna raised an eyebrow. "You didn't tell me you'd invited me along on an assassination."

"Dinner and a movie seemed so trite." He winked.

"This is *not* a date."

Her amusement added to his nerves. "I wouldn't have wanted to give you the wrong idea. Besides, it's not an 'assassination.' I'm not going to kill him unless he's guilty."

"I don't think it's a very good idea," said Anna. "As awful as they are, and as tempting as it is to prune off a few, the Syndicate doesn't forget easily. They'd be an inconvenience we could do without."

Acceleration pinned them to the seat for a few seconds as the little car left its protected lane and merged into city traffic.

"I got it covered." Shimmer winked. "All the security feeds in the building will show you in real time but record a different image."

"You can fake a Karsson-Neimand process?" Anna lifted a brow. "If the recordings test as false, it won't help."

"Not this much this fast, but I have done it. The police would determine it fake eventually, but it's not like the Syndicate is going to call them in. Even if they realize it's falsified, they won't be able to recover the real image."

"Impressive," muttered Anna.

"All right." Aaron rubbed his face. "Let's get on with it."

"Be careful," whispered Shimmer, before fading away.

Aaron tucked the NetMini in his coat pocket, leaned back in his seat, and closed his eyes.

"You never did say how you went from Britain's most hated man to a constable over here."

"You're right, I didn't." He smiled. "I wouldn't say most hated. I had my fans."

"Fine then." She huffed. "Why'd you quit frictionless?"

"Got tired of winning."

Anna muttered, "Twat."

"Have I been promoted from wanker?" He sat up and looked at her, his tone shifting serious. "It's a long story. CSB was involved."

Contempt on her face melted away to something approaching pity as the PubTran car came to a gentle halt outside a large tower building. The design was as plain as it was ominous, a basic rectangular shape. Its flattened corners deepened into grooves the higher they went, leaving the upper third of the building looking like four independent triangular sections. No name or logo adorned the plain, black front. Silver numbers above the entrance bore the street address: 1400.

"Right, let's hope no one inside thinks it odd the chief marketing officer of an interstellar shipping conglomerate arrives in a PubTran." Aaron flattened his jacket and fixed the button.

"The man lives on Mars," said Anna. "Do you think he'd buy a luxury car for a one day trip?"

"Depends on how corporate he is. Let's hope they believe it at least long enough to meet Julian." Aaron raised his arm in an 'after you' gesture. "You bring up a good point. Mr. Galbraith would likely have an assistant to do most of the talking."

Anna glared, though seemed to be fighting the urge to smile. "Twat."

He followed her across the courtyard, impressed by the evolution of her gait from perturbed trudge to arrogant sashay. She ignored the suited men watching the doors and went straight for the reception desk. Aaron tried to remember how it felt to walk into a media conference when most of Great Britain, and the frictionless-following world, adored him. She overtook and cut off a middle-aged man on his way to the same counter. The woman at the greeting station looked over her at the man with an apologetic cringe.

Anna tapped her hand on the false marble. "Ian Galbraith here to see Julian Cray. We've got a one o'clock and its ten minutes of."

"Excuse me," said the thick-bodied man.

"Our flight from Mars was as dreadful as you can imagine. Mr. Galbraith would rather appreciate Mr. Cray's promptness."

The receptionist appeared on the verge of hiding under her desk. She raised a placating hand toward the man. "You are?"

"Meredith Heath, executive assistant. Surely you've got us on Mr. Cray's itinerary."

The man got louder. "Excuse me!"

Anna shifted her glare to the rear and up. "Pardon? Did you sneeze or something?"

His face reddened. "You cut me off."

"Lose twenty pounds and walk faster. Mr. Galbraith doesn't have time to wait for the likes of you."

Aaron forced the irresistible laugh into a cough.

Anna faced the receptionist. "We'll just go up. What floor for Julian—"

"Do you know who I am?" roared the suited man.

"Obviously someone who fancies himself more important than he really is if you're asking that." She whirled about and glared at him. "Mr. Galbraith represents Halcyon Logistics Interstellar. Lenny, is it? We are here to discuss the facilitation of your network beyond Mars to dozens of colonies. Do you honestly think the handful of sectors you manage, rather cack-handedly by the way, matters one whit of fuck all in the grand scheme of things?" She took a step toward him.

Aaron grinned. Anna seemed to share in his practice of exploiting surface thoughts.

The six-foot-nine almost four-hundred-pound man leaned away from the five-nothing sprite.

"How do you think Mr. Benitez would react to learning *you* were the reason HLI walked out today?"

Lenny broke out in a sweat.

Aaron covered his mouth, trying to make the color in his face seem like anger and not the desperate need to belly laugh.

"Seventy-third floor, Miss Heath. Go right up."

After a final lingering scowl, Anna pivoted on her heel and stormed across the lobby to a set of burnished black metal elevators. Aaron made eye contact with no one until the doors closed them into a small space walled with crimson velvet panels.

Hold it together.

Aaron lost all urge to laugh at the sound of her voice in his mind. He broke out in a cold sweat as the strength left his legs.

What the devil's wrong with you now?

They had passed the fortieth floor before he found the ability to reply. *Careful. Something's not right with my brain.*

She laughed. "Really, you don't say."

I'm not mucking about. He scowled. *Trying to do anything mental to me could be... bad. Last time, I blew out almost the whole ground story of a casino.*

Anna blinked in a flutter. *I... Umm.*

Don't worry about it. He recovered his confident stance. *Good to know I can still have a telepathic conversation without knocking the building down. Where'd you learn to talk like that?*

Her cheeks went pink. *I've had the displeasure of enough executives' company to know what corporate types are like, especially ones who think they're as important as Galbraith.*

Aaron found himself speechless at the sight of her far-off look. Rhythmic bands of light pulsed from ceiling to floor as the magnetic capsule ascended in silence. His instinctive reaction to a woman wearing such a somber expression, reading surface thoughts, stalled. He lost a moment trying to convince himself he hesitated only because she'd have noticed him looking.

By the time the doors opened, Anna had recomposed her lethal outer shell and stormed down a cobalt-blue carpet flecked with a repeating pattern of tiny, black fleur de lis. Aaron put on his 'king of the world' affect and went after her, almost managing to keep a straight face when the holographic figure of a dark-skinned woman in an iridescent charcoal suit appeared in front of them. She had a certain kind of pleasantness about her, the kind that could turn on a pinhead to wrath.

"Mr. Galbraith?" asked the transparent figure.

"Yes." Anna stopped short. "Mr. Cray is expecting him."

Aaron tried to summon an imperious scowl and a look of impatience. The second part came easier; this entire side trip felt like yet one more obstacle cropping up in his path of revenge. He clung to the sour mood brought on by thoughts of Talis all the way down the corridor to the door the hologram indicated.

The left side of the outer office contained a number of silver spheres, hovering at various levels, each bearing a live plant. They ranged in size from eight inches to a foot and a half around, bobbing about with the slightest disturbance in the air. From behind a desk to the left, the real version of their holographic escort gestured at some chairs along the wall. A faint wisp of cinnamon perfume hung in the room.

"Mr. Cray will be with you momentarily. Please have a seat." She motioned toward a small table with a few silver cubes. "Please help yourself to refreshments if you like."

Aaron went for the chairs. "Miss Heath, be a dear and fix some proper tea."

Her plastic smile lingered until her back faced the executive assistant, whereupon it became a dire glare. "Of course, Mr. Galbraith."

"Do try not to muck it up this time, luv." Aaron made it a point not to look at her, focusing on his NetMini while muttering about a nonexistent presentation to the board of directors in three days.

Anna fumed, but forced a pleasant expression as she went to the table. Cray's assistant gave her a knowing look of sympathy. She fiddled with the food assembler.

"Would you believe these machines have no preset for Tim-Tams?"

Aaron looked up with genuine disappointment. "Shoddy."

"Uncivilized," muttered Anna, returning to sit with two cups of Earl Grey and some generic cardboard-flavored English tea biscuits.

If we wait more than ten minutes, you should throw a fit.

Aaron cringed as her voice entered his mind, eyeing the room with dread. Nothing moved. He exhaled. Three minutes passed, occupied with sips of tea and nibbles of the bland, crusty things Anna had brought back.

"Mr. Galbraith?" The woman at the desk tapped a few keys on a holo-panel, opening the inner door. "Mr. Cray will see you now."

Aaron set the half-consumed tea on a table to his left, got up, and crossed the room. The inner office was at least six times the size of the former, perhaps occupying an entire quarter-floor on its own. Water rippled in thin sheets down two massive granite slabs, falling into carved fountains brimming with koi. Small statues, Noh masks, Chinese fans, and European paintings (or excellent replicas thereof) adorned walls of burnished steel. Black marble columns ran in pairs down the center of the room, stopping twenty paces from a great onyx desk where two men waited.

The larger of the two looked to be in his later twenties, Asian, with spiky hair and a permanent scowl. He wore all black; his sleeveless shirt exposed the interface where his metal right arm met flesh; baggy pants concealed his legs. The artificial arm mimicked the shape of human musculature in such an exact match to his still-flesh left arm, it appeared like someone painted cybernetics over his skin. Silver squares embedded on each temple flickered with internal light. The sides of his head bore the telltale dark lines of embedded neuralware. He stood behind and to the right of the seated man, regarding Aaron with a frown as if debating the most efficient method to kill him. Dark grey plastisteel fingers fluttered as he opened and closed his fist.

Julian Cray seemed in his mid-forties, with brown skin and long, dark hair slicked back over his head into a ponytail. His features blended

Spanish and Asian, with a touch of Eastern European. He stood as they approached, extending a hand.

"Mr. Galbraith, I apologize for the delay. An unexpected matter came up that required my immediate attention. I hope your trip was pleasant at least."

Cray barely acknowledged Anna's presence, sitting after a handshake with Aaron.

"The ride was less than pleasant." Aaron eased himself into the chair. "I trust the day finds you well?"

"Well enough," said Cray. "I thought our meeting was tomorrow."

"It was." Aaron put on an annoyed expression. "Bloody military inspection of our facilities tomorrow, and Harrison demanded I be present to smooth things over with the brass. You'd think those simpletons could handle it. Considering the nature of our agreement, I thought it best not to call too much attention to this meeting by making a scene."

Aaron listened in on Cray's thoughts. The large man, whom he referred to as Tseng, spoke via an implanted device. Julian seemed pleased Tseng's scanning eye revealed no weapons or even any cyberware implanted in either guest. It made him feel safe.

Cray's lips teased at a smile. "Speaking of discretion, I was under the impression you would be alone. Who is this?"

"Meredith Heath, my new executive assistant." Aaron chuckled. "Horrible at making tea, but she's quite capable in other respects, especially discretion. I trust her implicitly. In fact, I can only think of one error of judgment she's ever made."

"Oh?" Cray raised an eyebrow.

Tseng tensed.

Anna glared at him.

Aaron steepled his fingers and flashed an aristocrat's smile. "She favors Manchester United."

Her eyes flared. Tseng furrowed his brow. Cray looked serious for all of two seconds before laughing, slapping the desk. The gesture reminded Aaron of the unstable crime boss from innumerable action holo-vids who could laugh at your joke and kill you a second later with a straight face.

Arsenal wanker rang out in his mind in Anna's voice.

He stifled a laugh.

"Damn Brits and your frictionless," said Cray. "I'm more of a Gee-ball man, myself. Full contact, guts and glory. There's danger out there, Galbraith, risk. Blood and spectacle."

"I take it you've never gone to a proper match then," said Aaron. "It's a bit rougher in person. The fans are... eh..."

"Dedicated," said Anna.

"Right." Cray clapped. "So, Halcyon's offer."

Aaron lifted the particulars out of Cray's immediate thoughts, as well as his intention to haggle. He needed the deal too much to turn his nose up at it, but he would threaten to walk. He glanced at his NetMini as though he sifted over contract documents. A text-only message scrolled along the bottom: ‹I'm in the cameras. That's the bastard. Do it.›

"Retainer of five hundred thousand credits per quarter, which includes a thousand one ton cargo pods per quarter to Mars and our network of outer colony settlements. Additional cargo beyond that to be billed based on our fee schedule according to destination. Halcyon agrees to honor your non-compete with other parties deemed detrimental to your business interests."

Cray flashed an appraising smirk at his terminal. "We had an offer from Parsons-Dormand for three hundred thousand a quarter."

Another text rolled by. ‹What are you waiting for?›

The answer shone clear as day on the tip of the man's brain. Aaron waved his hand around as he spoke. "Parsons-Dormand, on average, uses fourteen-year-old vessels with a host of mechanical problems. One in fourteen shipments they send never arrives. Plus, they lack the starport contracts Halcyon is able to leverage on the more established colonies. Not only do they pay per-landing berth fees, as opposed to a fixed yearly rate, they have no 'protection' from the scrutiny of local authorities upon unloading. With Halcyon, you're also getting discretion."

Anna gave him a sideways glance. *You could do this for a living.*

Except, what I'm doing to him is technically illegal.

Cray drummed his fingers on the desk. He scrambled to come up with something to offer in exchange for a reduced quarterly cost: sabotage to competitors, drugs, stolen merchandise, even sex slaves for some Halcyon executives. Not knowing how Galbraith would react to such suggestions kept the ideas from leaving his mouth. The man was definitely Syndicate.

"I do have one small question," said Aaron. "Something that got asked about in the boardroom while discussing possible liability and discretion. Do you remember a man by the name of Cory Braddon? We'd heard some unsettling rumors that you'd had a police officer murdered and didn't keep much of a lid on it."

To his credit, Cray kept a calm face. His thoughts gave him away in an instant. Images of a young man flashed by. Blond, green eyes, caramel skin, eager to be part of the Syndicate—until his cover fell apart. Once they sniffed him out as a police infiltrator, Cray had indeed ordered the man killed, though he had not been there to watch. Thoughts of Cory Braddon gave way to wondering who was going to die for leaking word of it to the outside world. A couple faces and names cycled across the forefront of his thoughts until he settled on a familiar looking faerie. In Cray's memory, she'd once appeared on every terminal screen in the Syndicate hotel, giving him a double middle finger.

Aaron suppressed the urge to facepalm. *Way to stay subtle.*

A trace of anger hardened Cray's eyes. "There are certain matters of business that many consider unsavory. One such area often involves hackers with monetary agendas. One such individual has targeted us for extortion."

Shimmer texted him again. <Bastard. Kill this fucker already!>

Anna must have been eavesdropping on Cray's mind as well. She tensed, ready for the proverbial shit to hit the fan.

Aaron smiled. "That's good to hear. My board of directors would like to enter this arrangement with open eyes. We are fully aware of the situation."

Are you just going to kill him? Anna held up her NetMini as if checking an appointment.

He glanced at her. *Me? No.*

"What... situation?" Cray leaned forward over his desk.

"Your employer's interests." Aaron dropped to a whisper. "The Syndicate."

He smiled at Tseng, gathering a sense of the man's weight in his mind and concentrating an overdone amount of telekinetic force on the metal fist. Enough effort to lift three cars hauled the limb straight up over the man's head. Tseng's face turned red with shock and exertion as he fought to bring his runaway limb under control. Aaron sucked in a breath as if about to battle constipation, and drove the metal fist downward. It hit Cray in the back of the head, detonating his skull in a shower of gore.

Most of which wound up splattering over Anna.

The impact cracked the slab, embedding Tseng up to the elbow in the expensive desk. Cray's body convulsed as spurts of arterial blood shot out of the mangled remnants of a neck.

Aaron leaned back in his chair. "An Arsenal fan would have seen that coming and ducked."

"You bloody idiot." Anna gasped.

"Actually." Aaron raised an eyebrow. "You're the bloody—"

Tseng roared, tugging at his trapped arm while screaming incoherencies.

Anna gawked at Aaron. "Feck me."

"I thought you said you were taken."

She zapped him in the knee, making him yowl and rub the spot. "No, you git. I just realized. You're a damn telekinetic. No sodding wonder you were such a star. You cheated!"

Aaron made a blasé face. "Yeah, yeah… Took the bastards awhile to catch on."

"I knew it!" Anna leapt to her feet. "The only damn way Arsenal could win so much is cheating!"

Tseng lifted the stone desk an inch off the ground before it cracked away from his arm, sending him stumbling backward into the wall.

"Luv, I don't think this is the time or the place to get into a debate about sports ethics. We've got a cyberspsychotic about to turn us into mince pies."

"You're a cheat!" Anna stomped in a circle. "They won sixty-eight of seventy-five matches over three years because you're a bloody cheater moving the stone!"

"You sound like a petulant schoolgirl. It really wasn't a big deal, just a little nudge here and there." Aaron stood up "We really should leave."

Cray's executive assistant appeared in the doorway, screaming.

"I say, Miss." Aaron gestured at her. "Your former employer's guard seems to have become unglued."

Tseng sprang airborne over the desk, leaping into a punch. Aaron redirected his flight with a subtle shove that could pass for a coincidental miss. Tseng's fist cratered the floor.

"Too much cyberware," whispered Aaron past the back of his hand while pointing at Tseng with the other.

"Mr. Cray!" screamed the assistant.

"He's a bit far gone for that, luv," said Aaron.

"How many goals did you really score?" Anna attempted to loom at Aaron, as much as she could at her height. "Or, did you cheat them all in?"

Aaron dragged her to the side as Tseng pounced like a human flea, cracking the floor again. The executive assistant ran from the door, screaming for security. Cray's bodyguard jumped up, sprouting a single fourteen-inch sword from the back of his cybernetic arm. Heat blur peeled from the edge and the high-pitched whine of a vibro-blade raised the hairs on the back of Aaron's neck. Oscillating at thousands of cycles per second, it could cut almost anything with little effort.

Tseng managed a step and half before a faint thread of electricity flickered between Anna's hand and his forehead with a loud *pop*. Aaron coughed at the strong ozone scent, jerking his hand away from her arm and waving his fingers as if burned.

The aug bodyguard went over backward like a plank, twitching and foaming at the mouth. Tiny panels opened and closed along his arm, and wirepaths beneath his skin glowed orange for a brief moment.

"Not a big deal?" screamed Anna. "Not a big deal? Are you serious? Do you understand what you did? You've destroyed the integrity of—"

Tseng howled past clenched teeth. "… Kill …"

"Oh, shut up," muttered Anna. Another hair-thin lightning filament snapped to his chest with a sound like a pistol firing. She jabbed a finger into Aaron's shoulder in time with each word. "You destroyed the integrity of the game. Arsenal's record for those three years was built on shit and bollocks."

"*Miss Heath*, we should not be here when the authorities arrive." Aaron jogged to the far end of the office, where dark tinted glass made up the entire wall. The street at the bottom looked clear.

"Oh, no you don't." Anna stalked after him. "You're going to contact the regulatory commission and—"

"They already know."

Her eyes went wide. "What?"

Tseng staggered to his feet, pivoting about with a lurching stride somewhere between a drunken frictionless hooligan and Frankenstein's monster. Aaron locked eyes with him, grasping Anna's shoulders.

"Why do you think I had an 'injury' and had to 'retire?' The CSB noticed. One of them was a bleedin' Manchester fan and kept doing parabolic analyses on the flight paths of the stone. There's no cybernetics in my leg. I never got hurt."

Tseng reared back and charged.

"Bugger…" Anna stared over his shoulder, off into space. "And they didn't rescind Arsenal's—"

Aaron leapt to the right, tackling Anna out of Tseng's path while simultaneously hauling the man forward with a severe telekinetic yank. The vibro-blade sliced the inch-thick reinforced glass as easily as foam. His roar of rage became a yelp of surprise, which cut out as his face made contact with the window, shattering the entire six-by-twelve-foot panel. An unconscious Tseng plummeted to the street far below.

"No, the club had no idea. I was after personal glory." He winked.

Lying on the floor, Anna looked up at Aaron and grasped his forearms. Flakes of broken silica caught light from outside and sparkled on the dark tiles around her head.

"Looks like pixie dust," he muttered.

"You're a cheat," she said, with a smirk.

He helped her up. "Just a little nudge here and there."

Anna stared at him for a second or two before she let go and took a step back, crossing her arms. "That's cheating."

The pounding of numerous bodies in heavy boots grew louder in the assistant's office. Whether or not anyone in the building believed Tseng had gone psycho didn't matter to his present aversion to being around cops. Aaron put a hand to her back and guided her closer to the window.

"Aye, but it worked." He threw an arm around her and leapt off the edge, dragging her along.

MENTAL SCAR

Anna's scream ended about halfway down when her lungs ran out of air. The effect of her terror manifested as a line of darkness following their plummet on the side of the building. Sputtering flashes and pops inside raced along with their fall, as anything electronic within fifty meters of her overloaded and died. Aaron's coat pocket caught fire when his NetMini committed seppuku. Unfortunately, the concentration necessary to maintain their telekinetic parachute prevented him from swatting at it until they reached the ground.

He landed facing the building, with Anna clamped around him like a koala bear. As soon as he relaxed his brain, he tamped at his left side while dancing in a circle and chanting the word "hot" repeatedly. Her trembling lessened, but remained audible in her voice.

"Aaron. If I've soiled my knickers, I am going to do something very, very bad to you."

"Bastarding thing." He clapped his hand over the smoking fabric. "'Mini's buggered itself."

She lifted her head; her shaking ceased. "Aaron?"

"What?"

"Are those friends of yours?"

Aaron sighed at rapid flashes of azure light reflecting from the corporate tower. He swiveled around as Anna disengaged from her death grip. Two Division 0 patrol craft sat half on the sidewalk, parked behind a pair of flowerpots as tall as a man, which held small trees. Four tactical officers had laser pistols leveled off at the pair, three E-90s and an E-86. The one woman among them looked angry enough to shoot him as readily as talk.

He smiled at the man holding the green-glowing pistol. "'Ello, Vernon. Still haven't upgraded that pea shooter?"

"He's *Sergeant* Ridge to you now," snarled the woman.

"Almost double the shots for the same E-mag," said Ridge. "Look, Aaron. I don't like this either, but we got orders to escort you in."

"I'll take a small bit of comfort in thinking you might believe me, since you're not just shooting."

The woman rounded the front end of the car, walking up to him, weapon raised. "I wanted to. Rios and Frost were in my graduating class. They weren't even there to mess with you, just getting tested. You killed them for nothing. Gimme a reason. I'm beggin' you."

Aaron glanced at her nameplate, Tactical Officer Nuñez. His gaze fell, as did his voice. "You know I had no control over that. I don't rightly understand what happened."

"They always say that," snarled Nuñez. "I was hoping you'd resist."

"Ridge." Aaron ignored the woman at his side. "How long did we ride together? You know me better than that. You knew Allison."

"Yeah." Sergeant Vernon Ridge shifted his weight, looking off to the side. "Like I said, I don't like it either, but you gotta come in so we can get everything straightened out."

"I can't do that yet." Aaron stared to his right, down the street. "The bitch that killed Allison got away. I'll consider coming in after I deal with Talis."

Anna raised her eyebrow at him.

Nuñez grabbed his arm. "You're coming with us now."

She dug her fingers into his bicep while making a constipated face, which melted to anger and then confusion.

"Oh, that's cute," said Anna. "She fancies herself an electrokinetic. I think she just tried to stun you."

"Hands in the air, bitch," screamed Nuñez, aiming at Anna. "She's an EK too; strong."

Anna winked. "How adorable. Let me show you how it's supposed to work."

Four streams of crackling lightning danced from the officers' weapons to Anna's raised hands. The pistols went dark. Anna thrust her arms forward at Nuñez, releasing two thicker arcs into the woman's chest that knocked her off her feet. Screaming, Nuñez skittered on her armor into the facing side of a patrol craft with a heavy *clank*.

The other three officers turned pale and clicked useless triggers.

Anna frowned, pouring more energy into the surge. Rage in Nuñez's howls faded to agonized, terrified pleading.

"Please, don't kill me..." Nuñez wailed, her body lost to electric convulsions. "I have a son!"

Aaron hauled Anna off her feet with a telekinetic shove, jerking her away from Nuñez and pushing her into the wall behind him. "Enough, Anna! Don't kill her."

"I wasn't going to." Anna faked a pout.

"You had me worried there for a tick. Wasn't sure a Man U fan could tell the difference 'tween a cop and a ref." Aaron grinned.

"You prick!" she yelled. "You cheating prick!"

Nuñez curled fetal, crying, muttering "ow" over and over.

"Did she just..." Ridge pointed at Anna.

The officer to his left blinked. "Throw electricity out of her fingers?"

"Are you okay?" asked the last officer, taking a knee at Nuñez's side.

The woman continued shaking, not even trying to speak.

Aaron offered an apologetic look to his old partner. "Vernon... I'm not entirely sure—"

"*Get in the car,*" said the man checking on Nuñez. His eyes glowed faint green.

No! Aaron twisted toward Anna, intending to shout at her to run, but couldn't get his jaw open. He strained to hold back, to resist the psionic compulsion, trying to contain the detonation millimeters away from escaping. His mouth hung open. Tears leaked from both eyes as his face reddened. Guilt at killing Allison hit him all over again as Anna's face flooded his vision, her eyes full of confusion and concern.

Run! Get away from me. Not again!

The command brought his head around, staring at the patrol craft he'd been ordered to get in, and the man before him. Energy filtered over Aaron's brain; painful waves rippled around the sides of his head and down his spine. He fell to a knee, grabbing his head, and screamed. A tremendous crash pierced the roaring din within his mind, snapping him out of his disorientation. Aaron straightened out of his cringe.

One of the patrol craft had vanished; twinkling glass brought his attention upward to the building across the street where a car-sized hole punched through the wall on the third story. Fragments of office furniture drifted out into the wind. The massive flowerpots had struck the building two stories higher, on either side of it. Distant screaming came from the damaged windows.

No... Anna...

The officer who attempted to use psionic suggestion on him also seemed to have ceased to exist, until a moan from above made him look up. A large advert bot struggled to remain aloft at the level of the fourth floor, impaled by a human projectile. Armor had prevented the man from dying, turning him into a living spear. Without a car to lean on, Nuñez had fallen flat on her back.

"What the bloody fuck..." Anna wheezed. "Was that?"

Aaron's heart resumed beating. With a gasp of relief, he looked over his shoulder; the glass wall behind him had disintegrated almost fifty feet in both directions from where he stood. Anna's boots stuck up from behind a bench seat in the lobby a short distance inside. The destruction seemed weakest around her.

Ridge and the other officer stood up from behind the remaining car. It sat about ten meters further away, in the middle of the road at the end of long black streaks from the tires. Another wave of pain gripped Aaron, knocking him to his knees and drawing a whimper.

"Don't use suggest..." He groaned. "I can't control it."

The advert bot let off a series of loud detonations and flashes. Aaron forced himself to look up at the exact moment the hover unit gave out. Calling on his telekinesis felt like someone had inserted a burning coal under his brainstem. He growled, face reddening, veins in his forehead rising, and pulled the semi-conscious man out of the plummeting wreck before it smashed a handful of parked cars into a tangle of warped metal.

Half-digested tea and biscuits sprayed out of both nostrils. Aaron collapsed with his forehead to the blessed, cold plastisteel sidewalk after setting the man on the hood of the remaining patrol craft.

"You're not making things any easier on yourself, Pryce," said Ridge.

Anna's boot crunched the glass by Aaron's cheek. "Are you all mentally deficient?"

The two unhurt Division 0 officers both grunted in fear.

"Your genius compatriot attempted to use suggestion on him. Something's gone bollocksed in his brain. I thought you people were supposed to understand psionics. Bloody *look* at him! Does that seem like somethin' he *wanted* to do?"

Aaron pushed at the surface beneath him; his effort to stand increased the war in his head to migraine proportions. White spots danced in his eyes as a trickle of bile leaked from his lower lip. He coughed, mesmerized by the once-straight line of the sidewalk edge blurring into a twist of reflected light.

"Bastarding hell," wheezed Aaron. At the touch of Anna's hand on his shoulder, he tried again to stand, and managed it. "Ridge…"

"You flung the goddamned PC into a building." Ridge glanced up and back for a moment. "You're rating ain't that high. No one's is. Logan's one of our stronger TKs, and she can't even get a PC off its wheels."

"And electrokinetics don't throw lightning through the air," added the other man.

"Don't poke me in the head." Aaron pressed a hand to his temple. "I've not got me legs, luv."

Anna pulled his arm around her shoulders, though her height left him in an awkward slouch. She gestured at all four officers. Glowing blue arc spiders appeared, dancing over their armor for a few seconds before dissipating. The two men screamed out of startlement, then exchanged a glance in silence.

"Can't 'ave you callin' for backup now. Be good little constables and stay out of our way. You're right. Electrokinetics don't toss lightning bolts from their fingertips, so you blokes must be hallucinating. Everything you just saw was in your imagination."

"You shouldn't antagonize…" Aaron lurched forward.

"Come on." Anna dragged him to the side like a drunk hauled out of a pub.

"I…" He pawed at his face, trying to pull at the sensation of a spike rammed into his brain, and vomited again. Before he could apologize, he blacked out.

15

DIRTY LAUNDRY

After the hot iron faded from his temporal lobe, Aaron found the dead Comforgel pad exquisite in its softness. Despite its gummy consistency and off-putting rubbery smell, it offered paradise compared to the past hour. He closed his eyes, focusing on the entrancing, repetitive *wubba-wubba-whirr* of the autoshower in the next room.

Minutes later, a metallic squeak echoed in the hallway outside, dragging him away from the precipice of some much-desired sleep. He cringed in preparation for the slam of the stairwell door, but it didn't hurt as much as he expected. Darwin's out-of-tune whistling grew louder until it entered the narrow entryway and burst into the main room.

A barrier of old clothes didn't do much to mute it.

"That's very far away from anything resembling music, unless you've been listenin' to alien species."

"Heads up," said Darwin.

A new NetMini sailed over the motley curtain, stalling in midair above Aaron's chest. Telekinesis didn't cause pain. A good sign.

"Thanks, mate."

Darwin's voice softened as he retreated to his room. "No problem, mon."

"You're about as Jamacian as I am, Darwin." Aaron laughed as he reached up to turn the little machine on.

"It's ready to go. I had 'em link it to the same dummy account as your old one." Something heavy hit the ground after a grunt. "Even pre-charged it."

"What the devil was that?" Aaron waved his hand at the holo-panel projected by the NetMini, scrolling through his contacts.

"Just a li'l somethin' I found," said Darwin.

He impaled the long string of letters and numbers Shimmer used for a PID with one finger, initiating a vid call. The sound of ringing filled the air. "Found?"

Darwin brushed an old dress shirt and a tattered chem suit apart, leaning into the space around Aaron's bed. His dark face and yellow toothy grin reflected upside down in the surface of a battered (and quite nonfunctional) frictionless orb. The upper half had undergone a recent attempt to restore shine to the chrome. A steady stream of crumbling dirt fell from four hover-ports protruding from small pentagonal hatches on the bottom, angled in direct lines away from the center point. The five-sided patches bore engravings of the Arsenal cannon icon.

"An old stone." Aaron slid to the end of the bed to get a closer look.

"Ain't stone, ya idiot."

Aaron frowned. "Na, ya fool. We call it a 'stone' since it's closer to a curling stone than a... umm..." He tapped his chin. "Right when frictionless started about, there was another... Football. Wait... they called it sucker here. No, soccer. Since it wasn't a proper ball, all heavy and hard and whatnot, some sodding tool wit the Association thought it was like a curling stone. It's lovely. She's going to be thrilled."

Darwin jerked his head toward the bathroom. "Thought you said you wasn't screwing that one. What'cha care what the shit she thinks?" He pondered for a few seconds with a nervous grin. "Can't say I blame ya. Too much risk to the boys."

"Some bints don't require the commencement of a shagging type relationship to subject you to incessant reminders of what they don't care for."

"Like frictionless cheats," said Anna from the bathroom.

Aaron hadn't noticed the autoshower cut off to silence. He clamped his eyes shut, muttering, "shite."

"What's that then?" she asked.

Darwin extracted himself from the hanging garments and stood straight. "Found a little trophy for him."

"Hah. It's as dead as his career."

"Bitch," whispered Aaron.

"An' not as dead as my ears." The bathroom door squeaked.

Aaron made a 'that figures' face at the ceiling.

Her voice got a touch louder. "Where's your damn towel?"

"There isn't one. Bloody tube's got a dry cycle. Use it. Assuming a Manchester tool can figure out how to work the panel." Aaron rubbed his forehead, cursing again when his fourth attempt to call Shimmer ended at a message stating her vid-mailbox had no free space.

Aaron didn't pay much attention to the door squeaking a second time until Darwin dropped the old frictionless orb with a heavy clank and scurried off with a frightened whimper. A second later, Anna shoved the curtain of hanging cloth to either side with a metal-on-metal *skshh* of ancient clothes hangers. She was dry—and rather naked—save for a pair of thin, black lacy panties. The steamy scent of autoshower soap clung to her, along with a cloud of warm, humid air.

"Very nice. Obviously real. Perfect shape to them, but a bit small." Aaron gave up on the NetMini and glanced at her.

"I don't need it for drying, you twat. You chucked all over me on the way here. Even managed to get it in my boots. My kit's flown off to the cleaners."

Aaron leaned forward, glancing around the floor. With a smirk, he concentrated and sent the red t-shirt floating to her. Anna let it drape over her chest and slip off.

"You're a funny one."

"It's a shirt."

"I'd rather loiter about starkers than wear *those* colors."

Aaron pushed the redial icon. "I'm not going to object."

She scowled. "I'm spoken for. Unlike you, *I'm* not a cheater."

"You wound me." He put a hand over his heart. "Still, it worked for three years."

Anna padded around the end of the bed, making sure to step on his foot on the way to the largest mound of clothing piled up against the wall. "Three years of undeserved wins, undeserved prestige, undeserved"—she waved her arm in a series of random gestures—"everything!"

"The best part… neither the Crown nor the Frictionless Association could say a damn word about it." He winked. "Think of the scandal."

"You should think about the amount of damage you could've caused. If it got out you were a psionic *cheat* at frictionless, the entire country would be up in arms about psionics!" She set her hands on her hips and scowled. "People have firebombed things over bad referee calls. Do you have *any* idea the kind of shitstorm you could've ignited? We'd have all been eyeball deep in cack! You endangered innocents."

"Tipping a wobbler into the goal now and then hardly endangers anything but a couple of turf accountants. I never did anything over the top."

"Your Pryce Slyder?" She scoffed. "No one could ever figure out how you got it to curve that sharp."

Aaron smiled. "That was a bit of genius, wasn't it? Made quite a bit of sterling off an endorsement for Bering Footwear."

"You really don't know..." Anna sighed and put her back to him, stooping to sift through the clothes. "Does anything in this shithole *not* have Arsenal on it?"

Aaron looked up at her ass, four feet in front of his face and right at eye level. Black silk pulled taut over porcelain skin as she leaned forward to rummage the pile. He rested back on his elbows, running his gaze up and down every curve of her leg, enjoying the view. It struck him as odd he *didn't* want to attempt talking her into a one-nighter. Regarding her as above that gave him pause. Ever since Allison, women had been the enemy. Yet in this tiny, white-haired, Manchester-loving sprite, he'd found an exception. Was it something about her, or had he been wrong about women in general? Morose thoughts gave way to amusement, and his grin widened each time she cursed at a tiny little cannon symbol or something generally close enough to Arsenal colors to earn her contempt.

"Could ya bend a little farther down, luv? Tryin' to see if you're a natural white."

She didn't, nor did she straighten. "You're a pig, Aaron. In every sense of the word."

"Thanks, luv." The enthusiasm leaked out of his voice. Her banter in the park, a friendly back and forth about an ancient song, had reminded him too much of Allison. Even the way she jabbed at him over frictionless had a certain playfulness to it amid the vitriol. His wife had never been one for the sport. She didn't hate it; the woman had no opinion. Manchester, Arsenal, or a jar of pickles—it didn't matter one whit. Granted, his wife had been much more innocent than Anna seemed. Then again, so was he back then. Perhaps Allison's hadn't been the only death that afternoon.

"I'm clueless why Lauren was so fecking insistent I recruit you. She's probably loving every minute of watching me squirm havin' to deal with a damn Arsenal wanker. I just don't fathom what women see in a chav like you. You're all charm and smiles and suave, but all you want is a one night fuck. It's all the same clapped out bullshit." She stood up with a plain black shirt wadded into a fist on her hip. "I mean... I can see it. You've definitely got the ability to talk the knickers off a girl, an' this on the lam scruffy bad-boy act has a certain appeal to it. But in the end, you're just a shallow, arrogant, selfish, prick."

Aaron sat upright, red faced, his pointing finger shaking with anger. "You've no idea who I am. Who the feck do you think you are to judge anything about me?"

She leaned back, one eyebrow climbing.

He slouched, head down, elbows on his knees. A hundred women flashed by in his memory, most blurred to smears of color and fragrance in a haze of alcohol. Every woman he used up and threw away became another mark on the scorecard, another victory over the gender. Why should any of them deserve his respect now? He'd lost the only one he'd ever cared about. No, he'd not lost her—he killed her. *It's my fault. I wasn't strong enough to resist.* Aaron's hands flew to the sides of his head, clenched to fists full of his hair. Talis's awful harpy voice reverberated in his consciousness.

Kill your partner.

He sobbed once, but swallowed it. His face soured to a sneer. The dead frictionless orb rocketed across the room and embedded half in the wall. She jumped at the sudden smash.

"I wasn't always... This isn't who I was."

Anna slipped into the shirt, which covered her to an inch above the knee. She eyed the flakes of pulverized concrete collecting on the floor and seemed about to snipe at him again, but her face softened. "Is this some ploy for a pity shag?"

"'Ave you always been like that?"

"Like what?" She shifted her weight onto her left leg.

"Cold and unfeeling. Of course, you're a Man U fan. D'you ever care about anyone, or is it all pissing and moaning about another lousy season?"

An instant of anger flared in her eyes. Dark, glinting sapphires bored into him. He looked up at her, ready to ride the lightning and be done with all of it. *Maybe Allison's gone off somewhere paradisiacal and hasn't seen what a shit I've been.* The scorn ebbed. Anna turned the same lost and forlorn stare he assumed had settled on his face to the window.

Aaron pondered an apology. As irritating as she'd been about the whole cheating thing, something about her had changed. For a moment, the woman before him had the presence of a lonely young girl, lost in a world way over her head. Anna scratched at her stomach, glanced at the floor by his feet, and wandered out of his field of view without a word.

Damn. Right. I bollocksed that up proper like.

Electronic music warbled at the window. Blinking lights adorned the chassis of a footlocker-sized hovering bot with the logo of the Geomatic Laundry Service. Creeping shadows drifted across the room, cast by the blinding glare from the grimed glass.

"I'll get it," muttered Aaron.

The dead frictionless orb shifted in its crater, gravity at war with the fading tensile strength of broken drywall. Aaron ignored it, letting it thud to the floor as he trudged to the patio. He paused, fingertips touching the glass, staring at the metal orb lying under a layer of white dust. Was that him? Some old Arsenal tool, used up, thrown in the corner, and discarded. He pushed the sliding door to one side, enjoying the burst of non-stagnant air despite the hint of piss on the wind. Automatic gestures took Anna's clothing from the interior of the robot while he continued to focus on the metal sphere. His hair fluttered in the blast of thrust as the delivery bot reversed from the opening and zoomed away. The tiniest bit of effort righted the old 'stone' and floated it onto the nightstand.

Anna took her clothes and retreated to the bathroom to change. Neither one of them dared make eye contact. She closed the door behind her, cutting off the light and leaving Aaron alone in the near dark. He stared at the bed, the hole in the wall, and out the window at the distant city full of uncountable glowing points. Billions of people went about their day, oblivious to his personal tragedy. Sitting around this shithole wasn't getting anything done. If he spent another hour here, he didn't trust himself not to do something rash.

"I'm off."

"Where to?" asked Anna from behind the door.

He frowned at his boxers and gathered some clothes. "Somewhere other than here."

16

RADIO SILENCE

U ncomfortable. The word rattled around in Aaron's mind the same way he jostled about the interior of the taxi. Several minutes spent trapped in the middle of traffic caused the self-driving vehicle to dart through the first-available opening and race into the PubTran dedicated lane on the far right side. A handful of pedestrians who had spilled off the walkpaths dove for their lives as the little wheeled box got up to a hair over sixty five. At least one coffee bounced off the roof.

Aaron risked a glance at Anna, sitting to his left. *Uncomfortable.* He nodded at nothing. The laundry chemicals wafting from her clothes scratched at the back of his throat, making him loathe the fixed windows in the public car. It would respond to a verbal request to turn up the airflow, but that would require breaking the silence. She'd not looked at him since he'd gotten a wonderful close-up view of her backside. He pictured the ebon silk stretched tight across her womanhood, surprising himself at the mood in which it put him. Rather than lust, the sight had struck him as beautiful, the way one might regard classical paintings.

He took Allison's nametag out and twisted it around his fingers, tilting it back and forth to play with the shadows filling the recessed letters. Desiring a woman, even though his wife was dead, felt as disloyal as if she were still there to cheat on. None of the one-nighters triggered that feeling. Of course, he didn't *desire* them. He wanted to conquer them. He wanted to prove to the world that Aaron Pryce hadn't been destroyed by the loss of his wife.

Anna shifted, making him look up. She stared at him; her expression could have been pity, contempt, or regret. His face must've been the same. Her cheeks pinked, and she returned her gaze to the window at her left.

The PubTran car squealed on a right turn, its diminutive wheels chirping as though it moved twice its actual speed.

A placid male voice flooded the cabin. "Debris in PubTran-only lane detected. Please disregard imminent impact."

Aaron leaned forward for a better view, blinking in shock at a sleeping, wounded, or dead man slumped on the ground. The car accelerated, intent on ramming the poor bastard out of its way. Aaron grunted and focused, flinging him into the dense crowd. The man's boot thudded off the corner of the car, adding a horizontal spin to the flying body. Aaron twisted in his seat, watching as a section of crowd went down like bowling pins, though slow enough to seem non-injurious.

He faced front and exhaled. "Bloody cruel thing."

"What's that?" Anna looked over.

"This car." He waffled a hand in the direction of the console. "It was about to run over a man."

"Oh. Yes, that does seem cruel." She picked at the hem of her coat where it rested over her knees. "Do you think that idiot will manage it?"

"Darwin?" Aaron shrugged. "As likely as he is to fail. He's got friends in places I don't."

She peered at the small, matte-black nametag. "I don't understand why Aurora waited so long to mention you."

"As if I'd know," said Aaron, sounding more tired than sarcastic. "Lightning from your hands. Can't say I've ever seen that before."

"You weren't listening the other day when I told you about the Awakened, were you?"

"A little. You know…" He flashed an uninspired smile. "I was too busy trying to work out a route into your knickers at the time."

She laughed.

"Good, I meant that as humor."

"Aurora's a clairvoyant. She helps us find others like us. Course, she's a fickle sort. Likes to play games."

"Games like sending a Man U fan to recruit someone who used to play for Arsenal."

"Aye."

The car came to a halt and the side door wound upward with a faint mechanical whirr. "We have arrived at your destination. Trip time sixteen minutes forty three seconds. PubTran Corporation regrets, but is not responsible for, delays caused by traffic conditions outside of our control. Thank you for choosing PubTran, have a pleasant day."

Aaron lurched from the seat and climbed out, tucking Allison's nametag in his pocket. *At least the doors are big.* He didn't miss Britain's Autocab. Talk about cramped. Anna's second boot touched the ground at the same instant the car wheeled itself forward so it could close the door without squishing them.

"Uppity thing," she muttered, gathering her coat and scurrying to the walkpath. "Where's it in such a damn hurry to?"

Aaron made a noncommittal one-armed shrug and forced his way through a thick river of pedestrians to the front courtyard of an open-air café. Despite the semi-fancy patio furniture, the rather ordinary phrase 'William's Bistro' glimmered in holographic gold script in both windows. The inside resembled a cross between a deli counter and a sit-down restaurant, while the deck outside looked like a scene straight out of the French countryside.

"Not many people 'ere, are there?" Anna followed him to an outdoor table.

Aaron coughed. "Some people find it hard to eat while smelling the city."

An orb bot, about a foot in diameter, glided up to their table. Someone had put a top hat and monocle on it, as well as a ridiculous brown handlebar moustache.

"Good day to you," it said, its voice dry and crusty like an elderly Brit. "Can I fetch you anything to drink?"

"Tea," they said simultaneously.

"Espresso actually." Anna rubbed her eyebrow. "Make it a double, please. Extra cream, no sugar."

"Very good, miss." It tilted forward in an orb's bow and pivoted to face Aaron before repeating the gesture. "Sir. I shall return momentarily." The floating sphere glided into a purpose-built hatch in the side of the building.

"Guess you 'ave been here a bit. Coffee?" Aaron cringed. "How can you stand it?"

She shrugged. "Never really thought about it. They *do* have coffee over there too."

"So, about that Awakened bit."

Anna looked up from a small menu projected by an emitter in the table. "The simple explanation is we're more powerful than other psionics. Archon thinks we're some kind of evolutionary leap ahead. He's certain the government will try and eliminate or control us."

Aaron rubbed his face, trying to blink away the fatigue of a few days' worth of bad sleep. "Given the way the ol' CSB's been toward us... he might have a point."

"Guess your thing is a bad reaction to invasive mental effects," said Anna.

"My 'thing'? Wot's that mean?"

"Most of us have little quirks. My EK runs away when I get emotional. Aurora's got a rather unusual appearance. Another little girl's eyes glowed, this one chap lit on fire when he used his abilities. The more overt ones seem like they're connected with some kind of early childhood trauma."

"I wasn't always able to fling cars around. I—"

The orb returned. A spindly retractable claw arm held a tray bearing two steaming cups. It set its cargo on the table and proceeded to reposition each cup by its appropriate person before gathering the empty tray and tucking it behind its nonexistent back.

"Would you like a little more time?"

"I'll 'ave the eggs, fried, with some corned beef hash and toast," said Aaron.

Anna switched off the menu. "Spinach and mushroom omelet for me, please."

"Excellent choices." The ball wobbled in a gesture possibly intended as a bow, and glided away.

"Perhaps that's why Aurora didn't sense you until recently. You weren't born Awakened." Anna made thoughtful faces at the smog layer for a moment. "Do you have any idea how it happened?"

Aaron glowered into the table. "I'd rather not dwell on it."

"S'got somethin' to do with that little trinket you keep fidgetin' with, doesn't it?"

The upwelling of anger made it to the veins in his forehead before he gathered it back. He couldn't get angry with Anna for not knowing. Rage became regret.

"I'm sorry." She looked off to the side.

"Hey!" Darwin leapt the fence into the patio area, ignoring the wide-open gate six steps to his right. He dragged a chair from a nearby table, spun it around backward, and draped himself over it. "I need your help, man."

As if the ambient fragrance of the city didn't make it difficult enough to eat, Darwin brought a resurgence of pungent 'back alley garbage' to the air.

"Did you have any luck finding Shimmer?" He smiled at Darwin. The man had excellent timing.

"Not yet. She's gone to ground. She'll turn up when she's ready. Look, I got a lead on something… Lot of credits to be made."

"First, go burn that jacket. Second, I'm not terribly interested in helping you commit crime, Darwin. Police officer, remember?"

Anna opened her mouth and closed it.

"No, I didn't cheat at that, too." He scowled at Darwin. Anna's expression drooped with guilt. "I've no interest in petty crime."

"Ex-cop." Darwin held up a finger.

The orb returned. "Good day, sir."

"I'll have what he's having." Darwin gestured at Aaron.

"Very good." The orb spun about and glided away, disappearing into its hatch.

"Thanks for lunch." Darwin winked. "Look, it's easy. Security's light 'cause you'd need heavy equipment to move the goddamned thing. It's worth a"—Darwin faked an awful British accent—"bloody fortune, mate."

"No dice, *mate*," said Aaron. "I'm not a thief."

"It's an old pre-war engine, like from a car. They used to call them vee-eights. Perfect condition, the bastard thing even runs. I know a guy'll pay six million for it."

"So why are you here?" Aaron gestured at the crowd. "Go steal it."

Darwin leaned forward, engulfing the table in caustic breath flavored in twenty years' need of dentistry plus fruity Nicohaler vapor. "The damned thing weighs a ton. They'll never expect two guys to pinch it. I need your… talents."

"Look, mate. I'm not a petty criminal. Shimmer's decided to drop off the planet, and at the moment, she's the best chance I've got at findin' Talis. Unless you can pull that faerie out of your ass somehow, I don't 'ave time for blaggin' some old relic."

Darwin rubbed a hand over his head, matting his spongy hair for an instant. He tapped his fingers as if playing the trumpet. "All we need's an open-back truck. We don't even have to get out. Just do your thing. I pull up, you float the engine over, and we take off."

The waiter returned with a tray of food clamped in its grippy-claw arm. It set the tray on the table and positioned everyone's meals. "Please let me know if anything is not to your satisfaction, sirs and madame." The orb folded its arm behind itself with the empty tray.

"Thanks, man," said Darwin.

Anna smiled. "Smells good."

"May I get anyone else anything?" The orb shifted side to side as if looking at everyone.

"He'll 'ave some common sense." Aaron gestured at Darwin.

"Right away."

The orb sped off before Aaron recovered from his surprise. Darwin attacked his meal as though he'd not eaten in a week. Anna picked. Aaron settled midway between gluttony and disinterest. All three looked up as the faint thrum of a hover unit neared. The spherical waiter deposited a glass in front of Darwin, eight-inches tall but only one inch around. Deep violet liquid at the bottom progressed in a gradient of various blues to pale cyan near the top.

Aaron chuckled at the realization 'common sense' was a mixed drink. He gestured at it with an open hand before pointing at Anna. "If he drinks that an' loses the itch to steal that thing…"

Darwin drained a third of it in one swig. "Naah, this is a foo-foo drink. It ain't strong enough to change my mind."

Anna stared at her plate, still with half her food remaining by the time Aaron finished. She took a hesitant forkful, looking up at the sound of Darwin's slurping.

He tilted the empty glass at Aaron. "So, I find Shimmer, you help me out with the thing."

"I'll consider it," muttered Aaron.

Darwin sucked at the ice once more, put the cup down, and jumped up with a smile. "Consider the bitch found."

A minute after he vanished into the crowd, Anna poked at her food and took a bite.

"A bit ripe, that one."

She muttered despite a full mouth, hurrying to swallow. "Aye. Before this gets any more awkward, are you willing to meet with Archon?"

"You've made it grievously clear you're spoken for." He put on a rogue's grin. "If I'd been trying, we'd 'ave shagged by now." As soon as he said it, he regretted it.

"Are you so sure of that?"

The hint of amusement in her face eased the tension in his back. "Either that or you'd 'ave killed me. Maybe this Archon's getting jealous."

She laughed, launching a particle of egg onto the table. "I sincerely doubt that. Does that mean you'd like to meet him?"

"Not just yet." Aaron set his fork on the plate.

As if sensing a disturbance in the balance of the universe, the orb waiter rocketed over to collect the empty dish, its spindly arm up to hold the hat in place.

"So what're you planning to do?" Anna waved at the orb. "Another tea, please. Earl this time?"

The orb pivoted, a disembodied head nodding. Anna held up a finger, glanced at Aaron, and made it two.

"I'm planning to wait for Darwin."

She blinked. "Right 'ere?"

"Aye. Unless you'd fancy going off somewhere to snog."

Anna's face went unreadable. A strange hope she'd take him up on the offer had left his tone ambiguous. He hadn't intended to sound serious, but it didn't come out quite like a joke.

"Are you really a sodding wanker, or are you just doing the typical Arsenal-fan thing and denying the obvious truth?"

Aaron looked around.

"What're you doing?"

He smiled. "Judging by the lack of random fires, and the still-working lights, I'll take it you were teasing."

She shifted and leaned back. Their tea arrived, and Aaron swiped his NetMini at the robo-waiter to clear the tab. The attempt at Earl Grey was on the low end of passable; he gazed into it like an ascetic using a divining bowl. Whatever communication occurred between the dark liquid and his subconscious didn't lead to any moments of epiphany by the time he drank it near to the bottom.

Aaron felt as though a teasing chance had slipped his grasp, like trying to catch an oiled-up catfish barehanded by the tail. Of course, it might've just been what women do. His question had not been serious—he blamed fear of her gift for his lack of interest—but that too seemed as much of a diversion as his bringing it up. At least she'd stopped mentioning Archon. He squinted at her innocent tea-sipping face. Was she as unavailable as she claimed to be? *Why do I care? She's too short. Bad attitude, wears her hair like a little boy, and she's a fecking Man U fan.*

He closed his eyes and tried to picture her. Allison had kept her hair short as well, though not a pixie cut, and brown instead of white. This woman was nothing like his wife. Anna had a mean streak Allison could never possess. Quiet, introverted Allison got along with machines better than people—until she'd met him.

Okay, maybe she doesn't look like a small boy. It's somewhat cute.

The curious glint in Anna's deep blues came too close to Allison the day they met, wondering what was going on in his mind. The more he thought about it, the less he wanted to subject Anna to the bastard he'd become.

He stood, staring off at the crowd so she couldn't see his face. "I've got some shite to deal with before I talk to your Archon chap."

Aaron didn't turn around; he didn't want to look at her again. Would any woman with short hair and large eyes have reminded him of Allison, or only Anna? He certainly couldn't call it a match of personality.

"Don't do anything rash." Anna slid her chair back. "Shall I call you?"

Aaron rushed into the crowd. No specific destination came to mind; he wanted to remove himself from regret. His mind lent more meaning than she'd likely intended to her parting words. An attempt to distract himself by focusing on the annoyance of the hacker's disappearing act cascaded through a multitude of emotions: irritation at Shimmer, anger at Talis, and feelings of failure at himself. At last, and most crippling, crushing guilt came with the memory of Allison's final, terrified expression.

He stumbled to a PubTran station at the end of the next block and fell into a waiting car. The world felt too heavy; he needed to get away from it for a few hours.

17

REMEMBERING

The clamor of bells pounded Aaron's head as though he'd slept in the clock tower of Westminster. His eyes snapped open. He tried to sit up, but failed; the weight of a sleeping woman pinned him to a luxurious, functional, queen-sized Comforgel pad. Two others lay on either side of him with nary a scrap of clothing between the four of them. He grunted, working his arm out from under the Asian girl to grasp the NetMini responsible for the racket. After pushing the cancel button on the incoming call, he levitated it back to the nightstand and let his head sink into the pillow.

None of the women stirred.

Ten seconds later, two metaphorical giants got to work on his skull with hammers. Aaron tried to form the requisite presence of mind to be angry at Darwin for setting his new NetMini's ring to the bell peals of Big Ben, but his mind refused to concentrate on anything but pain. The girl sleeping on top of him was as short as Anna, but larger in the bust and hip and had rather dark skin. Unlike her friends, the pale redhead on his left didn't touch him; she lay curled on her side with her back turned.

Aaron swallowed, staring at the ceiling. The sculpted tiles each had a rounded faux-wood egg jutting from a projection at the center carved to resemble leaves. They blurred in a nauseating dance, making him close his eyes again. The Asian woman on his right emitted a soft whine in her sleep and snuggled against his side. Almost at the same time, the pale one went flat on her back, slapping the dark skinned girl in the ass with a limp arm.

Fiona? Aaron squinted at the freckles across her cheeks. *I wonder how much that cost... I hear it's cheaper to go ginger as a baby. Siobhan? Fuck.* He spent a moment adoring the perfect holo-vid star face of the woman on top of him. Horror gripped him; aside from being unable to recall any of their names, his only memory of last night consisted of getting into a PubTran taxi and telling it to take him to The Imperial Hotel. Evidently, he'd met some women in the bar, and... well... Given the arrangement in which he'd come to, he could guess what they'd done, but it might as well have never been as far as his memory cared.

"Ugh," he moaned, rubbing his forehead.

A clunk from the bathroom snapped his head up again. *Is there a fourth?* When it happened again, he realized the autoshower probably ran a cleaning routine on its filtration unit. He imagined Anna standing in the doorway with her arms folded and a disapproving smirk on her face.

Feck what you think, lass. You're not in the running.

Morning urgency made the woman on top of him heavier. Aaron gathered a mental assay of her weight and distributed his telekinetic efforts across her entire body as he lifted her straight up. He untangled himself from the Asian girl and levitated himself over the redhead before easing the dark-skinned goddess back down. He landed on his feet near the nightstand and sighed at the three nudes.

Bugger. Aaron squeezed his temples. *I must've hit the gin a bit too much, can't remember a damn thing.*

The NetMini vibrated, adding a mechanical buzz to the peal of electronic bells drubbing his brain. He snatched it, ready to dash it to pieces on the carpet, until he saw the word Darwin in phantasmal letters.

"Oi, what?" Aaron mumbled.

Darwin's face appeared in hologram, six inches of shit-eating grin. "Where the hell did you run off to, man? I've been tryin' ta find yo' ass for six hours."

"What fecking time is it?"

"An hour 'til noon. They won't let my ass in the door of this place."

"Try wearing clothes that've been washed more recently than a year ago." Aaron rolled his head around in an effort to loosen his neck. "It works wonders on social acceptance."

"Yeah, whatever, man. Look, I found Shimmer. I'm outside."

Aaron gazed through the intangible head of his roommate, smiling at three perfect asses. "I'll be right there."

THE TINY CAR HAD PROBABLY SHED THE BULK OF ITS PAINT A DECADE AGO. Puny in-wheel motors lay exposed to the elements, their covers long gone. Clusters of coiled blue wiring sparked every so often, with the occasional lingering arc between the drive core and the ground. Aaron elected not to touch the handle and opened the door with a mental flex of telekinesis before hopping in.

Darwin jerked upright in the seat as the passenger door slammed. "I wasn't even there, man."

"Where?" Aaron raised an eyebrow.

His friend held his hands up as if expecting a fist in the teeth, squinted, and blinked. After a moment, he rubbed his eyes and laughed. "Oh, nothin'. It's been over an hour. What the hell took so long?"

Aaron settled into the seat with a Cheshire smile. "I needed to remember something."

Darwin stuck his finger in a hole on the dashboard, through a ring of black plastic bordering a button that had once been there. He shivered with a spasmodic shock and yanked his hand back. A second later, the dashboard lit up. A trace of burning silicon blew into the cabin from the vents.

"Think it's time for a new car." Aaron felt uneasy even touching it.

"Sure. You buyin'?" Darwin winked. His mirth faded. "Look. You're startin' to worry me. Cheap women and expensive booze ain't gonna bring Allison back."

Aaron glared. "The ladies weren't cheap, or shallow, or on the job."

"Ladies?" asked Darwin, leaning on the s.

"Aye." Aaron held up three fingers.

Darwin pushed the left control stick and nudged out of the parking lot. "Good grief, man. You're a slut. What would Allison say if she could see that?"

Aaron turned his sour face to the passenger window. "Don't 'ave much worry of that happening, now do I?"

"Are you angry with women in general, or is it Aaron you're pissed off at? Do you think she'd want you doing that to yourself?"

"Probably not." Aaron's throat tightened. He closed his eyes as her dying scream reverberated in his head.

Darwin kept quiet for a few minutes of driving, letting the grinding and scraping of e-motors fill the air. Eventually, he sighed. "Sorry, man. That's gotta be some rough shit."

"I have to do this. If Zero finds Talis, I can't take the chance of them looking the other way because she's strong and they want to recruit her."

"You know killin' her won't bring Allison back."

Aaron gripped his side, feeling her nametag under the fabric. "I know. But I'll feel better for a few seconds before the crippling depression comes back and I leap headfirst into a downward spiral that leads to my ultimate demise, probably on the floor of a PubTran terminal bathroom."

Darwin let out a bassy chuckle. "At least you're an optimist at heart."

"So what's all this urgency about Shimmer?"

"You're lucky those dudes want her to do shit for 'em. Syndicate found her in real time, dragged her ass to a place no one would hear her scream. I get the feelin' they forcin' her to hack for 'em. Probably gonna off her anyway when she's done."

The thought of a couple of Syndicate thugs working over an eight-inch faerie in some dark warehouse hit him funny. When he stopped laughing, he couldn't help but feel a wave of guilt. While some woman—Aaron felt mostly certain Shimmer was a genuine she—he depended on got the business, he went back for round two with three girls he *still* couldn't recall the names of. Three friends who'd just attended a baby shower and happened to be in the bar. The Princess wanted a baby but not a man; she'd been the easiest to convince. All Aaron had to do was agree with her new-agey distaste for fertility clinics and 'unnatural' custom genetic material. The Asian girl acted self-conscious about her unremarkable looks; she took a bit longer, but he found all the right things to say in her head. To be fair, her opinion of herself was overly harsh. Red held out the longest. She'd only gone along with it because she didn't want to be separated from her friends. He'd respected her hesitation and barely touched her all night or this morning.

Meanwhile, Shimmer endured who-knows-what. Yeah, Allison would be proud of him.

He pressed a hand to his face, focused on holding back the grief he'd been avoiding for so long. A gasp or two escaped as his emotion nosedived. Once again, anger saved him and kept his face stoic.

"You always been like that?" asked Darwin. "Did Allison tame you or something?"

Aaron's palm became a fist, pressed to his mouth. "No... You'll not believe me, but she was my first."

"Bullshit." Darwin jinked the stick about, skidding around a hard right turn right as the signal changed. "You're right, I don't buy it. All that Gee-ball money?"

"Frictionless." Aaron lacked the energy to get upset. "All those slags wanted was my bank or to get seen on the holo with the famous me." He let his arm drop away from his face. "Now, I bet few people'd even remember me."

"Met her on the force then? Lemme guess, your partner?"

Aaron flashed a wistful smile. "Not at first. Same squad though. Took us almost a year for me to find the stones talk to her. After we married, I kept harassing command to let us be partners. Captain Torres thought it was an awful idea." Warmth spread over his cheeks a second before a tear forced its way free. He slammed his fist on the dashboard. "I should've listened to him."

Darwin kept quiet as Aaron battled his emotions. Outside, the buildings went from shiny to normal to dilapidated. Ocean salt added to the scent of singed electronics. The car nosed into a parking space in front of a tall, abandoned building. Darwin squeezed it between a dead cargo transport covered in pornographic graffiti and an exploded upside-down bed that looked as if it had fallen from at least the fortieth floor.

A long breath pushed regret and misery aside, leaving room for controlled anger. Aaron shoved the door open and got out. Though he couldn't see any faces in the windows looming over him, the building had eyes. Every so often, one of the dark, glassless hollows held a wisp of sentience, a telepathic trace of a mind lurking in the shadows. Most of what he overheard criticized Darwin's ride as not worth stealing.

"This it?"

Darwin's door closed with a soft thud. "Naw, man. What do you think I am, stupid? Place we want is a block down and two over." He locked the doors.

"Relax, mate. No one here's gonna steal your Halcyon-Ormyr."

"Oh, you're a regular shittin' comedian. Not everyone can afford one of those things, Mr. Frictionless."

He grinned and followed Darwin along the street, hanging left at the first block. Squatters peered down at them from windows of various elevations. A small boy, perhaps six, leaned out far enough to snort and spit. Aaron stalled the glob in midair four floors below its maker, reversed it like a bullet, and slapped the boy in the forehead with it. The child vanished backward into the building, squealing and shrieking.

"That was cruel."

Aaron shook his head. "No, cruel would've been putting it back in his mouth."

Darwin gagged. He waved Aaron past him. "There… go past the alley. You want the place that looks like an old salon."

"You're not coming?"

Darwin leaned on the wall, arms crossed. "Not unless you give me some serious artillery. I can't mind-fu shit to death like you. Besides, *not* being seen in a place where Syndicate ass gets kicked improves my odds of living." He narrowed his eyes. "Unlike some people, I still give a shit if I see tomorrow."

Aaron scrunched his lips, about ready to punch Darwin.

"Hey, man." He unfolded an arm enough to raise a hand. "Just sayin' what I'm seein', get me? Can't say I wouldn't be there too if I had my woman go down like that. Course, mine took off with some military dude." He tucked his hand away. "What about that teeny one? Seems like she's more your speed."

"She roots for the wrong team," muttered Aaron.

"Ohhh." Darwin rolled his eyes.

"No, you twat. Not *that* wrong team. Manchester. Besides, she's got someone already."

"Shit, you're gonna let something petty like that get in the way?"

"Petty like her being in a relationship?"

"No"—Darwin's lamentable attempt at a British accent returned—"you bloody twat. The team crap."

"I don't have time for this." Aaron waved his finger in a 'wait right here' gesture before storming off.

A block later, a moan drew his gaze to the alley on his left. Four street punks lay scattered about on the ground, another draped out of a battered trash crusher. The sixth hung over the bottom rung of a fire-escape ladder, bent in half at the waist. Aaron raised his left arm to his face.

"Ops, I need a med…" He sighed at his suit sleeve. "Bloody hell." None of them appeared shot, looking either drunk or beat to shit. They could wait until he'd finished with the Syndicate. *Probably just gang warfare.*

He pulled himself away from the groaning figures and trotted across the street to his target. Two large windows fronted the fifth building. The lack of power reduced the normal bloom of holographic signage to a few small, dark emitters. However, the front room resembled a beauty salon, complete with chairs looking like they belonged on the set of a cheap horror vid. A patch of less-dirty floor and a scattering of broken bolts indicated a spot where someone had stolen one.

Aaron nudged the door open from twenty yards away. It let off a faint squeak as the sliding mechanism ground against its rails. When nothing exploded or blared, he crept up and ducked inside. The aroma of Chinese food hung in the air, swirling about with dust and whiskey. Faint whimpering of the feminine variety came from deeper inside. He grabbed at his hip, again forgetting he had no tactical armor. The E-90 didn't hang under his arm either. His rush to forget had sent him to the Imperial without it.

Bother.

Two interior doors led out of the front space, the one on the left an obvious closet. In the center of the wall opposite the entry, a pair of decorative faux-wood double doors fluttered in a weak breeze. He crept up and peered into a leaf-shaped window a little less than eye level.

Inside, ten stations set up as office cubicles held equipment for more advanced procedures than simple hair treatments. The first four seemed intended for pedicures. The next four had machines for cosmetic implants less permanent than NanoLED tattoos—the so-called 'forty-two day makeover.' The last two were the largest, their equipment the most complex. Sample images on the cube walls gave away their intent—facial restructuring. The same woman appeared in multiple pictures, with nine different noses, three alternate eye shapes, and four different jawlines. Aaron let off a noiseless whistle of disbelief.

The open ceiling stretched two stories up, giving a view into what used to be a mini-mall. A few stores had solid signs instead of holograms, coffee shops, cosmetic places, and a few clothing boutiques. All of it had overgrown with hanging ivy and weeds, watered by holes in the roof from which steady streams continued dribbling. Moss clung to angled slabs of concrete hanging on spindly rebar, glimmering with a sheen of runoff. He figured a pipe had to have burst somewhere above; far too much water than what simple rain could have accounted for pattered to the floor all around him.

Another whimper echoed off the ceiling of the atrium-like chamber. At the end of the stations, a writhing female body occupied the salon chair missing from the front room, facing away from him. A scrawny woman with a dark bag over her head struggled against some manner of cord securing her entire forearms to the armrests. A bit of short, green sleeve poked around the edge. Bare caramel-colored legs writhed in time with muted grunts. The same type of cord bound her ankles together and went under the chair to the hydraulic base. Green light glowed from the top of her left foot, a NanoLED tattoo of a scorpion about to crawl onto her big toe.

Two men in black suits occupied themselves with small electronics a short distance past the girl. One's face lit with flashes of fiery red and orange, his intense look focused on a video game. The other put down his NetMini and reached for a long sandwich. Aaron nudged the door open and slipped in. He stifled a cough at air so thick with the fragrance of vegetation he may as well have chewed on weeds.

Aaron focused on the man lifting the submarine sandwich to his lips. A telekinetic shove drilled his face into the desk through his lunch, flooding the room with a resounding metallic *boom* and a spray of shredded lettuce. He slumped forward. The other man, having looked up in time to see his friend deep-throat his sub to the point of unconsciousness, burst into laughter.

"Must be a damn good deli." Aaron strolled among the beauty stations.

Laughter ended with an incredulous stare. The Syndicate man pulled a pistol out from his suit jacket, but it never quite aimed at Aaron. As soon as it emerged from fabric, Aaron seized it with his telekinetic grasp. An outside observer would have assumed the man bashed himself in the face with it four times before sliding out of the chair. Aaron clucked his tongue at the man, face first on the floor with his ass in the air.

"Flying ostrich, so undignified, mate."

The girl tried to say something, but sounded gagged.

"Hang on, luv." Aaron looked around and up, seeing no one else. He levitated the pistol over and tucked it in his belt. "I'll have you out of there in a jif."

She mumbled something, shaking herself with a gesture of impatience.

Aaron kept a wary eye upward at a walkway around the second floor as he edged to the chair, grasped the seatback, and pulled it around. The young woman trapped in it didn't fit his expectation of what Shimmer would look like. Her lime green miniskirt was tattered and stained, and her half shirt bunched up under an X of cord that pinned her chest to the seatback. Bare feet seemed to be the cleanest part of her, with a lack of grime continuing to the midway point of her shins.

The stink of a street-dweller clung to her, rivaled only by the odors of booze and rotten food on the wind. Someone had tossed a pair of thick shin-high boots under the desk on top of what looked like a jacket and small backpack. He tore the silver tape from around her neck, freeing the cloth bag, which he pulled off her head. The girl seemed about eighteen. Blood trickled out of her nose, and her left eye appeared well on its way to being black. More silver tape wound around her head several times, over wild, black hair tinged with silver and red. A trace of dingy, pink satin protruded from the gag under her nose. Bruises in the shape of finger marks dotted her legs and arms.

Her huge, brown eyes widened with urgency. She pointed at her face and tried to say something. Aaron had to look away from her for a moment. Enough 'little girl' remained apparent despite her hard outer shell to reawaken a bit of the law officer left in him. Aaron had never imagined himself a cop while in London, but after a few years here, he'd grown to enjoy it. He snarled at the man on the floor. The body jerked upright, but he found control before rage made him snap the neck. She mumbled and wobbled. Even gagged, "Get me out of here" came through clear. Her biceps swelled as she pulled on the cords, fingers clawed at the air toward her face. Tiny round bruises with red points in the center decorated the inside of each forearm—the mark of autoinjectors. The girl's eyes didn't glow green; at least she hadn't dosed Lace.

"Tape's in your hair. It's gonna hurt a bit, luv."

She made noises and shook her head, bouncing.

Aaron recoiled from her surface thoughts, having no interest in knowing what her months-unwashed underwear tasted like. He clamped a hand over his mouth and gurgled.

Her glare hardened. The next attempt she made to yell sounded like "Do it." Already, traces of vomit dribbled down her chin. She seemed to be losing the battle to hold it in.

A surgical telekinetic pull tore all five or six layers of tape, and he unwound it from her head with as much gentleness as possible. As soon as the tape left her lips, a wadded pair of panties burst out of her mouth at the forefront of a sluice of orange-brown liquid, which splattered all over her. She lapsed into a gagging, coughing fit.

Aaron's patience attacking the knot at the back of the chair lasted for all of two seconds. Shimmer couldn't lean forward to throw up as long as the cords pinned her to the chair, and from the gurgling, he figured she had a lot more needing to come out. In an effort not to hurt her, he tensioned the cord with a telekinetic pull and gradually built up strength until the level of exertion reached the point where it felt like he could have lifted a full conversion cyborg. When the wire snapped, it gashed a six-inch slice in the steel desk to her left. Copper strands frayed out of the loose end with bits of cubicle wall cloth stuck to them. The girl slumped forward, still choking, managing to send the next wave of puke off the side to the floor. Though she cried, she looked more furious than angry or scared.

Aaron patted her on the back until she could breathe again. He pawed at her wrists for a few seconds, unable to find a knot in the thick mass of electrical cable. Breaking the binding or the chair with his psionic gift was possible, though dangerous. A quick glance at the rent in the steel made him decide against it.

"How the feck did they tie this?"

"I gotta blade. On the side of my boot. Cut me out before they come back."

"This wouldn't have happened if you didn't dodge my calls." Aaron held up a hand, catching the boots as they flew up.

"What?" She blinked, giving his suit an up-and-down glance. "Dodge your calls? I don't have a fuck of a clue who you are, upsec. Wait, I dunno a whole lotta guys as pale as you. You Mike?"

"No. It's me, Aaron. It's a bit past playin' elusive now, luv. This"—he waved at her predicament—"isn't my idea. Syndicate's found you."

A sense of indignant embarrassment came over her. According to her surface thoughts, she was grateful for his help, but ashamed to have needed it. She pegged him for an upsec, someone from a wealthy sector with too much money to bother with a place like this or a person like her. His heartbeat slowed at her complete lack of recognition.

"You're not Shimmer?"

The girl wrenched at her arms, squirming. "These assholes jumped my crew a few hours ago. This big son of a bitch goes right for me with that fucking bag. Gave me a shot, and I woke up here. What time is it?" She gave up fighting. "Fuck, what *day* is it?"

Aaron blinked. Both boots had a bright green icon bearing the words "Jade Scorpionz" in an exaggerated Asian-looking font around a jumble of geometric shapes attempting to resemble a scorpion. "Jade scorpions? Those six poor sots in the alley over there?"

"Six?" She looked ready to cry. "There's like almost thirty of us."

A man's voice echoed across the atrium from above. "Were. Past tense."

The girl gurgled up another mouthful of bile; her shiver rattled the chair. For several seconds, only the sound of trickling water broke the ominous quiet.

"Hold these." Aaron set the pair of boots in the girl's lap before taking a step back and looking up to the rear.

She struggled to reach a combat knife in a sheath strapped to the left one.

Eleven men, five per side and one at the end, stood on the second floor balcony. All had fancy suits, though the solitary figure had a white hat and no visible weapon. The other ten took their sweet time drawing handguns, checking ammo counters, stretching their arms, and aiming at him.

Aaron pursed his lips and felt like a jackass. "That isn't Shimmer."

"Very good, Mr. Pryce. She's a piece of throwaway street trash we borrowed to put on a little show for you. Nothing but a bit of cheese on a mousetrap. Like a good little cop, you ran straight for the innocent... or not so innocent girl." He pulled a Nicohaler out of his pocket and took a long drag. "Much cheaper rates than hiring an actress from an agency. She's got the screaming and whimpering down like a pro."

"Fuck you," yelled the girl. "I hope you fuckers all get like ball cancer and die."

Aaron held his arms out to the side. "Well, since you wankers appear to have set this whole thing up, you know I haven't a clue where Shimmer is."

"We're starting to believe you." White Hat took another puff and gestured at him with the Nicohaler. "This ain't about Shimmer. Does the name Julian Cray mean anything to you, Pryce? Or, should I call you Galbraith."

Aaron shot a quick glance left and right. "It's not my fault his hired meat-shield went nutters."

"You really must think we're stupid." White Hat blew a long plume of water vapor past his lips. Cinnamon roll flavoring made for a distasteful combination of scent with whatever the girl had last eaten. "Contrary to popular opinion, the Syndicate *has* heard of psionics. We know who you are, Pryce. We're sure Tseng's fist had a little help." He waved the

Nicohaler back and forth. "Kill him. Try not to hit the bitch. We can dye her Caucasian and sell her off to a colony."

"No!" she screamed, thrashing, and rambled off Spanish obscenities.

Aaron whirled, swinging one arm through the air. He seized upon the mass of the five handguns on the left side and pulled them with enough force to levitate a hovercar. Two men went over the railing, three lost fingers. He extended his telekinesis into the room, gathering a torrent of junk and trash into the air, which joined the five liberated handguns in an orbiting whirlwind of mismatched parts. The men on the other side opened fire.

Aaron condensed the junk field, moving away from the girl and hoping blind luck worked in his favor as he tried to isolate the floating pistols from everything else swirling around him. Incoming shots glanced off the heavier items and knocked lighter ones out of the turmoil. A hot fleck scored his cheek, something nipped at his leg.

The girl shrieked an unending stream of curses at White Hat, drifting in and out of English. Aaron almost got the feeling if she wasn't tied to the chair, the man would've had a serious problem.

It took him a few seconds to work out a mental map of the weapons' shapes. As soon as he did, five floating pistols erupted with a cavalcade of azure muzzle flares. What he lacked in precision, he made up for with quantity, pelting the right side railing into wood chips. The Syndicate boys abandoned shooting at him in an effort to get away from the erratic barrage. Once no one had a weapon pointed at him, he let go of the orbiting debris. Like a breaking ring of Saturn, the cyclone of steel bits and junk flew outward, pinging and clattering into the far reaches of the chamber.

One of the men who had fallen came out from behind cover after the wave of metal dissipated. He managed two steps before Aaron noticed him; five floating pistols perforated him before they ran out of ammo. He released his mental hold and the empty handguns clattered to the ground.

The other three above him on the left had stood in stunned silence at the supernatural display. He latched on to two of them, hurling them across the gap into a storefront on the opposite side. That time, he didn't throttle his anger. The bodies disintegrated a plate glass window on contact without slowing down before striking the cinder block wall behind it hard enough to leave holes. He raised an eyebrow at the red spatter and glops sliding down. *S'pose I've gone a bit over the top.*

A still-armed man on the right lunged away from the bloody carnage and took an ill-aimed shot at him between the fence rails. Aaron lofted the man up and over, driving him headfirst into one of the pedicure basins. He burst on impact, smashing the salon chair as if he'd gone off a high-rise building.

Aaron faced White Hat as the man whirled to flee, dragging him backward and over the railing. An invisible telekinetic 'hand' helped itself to the fancy custom pistol in a shoulder holster under White Hat's left arm and sent it gliding across the room to Aaron's grasp. He couldn't quite get his hand all the way around the massive grip, but he didn't plan to spend all day at the range with it.

While keeping White Hat floating helpless on his back, Aaron flung the remaining visible thugs at high speed into walls, one after the next. The girl closed her eyes, lapsing into a mantra of "Stop! Stop! Stop!" once a shower of blood hit her.

He didn't.

White Hat's gun startled him with unexpected loudness, which also made the girl jump and scream as he finished off two moaners with bullets. It seemed both wrong and relaxing to unleash the limit of his power on mere men. Body-shaped cracks in the tiled walls smeared with blood from where thugs had liquefied on impact. By the time he'd found where men nine and ten hid, the effort caught up with him, making him a bit tired. He flung them into the floor with only enough force to kill, rather than splatter.

After a moment, the room fell quiet except for the soft, disgusted whimpers of the girl and the pitiful whining coming from White Hat. Other, gloopier noises emanated at random in the dark. He stepped over a piece of desk with three bullet holes in it and lowered White Hat to the ground next to a corpse with a mannequin arm stuck in its chest. The girl squirmed, pulling at the cords binding her arms and ankles, but couldn't move.

White Hat crawled under the desk of one of the facial reconstruction workstations. Aaron tried to stuff the fancy gun in his belt, and it *clicked* against the one he'd first taken. He chuckled at his forgetfulness, set the huge gun on the desk near the girl, and took the knife from her boot sheath. The plastisteel blade would be more than a match for copper electrical wiring.

"So, who are you then?" He positioned the knife under her left arm.

"Andrea."

"How old?"

"Nineteen."

"Try sixteen." A telekinetic shove, far stronger than his arm could manage, sheared the entire wire bundle off in one stroke. "Don't lie to a psionic, luv."

Blood-spattered and shivering, Andrea stared at him for a long moment while he cut her other arm loose. "That was the most awesome, ass-kicking thing I've ever fucking seen."

A bit of 'new Aaron' poked out from under his anger, preening at the jolt of pride. He dropped the knife in her lap and left her to cut her feet loose while he glared at White Hat.

"Now what?" Andrea slid out of the chair and tore her vomit-covered shirt off before using it as a rag to mop puke from her legs.

Aaron pinched the bridge of his nose. "Right, get off the street. Stop doing drugs. Go back to school. You should go home to your parents, and so on."

"That was the lamest thing I've ever heard." She crawled under the desk to grab her backpack.

"Yeah well, the ones your age never listen. I'd be more enthusiastic about it if I thought it would mean fuck all." He let his arm fall. "If you were ten, maybe eleven, I'd almost be willing to try to talk you off the street."

"My parents are off-gridders squatting somewhere. I don't even know where the fuck they are. They're both crazy as bats, think the government is selling people to alien overlords as food and test subjects. I don't even *have* a home to go back to." Velcro ripped open. "You know they think the Beneath is where all the machinery is that keeps us alive. They don't believe this is really Earth. They have this elaborate idea we're on some kind of colony world, the descendants of space colonists kidnapped by aliens. Some kind of ant farm floating around in a giant ship."

Aaron looked away as she traded the miniskirt for a pair of pants. "You can get government assistance and all that."

"Lame. I'm not a fucking child." She clomped about, kicking her boots into place. "Are you gonna kill that shithead?"

"White Hat? No. He's goin' ta send a message for me."

Andrea slung her backpack over one shoulder and walked up alongside Aaron. She'd put on a black Netßunny t-shirt as well. "Spare me the bullshit about winding up as a druggie prostitute. You're too fuckin' late."

"If that's the life you yearn for in your heart, I won't get in your way." Aaron dragged White Hat out of his hiding place with a telekinetic yank.

Andrea scowled at the floor.

Aaron's weariness showed on his face. "You're disappointed I'm not riding you about getting off the street."

She glared. "I'm—"

"Can't lie to me, luv." He tapped his head. "Alas, I'm not a paladin anymore."

"Why not?" She blinked. "And what the fuck is a paladin?"

In his mind, he saw himself in the Division 0 armor, Allison at his side, guiding this girl out to a waiting patrol car. Another Aaron from another life. "Ehh, long story... Look, you wanna get your ass shot off out here, it's none of my business. You wanna dose a bad batch of chems, get high, and never wake up, go for it. You wanna have some sodding twit like this"—he bonked White Hat into a cubicle wall—"traffic you into off-world slavery, go right the feck ahead. You're not gonna change shit because I tell you to. If you want to, you want to. I'm done trying to save a world full o' people who don't want to be saved."

What's the point without Allison in it? He looked up from the blood-soaked floor, at the trying-so-hard-not-to-look-terrified girl next to him.

Andrea's surface thoughts teased at the idea of lying a year or two off her age and riding government assistance, even if it meant they would ship her off to a colony for adoption. "Can I have one of those guns?"

"If you at least talk to someone, you can 'ave the fancy one." He pulled it out and offered it, handle first. "Only a lady would carry something this gaudy."

White Hat started to say something, but Aaron bounced his head off a cubicle wall.

She hesitated.

"Remember, I can see what you're thinking." He dangled the handle at her. When she reached for it, he smiled. "You also have to promise not to shoot this guy, because I need him."

"He was gonna *sell* me." She raised her voice. "He killed most of my crew. Shit, bullets hit the fucking chair."

Aaron rotated White Hat upright and set him on his feet. "I need him to send a message on my behalf. Would'ya settle for a kick in the bollocks?"

Andrea moved to attack. White Hat guarded the wrong place as a roundhouse combat boot caught him in the cheek. She slipped in blood;

the spinning kick left her on her ass but set White Hat's nose gushing. He growled and lunged at her, but wound up dangling as if swimming in midair.

"Only prisses kick in the balls, an' I ain't no priss." She pulled the knife from her boot and lunged; a fatal strike to the chest became a painful but cosmetic slice to the arm as Aaron's telekinesis seized her as well.

Andrea glided away from White Hat, feet off the ground. "Put me down!"

He continued pushing her across the room, to the exit. "Get out of here. I'll deal with this bloke. Go... be safe or something."

"You're a fuckin' dead man," muttered White Hat.

Aaron looked at his chest, patting around for wounds. Aside from the stinging in his ear and a small piece of shrapnel stuck in his left shin, he felt fine. "Don't feel dead."

"Wiseass mother—"

The rest of the word distorted into a scream. Aaron flung the man out from under his hat into a blur. He stopped him short two feet from a tile-covered wall, already bloody from an underling. Aaron took a step forward and stooped to pick up the hat. The Syndicate lieutenant babbled and flailed.

"Now that I have your undivided attention... Do you 'ave any idea how much force it takes to liquefy a body from blunt impact?" Aaron rotated the man around and pushed his back into the wall. He stopped two paces away. "Even Division 0 has no idea what I've become, mate. I'm quite thoroughly unlike anything *you've* ever fucked with." He reached out and set the hat back on the man's head. "You've seen me mildly cheesed off. I'd advise against pushing me to the point of genuine anger."

"Y-you killed ten... You killed Cray... Do you have any idea how pissed off the big bosses already are?"

"You lot are all about 'It's no' personal, is business', aye? Well, it was business. I needed information, and Cray had to die for me to get that information. You sods kill for revenge, same shite comes back your way, you act all offended."

"The Syndicate had no problems with you until you made one."

Aaron took out his NetMini, trying to reach Shimmer again, without luck. "Not my revenge, you twat. That hacker you lot are so keen on finding. Cray ordered her brother killed."

"He was a damn informant."

"A police officer." Aaron narrowed his eyes. "I thought you boys had some sort of unwritten agreement to leave us… I mean cops alone?"

"You?" White Hat raised a bushy eyebrow.

"Ex."

"Oh. Yeah, well… Cray was pissed. Some money changed hands. The investigation led to a patsy." White Hat laughed. "Another bastard we needed dead. Got the cops to do our job for us. Sooner or later, we'll get you sleeping. How much is it gonna suck to spend your life, short as it may be, lookin' over your shoulder all the time?"

"I'll be honest with you, mate." Aaron levitated him close enough to kiss. "I don't much give a wank if I live or die, and I'm pretty sure I could do quite a bit of damage if I put my mind to it. How does that settle with your cost/benefit analysis? A little known fact about psionics is that our abilities feed on emotion. At a resting calm, I've managed a shade over four thousand kilograms." He paced about like a professor. "If the usual escalation holds true for awak—err, bother that. If the usual curve holds true, I reckon I'd about double that power if I was upset."

He tossed White Hat aside. The lack of telekinetic output after such a long period of constant use felt wonderful. Neither man spoke for almost four minutes.

"You go back to your boss, and you tell him to stay the feck out of my way." Aaron pointed at him. "I see one more of you chaps, and I'll knock down buildings lookin' for every last one of you roaches. I don't care what kind of no-touchy arrangement you've managed with Div 1, I'll bring the castle down even if it buries me too."

Your people can't keep secrets from me. I'll find every safe house, every stash, every operation you have and tear it to bits. He flung White Hat to his feet and into the wall again. *This is the last time I'm going to speak to you, Pablo.*

The unabashed violence in the room had not done as much to dim Pablo's sense of untouchability as did Aaron's voice echoing within his mind. Aaron walked away, leaving the shaking man to slide down the wall to sit in a puddle of his former associates. Aaron stopped short at a figure near the exit to the outer salon room. Darwin gawked at him, holding onto the doorway as if to keep from fainting.

He looked as grey as a zombie.

"What?" asked Aaron. "Well, I suppose that was a touch melodramatic, wasn't it?"

18

WITHOUT A TRACE

Awkward silence hung in the air. Aaron studied every scratch, gouge, and stain on Darwin's dashboard. He catalogued each missing button, broken toggle switch, and cracked holo-emitter—twice. A glance at zombie-Darwin in the driver's seat elicited no reaction but a faint *"hmpfh"* noise and a mild body tremor.

The image of a screaming dark blur zooming into the wall and bursting into a shower of liquid repeated in Darwin's mind. A pattern of red spots on Darwin's left side, a lingering reminder of the detonation. Aaron dropped the mental connection before too much of what it had smelled like made it across the link.

Light flooded the car along with happy chimes as an ovoid advert bot hovered by the driver side window, offering a number of cleaning products, favoring tissues. Aaron leaned forward to examine the ethereal screens as they cycled among different items.

"You've got somethin' on your cheek, mate."

Darwin made the *"hmpfh"* noise again.

"Right then. If you're going to sit here all night, I'm going to order food." Aaron fished for his NetMini.

The advert bot glided over the car to Aaron's window, displaying an array of snacks. He shrugged, indicated an interest in some pretzel nuggets, and looked back to Darwin.

"Nothin' for me, man."

With a happy chirp, the floating bot zoomed off.

"Well there's some progress. Actual words." Aaron patted his thigh. "Odd how they make those little blighters emotive, innit?"

"*Hmpfh.*"

"What's gotten you then? Was it what I did, or peeing in the Syndicate's porridge?"

"Six of one…" Darwin maintained his glassy-eyed stare straight ahead. "Man, you did more than pee in their porridge. You took an enormous shit right in their oatmeal, while the man was at the table."

"At least it's not me, then. Oh, bollocks." He used his NetMini to order two stimpaks. "Damn bit of metal in my leg."

"You shoulda killed Pablo."

"That, my good friend, would not have gotten my message across. I needed someone to do a proper job of explaining my position on the matter. Besides, they already know me. It's not like they couldn't have guessed what happened here." Aaron leaned left, raising both eyebrows. "Darwin, you can relax. I'm not angry with you for leading me to an ambush."

"You readin' my mind?"

"No. Should I?"

"*Hmpfh.*" Darwin added a chuckle. "Shim's made a career outta not bein' found. She's spent a couple years pissin' off the Syndicate. Them dudes can't even find her. I should'a had some sorta clue the post she left was fake."

"They"—Aaron pointed at him—"are not you. You can find her."

A shivering rectangular hover bot about the size of a meatloaf glided up to Aaron's window. It chirped a greeting, which his NetMini repeated. The little machine rocketed away after he removed the two stimpaks.

"Poor thing was afraid of the area." Aaron stared at the bit of metal sticking out of his leg. He grunted, trying to maintain focus despite pain. The shard wobbled and rose up in a well of blood. It was longer than it looked, more than three inches had gone into his leg. "Ouch. Oh, this is some kind of cartoon law, innit? Doesn't hurt until I look at it."

"Ouch?" Darwin blinked. "That thing just came outta your leg and alls you gotta say is 'ouch?'"

"I used to be a cop. I've been shot seventy… four times. Before that, I played professional frictionless."

"Oh, yeah… tough man." Darwin got close to smiling.

"How many times have you broken your shin?" Aaron jabbed himself with the stimpak. In seconds, the blood welling up from the injury foamed, then stopped. "A booster boot can punt a stone, err... frictionless orb at damn near forty miles an hour. What do you think that boot does if it hits a leg? Eighteen times here. Stops hurting after the... oh, never mind. Hurts like balls every time."

Darwin cringed, took a breath, and stuck his finger in the broken start button. The car thrummed to life. Aaron hadn't realized how badly Andrea stank until the burnt silicon air conditioning brushed his face.

"I appreciate the vote of confidence, but I don't think even I can find her." Darwin got the car moving. An easy task with the total lack of ground traffic in the grey zone. "Last thing I heard, Syndicate's got two million on her head."

"Assuming they take offense to the loaf I just pinched in their oatmeal, do you think I've outdone that?"

Darwin laughed. "Can't say. Tell you in a few days. I know you ain't wanna hear this, but might be time ta pack it in on the whole Shimmer thing. She's the kind of supergeek that only gets found when she wants to get found."

Flashing lights lit up the rear-view monitor.

"What the fuck? I ain't..." Darwin glanced at the screen twice. "Oh, damn. It's just a bot."

"Slow down. Probably my pretzels chasing us."

It was.

Darwin declined the offer of an open plastic bag.

"You sure? Mustard and onion." Aaron chomped away.

"How can you eat that?"

Aaron laughed before stuffing another handful into his mouth. "There's gotta be some way to find her."

"Your guess is as good as mine." Darwin took a right turn, slowing as they joined traffic where the quality of the city improved. "I'm gonna go ahead and guess that little situation's changed your mind about that engine."

Aaron chuckled. "Well, you got over it pretty quick." He pondered a pretzel nugget for a moment before tossing it in his mouth. "You still lookin' to give most of it to your son?"

Darwin swerved; when he recovered control of the car, he divided his time between watching the road and glaring at Aaron. "How the—"

"Psionic. The only reason I went along with the casino thing. I thought you were daydreaming about fancy cars and a nice house."

"Heh." Darwin grinned, leaning back with one hand on a control stick. "I was, but not for me. My ass is beyond help. Kurtis was nine when the old lady got stars in her eyes for this Marine motherfucker." He raised one hand. "Now, I ain't got nothing 'gainst the Marines as a whole... just that one motherfucker."

"Understandable," mumbled Aaron over a mouthful of pretzels.

"Guess she got tired of my side business. Her ass was convinced I'd wind up incarcerated." He chuckled. "She's almost right, but I slipped through their fingers. Spose that's why I'm in the grey now. She wouldn't let me see my own son. Took him right off the damn planet. He's twenty now." Darwin seemed to deflate. "I know I ain't made all much of an effort to contact him, but that guilt gettin' heavy, ya know? I just wanna make sure he's good while I still can."

Aaron jostled the bag, looking for a large piece. "You're certain you can cash in that engine? Something like that is going to stand out. Even if you manage to sell it, people might follow the money trail to your boy."

Darwin grumbled as he turned right onto a major ground-level road, three lanes in either direction. Pushcart vendors, beggars, and vagrants dotted the ten-foot wide strip separating east from west traffic. Quite a few had tents, or more permanent dwellings made out of old shipping crates. They drove four blocks before coming to a standstill amid a sea of bright red taillights. Aaron gestured at the logjam of cars. He tried to say, "Aww, now what the feck is going on?" but only sprayed pretzel bits while mumbling. Their retreat closed off as another driver crept up within inches of their back bumper.

"Yeah, exactly." Darwin leaned back and closed his eyes. "Wake me up when this shit clears."

At the head of the stopped cars, a pair of cargo transports had entered an intersection up ahead at the same time. One from the left, one from the right. They sat cab to cab in the middle, cutting off all four directions while the drivers shouted at each other about who should back up.

"Bloody well lucky I forgot my E-90." He flagged down an advert bot and ordered a large bottle of iced Earl.

"That ain't smart. We'll still be sitting here when you gotta piss."

"Cmff you fnmff wakfmafi?" Another spray of white crumbs flew everywhere with the last word.

Darwin tapped his fingers on his legs. "For a psionic, you's dumb as shit."

Can you find Rakshasi? Aaron gave his friend a light punch in the arm. *Skip Shimmer altogether.*

"Maybe... I gotta do it the hard way though, could take weeks."

Take weeks. That phrase planted the seed of discontent at delays in Aaron's mind. The concept of losing the next twenty minutes in traffic grew intolerable. His foot got to tapping, which led to his entire leg bouncing, which led to him turning red in the face two minutes later.

"Come on you sodding wankshafts, flip a bloody coin or something!"

"Yellin' at 'em would work better if you opened the windows."

"Bugger it." Aaron glared at the cargo mover on the right.

The fifty-plus ton vehicle shuddered and twitched. Aaron grunted; exertion darkened his already anger-brushed face.

Darwin glanced at him. "If you shit in my car, your ass is buying me a new one."

"Gaaaaah!" roared Aaron, spittle flying from his teeth.

He panted. Lifting it was too much. He concentrated again, focusing on lateral motion rather than vertical. Fingers dug into the seat as he strained. The metal beast wobbled and let off a loud *boom* as though a giant had kicked the trailer. Both drivers and twenty some odd people who'd gotten out of their cars to watch jumped and spun around to look. With a great squealing howl of rubber on plastisteel, the cargo hauler on the right skidded back into the lane it came from. Small cars crumpled together behind it, brushed aside like dead leaves. A surge of light-headedness almost made him faint when he 'let go' of the truck's mass. He flashed a euphoric grin, despite a mild nosebleed.

The driver of the moved truck blamed the other driver for 'doing something fucked up' and threw a punch at him. Other motorists returned to their cars.

"You get points for subtlety."

"Bugger subtlety. Those two idiots would've been there for hours, and all these useless people beeping weren't doing—" Aaron opened his window and leaned out to yell, "All you sodding wankshafts beeping are doing precisely fuck all to help the situation."

Between the horns and the aftershock of truck sliding backward, no one reacted to him shouting.

A flying bot arrived with his iced Earl.

"Perfect timing," wheezed Aaron. He sucked down a third of the half-gallon in one breath and held the frigid bottle to his forehead. "Darwin, I think I might've overextended myself."

Aaron lost a few minutes. The next thing he knew, they cruised at a decent speed, far from the intersection. He squinted at his surroundings, struggling to figure out where he was.

"Darwin's car."

"Yeah," said Darwin. "You noticed."

The bottle of iced tea rolled around on the floor between his feet. At the mere thought of levitating it, he felt ready to pass out again. Aaron did it the hard way, bending down to grasp the plastic. It wasn't cold anymore, but he drank a few mouthfuls anyway. When the buildings passing by his side struck a familiar chord, he patted Darwin's arm with the back of his hand.

"Oi, Darwin. 'Ave we been 'ere before?"

"Yep. Just gotta make a stop here real quick. Gotta drop some shit… oh fuck."

Aaron lurched forward as Darwin stomped on the brake. A Division 0 patrol craft took up two spaces in the parking lot of a dive hotel. The same dive hotel Aaron had found himself in after the Infinity Casino fiasco. They'd gone too far to change course without attracting attention, one tire had already crossed the walkpath. Aaron sank low in the seat. Darwin chose one of the outer spots, closest to the street.

"Oh, that doesn't look suspicious at all," whispered Aaron. "Three whole cars in this lot, and you park at the ass end of nowhere."

A slender man with dark hair and pale skin walked out of one of the rooms on the fifth floor wearing a cocky grin, Aaron's cocky grin. His eyes were more closed than open, and he made a series of odd gestures as if putting on a hat he didn't hold.

"Oh, this is great." Aaron went from nervous to excited. "Watch this."

The officer took a step to his left, performed a military about-face, and smashed his head into the wall. He slumped to the floor, cheek squeaking over the metal on his way down. Aaron doubled over, cackling. A dark-skinned woman with short, bleached hair rushed out of the room and took a knee by the man. Aaron didn't know her, but her wearing a standard Division 0 cloth uniform instead of armor meant she was Investigative Operations, a commissioned officer.

He scooted lower. "Go on, I'll wait here."

"Are all you psio cops batshit crazy?" Darwin gestured at the windscreen. "What the fuck was that?"

"He was tracing me. Remember the helmet?"

Darwin blinked.

"Some clairvoyants can relive the past motions of someone... Bastards have been trying to track me for months. Little things like this make 'em hesitate. Couple months ago, I put a pillow in my lap and bashed the devil out of my bollocks. I doubt the tracer had a pillow handy."

"You're one sick motherfucker." Darwin let off a wheezy chuckle.

"Well, it took him a month to dare doing this again, didn't it?"

Aaron opened his door. "You do what you gotta do. I'd rather not be around here when he wakes up."

"Probably not a bad idea." Darwin offered a hand. "Keep yo' ass safe."

"I plan on keeping more than my ass in one piece."

Aaron slid out of the car doing the limbo and flipped his back to the two investigators as soon as he got upright. With his hands in his pants pockets, he wandered away, whistling "God Save the King."

DANGEROUS REGRET

Aaron's aimless wander had left him slouched on the floor of a PubTran maglev terminal. A few still-working overhead lights painted the dingy white tiles behind him with glare. The station had only a few people in it, but appeared functional despite its proximity to a grey zone. None of the merchant stalls along the concourse still operated, not even the CaffeiNation. A feeble holo-emitter continued to animate a handful of tiny flags, recreating the retired Stars and Stripes, with coffee beans in place of stars. Next door, three fringers had made a home of the gutted remnants of a fast food place. Someone had drawn a moustache and an exaggerated penis on the giant cartoon chicken mascot etched on the window.

Three grimy boys trudged up the street-access stairway twenty yards to his left. The youngest looked about nine, the oldest no more than twelve. All three eyed the sparse group of commuters with calculating eyes too old for their small bodies. Judging by the shoddy condition of their clothing, Aaron assumed them the offspring of squatters in the grey. They had the same saddle-colored skin and bushy brown hair; they might've been siblings. The boys disregarded Aaron, evidently assuming a man slumped against the wall of a PubTran station had nothing worth stealing or begging for.

He watched them go from person to person. A thin, intellectual-looking man ran into a column to get away from them, earning laughter and mockery when he fell. Their next target, a wild-eyed man with frizzy hair who muttered incessantly at thin air, reacted no better—he ignored them as though they weren't real. They scored a few credits from a sympathetic woman who fell for the youngest child's pouty stare before crossing thirty yards of open space to the next cluster of waiting people.

A middle-aged man became worked up at the sight of them and took out a NetMini. He asked about their families, why they were on the street at their age, and what sort of food they liked. Aaron wasn't sure if he felt guilty or disappointed at their choosing to beg rather than mug. Granted, since money went digital, mugging wouldn't have gotten them much, unless they fancied crappy suits or a battered briefcase. The look in the eye of the eldest seemed malicious at first, and Aaron had looked forward to a little entertainment. Then again, they lacked the size to mug anyone but other children; the most they'd manage would be a grab-and-run. Allison's mental ghost chided him for not being the one to feed them. He tried to rub a building headache out of his temples.

She'd have wanted to take them home.

He daydreamed about her approaching them, chattering away in Spanish with wide eyes and a big smile. The boys would have gotten whatever they wanted from her.

Aaron stared at the trio, wide-eyed with gratitude. One man's willing charity had caught the brothers so off guard they lost the ability to speak. Surely, life on a hydroponic farm off on some colony world or a frontier settlement held more promise for them than being swallowed by the city's bowels. He pondered calling Division 1 for a social service intervention, but looked away with a sour frown. Allison's nameplate seemed to grow heavy in his pocket. His fingers teased at the NetMini. Bringing police here could bite him in the ass. The kids looked happy enough with their squalor; who was he to transplant their lives? Aaron closed his eyes and let his head lean back against the warm tiles. If he didn't watch the miserable waifs begging, he wouldn't feel Allison's demanding stare.

Ex-cop, remember.

Soft footsteps approached; neither volume nor pace felt threatening enough for him to stop attempting to nap. The image of Allison glowered at him out of the darkness, gesturing in the direction of the three beggars. Her lips parted.

"You look like an Arsenal player."

Aaron's thought processes ground to a screeching halt. "What's that then?"

"I'd 'ave said homeless," said Anna, "but I didn't want to insult the tramps. S'pose you didn't catch the game last night then. Your boys got drubbed."

Aaron abandoned the idea of sleep and glanced up at her. She hovered close, navy blue coat fluttering about her shins, hands in her pockets, and a smirk of amused superiority on her lips. Knee-high boots of dark blue suede had short, elevated heels. He pondered a remark about her trying to fake an inch or two of height, but didn't have the energy to spar. Her head wound up aligned with a still-working overhead light, creating a squint-inducing glow in her hair.

"Homeless, eh?"

"Did you decide to go a few rounds with oncoming traffic?"

"Something like that."

"Run!" shouted one of the children.

Ratty sneakers squeaking on the metal floor, the boys scrambled away from a woman in blue Division 1 police armor. She'd taken a knee and tried to put on the most reassuring face a person could manage after military training. Seems the man who'd fed them had more of a conscience than Aaron... or at least, less apathy.

He made a feeble attempt to grab the boys, yelling, "Wait!"

"You're not in trouble," yelled the cop, to no avail. *"No estás en problemas."*

Aaron tracked them as they ran to the left until the eldest stopped short, triggering a pile up. Another police officer emerged from the stairs on the opposite side. He had his hands up in a reassuring gesture, but the man was so massive the sight of him turned the urchins white. The boys spun in place, staring back and forth at the two cops trying to calm them down. The closer the officers got, the more frightened the kids looked.

The youngest ran to the edge of the platform, eyeing the maglev rail. At the instant the boy jumped, Aaron borrowed a disinterested passenger waiting for his ride home from work. A bit of telekinetic finesse moved him and made it look as though the man dove in time to catch the boy in midair. Aaron guided them into a tackle and held all four down until the cops were on them.

"Well, that bloke'll be a hero for a few hours," muttered Anna. "I thought you liked the limelight."

"I used to." Aaron wobbled to his feet. "Course, I wasn't a fugitive then. That's the nice thing about TK, easy to pass off as coincidence."

She narrowed her eyes but couldn't suppress a smile. "Cheater."

"Guilty."

"Care for a spot of tea?" Anna held out her hand but thought better of it. "After you scrub up a bit."

"We best get out of here before their backup arrives. I don't fancy an interview."

He stood, gestured in an 'after you' manner, and followed her away from the chaos on the platform. The hapless good Samaritan had the look of a groundhog staring up at a diving eagle as a swarm of news-bots and applauding eyewitnesses formed around him.

Sector 3011, near the southeastern corner of West City, was home to the Twenty-Nine Pines Mall. One of, if not the largest shopping-plex in the entire country. While some management companies chased exclusive markets, the one responsible for this place catered to the masses. What 29P, as the locals called it, lacked in high-end merchandise, it made up for with choice. The entire five-mile square of Sector 3011 contained sixteen stories of shopping, food courts, and entertainment venues, all arranged around three open-air plazas often used for concerts or other live events.

Humor abounded; as far away as East City, citizens would often joke about the 'type of people' who shopped at 29P. Entire sites on the GlobeNet sprang up, dedicated to image and video captures of the creatures who roamed the mall. To be fair, the lower-end stores on the ground level, especially in the north end, did attract a certain quality of shopper, but for the most part, it was the haven of the lower middle class.

They occupied a small table close to a wide-open shaft that ran the entire sixteen-story height of the mallplex. Through an inch-thick plastic window at his left, Aaron gazed out at a dizzying array of stores arranged on multiple floors. The din of ten thousand people carried up from below, fading into an indistinct murmur of ambient noise punctuated by the occasional squeal of a child.

Aaron leaned back in his seat, fidgeting.

Anna, seated opposite him, bobbed a hydroponic-grown teabag in a cup of hot water. "Something the matter?"

"I'm tryin' to suss out if this chair is uncomfortable, or just not comfortable."

The teabag paused. She stared at him for a long, silent second. "What?"

His gaze settled on a pale woman in a distracting tiny black dress made of cloth strips one level down. She carried a small brownish furry thing under her left arm, and lingered by a storefront window full of mannequins modeling equally skimpy outfits. "Is that a dog or the head of a mop?"

"What?"

"Never mind." He squirmed. "I'm trying to figure out if this chair is painful to sit in, being outright uncomfortable, or if it's just woefully basic and lacking in comfort."

"You are a strange man." She resumed bobbing her teabag.

Aaron levitated his out of his cup. Tea oozed as telekinesis compressed it into a tiny sphere. When it ceased dripping, he dropped it on the table. He took a long sip, and gave it an impressed frown.

"What do you think?"

"I've had better, but it's not bad for twenty credits." He shifted in the chair again, left arm draped over the railing to his left where half-inch thick glass came between him and a five-story fall. "So, where's Archon?"

"He's a busy man, Aaron. He's trying to protect a lot of people."

"Busy?" He took another sip. "Not that I object to your company, but I do find it odd that he's too busy for his lady. Has he been having a rough time of it?"

Giggling children ran by, out of sight somewhere below. The name "Brandon" lofted from the crowd noise on the voice of a frustrated woman.

Anna glanced over the side. "Not as rough as master Brandon's about to have it. Look, Aaron"—she stared into his eyes—"Archon is running back and forth from East to West, trying to gather as many people as he can. There've been some… issues."

"Issues?" He leaned his elbows on the table.

"We've lost contact with two Awakened. One's a rather dangerous pyro who also disappeared. The other is… well, she's a bit…" Anna grumbled. "Dammit, James. Lauren told you to leave that one alone."

"Who's James?"

"Archon." Anna added sweetener to her tea and held the cup to her lips. "His real name is James Mardling, but don't call him that. He's Archon now."

"That sounds damn familiar." Aaron tapped all ten fingers on the table. "I think he spoke at some event… The team got invited to a dinner. Oh, yes. Wasn't he some boffin from Oxford doing research for the Crown?"

Anna laughed. "I thought him a boffin when I'd first met him, too." Her mirth faded. "It's an act, you know."

"I suppose we all have to act a bit." A whirring bot in the shape of a large bird flew by out in the open space. Its garish yellow and green feathers were reflective to the point of luminosity, and a six-foot trail of fluorescent blue plumage trailed it. "Nothing's what it seems. Take that bird... Some manner of drivel from that Monwyn nonsense. Everyone 'ere knows it's a fixture of 29P. It roams about day and night. Sometimes, it'll take a fancy to some random person and circle them. Supposed to be some rare thing wif prizes and whatnot. How do we know it ain't the government watching us all?"

"What's your point?"

He leaned back. "Well, everyone thinks it's some 'armless thing from a kid's movie, right? It acts like a made-up fire-breathing bird what never existed. No one pays it any attention. Perfect thing to use to watch us all."

"You do realize the city is full of cameras that they don't even bother hiding."

He chuckled. "Aye."

"Aaron?" Her fingernail traced lines through some of the spilled white crystalline sweetener on the table. "Can I ask you something?"

"I thought you weren't a cheater." He winked.

She threw a sweetener tablet at him, bouncing it off his forehead. "You are incorrigible. I want to know why you're like this. You could've left that scorpion girl to get shot to bits, but you didn't. You didn't have to interfere with those boys on the tram... but you did. Are you really Aaron Pryce, charming arsehole of the highest order?"

His teeth showed as he made an expression that would've been appropriate for sitting bare assed in cold pudding. He stared at the top of her head while she gazed at the table, one finger tracing patterns in the spilled powder.

"I've been trying to suss out if you're as cold as you act sometimes." He decided to consider the chair's uncomfortableness a matter of fact rather than speculation. "What difference does it make?"

"Archon got me out of a fix... I wasn't in a great place, and he put me back together. No, I wasn't always this... confident."

"Confident? Is that what you call being able to melt a man's bollocks off without battin' an eyelash?"

Anna's gaze flicked up to meet his. "I didn't do it, did I? If I *was* an 'ice queen,' I'd have killed him."

Aaron covered his face, staring into the unfeeling eyes of Talis as she mocked him for murdering his wife. Two seconds later, everything went dark. "Maybe they're right." His cheeks warmed. He pressed a fist into his mouth. Emotion tainted his voice. "Maybe we are all too dangerous. I mean, look at me. I could kill anyone around us and make it look like some other sod went nutters." His voice raged in his mind, screaming "No!" as he replayed the azure streak piercing Allison's forehead. The terror in her expression remained even after death. He rubbed his eyes. "They'd be right to get rid of us all."

Anna stopped drawing in the dust. "How'd you manage to get out of London if they discovered you cheating?"

His short, harsh laugh sounded like an electrocuted goose. He sniffled, bit his lip, and let out a long sigh. "They'd been watching me for months and I didn't even know it. I took a chance on a freak ground out that was on its way to missing. The stone came off the turf at a 'lucky' angle and curved into the goal. Computer models got me; they proved external influence. They thought I had a hacker controlling the stone, but when everything there checked out, they brought the CSB in on a lark."

Her eyes went wide. "*Oooh...* I remember that! They called it the Wembley bounce. It's still being dissected in the media. The bastards at Bristol City used to get into fistfights over it."

"Bristol City?"

She turned bright red. "Umm."

He looked away, staring out at the mall. A faint reflection of his face hovered on the surface of the clear barrier. "I know of the place, was just shocked you did." His concentration failed at the sight of a man wandering out of a Reinventions clinic. His clothes would fit a six-hundred-pound behemoth, though he didn't weigh a third of that. "Well I can tell why that one's happy."

"Can we not talk about that place?"

She sounded so fragile he couldn't help but stare at her for a moment in silence.

"Of course." Aaron gulped a mouthful of hot tea that hurt going down, and hissed air between clenched teeth. "The CSB didn't release their findings to the public. A psionic in frictionless? King William would shit himself right on the throne, and every Member of Parliament would toss bangers at each other and harrumph."

Anna burst into giggles. As tempted as he was to eavesdrop on the mental images she conjured, he wasn't in the mood for that sort of humor.

"The undersecretary of the CSB is a big Arsenal fan."

Her joy faded. "Oh, that figures."

"So's Prime Minister Torrington. Would you believe she walked in on my 'interview' with one of the CSB stooges to get an autograph?" Aaron made a sound dangerously close to a giggle. "She didn't even care about the whole cheating bit. Honestly, they could pick any bloke and make a celebrity out of him, regardless of talent or merit. It's all dogs and ponies anyway."

Anna set her tea down. "I never did like that bitch."

"Anyway, there were a couple of 'I solemnly swears' and whatnot, and I was whisked out of the country in the middle of the night, sworn to secrecy, and deposited in Division 0." Aaron bit off half a chocolate chip cookie, the closest thing they could find to biccys in 29P.

"What'll they do if you talk about it?"

Aaron sipped tea over a mush of half-chewed dough, swallowing the slurry. "I've no idea. Probably say 'don't do that again' in a louder tone of voice."

The fancy false bird glided by, closer this time.

Anna gestured at it. "Maybe you'll win something. You know, they're starting to lighten up a touch back home. I wound up on the desk of Lord Thompson."

"Oh, I *have* to hear this story."

"Not like that, you pervert." She kicked him in the shin. "CSB got me. Said they'd kill me if I didn't assassinate the man. I figured I'd be dead either way, not that I wanted to kill the sod… I wound up diving on him to get him away from a sniper. Course, he turned out rather grateful afterwards."

"Savin' a person's life can alter their perception of you."

"His son's gifted." Anna examined a cookie, holding it to her mouth while Aaron feigned high-society shock. "Thompson launched an inquiry into the CSB last I heard." She bit the top off. "So, why are you so glum? I doubt it's your team's record as of late, though that's quite worthy of glumness."

Aaron sucked sugary bits out of his teeth. "I'm at a dead end. The only person I've had any hope of helping me's fallen off the planet."

"Who is it? Why do you need to find them?"

He waved her off. "Nothin' you need worry about."

"Really?" She uncrossed her legs and leaned forward. "Maybe we can help?"

Frustrated, he couldn't settle on a place to put his hands. "I... I just don't want to talk about it."

"This is it, isn't it?" she asked, her voice bereft of its oft-accusatory tone. "It's got something to do with how you're such a chav."

Aaron stared at her. A glimmer of someone else lurked millimeters below the surface of her sapphire eyes, a girl who never was. A woman who'd clearly suffered a deep emotional wound. He let his gaze fall to the table as he pushed a cookie back and forth in the cheap plastic packing tray. They'd killed at least half the box. He'd lost the urge to eat.

"Allison," he whispered.

Anna slid a hand through the sweetener dust toward him. The electronic bird hovered up to the railing by their table, a long rainbow train of holographic tail feathers glided behind it.

He watched her fingers creep closer for a moment, looked up at her face, and thrust his jaw forward, unsure if he liked the feeling of absorbing her pity. "There was a"—four Division 0 tactical officers, in full armor, walked out of a distant hallway and looked around—"shit."

"What?" she perked up like a meerkat. "There was a shit?"

The woman leading them spotted him and pointed.

"Zeroes." Aaron jumped up.

"Pryce!" shouted a woman's voice, amplified by helmet speakers. "We just want to talk."

He shoved his arm forward; a telekinetic wave knocked the police flat and sent them skidding into a toy store. Two spikes of mental effort toppled shelves, burying them in a massive pile of stuffed animals and children's dolls. He grabbed Anna's wrist and ran, dragging her along.

"Is that necessary?" Anna scrambled to keep her feet under her.

"What?"

"The arm waving thing."

Aaron stopped and gave her a matter-of-fact look. "It feels more dramatic."

"You are such an idiot."

"It does, doesn't it?" He smirked. At the sight of a two-foot red ball bouncing past, he sprinted off. "Come on!"

"Not going to fly?"

"No, that'll draw too much attention." He ran down a moving stairway.

"Oh, and sprinting about won't?"

A spread of octagonal tables in the court at the bottom threw off a blinding glare. Half of them shifted from painful gleam to black as they descended, forming an alternating pattern. He swayed from the disorienting optical illusion of a moving spiral and bumped into a table, startling several people away from Asian food. A short sprint later, he knocked a man into a pond full of holographic koi and ducked past an archway resembling wooden posts carved into dragons.

"Dammit, Pryce, stop!" shouted a man somewhere above and behind.

Telekinetic force grabbed him. Aaron whirled about, threading his power into the intangible hands grasping for him. The Division 0 officer at the top of the escalator sailed out of sight as Aaron overwhelmed him in a contest equivalent to an augmented assault Marine arm-wrestling a two-year-old. For a few seconds, Aaron stood still, blinking at his own strength.

"Well, I'll be…"

Anna prodded him into running again. They weaved among the crowd for another hundred meters or so, ducking snack food carts and random unlicensed vendors selling refurbished junk. The Division 0 officers had the advantage in the sea of people, as most who saw police armor got well out of their way.

"Sorry, Anna." Aaron stopped, squeezed her arm, and let go. "You don't need to get dragged into this."

"Who's Alli—"

She made a noise like a kicked chicken as he telekinetically launched her down a wide corridor lined on both sides with kid-tainment shops. Her distancing shriek drowned in a thousand explosions, beeps, and starship noises from holo-sims. A shower of sparks burst from the ceiling overhead, wherever lights bore the brunt of her surprise. Electronics faltered, creating the illusion of a sphere of shadow racing down the corridor. He slowed her to a gentle stop some two hundred meters later near a bank of doors, targeting someone in a giant rooster costume as a landing cushion. On impact, the suit's electronics emitted a loud squawk.

He struggled to resist laughing at the ungainly flailing of the poor man, though the sight of Zeroes reaching the bottom of the escalator on the far side of the food court did the trick. Aaron cast a brief glance at the ensuing chaos down the hall, hoping he'd moved her away fast enough to escape notice. He gestured at the police, who flinched despite him doing nothing psionic. He gave them a 'gotcha' smile and sprinted in the opposite direction from Anna.

Opportunity for salvation came in the form of an 'employees-only' door at the end of a hallway of rental lockers and public bathrooms. An unpainted corridor between the exterior wall and the rear exits of numerous stores ran in both directions on the other side, flooded with the stink of rotting food and industrial chemicals. Aaron used his sleeve as an emergency air filter. Not trusting his former friends' motives, and with no crowd to dissuade the use of weapons, he sprinted to the left, which offered a shorter distance before a ninety-degree turn.

They've probably got at least two units in the air if not drones. I can't just run out the back.

He jumped a pile of pungent trash bags at the rear door of a restaurant, tossed against the wall by a lazy employee who couldn't be bothered to walk to the exit. An oblivious teen girl in the white and green polo shirt/skirt uniform of a Chinese food vendor sang along with whatever music pumped into her ears while propping open a door decorated with a cute, painted panda face. A wheeled robot jostled and thrummed as it processed something, the smell coming off it a clear indicator of their reason for bringing it to the back hall. The voice of an older man yelled in Cantonese from inside. The girl didn't notice him as he shot by.

Aaron gagged; the stench came close enough to food to transcend from merely bad to abhorrent.

The straightaway led to a switchback left turn and an unexpected group of mops, brooms, and plastic pipes stacked against the wall. He windmilled his arms, managing to avoid landing on his face despite tripping and sliding through the mass of junk. His mind tracked at least seven or eight objects at once, mostly the ones tangling his legs, and forced them out of his path while holding his body upright. He kicked his way out of the debris and made it to the end of the section of hallway, where it opened into a room with fuse panels, generators, and a large metal rolling door. Numerous empty pallets littered the floor, with more stacked to his right.

Three teenaged boys in three different store uniforms leaned against a broken cargo lift parked atop a Cryomil stain. A case of synthbeer canisters perched on one of the loader's fork tines. One sucked on a Flowerbasket inhaler and stared into space. The other two slurped their drinks; their continuous complaining about weak drugs and weaker beer came to a suspicious halt as Aaron skidded to a halt by the door.

Strong telekinetic encouragement forced it to roll upward, breaking the magnetic locks and sending sparks flying from the motor at the top. Two of the three slackers went running back into the mall screaming while the one hitting the Flowerbasket laughed. Aaron slipped under into a loading dock. As soon as he 'let go' of it, the magnets slammed the door down hard enough to crack the concrete. He didn't expect the loud, echoing *bang*, and jumped. Nine smaller doors designed to accept cargo transports ran across the right-side wall. Automated cargo loaders rumbled back and forth past rows of merchandise, while refrigerator-sized hover bots ferried items from shelving stacked to the ceiling to conveyor belts at the distant end of the room. A continuous stream of delivery bots floated in via purpose-built doorways at the fourth-story level and picked up outgoing shipments from the belts before flying off into the city.

The well-oiled machinery of commerce mesmerized him for a few seconds.

He frowned, realizing he couldn't take any of the truck doors. He figured it a veritable certainty more police—or at least some manner of electronic spy—would see him. For a moment, he entertained the thought of hitchhiking on a delivery bot, but none of the ones coming in looked large enough to carry a man.

Armored bodies clattered in the hallway, urging him deeper into the room. He ducked among the cargo movers, which seemed to disregard his presence. Everything from small pieces of furniture to clothes to snacks floated past him on its way to someone in West City. Banging at the door grew louder, urging him to a careless run. One of the large movers came out of a blind corridor, hitting him broadside and sweeping him off his feet. He let off an *oof* as he crumpled over it, clinging to a seam in its paneling. Fortunately, it wasn't moving too fast, and the collision hit him no harder than a pair of frictionless players having a head-on encounter at a full sprint.

With the wind knocked out of him, he could only cling and try to breathe as it flew up to the ceiling and gathered a number of one-gallon plastic canisters with a cartoon goat's face on the label. Aaron's stomach did a backflip at the idea of synthetic goat milk shakes, in powder form. Some manner of high protein supplement for a muscle-head. He wanted as little to do with imagining how it tasted as possible, but his evil brain tried to figure it out based on the cloying smell leaking out of the containers.

He still choked on it twenty seconds later when the product-fetcher bot descended upon the conveyor belts. Aaron jumped free the second it came within two stories of the floor. He caught himself on a telekinetic cushion, floated to the ground, and ducked under the nearest row of shelves, hiding beneath patio furniture.

The sound of dripping water attracted him toward ever-narrower passages in the tangle of merchandise, into a dark space under sixty-foot tall shelves packed with yet more consumerism. He helped himself to a pack of instant self-heating hot pretzel nuggets and crawled to the back corner. The spot was dark and hard to reach, but a telepath would be able to sense his mind regardless of light. Dripping echoed louder here, leading him to a grating in the floor.

Aaron crouched, peering down into a shaft full of wire bundles and corroded pipes descending into the dark, at least twenty meters down into the city plate. Laser pistols went off in the not-distant-enough loading area, leaving him precious little time for pre-regret over what the trip into The Beneath would do to his fresh suit. The clatter of the once-door striking the ground erased the last of his doubt. He scowled. His need to escape didn't come from fear. If Division 0 got a hold of him, Talis would be free and clear. They'd never bother going after her. Most of them likely hadn't even believed she existed.

He frowned at the grate and gathered a sense of its mass in his mind before tearing it off its bolts. The metal warped from the force needed to move it, no longer able to fit back over the shaft.

"Bugger all."

Aaron set it aside and levitated himself into the foul darkness, before a telepathic ping could find his thoughts.

DOMINOES

With an unceremonious shove, Aaron flung the door to his current piece-of-shit squat apartment to the side. It slammed into the wall, knocking some unknown object to the floor. Various awful fluids coated every inch of him, sliding into places and crevices he would not have otherwise known existed if not for the sensation of creeping sludge. The maddening trek through the interior of the plate had indeed kept him away from police detection, but at the cost of a stink able to stain a man's soul.

A reek like metallic fermented raspberries blended with a full-bodied aroma of fetid beef permeated his senses, both smell and taste. He swallowed bile for the fortieth some odd time and trudged into the bathroom. The first fifteen-minute cycle of the autoshower happened with clothes on. He stripped for the next two.

At the halfway mark of the first naked shower, he stopped fighting and puked into the spray of water. When the third dry cycle stopped, he stood motionless in the steam-filled enclosure staring at the mass of fabric on the floor. Puddles of industrial sludge had an awful lot of nerve disguising themselves as safe ground. He contemplated burning the suit, but lacked the energy.

The entirety of his food intake for the day consisted of about a half-dozen cookies and a cup of tea. His purloined pretzels still floated somewhere in a pond of vileness, lost the first time he'd gone under.

Getting out had been more important than recovering a snack of opportunity. A second glance at his clothes chased away any inkling of desire for food. If not for the 'hot water low' warning on the shower's console, he would have run it a fourth time. Aaron grumbled the entire way from the safe, warm tube to his cold 'bedroom.' If he missed anything from his real home, it would be the white machine on the wall, which provided a constant supply of clean knickers... as long as he kept stuffing dirty ones in the top end.

The entirety of his clothing stank—not that his sense of smell had much recovered from his foray below the city—even the unworn ones, having absorbed the ambiance of the place. Aaron remained nude while pacing back and forth with his NetMini, ordering new skivvies as well as laundry service. Minutes later, he slipped into a brand new pair of boxers and a t-shirt before loading the rest of his clothes into a service bot. With the bulk of his emergency clothing on its way to be cleaned, he fell face-first on the clapped out Comforgel pad with a dull *splat*.

ONE EYE POPPED OPEN. SOME THREAD OF COGNIZANCE HAD REACHED INTO his skull and tricked his brain into separating itself from a wonderful dream of breakfast with Allison. He seemed in much the same orientation as he last remembered, face down, lips mushed to one side, and arms limp. In the odd sort of way the human mind tends to process information in the first moments of wakefulness, he realized he heard a sound that did not belong in his apartment, but couldn't identify what it was.

Hissing.

Snakes? He forced himself to blink. *No, too constant. Perhaps there's a steam pipe blown? Steam pipe? What century are you in?* He sucked in a breath, which added a smell to the list of suspects accused of criminally causing consciousness in a sleep-deprived idiot. *Sausage? Oh, someone's broken in to steal the use of our stove.*

Aaron disregarded it as a lunacy of exhaustion and closed his one open eye.

Whirring and rhythmic banging woke him a second time. *Criminal wakefulness in the first degree.* He dragged a hand up to wipe the drool from his lips and used it to push himself over onto his back. The hand remained pasted to his cheek. *This lack of hangover thing is becoming annoying. I need to drink more.* He lay there for a moment, breathing. *Yes, that's definitely sausage.*

"Darwin? Is that you cooking?"

"Not quite," said an unfamiliar female voice, deeper than Anna's and brushed with a dash of haughtiness. She also sounded British. "I see you're up then. Your laundry's back. I took the liberty of stacking it by the duffel."

Against the vehement protests of his central nervous system, Aaron scooted to the side of the bed and sat up. He brushed a portal open in the wall of ancient clothes at the exact moment a statuesque nude woman with paper-white skin strode out of the bathroom. Lemon blonde hair trailed behind her, long enough to gather at her calves when she stopped to smile at him. He lost himself ogling her generous hips and bosom, but as soon as he caught sight of her eyes, his libido hit the panic button, and he stared open-mouthed.

Entirely black, as though someone had replaced her eyeballs with onyx spheres.

"Come on, I've made you some bangers n' mash." She glided into the kitchen with the grace of a sylph.

"Darwin," yelled Aaron. "Did you slip me some fecking absinthe?"

"Your associate is out. He's run into a bit of trouble with those drugs he dropped off at the hotel. Apparently, there was some tampering type wankery afoot, and someone blamed him for it." Her head peeked around the doorway. "He's off tryin' to make it right before they lop his 'ead off."

Aaron slapped himself. She was still there.

He blinked. The woman remained.

"Are you nutters?"

"Are you real?"

"No. I'm a figment of your imagination." The woman dissolved into a cloud of silvery-white mist, which faded away.

"Bugger." Aaron sighed, holding his head in both hands and staring at the tattered carpet between his feet. "I have got to stop doing"—he waved his hand at nothing in particular—"whatever I'm doing that's making me go crazy."

A cold breeze ran across his back. He ignored it until the rubbery Comforgel moved.

"Just kidding," said the woman, kneeling right behind him.

"Gah!" He leapt off the bed, tearing down a large portion of the clothing wall and pulling it with him to the floor. "Bloody…. Shit… Feck.

Hell!" He flipped over, clutching a decaying yellow nightgown up to his face like a little boy hiding under his blankets. "What on Earth?"

She crawled to the edge of the bed, moving like a panther stalking a groundhog. After a lingering glance, she dispersed into fog a second time and reappeared standing. For the first time in his post-Allison life, he found himself six feet away from a nude woman with sex the furthest thing from his mind. The alabaster vixen padded closer. He leaned away from her advance until he wound up flat on his back, her feet on either side of his head, staring up between legs as smooth as a white marble statue.

Under normal circumstances, he'd have adored the view, but he was too out of his wits to notice any part of her anatomy other than those creepy all-black eyes.

"Your breakfast is getting cold." She leaned all her weight on her left leg and poked him in the gut twice with her right big toe. "And by the way, I'm real. Just takin' the Mick."

He shifted his head to watch her upside-down figure sashay to the kitchen. He rolled onto all fours and knee-walked to the doorway. She rounded the table and sat at the pathetic excuse for a table, where two plates of sausage and mashed potatoes waited, doused with gravy. She crossed her legs and dug in, not waiting for him.

"Are you planning to join me or just kneel there staring? I'm Aurora, by the way. Anna must've said something about me by now."

Aaron used the wall to pull himself upright, but continued gawking at her. "Aye, she's mentioned you."

"You might as well sit down and eat. Of the trillion-billion possible things that might occur within the next few hours, our having a shag is about as likely as the ghost of Churchill himself grabbing my ass."

She stuck a forkful in her mouth and winked at him. Before she could chew twice, she bounced in her seat and made a high-pitched *"Oomff"* noise. She swallowed before scowling at empty air behind her. "Honestly? Unbelievable. Go away."

Aaron pinched the bridge of his nose. *I did not just smell cigar smoke.* "Was that…?"

"What do you think it was?"

"I *don't* think it was a man who's been dead almost five hundred years pinching the bum of a naked… woman in my kitchen at…" He looked around. "What damn time is it?"

"You hesitated? I assure you, I'm all woman."

"I was 'aving a momentary debate regarding the reality of succubae."

Aurora laughed, clamping her hands over her face to avoid spraying food.

Okay, not a succubus, just a tart.

"Your breakfast is getting cold. Sit. Eat." She pushed the other chair out with her foot.

He zombie-walked to the table and fell into the seat. The food wasn't bad. He managed half of one of the sausages before he pointed a potato-laden fork at her. "Why are you naked?"

"Do you want the basic answer or the full?"

"I'll 'ave the lot."

"Solid objects don't follow me into the astral world. I'm far lazier than I am modest, and all the shite hanging up around your bed is dreadful. The stuff that would fit either would fall apart or has mold growing on it. I'm also rather amusing myself at making you uncomfortable." She dribbled a small amount of gravy on her right breast, clearly on purpose, but pouted anyway.

Aaron almost dropped his fork when she leaned down as if to lick it away. He gawked. She laughed and wiped it with a napkin. At the look on his face, she burst into laughter while he propped his head up on one fist and stared at his food. That lasted all of a minute until her foot slid up his leg.

He looked up at her. "Must you?"

"Is this making you feel awkward?"

"Aye, a wee bit."

"Then I must." She winked, sliding her toes up along the inside of his thigh.

"'Ang on a minnit. You said... and Churchill just grabbed your bum. Does that mean?"

"Oh, that wasn't Winston. He's in the Abbey. He's not going to pop over here that fast just to play grabass with the likes of me. Not with the Germans coming any day now."

"Right, yeah." Aaron nodded as though the continued existence of the ghost of Winston Churchill made complete and total sense. "Of course not. Not to imply your ass isn't worth an intercontinental trip to pinch."

She broke up in a fit of giggles, clamping her hand over her mouth to avoid spraying him.

"Germans? You do realize that was centuries ago?"

"Aye." She moved her head as if rolling her eyes. "He thinks they're trying to lull us into a sense of complacency by faking it."

Aaron blinked. "For almost five hundred years?"

"He's a patient man." She took on a thoughtful look. "Though, if you think about it... Half of the major power within the ACC used to be Germany, so... it does make one wonder."

"That's a bit imprecise. The Corporates have most of Europe. Bah. I appreciate the cooking. It's been awhile since... Ghost?" He gazed into space.

Aurora gave him a somber look. "No, I haven't seen her. I'm sorry."

"Right, of course." His breakfast lost some appeal.

"That's a good thing, Aaron. Few dead people linger. Not seeing her about means she's not upset at you. She knows it wasn't your fault. If she had issues, she'd likely be all over you."

He went red, pale, and red again in the span of a breath. Anger, confusion, rage, and sorrow all got in sucker punches, leaving him open-mouthed and stunned.

"I'm a clairvoyant. Awakened, of course. Take whatever you know about seers and..." She bobbed her thumb upward.

"Anna gave up with the sales pitch, now it's your turn?"

Aurora sliced off a bit of sausage and used it as a shovel for some potatoes. "Not entirely given up. She's a bit sore after you had your way with her in the mall. She's not used to that much cock."

He barked a laugh. "A man in a chicken suit! It was a soft landing."

"Mmm."

Aaron stayed quiet during the considerable pause while she chewed.

"I find people for Archon, other Awakened. No, Anna's not upset with you. Archon wanted me to thank you for keeping her under their radar."

"Find people?" He raised an eyebrow. "What if I asked you to find someone for me? Can you locate Shimmer?"

Aurora dragged a finger through potatoes and gravy and lifted it with a flourish to her lips. He shifted in his chair as she sucked her finger clean. Aurora tapped her nail against her teeth, breaking the silence with two sharp clicks.

"I'll find that little hacker for you, but I want you to do me a favor in exchange."

"Meet Archon?"

"I'd appreciate that as well, but no... I want you to tell Pixie about what happened."

"Who the devil is Pixie? Wait, you mean Anna?" He picked at his empty plate. "I got the impression she's rather not fond of that name."

"I suppose. Yes. I want you to tell her what happened with your wife."

"What the feck for?"

Aurora's lips spread into the grin of a succubus. "Dominoes."

"What?" He blinked.

"Dominoes." She flicked at the air.

He stared at random objects in the cramped kitchen while mulling it over. At the mall, before the police showed up, it had almost come out. Why he'd come so close to opening up about it eluded him. Not only had he known Anna for less than a week, she was a woman—a physical manifestation of pain, suffering, and loss. He had to protect himself from them. They'd all become Talis in his mind, every single one of them out to jab the knife in deeper. A woman had forced him to kill Allison. Every time he laid eyes on one, he saw either Talis and felt rage, or his wife and felt loss. Pre-emptive callousness had become his armor.

He lifted his head, gazing between his clawed fingers at Aurora. She wore the expression of a sympathetic soul, nodding as if in reaction to his inner argument.

"Dominoes?" He asked.

"Aye."

"All right." Aaron cradled his head in both hands, searching for meaning in the pattern of smeared gravy.

Aurora slid out of her chair and moved around the table. The white of her stomach glowed in his peripheral vision. "Care for a grope before I get going?"

"I'm not honestly in the mood, luv."

When he raised his head to look at her, he stared at an empty kitchen.

BARELY HANGING ON

Aaron swirled wine around the bottom of a tall glass. Faint electronic music buzzed and beeped at the edges of his awareness, the sort of thing the hoity-toity crowd preferred. It amused him to think about how, sixty years ago, the 'proper' crowd decried the same stuff as noise. He looked up from the sloshing burgundy liquid, watching a lone waiter adjust napkins on empty tables.

Everything not metal or glass was white: tablecloths, napkins, and candles, which turned out to be exceptional holograms. Only their lack of radiant heat gave them away. He decided these cushioned chairs fit quite comfortably in the zone of being comfortable. A vast improvement over the 29P food court. Then again, the price of one plate here would feed a family of sixteen at the mall.

The waiter offered a pleasant bow as he passed, continuing his life's mission of napkin tending. Aaron wasted a minute staring at the facing, empty chair before looking out over the room. Everything curved to the right until the ocean of tables vanished beyond a bas-relief of angels and demons locked in battle. The Spire, the restaurant he had suggested, occupied the interior of a torus-shaped building, elevated a hundred and ninety-two stories above West City. Glass composed the majority of the outer wall, angled outward at the top to allow an unobstructed view straight down. Celestial battle in bas-relief wrapped around the inner wall. Except for the plain white elevator doors, nude muscular figures with wings and swords, kept modest by convenient ribbons of billowing cloth, clashed with grotesque creatures rising out of the pits of Hell. He thought he'd remembered reading somewhere the installation cost three or four million credits and took a team of artists two years to finish.

Much of the city hid behind a rolling haze of cobalt blue. Hovercar lanes at or around the fiftieth story created a dark, shifting grid within the distant murk below. The orderly migration of thousands of vehicles formed eerily straight lines by a combination of distance and electronic navigation aids. If he were a hundred stories lower, the traffic would be a frenetic scramble of disorder. Far removed, it looked serene.

Each time the elevators opened, he looked over, hoping to see Anna, though only waiters emerged with food on its way up from the kitchen below. He glanced at the time, debating if she'd even bother. The twenty-somethingth time the elevator chimed, he didn't bother peeling his gaze off the window.

"Sorry I'm late." Anna removed her coat, draping it over the back of the chair.

He looked up, too surprised and relieved to speak.

"Archon decided to give me another errand. How good are you at locating people who know how to work a jump-capable starship? I'm having no luck."

He smiled at her gown, two swaths of deep blue fabric crossed over her chest, suspended by silver chains over bare shoulders. The hem fell mid-thigh in a purposeful attempt to create the look of a tattered pixie dress. Silvery flecks glinted from her cheeks and around her eyes, the lightest touch of body glitter spread away from her azure eye shadow. Her dress, her lips, and her eyes matched.

Aaron spent a moment staring. "You look magical. Are you sure your man is all right with us meeting?"

"Yes, he's aware I don't cheat." She winked.

"I can't say I'd be so trusting of other men. You're ephemeral. All that's missing are the faerie wings."

Her mood seemed to smash through the floor.

"Umm." He coughed. "Sorry?"

"It's all right. You couldn't 'ave known." She held a small purse composed of several thousand tiny dark grey metallic squares.

"Interesting bag."

"It's dielectric. Keeps the 'mini safe." She brightened. "Interesting suit. Is it blue or black?"

"Depends on its mood." Aaron smiled. "Lately, it's been a bit of both."

"Good evening," said a waiter in a long-tailed white coat. Six silver rods down his chest held the garment closed, tiny jousting lances pointing in alternating directions. "Are you ready to order?"

Aaron gestured at Anna.

"That's fine." Anna offered the waiter a polite smile and took her seat.

The waiter reached out, waving his arm in a gesture that appeared to unroll an ancient paper scroll in thin air. The hologram cycled among several pictures, each featured a main course with smaller images around it indicating the supporting dishes. With each image came a wearisome description of ingredients, down to the region from which they were imported as well as statements of how much care and love went into the preparation.

Aaron ordered lamb chops covered in a garlic and rosemary drizzle spritzed with ground mint leaf. Anna chose the steak kew. She forced an interested smile as the waiter explained their sourcing of genuine Asian beef from the best growers.

"Excellent choices." The waiter bowed.

Anna helped herself to the wine, pouring her glass up halfway. "What are you smiling at?"

"Your nails are blue, with silver doves."

A trace of pink filled in her cheeks. "I had to look the part. This isn't a food court."

"Indeed." He held up his glass. "Well, after three of these, I think I'm going to tell you something."

"I'm listening." She sipped some wine. "I'm still taken, no matter what you're going to say."

He shook his head. "Not at all where I'm going with this, but, I understand." His hand emerged from his pocket, setting Allison's nameplate in the center of the table. The matte-black metal looked like a hole in the snowy tablecloth. "That was my wife's."

She touched it with a fingertip. "It's cold."

"Always is. Not sure if it means anything. Aurora said she's not loitering about."

"Sorry." Anna withdrew her hand. After an awkward moment of silence, she glanced at the window. "I used to be an exotic dancer. My costume had holographic pixie's wings." Her face went from pink to crimson. "Costume... bother, it was just a harness with a projector."

"The reason I've been delaying meeting your boy Archon is I'm hunting the woman who forced me to kill my wife."

Anna's cheeks matched the tablecloth. "Oh, Aaron." She grasped his hand. "I'm so sorry…"

He bristled at the incoming pity, forcing his expression not to project his distaste. Anna's doe-eyed stare offered a glimpse at someone she used to be. "We'd gotten a report of a robbery in progress at a jewelry shop. A couple of their security people in the back room watched a woman walk in and tell the clerks to put the valuables in a sack. No weapons, no threats, all smiles. When the salespeople did what she asked and seemed overjoyed to do it, Div 1 kicked it over to us."

"Suggestive?"

"More than that, I think. Telempath as well. The clerks looked like they adored her. Anyway, I'd spent the better part of my time on the force begging our captain to let us ride as partners. It's against all sorts of regs, you know."

"I can imagine."

Aaron paused as the waiter returned with a ginger salad for Anna and a bowl of potato and chive soup for him. The man insisted they taste and be pleased with the offerings before he departed. He sampled a spoonful and gave the man an approving nod. After a mild bow, the waiter walked away.

"We'd been riding together for only a month, and we got this call. Honestly, I didn't expect too much difficulty with it. Surveillance footage looked like a nonviolent event, despite that she had a bunch of thugs with her. I should've been more careful. The authorities don't fancy suggestives much."

Anna mumbled with a mouthful of greens. "Mmm."

"So, we show up and do the usual routine. Police, keep your hands where we can see them, the whole spiel. They take off out the back into an unfinished space. To make a long story short, we cornered her and well, this bitch looks right at me and says 'kill your partner.'" He gripped the tablecloth, once more seeing Allison's terror replay itself. It got a fraction easier when Anna squeezed his hand. He swallowed. "The instant her eyes flashed white, I braced myself. Her voice hit my brain like a hot knife. We'd been required to work with a department suggestive to develop a tolerance against it, such as you can…"

Anna handed him his ice water. "Drink this; you're sweating."

He drained the cup in one pass and took a moment to gather his breathing. "They say it's easier to resist an implanted compulsion to harm someone you love. Spouse, parents, your children… I heard myself shouting 'no' over and over, but my arm moved to aim at her. The harder I tried to fight it off, the more desperate I became." His reflection in the silver vase had turned cherry red. Tears fell from his eyes. "She just stood there. She didn't expect me to…"

"I get the idea." She gripped his hand again. "You don't have to go through it again."

Aaron wiped his face. The waiter stopped at the table.

"Is everything all right?"

Anna flashed a broad smile. "Oh, the soup is just so exquisite it's moved him to tears. His late grandfather Marley used to run a chive farm out of Oxfordshire."

"Wonderful! I shall let the cook know." He zipped away.

"Oh yes," whispered Anna. "He can't resist a good chive. Gets quite emotional about watery potatoes and green bits."

Aaron cracked up, though he still sniffled. "You're insane. Do you realize that?"

"How is your grandfather, anyway?"

"I dunno. I came along rather late. The old man was wheezing and bedridden before I was walking." He stirred the soup, almost ready to take another spoonful. "I remember seeing the shot. She fell. The screaming in my brain got so loud, I thought my grey matter had split in half. It felt like an explosion in my head."

Anna stabbed at her salad. "I think Archon may want to hear this. You might've cracked at that point."

"You think I'm a nutter?"

"Not that kind of cracked. Though"—she tapped a finger on her cheek—"a man who cries over chives might be."

"Now you're reaching. I appreciate you trying to cheer me up, but… I killed my wife. She didn't deserve it. Allison was the sweetest, most loving… innocent." He dropped the spoon against the bowl. "When I came to, the place was a hames. Two of the walls were open to the outside, they said jewelry'd flown a quarter mile. They found sixteen cars in offices across the way. Two of the sales clerks are still unaccounted for. Six customers were crushed to death."

Anna gasped.

"I was in the hospital for a few days. They thought I'd gone murderous and wanted to know why. I tried telling them it just… happened. I figure it was the display of extreme power that kept me alive, on account of their curiosity. Cop killers usually get the summary. Cops who turn traitor don't last too long either."

"But you didn't... right?" A bit of tomato burbled out of her mouth as she bit down.

Aaron found a smile. "No. It happened again in the casino. One of their security people tried to use a suggestion on me, and it set me off like a bomb."

"That's why you almost shat yourself when I sent you a telepathic message."

"Yeah... I didn't know if that would have the same effect." He held up a hand. "Before you go running off to tell Archon about this amazing new weapon, it hurts like hell. Worse than two hangovers wrapped up in a car crash. Leaves me in bed for a day."

"He could probably suss out how it works."

Aaron took a few mouthfuls of soup. "He could also set me off and... well... I don't want to be responsible for ending your little uprising."

She made an indignant face, despite looking about ready to laugh. "Little uprising? Are you serious? We're not 'uprising,' we're leaving. Archon doesn't want to hurt anyone; he's trying to protect us."

Over the next few minutes, he finished the soup in silence and stared at the bowl.

Anna leaned closer. "What're you thinking?"

"Those chives were..." He sniffed, dabbing at his cheek with the napkin. "If only grandpappy Marley could have been here."

"Stop." She laughed. "Why don't you come with me after, and you can meet the others?"

"I can't. Not until I find Talis." His expression hardened. "I don't care what else I do, that bitch is going to have a reckoning."

"Are you so sure the same thing won't happen again?"

"I'm planning to go alone."

"Oh, so she'll just tell you to jump off a bridge then."

"She won't see me coming. You don't need psionics to handle a psionic. A firearm works wonders."

"Archon..." She half-rolled her eyes, grinning. "As he likes to remind everyone, he's a rather powerful telepath. He's also quite good with suggestion. You're far less likely to run off and get yourself hurt if you have help."

"That earnest look you're giving me makes you look like a schoolgirl."

He chuckled. "Truth is, I never much cared about coming back. I just had to try."

"Why all the womanizing?" She glanced off to the side, fighting the urge to scowl. "Something to try and deaden the pain?"

"You've been talking to Darwin, haven't you?" A moving white blur out of the corner of his eye stalled his words. He leaned back, allowing the waiter to clear the table and walk away. "No. I… suppose I've blamed women for everything. For being too trusting not to duck, for being too painful to lose, for being so evil to make me do that. Whenever I laid eyes on a girl, I'd see my wife dying all over again and hate the one in front of me for still being alive when Allison was dead. Sometimes, they'd remind me of Talis, and I'd regard them as something less than human."

Anna blinked, her expression blank.

"This is going to sound corny, but I didn't get the same feeling from you."

She refilled her glass. "You're right. That does sound corny. What kind of feeling did you get from me?"

"Well, first I was wondering if you were old enough to be in the bar."

She coughed on the wine. "I'm not that damn short."

"Of course not. As soon as I saw your face I knew, but you also looked ready to kill someone."

"Aurora insisted I be the one to make contact with you. Made me miss a damn live match."

"Don't like replays? You know they have these things called video recordings now. Full 3D, you could be at any angle, even on the field."

"Terrence would have ruined it for me."

"Who?"

Anna waved her hand about. "One of the unfortunates that've joined our little 'uprising.'" She chuckled. "He's a telekinetic, not Awakened. Been in a shit mood since he got out of jail."

"Jail?" Aaron raised both eyebrows.

"He got picked up for attempted luring of a minor."

Aaron glared.

"No." She swatted at the air. "It wasn't like that. The 'minor' was a girl we were trying to recruit, but she'd run off. She's a healer and a telempath. Terrence tried to grab her on the sidewalk, but she made everyone in the area all sorts of panicked. They took one look at the little sprog, she had this ratty little half shirt on and a skirt made of scrap leather that barely covered her, and assumed the worst. Poor Terry got quite a beating."

"Oh, I think I heard about that one. They set up an outpost in the Badlands. At first, they tried to be picky about who they approved to know about it, but when no one volunteered, their selectiveness diminished. Almost wound up there myself, but Allison was afraid of leaving the city, so we passed."

The waiter returned with a friend and the entrées. Aaron's looked like a work of modern art. Three pieces of meat, each bunched up at one end of a long, narrow bone formed a teepee in the center of the plate. A colony of tiny egg-sized potatoes drizzled with a reddish-orange sauce surrounded them. Anna's plate was more active; chunks of meat and vegetables sizzled and popped in a metal-in-Epoxil tray.

After an obsequious insistence on checking to make sure everything was perfect, the waiter left them to eat in peace.

"I'm not sure if you should eat that or charge people admission to look at it." Anna grinned. "Anyway, the girl's confused. Her entire life, everyone's been cruel to her. She assumed all we wanted from her was to exploit her power, so she kept running off. I don't know where the devil she got this augmented oaf from." Anna stumbled over her words, near to crying. "He almost killed James."

"She evidently found the police..." Aaron angled over his plate with a knife and fork, looking for the least awkward angle to start. "They set up a veritable colony out there all to watch her."

Anna couldn't speak for a moment and held her hands over her face as if trying to push tears back into her eyes. "Aurora's convinced the next time that girl and James are in the same place, he's going to die. So far, he's been content to let her stay behind, not that he's fond of leaving her to the machinations of the government. Her healing ability is beyond anything that's been documented. He's got it in his head that she can alter the brain structures of 'normal' psionics and turn them Awakened. James is trying to protect us, but if someone's too daft to understand that and wants to suffer here on Earth, we're not going to force it."

"What do you think Aurora meant by dominoes?"

"Little bits of plastic that people set up in lines and tip over?" Anna's shrug turned into a cringe as her food emitted a loud *snap*. "Cripes, it's trying to assault me." She poked at it with a fork while leaning away.

"That looks hot."

She winced. "It's not spicy."

He waved his hand about while he finished chewing. "No, I mean thermally hot."

"Oh… right." Anna ate for a moment in silence.

"So, what about this Aurora person? She paid me a visit the other day. Said something about dominoes."

"The woman's quite strange sometimes. Your guess is as good as mine what she means."

"I see."

A few minutes passed where the food absorbed most of their attention.

"Aaron… did your parents have a fit when your gift manifested?"

"Not really. Mother thought I'd just gone into a phase that would pass. Still does. Father thought it 'brilliant.' The whole frictionless tweaking thing was his idea, if you must know." Aaron lowered his voice to a whisper. "He's a betting man."

Anna's jaw hung open. "Are you taking the piss?"

He shook his head due to a full mouth.

"Well, you're still a cheater since you did it."

"Aye." He dabbed a napkin at his lip. "What about yours?"

A shiver took her, as if a burst-into-tears moment was imminent. She collected herself and went steely. "CSB killed my Mum when I was two or three. I don't remember her at all. No idea where my father is, or if I even have one. For all I know, he was a petri dish."

"Sorry." He tilted his head, wondering how the exotic dancing bit came into play.

"What?"

"Oh… I don't want to pry. Was just confused about what you said earlier, 'bout the wings."

"The stripping?" She gestured with both hands. "Might as well be out with it since we've gone this far. CSB had a watcher on me. I thought he was my dad, but the bastard wasn't what you would call a kid friendly person. My little habit of emotion equals fried electronics got expensive. Add a constant flow of beer to that… Screaming turned to slapping, then beating. He came after me bad one night when I was twelve, and I must've thought he planned to beat me to death for torching the holo-bar. Fried the sodding thing right in the middle of a frictionless match. He got awful cheesed off he'd miss the rest of it and came after me worse 'an ever. I panicked and killed the son of a bitch by accident. Wound up on the street."

"No social—"

"Ran away. Didn't want to get found out as a psionic. My little monster makes electronics freak out if I'm not perfectly calm. Emotions, good or bad, make it play... and right after that night..."

"Ahh, right. Ahhh..." He shot a guilty look at the table. "I didn't ask for special treatment, honestly, I..."

"Oh, it's not the same climate when they found you as it was back then. The business with Lord Thompson was two years past by the time you had your 'injury.' Moderates were already backing off on 'The Directive.'"

A shadow drew Aaron's glance to the right, at a pair of augmented thugs in long, black coats. "Well, look at that."

"What?" She perked in her seat, indignant. "Little me changing the course of British history?"

"No, those big bastards pointing rifles at us."

A beep at floor level drew his attention to a silver canister about the size of a synthbeer bouncing and rolling at them. The charge detonated before his brain could react. An ear-splitting *bang* cracked the air as a concussive wave threw him, the table, and Anna onto the angled window. Aaron's world became a haze of white accompanied by a constant high-pitched tone. She hit the glass face first, not moving. Shots rang out, jarring him back into reality. Bullets punched holes in the inch-thick glass on either side of his head, spraying him with silica dust. Despite the stun grenade, he found enough presence of mind to push their rifles to the side and up.

The crunch of bullets chewing on window turned into clanks. A metal band between two transparent panels gave out like a noodle under the barrage. High-pitched squeals ran with cracks zigzagging in the glass beneath him, adding a spike of fear to Aaron's telekinetic yank at the rifles. Neither lost their weapon, but they did stop firing. He cocked an eyebrow, impressed by the strength of the boosted thugs.

Shattering preceded a blast of cold air from the side, which shoved him off the angled window to the floor. Napkins went flying from the force of the gusting wind. He looked on in horror as the square of glass supporting Anna broke away from the mangled spar and dumped her out like a trapdoor. The thousand-pound slab of glass slid out of its socket and followed her, spinning like a gargantuan shuriken.

His primal want to pull her close resulted in a brief release of telekinetic energy and a dull clank below the level of the gaping hole where a window used to be. She screamed. A strip of tablecloth material snagged on the spar went taut, as if it supported weight.

"No!" he roared, scrambling to crawl at the hole.

Aaron flattened himself as another burst of gunfire rang out behind him. Metal rattled outside, almost lost in the howling gale.

"Anna! Hold on."

Her answering scream sounded close. He flipped on his back ready to kill, but a second concussion grenade landed on his chest. Panic, quite similar to the way one might react to a dinner-plate sized spider appearing out of nowhere on one's testicles, manifested in a telekinetic launch of the stun grenade. It detonated a few feet away, plunging him into a world of white light filled with a horrible blaring screech. He thought he flailed, though he couldn't tell if his arms moved for real or if he only imagined it. Reaching out with telepathic feelers pinpointed several minds in his vicinity. Two contemplated murder, the rest occupied various states of fear or panic.

Aaron projected random surges of telekinetic force in the direction of what he believed to be their assailants. With all the grace of a blind man fumbling in the dark, his mind latched onto the inconsequential mass of tables, and flung them. A few seconds later, the squeal in his ears lessened enough to allow in the screams of the wait staff as well as Anna's terrified cries.

"Aaron!" she shrieked. "I'm slipping. Help!"

He found himself lying on his side under the broken remains of several chairs. Guns went off, tiny pops sounding far away and under water. Above and behind him, more glass exploded in fist-sized plumes of glittering dust. Aaron rolled on his back, twisting his head around to search for the source of the terrified screaming.

The tablecloth ripped, unraveling and sliding a few inches out. Her cries for help turned into a wild scream as every light in the ceiling exploded in a shower of plastic bits and sparks. Both men shooting at them gurgled and howled; lightning crackled around their faces, lapping from their implants to any nearby metal surface.

Aaron dove across the metal radiator strip at the base of the ring window, landing flat on his chest with one arm over the edge. Anna dangled five feet down, her two-handed grip failing in a slow, continuous slide down the length of imitation cotton. She half-heartedly kicked at a narrow walkway ringing the restaurant, which probably hadn't seen boots since the place was first built. A colony of pigeons watched her with disinterest.

Time seemed to stall as she lifted her head to scream at him. He didn't hear her voice or comprehend any words coming out of her. Anna's face had the same expression as Allison's.

Blind-fired bullets peppered around him, shredding furniture and shattering another piece of glass to the left. Less concerned with gentleness than success, he telekinetically jerked her closer to the building. She slapped into the metal beneath the window and crumpled onto the narrow catwalk.

"Pull me in, dammit!" She howled, clinging to the thin superstructure.

"Minute, luv. They've got guns."

Aaron sat up at the same moment the backup lighting painted the room crimson. He let off a war cry and focused his power at the man on the right. A vicious surge of telekinetic force hurled him at a still-intact section of window, feeding on the rage summoned at the 'I'm going to die' look in Anna's eyes. The leg breaker smeared into a streak of black as if fired out of a rail gun. Glass disintegrated to shrapnel on contact; the metal-infused body hit a spot between two panels, where a bracing strut acted like a blade and sheared a leg off. The free limb vanished into the fog as the man careened in an arc for the ground more than two thousand feet below.

Ignoring Anna's alternating pleas and angry demands, Aaron stared death at the remaining assailant, but tempered his killing urge with reason: he had to know who sent them.

Since the cybernetic hands had withstood his attempt to disarm them once already, his next telekinetic exertion mangled the thug's rifle into an explosion of twisted debris. With a snarl, he slammed the huge man backward into the wall, smashing the left arm of a titanic sculptured demon holding a trident. White plaster bits fell around dark metal biceps that cracked open in a flurry of sparks. The assassin's limbs smoked and shuddered. Myofiber muscles exceeded their stress limits, snapping like bundles of dark grey rubber bands as the metal limb flailed about. He managed to get a pistol halfway out of a belt holster before Aaron torqued the wrist around, breaking the hand off and flinging it. Gun and metal fist pulverized the wing of one of the sculptured angels while dark green fluid sprayed from a bundle of ripped wires.

"Aaron!" screamed Anna. "Please..." A sharp *bang* came from an advert bot that made the mistake of getting too close to her.

Damn, I can't leave her sit out there.

"Elevator or express?" Aaron leaned forward, bug eyed and looming. Every vein in his forehead swelled.

The thug hauled ass for the elevator, jabbing his metal stump at the call button.

Once the doors closed, he rushed to the edge. Anna clung to a metal spar about five feet below the floor level. She'd managed to get one leg hooked over the metal superstructure, likely a catwalk used by window cleaners or maintenance crews. He grasped her in a telekinetic embrace and gave a light tug, but she refused to let go.

"Anna?"

She looked up at him. For an instant, she had the same expression Allison had when he'd pointed a gun at her. Irritation brushed it aside. "Oh, finally got 'round to rememberin' me out here?"

"Aye, sorry. Couple o' dogsbodies weren't in the mood for a chin wag."

He levitated her up and in the missing window. She clamped onto him, trembling hard enough to make it difficult to stand. Smears of glittery eyeliner ran down her cheeks, her teeth chattered, and she gave him the most pathetic stare. An all-too-familiar pathetic stare.

He pulled her into a hug, rubbing his hand up and down her back and ignoring the constant prickling sensation of electrical discharge. The distant sound of sirens didn't matter. From the looks of things, the plummeting body caused a hovercar accident a few blocks away. He didn't even want to think about what the massive hunk of glass had done.

"T-thank you..." She squeezed him.

The Spire's staff had fled, leaving them alone in the damaged torus.

After several minutes of clinging, she stopped trembling.

"Aaron?"

"Yes?"

"You know this isn't a hug... This is me bricking it."

"Aye. Don't blame you. I can probably fly, and I'd sign cloth if I fell out that window too."

She swallowed. "I'm not afraid of much, but I can't zap gravity."

Another minute passed in quiet. Neither made a move to let go.

"Anna?"

"Yes?"

"You had the same look in your eyes Allison did."

She pulled away enough to meet his gaze. Her expression hadn't changed much. He squeezed her arms, fighting the urge to do more than hold her upright.

"Don't make that face at me. I'm not your reincarnated wife. I'm older than she was."

He glanced down. "She was twenty-four."

"Twenty-eight 'ere."

"Twenty-nine."

"Not for eight months yet."

Aaron glanced down at her painted toenails and chuckled. "No, I meant me. Oh, you seem to have lost your shoes. I hope they didn't kill someone when they landed, though I have to say the barefoot look works with that dress."

She frowned at her feet. "Dammit. I just bought those today."

"You nearly fell from a two-hundred story building, and you're worried about shoes?"

Anna clamped onto him again at the reminder. "You said that on purpose, didn't you?"

"Aye."

"That was unfair." She backed up. "Taking advantage of me. You know I'm not some helpless little flower. I could've taken out those cretins myself."

"Sorry. We should probably get out of here." He motioned at the elevators.

She brushed a smear of dirt off her left arm. "Yes, let's."

ILL-EQUIPPED

T hings had been worse at ground level than he'd anticipated. The slab of glass had hit a passing hovercar, shearing it in two pieces, each of which wound up striking nearby office buildings. Given the late hour, only a handful of people were at work, which reduced injuries on the ground… but the poor bastard in the hovercar hadn't survived.

They made it out of the immediate area before enough police arrived to set up a perimeter to trap people for interviews. Anna's special purse had done its job, protecting her NetMini from the electrical storm her terror had unleashed. Aaron's wasn't so lucky. He cradled the scorched device in his palm, shaking his head at it, not paying attention to where the PubTran taxi went.

"Sorry. Would you care to stop for a replacement?"

Aaron made a face of resigned acceptance. He couldn't be angry with her given the situation. "Might as well. Hopefully, they can extract the PID from this one and program a new one. Darwin set me up with a false identity so Div 0 doesn't track me."

"What if they identify the one you're using?"

"It would take Division 9 to find it. There's a decoy routine set up in the GlobeNet that creates a thousand clone traces using randomly selected PIDs. Each time a trace is started, the sample set changes." Aaron dropped the dead NetMini in his pocket. "Even with their tech, it would take months... I hope."

"Well, with any luck we won't be on Earth anymore in a couple of months." Her face lit in hologram-green as she ordered herself a pair of basic sneakers and him a new NetMini.

Fourteen minutes later, the PubTran car pulled over outside a disused-looking warehouse adjacent to a wharf. Salt air mixed with the decaying structures, flavoring the environs with the taste of metal and rust. Two delivery bots, which had been chasing them for the past ten minutes, caught up and dropped off her purchases.

She tossed a box to Aaron and put the sneakers on.

"How many of these things have you gone through?" He unwrapped a new NetMini and turned it on, frowning at the low charge level.

"You don't want to know." She slipped into a gap in the gate and trudged across a rain-soaked courtyard full of dead robotic forklifts. "Too many. I went a good few years not bothering to 'ave one at all. I'm still not used to bein' able to call a ride from anywhere."

"That had to be rough."

"You've no idea. It was like living primitive."

"C... ritical error." A digitized male voice emanated from a massive metal cube on tiny wheels.

Aaron jumped to the side, reaching for a gun he no longer carried.

"System failure." The cargo pallet on the loader's spurs shuddered and dropped an inch. Three tiny green LEDs at the corners of the boxy robot winked out.

"Did you do that?" Aaron found it difficult to look angry and accusing so soon after almost fainting.

She hid her grin with a hand. "Possible. My little runaway zaps don't only come from bad feelings. Any strong emotion'll do it."

"Right." He shot a wary look to the ancient forklift, pointed at it as if to remind it to stay still, and followed her to the building. "Does James have a dielectric nodder?"

She punched him in the shoulder, but laughed.

Anna ducked a half-open garage style door, walking into a cavernous space full of emptiness and dripping sounds. Six people sat around a long folding table against the far-right wall. Their mismatched clothes and wild hair gave them the look of a street gang, though they seemed more into the pile of technology in front of them than drugs.

Four of the six opened telepathic links to Aaron's surface thoughts. He cringed and blocked them out, causing them to pull handguns. The youngest of the lot, a girl of about fifteen with long, dark hair and pale skin, levitated four pistols in a cloud around her.

"It's all right." Anna held up a hand. "He's got a dangerous, involuntary reaction to mental connections. I don't want anyone trying to do anything to him, is that clear?"

Murmurs of discontent spread among the group, but they relaxed. Gun-cloud girl took the longest to stand down. She squinted as if daring him to give her an excuse.

"Oh, that *little girl* over there is precious." He pointed.

"Melissa," said Anna in a stern tone. "We've talked about this."

The teen sneered at Aaron as her guns flew back to individual holsters of pink and purple, some bearing Hello Kitty stickers. She whipped around to face the table and resumed soldering something. A cute cat-eared skull and crossbones with a little pink bow on its head took up the entire back of her jacket.

"Sorry." Anna patted him on the arm before moving in the direction of a small office. "She's trigger happy."

"That looked territorial. Like she's jealous of another telekinetic."

"Oh, don't be silly." Anna opened the door for him and followed after he passed. "She just wants to kill someone."

He blinked at her. "Aye, right up until she's done it."

The tiny space looked as though it had once been a manager's office. Aurora sat at a table against the interior wall, barefoot and wearing a black cheongsam with gold trim. She held a NetMini, which projected a holo-panel in front of her. A game with multi-colored glowing pieces in the shape of animals absorbed the entirety of her attention. The sight of it made Aaron crave gummy candies.

A man with thick shoulder-length chestnut hair sat behind the manager's desk. His brownish-grey suit gave him the look of a dowdy old-school professor. He glanced up as Anna approached and leaned forward to exchange a polite kiss. She sat on the corner of his desk, facing Aaron, and crossed her legs.

That's James? Aaron raised an eyebrow. *He's almost old enough to be her father.*

"Ahh, Mr. Pryce." The man stood and extended his arm.

"You must be Archon." Aaron approached, shaking hands. "I've heard quite the lot about you."

Archon gestured, and the unused chair at the table slid up behind

Aaron. "Please, sit."

"Telekinetic as well?" Aaron sat.

"I dabble at it." Archon leaned on the desk, giving him a once-over. "Anna tells me you have a rather unusual reaction to mental powers."

"Unusual." Aaron chuckled. "That's one way to put it. More like disastrous."

"Telepathic communication appears to be safe," said Anna.

"May I?" Archon eased himself into his chair. "I am quite curious."

"Your funeral if you poke the wrong neuron." He cringed. "As well as everyone in 'ere."

Archon glanced at Aurora who still had not looked up from her game. After she ignored him for a few seconds, he looked back at him with a smile. "Would you be so kind as to recall the last time the 'unusual reaction' manifested itself?"

Images of the casino filled his thoughts. The sense of Archon eavesdropping on his mind came on as though someone had balanced a giant, warm water balloon on his head. He fought the instinct to resist the observation and concentrated on the memory of the eruption of uncontained fury.

A wave of vertigo swam over him, forcing him to grab the armrests as his head throbbed. Whatever Archon did, his mode of 'reading' the memory brought him back to the moment. The tiny office vanished, leaving Aaron on his knees in the gaming room. Frozen, he clenched two fistfuls of hair, mouth agape with a scream he could not hear. Debris, bodies, dice, and drinks hung in midair, jerking and stalling as time warped backward and forward. He had no conscious recall of the scene, and gazed around at what his subconscious had kept hidden with a paralytic sense of dread awe.

The roulette table sailed away from him, passing through the croupier and the telepath, disrupting their bodies like liquid suspensions in human form. Falling objects appeared to hang motionless while the gambling machine glided past a cloud of blood at the pace of a brisk walk. Neither man's expression showed a reaction as the table crushed them. They had died so fast they never knew what happened.

Rippling carpet peeled up in a radial wave spreading from his feet. Everything burst outward from him: shot glasses pierced bystanders like bullets, a Nicohaler embedded in a man's skull, larger drinks blasted holes in concrete. A momentary sense of relief came amid the carnage as he caught sight of Aurelia diving for cover inside an elevator. She hadn't been in the room when he'd gone off, likely on her way to meet him at the bar when the room exploded.

Every person, gaming table, machine, chair, and piece of furniture tore up from the ground and joined the expanding ring of devastation. Bashed by a wave of telekinetic force, the security man came apart in sparking pieces, confirming Aaron's suspicion of his being a doll. Cracks rippled across the ceiling, suggesting the presence of an invisible sphere growing around him. At the instant the outer wall exploded away from the building, unconsciousness rendered the scene dark.

The casino faded back to the mildew-scented air of the warehouse manager's office. Aaron groaned and slumped in the chair. His eyes happened to point at the wall where a metal wire guide stymied a beetle's attempt to climb. It reared up, trying to get its legs to purchase on the rod, shuffling to one side in search of an opening. Fatigue washed over him, rendering him tired to the point where breathing seemed an unwanted exertion.

Archon's voice existed in his head and reality simultaneously. "My word, man. What on Earth could have gotten you so angry?"

It was an old telepath's trick, one he'd used innumerable times—first as a cop and then as a one-night-stand artist. Archon asked it, and he thought it. As before, whatever Archon did made the moment seem real again, bringing back every ounce of sight, smell, and emotion. By the time he finished reliving Allison's last moments, he blubbed like a schoolboy with a skinned knee.

Archon kept a respectful silence. Anna bit her lip and glanced between the two men. After an apologetic stare, she examined her lap, making no move to comfort him. She kneaded her fingers and snuck another peek at him.

The game floating over Aurora chirped and beeped.

Aaron pushed himself upright before he slid to the floor, and wiped his face. The abnormal vividness of the memory faded fast, leaving him in control after a few breaths.

"It is my theory that all psionics have the potential for awakening." Archon gazed at Aaron over his steepled fingers, leaning back in his chair. "The death of your wife was a uniquely powerful emotional scar that broke down the wall holding you back."

"People die all the time." Aaron glared at an exposed patch of floor where carpet had torn. "Wouldn't that 'awaken' more?"

"Your situation is unusual, Mr. Pryce. I am sure you are well aware, having been in the employ of Division 0 for some time, suggestive commands have certain limits. Impulses to inflict grievous harm upon loved ones rarely succeed."

Fire warmed Aaron's cheeks. "Are you saying I didn't love her?"

"Oh, no." Archon offered a condescending smile. "Not at all. I could see your feelings quite clearly. The unusual part of what happened was how that woman's suggestion overcame you. If anything, your wife's complete trust in you should have made it even easier to fight off."

Aaron gnawed on a knuckle as a lump swelled in his throat. "She was… She knew."

"If she understood how suggestion worked, her show of faith in you was deliberate. It should have let you resist, but it did not. Your mind cracked a touch."

"A touch?" Aaron blinked. "I gutted the bloody building. That's 'a touch?'"

Anna smoothed a hand down her dress. "James is fond of understatement."

"That's an understatement," muttered Aurora.

Aaron shifted in the chair. "So, what is it then?"

"As far as I can tell, this is your mind's reaction to invasion. Rather than gamble on failing again, it counteracts any attempt at mental tinkering by destroying everything around you. Since the effort originates from deep within your subconscious id, it is unburdened by factors of morality, conscience, or hesitation. That's why it is so powerful. It is your raw, primal caveman self-preservation."

"Why's it feel like I've drunk The Isle free of whiskey?"

"Simple overexertion, like operating any machine outside of its tolerances." Archon smiled. "Let me assure you, I have no interest in attempting to weaponize your mental scars. It is indiscriminate, not to mention quite unhealthy for you. You're no good to anyone burned out or dead."

"Can you fix it?"

Archon tapped his chin, glancing up and to his right for a moment. "I dare say I would need a lot more study to render an opinion on that. My initial suspicion is that any attempt to correct the issue would require the use of abilities that would trigger it."

"'At's a bit of a connumdrum, innit?" muttered Aurora, sounding half-interested.

"There is also the possibility it would diminish you." Archon brushed at his eyebrows.

"Diminish me?" Aaron leaned forward. "What, like no longer being one of these 'Awakened?'"

"Essentially, yes. I'd need to study your mind at length to properly understand all the ramifications."

A knock came from the door.

Archon raised his voice. "What is it?"

Parrot-green hair adorned the head of the stick-thin man leaning in. "Oi, Hughes is on the Vid. Says he's got six more on a shuttle, smuggled out of the ACC."

"Are they at least old enough to be useful?" Archon balanced his chin on his fist.

"James!" Anna glared at him. "Those kids need our help. They'll be executed over there."

"Yes, yes." He waved his hand about. "We're collecting an awful lot of little ones and running out of room as well as people willing to play nanny. What we need are men and women old enough to fight, should the need arise."

"Three adults," said Parrot. "Not sure what their abilities are. None of 'em speak English. He's askin if it's time for him to cast off."

"Not yet. Tell him things are progressing as expected, and we're in the final stages of preparation."

"Aye, boss." Parrot ducked out.

Aaron looked from the closing door to Archon, to Anna, and back to Archon.

"The Corporate territories consider psionics illegal and often execute them on sight. I maintain connections to some rebel groups in various parts of the world willing to smuggle gifted individuals to the UK in exchange for financial assistance. The little ones wind up being the easiest to transport."

"Don't sound so disappointed, James." Anna frowned. "And don't make it sound so much like you're purchasing children."

"Aren't we?" asked Aurora. "Some of the resistance fighters are separating families to send the sprogs to us. They want the money, and the parents are either non-psionic, too difficult to smuggle out, or want nothing to do with their 'demon children.'"

Archon stared at the ceiling, sighing. "They're better off here. I would so adore a few more adults, however. I'm not about to arm schoolchildren and put them on guard."

Anna gestured at him. "If you're concerned about gangs, we can move our base of operations."

"I selected that facility to avoid detection by the authorities." Archon tapped his fingers on the desk. "I would rather not have to strip this city of its police to ensure our success."

Aaron raised an eyebrow.

"He's being melodramatic." Anna squinted at Archon. "Aren't you, James?"

"Of course." He kissed the back of her hand before giving Aaron an expectant look. "Aaron, your telekinesis is most impressive. It would be an honor to have you among us. Shall we be off?"

"I'm not quite ready to commit to anything."

"Leave the woman to the authorities. You're not equipped to deal with someone like that." Archon attempted a sympathetic smile. "In all likelihood, she'll poke you with a suggestion that will set off your... bad reaction."

"Aye. That's what I'm hoping for. If I'm close enough, it'll kill her."

The face of the teen girl with a chip on her shoulder appeared in the window, glaring at Aaron. He exaggerated a smile and waved at her. Her eyes narrowed in a silent command to 'die.' She stomped along the window and burst in the door.

"He's a cop!" She pointed.

"We know that, Melissa." Anna made shooing gestures at her. "Ex-cop."

"Oh, I remember you." Aaron laughed. "That one ran away from the dorms twice. She's got a problem with little things like laws, manners, and sobriety. You sure you don't wanna go back to school, luv?"

Her pistols wobbled in their holsters.

Archon gave the girl a look that sent her sulking off. "The girl is concerned about you being a police mole."

Aaron laughed. "The bastards didn't believe I was compelled." Anger and depression crashed into a blanket of apathy. "As you said, I should've been able to resist a command to kill my wife. Command thought I wanted to. To hell with them. They're not going to find Talis. I doubt there's even a hunt on for her. Everyone's looking for *me*."

"We can help you with that issue." Archon smiled.

Anna edged forward; the pity in her gaze tilted him in favor of anger.

"Look, I appreciate your offer. Honestly, what you're doing sounds rather appealing, but this is something I have to do. For Allison."

"Oh, I almost forgot." Aurora waved her NetMini at Aaron. His chirped. "I found your hacker friend."

Aaron dug the vibrating device out of his pocket. White letters formed an address on the physical screen. "You've got a lot at stake here, mate. If what I need to do goes pear-shaped, better my mess not come back to ruin it."

"You are not equipped to handle someone like her," said Archon. "*I* can."

Anna gazed at the floor, picking chips of plastic desktop away.

"Let me check this out." He stared at Anna, trying to will her to make eye contact. She didn't. "I, uhh... I'll try to be careful. I'll be in touch."

Archon mumbled something unintelligible. "Kindly do not take all month. We are on a schedule." He returned his attention to the terminal.

Aaron walked to the door, watching Anna fidget at the desk. "Care to join me, Anna?"

"I shouldn't." She didn't look up. "I've some things to do here."

Aurora poked at her game. "She doesn't want to miss the match. Man U is playing in two hours."

"Right. I'll try not to get killed, like Manchester's going to."

Anna's head snapped up. The lights faltered.

The game hologram above Aurora's NetMini swirled from a landscape of tiny gem-like animals into a blur of ascending numbers, accompanied by a triumphant musical score. She looked over a rain of golden coins at Aaron, wearing a winner's smile.

SHIMMER OF HOPE

Aaron missed hovercars. More to the point, he missed the Division 0 patrol craft, a super-high-performance hovercar he didn't have to pay the insurance for. Fingertips thumped upon the thin plastic bench of the PubTran taxi. As if sitting in crawling ground traffic wasn't bad enough, this ride had flung him out of his seat twice when the little car stopped to avoid clipping errant pedestrians. Evidently *moving* people ranked high enough in the car's AI to be avoided. Unconscious or dead people, not so much. He had hoped his destination would be free of annoying traffic given the affluence of the area, though somewhere in the back of his mind he had a vague recollection of an old environmentalist movement. Someone with a wild excess of money and time started raving about how hovercars were bad for the planet.

To 'stay trendy,' the well-to-do locals all ran out and got land cars. Aaron stared up at the regular ebon obelisks passing by at a pace that made him want to walk. Aurora's information led him to Sector 18935, close to the northern end of West City and thirty miles in from the coast, where the same repeating pattern of identical, black century towers full of high-end apartments spread over a number of adjacent sector squares. The sort of home frictionless star Aaron Pryce might have lived in—if such a man still existed.

It had taken him forever to get used to the UCF NavMap system after arriving from Britain, and no sooner had he'd gotten the hang of it, everything went to hell. The city reached an approximate 260 miles in width, and 1880 from end to end. Sector 1 sat in the lower left corner, the first city plate. They counted to the right, with Sector 53 being the bottom right corner and Sector 54 the westernmost grid square in the second row. Of course, the legal city extended past the elevated portions, though the lower parts didn't exist on the sector map. Down there, things didn't look much different from how they'd been before the war, a rustic combination of Mexico-meets-Badlands, without all the genetically-engineered war machines or raiders.

The function of it remained a matter of obliviousness to most citizens. Travel, for most, entailed telling a computer what sector number they wanted, and an automated vehicle would bring them there. With so much of the city looking like every other part of the city, one could easily lose track of where they were in relation to the actual land.

After a laborious forty-minute ride, the little car jammed to a stop in front of his destination, flinging him to the floor for a third time. It made a faint whirring noise before sliding sideways to the right until it bumped the curb. Cold air rushed into the cab, carrying the scent of metal and glass. He ducked out of the impatient car, which eased away and zipped off before he'd gotten all his weight on his leading leg. Aaron had half a mind to flip the bastarding thing over, but decided against drawing attention.

His dark suit did not feel as out of place here as it did in his new 'home.' Everyone in sight wore similar attire in either grey or black and walked fast, as if late for a meeting. Silver walkpaths between the onyx columns contained only wealthy adults. The lack of children, beggars, or anyone in anything even approaching a good mood struck him as eerie.

Oh, right. At this hour, kids would all plugged in to school. He took a deep breath of freezing air. *These people have money.* He debated the advantages of online primary school compared to his childhood in the UK, being required to attend a physical classroom.

Makes for better character! shouted the headmaster out of his memory.

Parents routinely complained of the hassle, but the Crown agreed with Mr. Collingsworth. Truth be told, all the entertaining trouble he'd gotten into as a schoolboy would've been impossible by virtual reality. With a nostalgic smile, Aaron reached for the gloss black door, but it opened before he made contact. The lobby was quite a bit warmer than the outside, a velvety curtain of comfort hung at the entrance. Music

202 | ZERO ROGUE

lurked in the background of notice, only loud enough to remove silence, but faint to the point of being unrecognizable.

A single desk attendant looked at him. Her black flare-shouldered suit matched the status quo of the area as well as her raven-colored hair, gathered into a neat coif. Pink-tinted overhead lights caused her Marsborn-white skin to glow and added thin stripes of glint to glossy dark red lips. For a moment, she distracted him from his mission with a bout of mental math at how easily he could talk her into something more fun than sitting behind a desk. The idea faded when a telepathic poke found no surface thoughts.

A doll.

A good one, too. Maya-6 most likely. The quality of her motion coupled with the faces she made gave him the impression he ogled a self-aware AI, not one of the cheap 'human-shaped-computers' so often relegated to menial jobs. King William despised such machines, banning dolls from entering London. They told the public the ban had been enacted to preserve jobs for the under-educated, but most believed him a paranoid fool who took to heart a story told by a fortuneteller claiming a doll would kill him. After some of the things he'd seen in Division 0, the idea of it seemed less farfetched.

He couldn't suppress the chuckles at the thought on his way to the elevator. The 'girl' at the desk smiled at his polite wave.

"Visiting a friend."

Bright green light flared within the woman's eyes, shining out from her expanding pupils. He hadn't noticed how *blue* her irises were until then, a shade of rich, luminous cerulean that no human possessed naturally. The glow faded in seconds.

"I'm not armed. No implants." He smiled.

"So I see," said the woman.

Her piercing gaze and coy smile lingered in his mind as a wall of metal slid in front of him. The elevator was a large cylinder, which rotated clockwise to close. Aurora described Shimmer's home existing in a space removed from the building's map, with no official entry. Semitransparent plastisteel where the opening had been reduced the lobby to a blurry haze before it lit up with numbers and a wireframe model of the tower.

Aaron touched the display for the 89th floor and waited as the capsule shot upward. He went over the graphic Aurora sent to his NetMini. For an hour that morning, he'd sat in bed and stared at the schematics, trying to work out how to get into the place. Floors 50 to 89 contained what passed for 'middle of the road' apartments in this area. Each had more square footage than an average single-family home, and occupied one quarter of the entire floor. Two of the apartments on the 88th floor were smaller than their neighbors, though not by so much that someone inside one would notice without measuring. Shimmer lived in the stolen space, a modest, concealed chamber.

Aurora's digital sketch depicted two ways in. A narrow shaft from the hidden apartment straight to the roof, and a small corridor accessible from the elevator tube. The 'luxury' apartments had six dedicated elevators that expressed from the lobby to the fiftieth floor and up, bypassing the cheaper dwellings below. On the upper floors, a central neutral space existed between the four apartments, de facto front yards, complete with artificial grass. The access to her home was hidden in the elevator bank, at an angle the capsule would never face during normal operation. He figured she had a special code to get in, but Aurora said she couldn't obtain it without being detected.

Hyacinth scented air greeted him on the 89th floor courtyard. A space fifty meters square, with truncated corners, occupied the center of the building. Each flattened corner bore the façade of a house, and a door with an apartment number. Polished metal formed a circular walkway around the elevator building and led in straight lines to each dwelling. Fortunately, the only occupant of the chamber aside from him was a small schnauzer dog frolicking in the artificial grass by 89-2.

The capsule rotated closed with the faint squeak of a pneumatic seal. Once the sound of its return to the ground floor faded, he studied the door. For the first time since his life fell apart, he missed carrying the official authority (and equipment) of a police officer.

An override code would be lovely here, wouldn't it?

He rubbed his left forearm, grumbling to himself about how much easier this would be if he still had his gear. Alas, without it, he had to resort to more basic methods. It took him a moment to telekinetically probe out the shape and mass of the rotating cylindrical elevator shaft door. Once he felt confident, he concentrated on his desire to twist it out of his way. Gumminess in its motion suggested magnetic actuation rather than gears, which worked in his favor. He could force it open without breaking anything; hopefully, it wouldn't set off any kind of alarm. After tentative pushing got nowhere, a spike of irritation torqued it to the side. He grunted with the effort necessary to hold it open, fighting a magnetic field that presented constant opposing force.

Bereft of light, a dark metal shaft six feet in diameter ran the length of the building. Shiny silver-grey walls reminded him of raw silicon, with the exception of four hand-wide strips of white enamel. Aaron figured those rails contained the magnets that propelled the capsule up and down.

He leaned into the space, smiling at the half-height hatch a few inches below the level of the floor, as described in the hand-drawn wireframe model he'd spent the morning studying. Given the absence of ladders in the smooth shaft, a normal person had no way to get to it without knowing the code to force the elevator to face it. Aaron levitated himself, juggling effort on the capsule as well as his body as he glided in and down a few feet. Once he reached the shaft, he released the outer door. It flung itself closed with enough force to spin all the way around twice before wobbling back and forth with a dull hum.

A simple mechanical wheel lock secured the hatch. He nudged the mechanism around and pulled the metal flap open. Beyond it, a dingy black-walled shaft four feet square led about thirty meters to another door. He crawled in, pulling the door closed behind him to avoid a crash in case the elevator went by. Here and there, missing panels exposed pipes where thick cables spliced into the building wiring, carrying either data or power. He pulled out his NetMini to use as a flashlight and duck-walked to the end.

The ceiling over the last four feet of shaft expanded enough to allow him to stand. Two metal rungs jutted out from the wall below a thick, armored door that looked like she'd stolen it from a military starship. Shadows crept around as he moved the NetMini over an unlit keypad.

Feck. It would've been nice if she warned me about this.

With no idea how long a code it wanted, four, five, six, maybe ten digits, he turned his attention to the door itself. In a stroke of luck, a chromed locking bar glinted from his improvised light source. Aaron didn't need to use much power to slide it aside, freeing the door. The hatch glided inward with a faint squeak, revealing a chamber almost as dark as the crawl shaft. A matte-black coating, like the skin of stealth combat aircraft, covered the floor, ceiling, and walls. Stagnant air swirled around him, thick with the scent of a person and cheap ramen.

Ribbed hoses and smooth wires crisscrossed the floor like an explosion of technological plant growth, some as big around as his leg, others as thin as a lightpen. Despite the apparent chaos, they all wound their way to an island of technology in the middle of the dim room. Here and there, LED lamps, the handheld kind used by construction workers, lay scattered about, creating pale spots on the ceiling.

A ring of space heaters surrounded three folding tables and a huge, cushioned chair tilted back so far it became more of a bed. Stacks of cyberspace decks on the tables blinked and flashed with holographic panels. One looked like a feed from a low-flying drone sailing over desert scrub, another had text scrolling by too fast to read, the rest contained windowed readouts of stats for various programs.

Aaron tilted his head, appraising the slender body of a young woman lying on the chair in a ratty tank top and panties. Her olive skin displayed an obvious lack of muscle tone from many hours spent in a virtual world, and more than one skipped meal. Fluorescent blue hair draped over the headrest, hanging to the floor. He thought it long enough to reach her knees were she standing. At a guess, Aaron put her age around twenty. Two wires came out from behind her ears, draped over her chest and along the chair between her legs to a central interface box on the table at her feet. Patch cables ran from there to the seven or eight decks.

Aside from being full size and lacking wings, she looked like Shimmer's holographic faerie avatar.

It struck him odd from Aurora's notes how the girl had reacted to her visit. Despite Aurora remaining in the astral world, the woman had looked around and called out asking if someone was there. Shimmer—this time he felt certain he'd really found her—showed no reaction whatsoever to Aaron's presence. Her notice of Aurora hinted at possible psionic ability.

Plastisteel shipping cartons stacked everywhere, mostly against the walls, overflowing with circuit boards, wires, cyberspace terminal parts, and random junk. Techno music pounded behind the wall in the far left corner from the legal apartment on the other side, rattling the autoshower door with the bass. A few feet to the right, an exposed toilet sat by an opaque green plastic curtain bunched up against the wall on its track.

Aaron cleared his throat. When she didn't react, he did it again, louder.

One of the holographic panels morphed into a ten-inch faerie, the tiny version of Shimmer he'd seen before. The false woman swiveled to face him, went open-mouthed, and screamed.

Aaron waved.

Chaos swam over the various displays; some windows closed while others erupted in red text. Two pie charts collapsed. Shimmer's real body shot upright in the chair as though she'd been shocked with a defibrillator. She struggled to keep her head up, but kept slouching forward, almost falling off the seat. Her brown eyes seemed oversized in her moon-shaped face, wide with radiant fear. Sporadic twitches made her shake and convulse like a creature from a zombie vid. She drew her knees to her chest, squirming to cover herself while reaching for a pistol in a black canvas satchel hanging on the armrest.

Aaron held his hands up. "Easy, Shimmer. It's just me, Aaron."

She left her hand on the gun but didn't pull it out, staring at him for another minute before attempting to speak. The stuttering squeak that leaked out of her throat didn't come close to speech, though her words drifted clear in her surface thoughts. *How did you find me?*

"A friend found you. She's clairvoyant, a psionic."

Shimmer shifted toward him, letting her feet slip off the chair to the floor. The convulsive, disorienting effect of rapid disconnect faded, and her terrified affect changed to one of anger.

"W-what the fuck? Do you just walk into people's homes?"

Aaron gestured over his shoulder with a thumb. "Couldn't find the doorbell."

She scowled, twisting her head left and right as she pulled wires out from behind each ear. "That's because I don't fucking have one. How about a little privacy?"

"I wouldn't be here if you'd have answered my calls, and you know they invented these things called clothes. Do you live in your skivvies?"

"You're the first person other than me to see the inside of this box for six years. What's the point? It was *supposed* to be private." She slid off the chair and stretched. Her hair fell down around her ankles. "I had a bit of a close call the last time I tried to vid you. Someone was watching your NetMini for incoming connections and tried to send a Traceweasel after me."

She stomped across the room, rummaging among the boxes of electronic gear in search of something more to put on.

"A weasel?"

Shimmer stepped into a pair of white shorts that stalled at her knees since they were sized for a preteen. "Dammit." She offered up a cheap smile and threw them into a different box. "It's been a while since I've had a guest. Traceweasel is a net soft that backtracks a connection and translates it into a real-world geolocation tag."

Aaron removed his suit jacket and handed it to her. "Might want to order some new things."

"Thanks." She wrapped herself in it and took a NetMini out from between the pile of decks. "So, yeah... I was gonna call you as soon as I dealt with whoever was trying to find me." Pale grey light bathed her from the little device's holographic panel. She poked at it while wandering to the middle of the right wall, navigating the maze of wires and tubes without looking.

"You should probably get out more. This can't be healthy."

Shimmer grasped a handle on the wall by a stack of old food cartons. With a twist, a section pulled away, revealing a small chamber with a ladder. She took a step in and leaned around the door to wink at him. "Neither are Syndicate bullets."

Aaron glanced at the room while she disappeared. Echoing metallic sounds conjured the image of her climbing a ladder up a narrow shaft. He picked at some of the junk in the crates. Amid the carcasses of evolving, upgraded tech, the trappings of a once-childhood emerged. Dolls, old clothing, toys, and a couple of holo-bars. Aaron reached into the junk and pulled out a small silver bar. Three inches long and about as big around as his finger, it could hold thousands of photos. He traced his finger over the device and held it flat in his palm, as though it sat on a table. A three-dimensional image formed above it, depicting an important looking man in a suit seated in a fancy leather chair. To his left, Shimmer at around age six stood like a dutiful daughter in a white silk dress and kitten heels. A boy, maybe sixteen or seventeen, a younger version of the sitting man, posed on the other side. All three wore huge smiles and expensive outfits.

The bar contained several more portraits of the girl; he thought she looked strange with her natural hair color of black. One image had her at about eight or nine in the lobby of a corporate office tower. A stylized symbol hung on the wall in the distance, a series of round-ended rectangles of increasing size hinting at a segmented grub or some manner of insect larva.

Air rushed out from the shaft as the upper hatch opened. The sound of hovercar traffic and advert bots filtered in. Aaron dropped the keepsake back in its box and wandered to the desk where her 'current technology' resided. A few steps past the desk atop a nauseating coral-pink foam mat, a datapad projected a hologram of an Indian man in the midst of an extreme yoga pose. At the edge of the pad, two small porcelain vessels held the ashes of incense. Every few seconds, a thin line of left-shift glided upward through the motionless man, revealing him as a hologram on pause.

Between the GlobeNet interface decks, one picture-bar held a place of prominence. It contained twenty some odd images of the boy from the family photo, only later. At his oldest, he seemed to be in his twenties and wore the uniform of a Division 1 police trainee. Shimmer at about twelve clung to his side, grinning from ear to ear.

Two boxes slapped to the floor inside the shaft. Aaron jumped, swatting at the holo-bar to turn it off as the rattle of the ladder grew louder. The photo went dark a split second before her bare feet appeared, and Aaron folded his hands behind his back in an exaggerated gesture of innocence.

Shimmer emerged from the shaft and stepped over the boxes. After closing the door and locking it, she gathered them and returned to the chair.

"Turn around. I'ma change."

Aaron obliged. Plastic crinkled behind him for a few minutes while he tried to make sense of all the wiring on the floor. Footprints in various substances from food to neural memory fluid appeared here and there. She tapped his arm with a bundle of cloth, returning his jacket. He assumed it safe to look and turned around. A stretchy black top that left about two hands' width of stomach exposed replaced her ratty undershirt, and she wore a new pair of modest white panties.

"Thanks."

Aaron put his jacket back on while she slipped into a loose pair of white/grey camouflage fatigue pants. The drawstring closures at the foot end flopped about as she went over to a small food reassembler, hidden among the storage boxes. She touched the door with her toe and closed her eyes. Seconds later, the machine beeped.

"Son of a..." Aaron laughed. "Well, this certainly explains how a kid's been able to avoid the Syndicate."

"I'm not a little kid, Pryce. I'm nineteen." She squatted and took a plate of brown goo and yellow triangles out of the machine. After standing, she kicked the door closed. "Don't get any ideas either. I know how you are with women."

Aaron put both hands on his chest in a 'Moi?' gesture.

"Yeah, you."

"What in the name of holiness is that mess?"

"Nachos with taco meat and beans." She munched as she sauntered over to her chair and leaned on it. "Extra jalapenos, no sour cream."

Her toes peeked out from the oversized pant legs, traces of blue polish in combination with her posture made her seem younger than she claimed. Aaron watched her eat for a moment, gripped by distinct unease. In the months since Allison died, he'd probably manipulated several nineteen-year-olds to bed. At the time, he'd been too drunk to care, and the girls had been happy to enjoy some of his fortune and fame.

Shimmer had nothing in common with those women. She hid in a self-imposed prison, avoiding the outside world, barely containing her urge to run away from even Aaron. She didn't care how much money he had or who he was, and the way she shrank against the chair nagged at his wounded conscience. Division 0 had been an escape route from the CSB, a means of asylum. Somewhere along the line, he'd developed a sense of duty. Frictionless had been one big game, a great stonking raised middle finger at the world, a pack of tossers running around a field and getting paid gobs of credits for it. Did the things he'd seen as a police officer change him or had it been Allison? The wretched, beaten, mess of his former self reached a hand out of the murk, trying to get his attention.

Shimmer pushed a mass of brown paste and green bits around the plate with a chip. "Yeah, I'm psionic. Tech always liked me. The implants don't even interfere with it. So, is this where you haul me off to the dorms or something? I don't have to go, right? I'm nineteen now. Not a kid. I'm, uhh... not breaking *that* many laws."

He moved to her side, lifting her hair away enough to examine the M3 socket behind her earlobe. Her toes turned white with tension, the plate trembled. She refused to look at him.

"Interesting. I've heard of a few people with technokinesis who opted for cybernetic augmentation. Most people think it makes us weaker... 'course I suppose you have to believe in all that 'natural aura' stuff for that to make sense. Either it's bunk or I guess your mind rather likes tech." He let her hair fall. "Sorry, I don't mean to make you nervous. You're right. A bit old for the dorms, though they would still take you in." He frowned. "I don't really recommend it, though. Seems they're a bunch of wankers after all."

She risked a glance at his chest, shying from eye contact. "I'm safe here."

"Is it worth all this?" He waved around. "Shutting yourself away from the world."

"I'm still part of the world." Her tension faded as she crunched another chip. "I'm free on the net... and I don't have to wear pants."

"You've been after the syndicate since you were what, twelve? Someone with your psionic abilities would do well in the legitimate world."

Her face darkened. She set the nachos down on the chair and jabbed a finger into his chest. "I'm not some wannabe coasting on psionics. I *am* a real operator. Do you have any idea how much more effective psionics are when the person using them knows what the fuck they're doing? I've pirated enough technical CBTs to run through university in two years and come out with a master's degree in electronic engineering as well as software design. I could rewrite the operating system of a Nishihama Berserker in six days. Short of StarPoint, there's not a network in this city I can't have my way with. You think just because I'm this skinny kawaii chick with blue hair, I'm some kind of airhead that coasts on psionics?" She shoved away from her giant chair and paced in a random orbit, fuming. "Okay, maybe C-Branch is over my head, but still."

Aaron held his hands up, leaning back. "Sorry... didn't mean to imply you weren't talented. I said it because most who have an easy route take it."

She folded her arms. "I'm not coasting on psionics. I *am* a tech head. I don't know how the hell you found me here, but I swear, if you blow my cover and make me move..." Her gaze hardened. "I know all about your private ICFC accounts, Dr. Yuichi Omaru. Maybe should I call you Sean Burke, or Jake Tanner? Or... what was the other one... Arturo Tyrondus?" She pointed. "I swear I'll ruin your fucking life if you rat me out."

He slouched. "Too late."

"You're a bastard," she yelled. After a few seconds of looking for a suitable target, she kicked a stack of boxes over and then grabbed her foot. "Ow. Fuck."

"No," said Aaron. "I mean my life. It's already ruined."

"Dammit." She limped back to the chair and rubbed her toes.

"You shouldn't kick metal crates." Aaron chuckled. "Look, I need to find Talis. I'm not going to drag you off or anything. The only other person who knows where you are is not going to say a word."

"You're giving me that look."

"What look?"

She slid backward onto the chair, letting her feet dangle. "That pitying, 'oh, you poor thing' look. I'm fine."

He glanced at the door he'd come in from. "Do you really want to spend the rest of your life in a windowless prison?"

Her legs drifted back and forth. "I'm free in cyberspace. I don't have any desire to be rich again. I find enough credits to get by. With Cray dead, I just gotta wait for the Syndicate to forget about me."

"Again?"

"Dad was an executive. Pretty high up. We had money coming out of every orifice, but he never had time for me or Cory. He got me a synthetic unicorn when I was eight. I mean, we had more credits than we could spend. I grew up with nannies and live tutors and vacations... But it was all hollow, ya know?" She fidgeted with the pockets on the side of her pants. "I've met people online that I'd kill to protect. My dad? Whatever. I mean, he wasn't mean or anything... just uninvolved. Felt more like 'the guy that owned the building we got to stay in' than a parent. Besides, he's already dead anyway." She made a sarcastic face. "Hostile takeover."

The name 'Chrysalis Corporation' floated around her mind.

"So who are you, really?" He stared into her eyes.

'Lily' whispered in her thoughts, in a man's voice. Her brother had been the last person to call her that.

"I'm Shimmer." She scooted back on the chair, faced the wall of light, and sat cross-legged. "I found your tiger lady, Rakshasi. She's doing mercenary work for Preston Cryogenics. The files I was able to get into make it look like she's on retainer to deal with defecting researchers. An assassin. I managed to track down her true identity. Aparna Devi is originally from India, former military intelligence. They tried to cover it up and make it look like a retirement. In truth, she humiliated them with the theft of several petabytes of sensitive information that wound up in ACC hands."

Shimmer took one of the wires off the chair and plugged it in behind her right ear. The curtain of holo-panels flickered and changed, showing camera feeds, personnel records, and maps. A woman's face filled in, narrow and tall, with harsh angular lines. Dark stripes reminiscent of a tiger's marked both cheeks. Waist-long black hair swept back into a ponytail, and both eyes had metallic gold irises with vertical slit pupils. Three hexagonal indentations on her right temple, progressively smaller, contained tiny numbers written in black. Shimmer leaned forward, taking a container of hours-old lo mein out of a drawer.

"This bitch is wired to the nines." She bundled a wad of cold noodles on chopsticks and stuffed it in her mouth. One of the screens went black with gold wireframe depicting a woman's arm. Six-inch narrow transparent blades emerged from each finger. "Nano scratchers, reflex boosters, both eyes replaced, toxin filtering in her lungs and liver, bone reinforcements"—the hand shrank as the display became a full skeleton; patches of white flashed to indicate where metal had been grafted onto bone—"military grade speedware"—a hairline network of wiring flashed white throughout the entire body—"Flea mod for jumping." Shimmer slurped more noodles. "I'm surprised she skipped the tail and cat ears."

Aaron pinched the bridge of his nose. "Tail gets in the way in a fight. One more thing an opponent could grab." His initial disgust at the food gave way to a raised eyebrow. "That food isn't slime."

"Nopf." She mumbled past a full mouth. "Real."

"How do you afford that?"

She grinned. "A hundred and fifty people are kind enough to donate half a credit each."

He shook his head.

"What?" She jammed chopsticks into the mass of brown noodles and chicken as though slaying a dragon. "You're going to go kill this bitch, and you're giving me that face over a dinner stolen from people who won't even notice?"

He blew air between flapping lips. "Yes, I suppose when you put it that way it does seem a bit hypocritical."

"Oh, don't waste your time trying to charm this one." Shimmer squinted at the fifth screen from the left, where a platinum blonde woman with Eastern European features appeared. "This is the agent that turned her traitor. Rakshasi isn't going to find you appealing."

Aaron closed his eyes. "I had a feeling."

He thought back to the one time he'd almost caught up to her, about two months after Allison's death. He'd chased them from one end of an automated manufacturing facility to the other. When they'd run out of factory, Lucky had made it out a door, which he had a clear shot on, trapping Talis and Rakshasi behind a plastisteel machine press. After the women kissed, Talis sent Rakshasi on a suicide run to buy herself the opportunity to escape. Now that he thought about it, the blade-fingered woman charging at him had the same terrified look that must have been in his eyes when he turned his weapon on his wife.

The last he'd seen of Aparna Devi, aka Rakshasi, his telekinesis had boosted her charge into flight, sending her right over his head and into a vat of industrial lubricant. Before he'd 'cracked,' flinging an adult woman off her feet at all would've been near the edge of his power. He'd always had a lot more finesse than brute force.

She stared at the pocket where his NetMini lurked. It beeped. "I've sent you all the info I found. Now I'm going to have to go into the net and make sure no one's tracked your ass here." She started to give him a threatening glare, but softened into a pleading stare. "Promise me you won't sell me out?"

Shimmer had read him like an online training course. Whatever talent young Lily Braddon had once employed to wheedle things out of her billionaire father came to the surface. He managed a dumb nod as he backed toward the door.

"Aye. Thanks for the info, luv. You..." He sighed. "You sure you want to stay here?"

"Yeah." She drew her knees to her chin.

"Right then, take care of yourself."

Shimmer hid her face against her knees. "Yeah, no one else will."

He stared at her for a moment. "Awright, now you're laying it on a bit too thick."

"Sorry." She looked up with a grin. "I'll call the elevator for you."

"Thanks." He stumbled over the wires and tubes to the exit corridor.

"Aaron?"

"Aye?" He stopped halfway out the door.

Shimmer connected her second wire and reclined on the chair. "Try not to get yourself killed."

The sound of the elevator arriving made him jump. "Yeah." He started not to care if he made it or not, and wound up thinking of Anna. *Bother. She's taken.* He hung his head. "Right... I'll see what I can do."

24

CORNERED TIGER

Preston Cryogenics headquarters occupied forty percent of Sector 19039, fifty miles away from the upper reaches of West City and about thirty-five inland from the ocean. Twin office towers stood at the northeast corner of the grid square, overlooking three long, rectangular production facilities a mere six stories tall. At the southern end of the company property, a farm of ten-story orb shaped tanks lurked in a perpetual fog of water vapor. Between the office towers and the manufacturing buildings, a pleasant courtyard offered a place for workers to relax among a few miniature potted trees, an artificial lake, and a statue of the company's founder. The west portion of the property contained storage and warehousing, as well as an army of cargo transport vehicles.

Aaron crept along a gridded catwalk, suspended from the underside of an elevated roadway linking two high-rise towers at the fortieth floor. Preston Cryogenics had enough pull to purchase the permits necessary for a dedicated off ramp from The Highway. Aaron's plan had felt solid until he'd spent more than five minutes on the exposed walkway in the gusting winds of what used to be British Columbia. He huddled against a support and fished out a sleek, silver-framed visor.

Within a second of slipping it over his eyes, the glowing light-trail of an eight-inch faerie appeared, leading his gaze to the right past an array of pipes and struts. She zipped to a halt a foot away from his face, causing an involuntary flinch from a spray of pixie dust that didn't exist. His knuckles whitened on the freezing metal, and he glared at her once the look of terror left him.

"What are you worried about? You can fly, right?"

He swallowed. "Not exactly, and that doesn't mean I'm fond of heights."

"How does that work anyway?" Shimmer folded her arms, tapping one finger on her chin. "Isn't that like lifting yourself up by your boots?"

Aaron pushed off from his place of safety, moving at as fast a stride he could tolerate on the bouncing metal grate. "I'm not just lifting myself. I'm holding onto stuff nearby. Like, I'm trying to telekinetically move the building, but since it weighs so much it winds up moving me instead."

"Oh, so it's like you're swinging on an invisible vine?"

"More like doing a pull up." He stopped to clamp onto the railing as a car rumbled overhead. "Or a pull down. When I'm falling, I reach out against the ground, pushing. It's still all quite new to be honest. Telekinetics aren't supposed to be this strong."

The headset simulated Shimmer's faerie-pitched voice zipping back and forth behind him. "You should get a costume, fly around doin' stuff."

Aaron laughed, but more from nerves than mirth. "Aye, except I'd have to wear a mask so I don't look shitless when I land." He ducked behind another large strut. "How does the parking deck look?"

"If I say bad, are you gonna jump?" She giggled behind his head.

"Yes, but it would be tiring for no reason if you're just takin' the piss."

"I don't have to go."

Aaron grumbled. "It means messin' with me."

"Why didn't you just say that?"

He tried to grab the faerie out of the air. "Do you 'ave a sister named Strawberry? The two of ya."

Shimmer shrugged. "There's the usual security in the parking deck, nothing cereal."

"I'm not in the mood for breakfast."

"Ass."

"What?" Aaron got moving again.

"It means serious."

"Then why'd you not just say serious?"

A faint raspberry fluttered in his left ear.

By the time he reached the point where the elevated strip of road met the forty-fourth story of the primary office tower, he'd lost feeling in all four limbs and his lips. Despite the presence of a ladder and a hatch, he didn't trust his fingers to be able to close around the rungs. Shimmer whirled about in circles laughing as he telekinetically levitated his body up and over the guardrail onto the road surface. The electronic version of a faerie's voice became needles at his eardrums.

"Got it," she chirped.

Aaron walked into the parking deck, heading for a door a few feet inside on the left that opened for him and led to a utility stairway. According to the information she'd sent him, Rakshasi lived in an apartment on the ninety-first floor of the secondary tower, among the residences of executives stingy enough to accept company housing and critical engineers the company refused to let out of their sight. He jogged down the plain concrete steps, the skiffs of his shoes echoing off unfinished walls.

"Do you think those people know they're living a few floors away from the person who'll be sent to kill them if they try to leave?"

"I'm sure they do." He eyed a head-sized onyx orb set in the ceiling. "I'm betting they've put her here as a warning."

"Relax. I've got the cameras and the pea shooters on a short leash. As far as Preston Cryo's security people know, you don't exist."

"Pea shooters?" He held on to the railing at a corner.

"Fully automatic ballistic turrets chambered in eight millimeter. Two hundred rounds each, dual mode operation. IFF selective or manual control from a security station. Since you don't have a Preston Cryo employee ImDent chip, they'd try to aerate you."

"Great."

The faerie zoomed in front of him, posed as though holding back a great weight. Her tiny voice growled with effort. "Don't panic. I'm protecting you."

He jogged down the remaining thirty and change floors, warmed and invigorated by the time he reached the bottom. As much as he wanted to avenge Allison's death, the sight of a door to the outside made him hesitate. He didn't want to go back out into the cold so soon.

"Wait!" yelled Shimmer. "Sentry orb going by. Shit."

"What, shit? Shit sounds bad."

Her little face scrunched in a variety of expressions. "Go. No big deal, some idiot on their network seems to think there's an unauthorized access."

"Isn't there?" He edged the door open, peering out over a concourse.

Wind howled through an outdoor 'corridor' between the buildings, where a number of benches sat in pairs, interleaved with small trees emerging from mounds of brown mulch ringed with tiny flowering shrubs. A quick glance revealed nine security cameras, some on the side of the facing building and some on lampposts, as well as two spheres embedded in the opposite wall he suspected to be guns in hiding. He would have sprinted to the other tower if not for a man in scuffed white armor relaxing on a nearby bench.

"Oh, wow, these defense people are getting irritating. I'm gonna be quiet for a minute. Gotta slap a couple bitches around."

The faerie faded away.

Aaron studied the man for a few seconds, settling his gaze on the stunrod hanging from his equipment belt. The guard also had a sidearm, but he had no need to turn deadly on a poor sod doing his job, or slacking off his job. He focused on the stunrod's cushioned handgrip, working out just how to flex his telekinetic grip to simulate a squeezing hand. The man startled when the tip erupted with sparking blue light.

"What the—"

A gentle telekinetic twist flung the device upward and touched the end to the man's cheek. In an instant, the guard lost control of his muscles and bounced off the bench to the metal ground. He convulsed for a few seconds, armor clattering and spittle flying. Once he went still, Aaron released the weapon and shoved the door open. The clank of his shoes on plastisteel tiles faded to several muted thuds as he jumped a row of foot-tall hedges and cut across the mulch-skirt of a tree.

He hit the wall of the target building breathing hard and huddled in a strip of shadow. A fern-lined red brick walkpath connected the towers in a straight line from entrance to entrance across the park area between them. The security/maintenance door he'd emerged from had a companion on this building a few meters away, right in the middle of a bright patch. Aaron edged up to the limit of the dark and stared at one of the gun pods on the wall. Its barrel sat retracted behind a hexagonal door, though the spherical housing panned left and right, a small yellow light high and center. He contemplated smashing it in case Shimmer wasn't faring well in her electronic duel.

All the lamppost lights in the narrow courtyard died at the same time, as did the sensor on the turret. Aaron had to bite back a cry of startlement. Hoping Shimmer was responsible for it, he ran to the door, trying to rub warmth back into his hands.

A strip of holographic light, four inches wide by one tall, glowed red atop a physical keypad. He tapped his foot, glancing left and right.

"Come on, come on."

Glowing text appeared in front of him as if drawn in pixie dust: ‹15732›.

His hand shook, but he jabbed his numb finger into the metal buttons, filling white numbers in on the red stripe. When the final digit appeared, it turned green and the door clicked. No sooner had he pulled it open than the entire western part of the Preston Cryogenics complex exploded in an array of flashing multicolored light and deafening techno dance music.

He let off a shout of surprise while hurrying inside—not that anyone heard.

The door slammed behind him, trapping him in darkness. The distant music was so loud it robbed him of the ability to think even with a two-inch thick plastisteel plate between him and the source. Deciding against ninety stories of stairs, he ducked into the corridor leading to the ground floor. It ended at a security guard's break room. A cup of coffee lay spilled on the floor atop a scattering of popcorn. Two large holo-bars in front of a couch flipped on its back flooded the left side of the room with the flashing glory of Gee-ball games. A row of lockers hung open, exposing four rifles and two sets of security guard armor.

Aaron smiled, imagining the hasty scramble of lazy guards.

"Not enough time," said Shimmer. "Go. They'll be back before you're done changing."

"What the hell was all that noise?"

Shimmer planted her hands on her tiny hips and scoffed. "You have heard of a distraction, haven't you?" She pivoted away from him. "They already thought they had an electronic invader, so they got a little boy out looking to play pranks."

"Loud music got all the security staff to run out of here like this?" He jogged to an interior door composed of tinted glass.

"No, that would've been all nine high-security storage vaults showing break in alarms at the same time." She giggled. "I added some Wild Boyz to the security video, too."

"Do I want to know?" He sprinted through a sparse, utilitarian lobby, twitching each time a ball turret in the ceiling panned left or right. "Cripes."

"Oh, relax." Shimmer sailed along at his side, leaving a trail of glowing green light. "I own those guns. Nothing serious, the Boyz are a local street gang up there. I couldn't use anything too dangerous, or they'd call in the police."

The elevator opened before he got to it, and the doors squeezed off his view of the lobby at the exact moment a dozen white-armored figures came in the front. Even with half their faces obscured by their helmets, they looked angry.

"Up, up, and away!" cheered Shimmer.

"You're enjoying this entirely too much," mumbled Aaron.

Her enthusiasm fell to a lip-quivering pout. "I don't get out much."

"Oh, stop."

She laughed. "Ninety-first floor. She's in the sixth apartment on the left. Be careful."

"Of course." He winked.

ONLY A PLAIN GREY DOOR MARKED 91-11 STOOD BETWEEN HIM AND answers. The quiet of the hallway made his heartbeat noticeable. White walls and charcoal carpet as bland and boring as he expected from corporate housing stretched out before him. Strips of baleful light ran in metal gutters along the top of the walls, muting to a soft glow by virtue of reflection from the ceiling.

Aaron pondered ringing the bell, knocking, or just smashing it down. The last time he'd met this woman, she'd tried to kill him. Of course, she'd been under compulsion as well, so it wasn't her fault. His indecision ended when the door clicked and slid open to the left.

Thanks, Shimmer.

He stepped into a spacious living room thick with the scent of East-Asian incense. A giant U-shaped sectional sofa big enough to seat twelve adults wrapped around an object that could've been a table or a piece of modern art; three oval slabs of dark silvery material jutted out of a lump of jet-black rock that looked like it came from an alien world. Atop the largest slab, a narrow vase held three roses sculpted from metal. Shag carpeting the color of pewter ran wall to wall, ending by plain white linoleum where the space gave way to kitchenette. Floor-to-ceiling window spanned the opposite end of the room, covered in chromed blinds, which rotated closed as soon as the door shut behind him. He hoped Shimmer covered his presence, and he hadn't walked into some trap.

Something beeped in the distance, and the scent of chai tea slithered under his nose. He stood motionless as a woman emerged from the back hallway. Her delicate features resembled a sylph carved from rich brown stone, and she wore a black robe with the sheen of silk. It covered her to the middle of her thigh, tied with a floppy belt reminiscent of a karateka. More stripes decorated the outsides of her legs to an inch above each ankle. Aside from her black hair flowing loose, she matched the image in Shimmer's data.

Rakshasi went to the kitchenette and removed a cup from a small white appliance. As soon as she turned to walk out, they made eye contact. Her vertical cat's pupils narrowed, reducing the amount of crimson light leaking out. If he hadn't known she had cybernetic eyes, the demon-tiger affect would've tightened his throat.

Aaron held up his hands. "I'm only here to talk."

Her surface thoughts held onto the kind of repulsed feeling one might get after stepping barefoot into a pile of dog shit. Only, in her case, the skin-crawling sense of disgust came from having a man inside her den. A rambling internal diatribe went by in another language, Hindi he assumed, which he could not follow.

"Where's Talis?"

Rage, love, and betrayal whirled into a clawing furball in the woman's mind. Based on the scenes and feelings playing out in her thoughts, he could tell she understood Talis had abandoned her to the police to get away; she knew the woman had manipulated her emotions, but still harbored a sense of love and loss. Unfortunately, she hadn't seen Talis since crawling out of the syrupy mess in the vat. Numerous glimpses of attempts to find the woman she believed loved her flickered by, before she settled on working for Preston Cryogenics.

"I'm sorry, but that woman never loved you." Aaron held up both hands. "She's psionic. It was all manipulation."

Rakshasi's brain twitched in a way Aaron had not observed before. Confusion at the gesture evaporated as her body blurred into a smear of brown and black; she leapt with claws outstretched, raking her bladed fingers at him. Her unusual mental flex had activated speedware. He got his telekinesis around her, stalling her leap. The tip of her middle finger claw, the longest of the lot, sliced his chest before the cup of chai had started falling. He leaned back from a handful of Nano claws. His multitasking mind saved the tea, pushing Rakshasi away while floating the cup toward his waiting hand. The shallow cut proved more painful than deadly.

He frowned at the slash in his jacket. "Damn, this suit was nine thousand credits." *Slurp.* "Thank you for the tea."

She shrieked at him in Hindi; boosted reflexes rendered her frenetic claws into an imperceptible blur of glinting metal. Crimson light flared out from widening pupils. Aaron had gone from nervous to a level of anger far beyond what facial motions or a reddening of the cheeks could convey. To an outside observer, he looked the perfect picture of serenity. All his effort to find Rakshasi, and she turned out to be another dead end. He pictured the Syndicate thugs bursting like water balloons on impact with the floor. Telekinetic energy pressed her into the wall and tightened around her throat. He forced her arms flat at her sides and spread the crushing force over her entire body, pinning her still except for allowing her head to thrash side to side.

"Aaron I—" Shimmer's little voice chirped in his ear, but an odd digital warble consumed it to silence.

"I'm only going to say this once." He set the chai down on the table by the sofa. "I came here looking for Talis. I thought you might have known where she'd toddled off to. Since you do not, we have no further business."

Rakshashi dug her scratchers into the wall, the thin synthetic diamond blades sank in as if plasticrete offered no more resistance than cream cheese.

"You may be a twisted individual the world could do without, but I am not terribly interested in liquefying you."

She stopped resisting.

"I will find her, and I will kill her for what she did."

"No!" yelled Rakshasi.

He peeled her away from the wall and sent her across the apartment to the farthest point in the room. "She didn't have any feelings for you beyond how useful you could be. Whatever you think you feel is an implanted idea."

"You can't kill her." Rakshasi screamed as she fought to stand up against the unseen force holding her down. "*Neend kohra!*"

Aaron shook his head. "Must you be a pain in the ass?"

He fished out his NetMini, which already displayed the translation of her words. Her continued primal grunts took on a blurry, distant quality as his surroundings hazed. The text hovering in front of his eyes—‹sleep fog›—barely registered meaning. His focus weakened; his brain pulsated at the sensation of her slipping out of his telekinetic field.

Rakshasi sprang to her feet. Aaron stumbled to the side, trying to hold his breath while lashing out at the closest, most lethal object he could find. He launched the onyx coffee table at her, spinning it like a three-tiered saw blade. Her lithe body shot upward so fast she seemed to disappear and reappear with her back to the ceiling as the thousand-pound stone stuck in the wall. She landed in a crouch, red eyes glaring at him.

"Oh, of course. Noxious gas... you've got a tox filter."

He gasped and shoved her away. Her bare feet squeaked over the smooth white floor in the kitchenette. Unable to summon enough clarity of mind to kill, he flung her into the cabinets with barely enough force to leave a bruise.

"*Aapaatkaal andhera!*" she yelled.

Aaron leapt for the door. The console ignored his touch, offline as though it had lost power. The window blinds whirred tighter with a click.

The lights went out.

‹Emergency Darkness› hovered over his NetMini, the glowing words throwing off enough light for him to make out the shape of his hand. Wobbles crept up his legs. Distant red cat-eye slits turned green. Soft thumps raced toward him, followed by the delicate click of deploying claws. Aaron released an omnidirectional pulse of telekinetic repulsion, but felt no resistance.

A bare foot caught him across the face, spinning him chest-first into the wall. Unseen blades speared his left forearm; the NetMini slipped from his grasp and clattered to the floor. Searing pain lanced his left thigh from a stabbing wound, a surgical strike that severed his femur in four places. Aaron wailed, gritting his teeth at the feeling of bone pieces grinding over each other. His cheek squealed on the metal door as he slid down. After another faint *click*, fingers dug into his shoulders and flung him onto his back.

Dazed by the chemicals in the air, he flailed at the endless darkness with one arm. She stepped on his thigh, triggering a blinding flash of pain and a throat-ripping scream. He rolled onto his side, cradling his wounded leg. Angry muttering came from everywhere. Panic set in, and he fired off telekinetic thrusts in random directions. Aaron cried out as four searing lines of pain plunged into his right thigh and withdrew as fast as a wasp's sting, severing the bone there as she had done with the left.

He grabbed at the rug with his one usable arm, dragging himself in the direction he believed would bring him closer to the door out. Whatever chemical he'd inhaled left him disoriented and feeling as if he floated in an endless morass where up and down meant nothing. Perhaps its effect also explained how he hadn't yet passed out from pain. The rasp of her breathing faded to the corner of the room. Fleeting impressions of a sentient mind circled him, fifteen feet away. Between the chemical vapor and the agony in his legs, he couldn't even concentrate on her surface thoughts. Weak light welled up out of the floor on the far side of the room, a faint presence hinting at a woman's outline.

"Allison," he whispered, reaching.

"You think you're so impressive with your mind powers." Rakshasi's thick-accented English surrounded him. "You think you're so much better than us. All it takes is a little poison in the air. Go to sleep, bastard. Wake up in Hell."

Ten burning nails sank into his back, flooding his throat with hot blood. He ceased feeling the blades, instead reaching for the ghostly figure drifting closer.

"You are a strange man," said Rakshasi. "Never have I seen my prey smile."

He let off a wheeze as she jerked her talons free, and blacked out.

25

A RIGHT HAMES

"Aaron, what are you doing?"

"Allison..."

Aaron felt weightless, nonexistent. He couldn't perceive limbs or any sense of being able to move.

"Aaron, why are you doing this?"

"I'm sorry..."

Cold fingers slid over his cheeks. A woman's hands cradled his face. "You're a bloody idiot, Aaron."

Night faded to a grey blur. A thick, coppery taste flooded his mouth. Blood and chai-laced bile dribbled between his teeth. The haze gave way to distinct carpet fibers the color of pewter. Ozone hung thick in the air, mixed with the scent of overcooked meat and burned hair.

"I'm being literal this time. You are an idiot and you're bloody."

Allison's voice changed, deepened. Less innocent, haughtier.

The ghostly figure solidified into Aurora; naked as can be, kneeling with his head on her thigh. His attempt to speak sent a crimson sluice down her pure white legs. His head throbbed; the feeling of air moving inside several holes in his back made him shudder.

"Oh, that's disgusting."

She turned into a silvery mist, letting his head fall to the ground with a muted *thump.* More fluid came out of him to join the glop that had passed through her ghostly form. Aurora coalesced a pace away, clean and standing. His skull felt as though it expanded and shrank in time with his heartbeat. Continued effort to breathe speared him in the chest with icicles. Aaron wheezed, flapping his one movable arm.

"He's got a sucking chest wound," said Aurora. "Looks bad."

"Bitch," said Anna, right before the faint *pop* of an electrical shock occurred somewhere out of sight.

She skidded to a halt on her knees at his side, fumbling with a stimpak. He grunted and gurgled, failing to speak and unable to move. One after the next, Anna stabbed him in the shoulder blade with four autoinjectors. The portable medical devices weren't supposed to cause pain, but they also hadn't been designed for repairing serious internal injuries. He howled and rolled flat on his back as the ragged wounds flared up with a feeling like thousands of tiny mouths gnawing on his flesh. Burning became itching, causing a soundless scream. The second time he attempted to howl, his lungs managed to hold air.

"Hang on, Aaron. We'll call for a MedVan." Anna scrabbled at her purse, stymied by the closure.

"Sih…" he wheezed.

"What?"

"Sih…" Aaron coughed up blood.

"What are you trying to say?" She wrenched the purse open and gathered her NetMini, spilling a number of other random items to the floor in the process.

"Six… Six of one." Whatever the stimpak fluid attempted to do to his femurs felt like an army of furious fire ants going off on a drunken bender. "Oh, fuck this hurts." He grabbed at the sectional.

Anna clamped onto his arm, squeezing. "Hang on, luv."

"MedVan'll bring me to Prince George Regional Medical… Zero'll be waiting for me. I… Might be better for everyone if I just kicked off. I saw Allison."

Aurora's face lit up with inspiration; she vanished in a cloud of luminous fog.

"Dammit, where the hell is she going?" Anna clutched his arm to her chest, rubbing the back of his hand. "Don't give up, Aaron."

A feminine gurgle came from behind her.

"Look out," he rasped.

Anna twisted her head around to peer at something. "Don't worry about that bitch."

He tried to chuckle, but the attempt only triggered a coughing fit. "Looks like Manchester won this match."

She gave him a look as if she wanted to punch him and cry at the same time. "What were you thinking coming here alone?"

He interlaced his fingers with hers and held on. "Wasn't expecting the gas."

"Gas?" Anna smirked at a scorch mark on her coat sleeve. "That explains the fireball."

Though his legs remained numb and unresponsive, and his chest felt like a pub dartboard on Friday night, he managed the strength to prop himself upright—or maybe Anna helped.

Chemical fumes replaced the smell of incense. The formerly white sectional had browned in places like a tortilla. Tiny flames licked up from the carpet at the kinks in a jagged lightning-like burn, and the front door control panel was missing, the space it once occupied a charred ruin of smoking wires.

Rakshasi lay on her back near the kitchenette. Her unfocused gaze searched the ceiling without sentience, while her body twitched in the throes of random convulsions. The blade on her right forefinger snapped in and out. White foam dribbled down both cheeks.

"Which one of you is the mind blaster?" Aaron coughed.

"Didn't need that. The ones with that much 'ware are rather vulnerable to me. Neuralware is basically conductive wiring all through the body. She's alive, but I'm afraid I've made a hames of her."

"Fuck." Aaron let his head sag back. "She might have some idea of where Talis went. If you've cooked her brain, I've got nothing to work on."

"Bother that wench." Anna went for her NetMini.

He put his hand over it. "Don't. I'm done. I'm so fucking done. Spare me the five minutes of NewsNet infamy. No MedVan."

"You bloody coward," she yelled. "We'll get you out. Even if they stick you on the Moon somewhere, we'll find you."

Aaron winced from a ripple of pain. His left leg set about a rhythmic tremor that caused the separated bone segments to grind. He wondered for a moment how he could still be alive, having a vague recollection of a major artery right around there in the leg. Missing one could have been luck, missing it on both sides wasn't. He scowled at the twitching body, but no matter how much he tried to smash her into the ceiling, all he managed to do was lift her an inch before his head throbbed.

"Save your strength." Anna pulled his hand away from the NetMini.

"You're right." He slumped to the side. "I'm an ass, drowning my sorrows in cheap booze and cheaper women. I deserved this."

"Don't," said Anna.

"I deserved to get chewed up and spat out, just like I did to all those ladies." He thought about gesturing with his left arm, since Anna clung to the other, but it didn't move. "Bollocks, look at me. I'm... Probably losing both legs, half my arm"—he coughed to the point of seeing spots—"and a lung."

"You'll be alive."

"Will your Archon boy still want me if I'm barely psionic with all that hardware in me? Why'd you have to pull me away from Allison?"

"That wasn't Allison, you twit." Anna gave him a light slap on the cheek. "You're fading out. You saw Aurora scouting the room and hallucinated. She went into a trance and started screaming, said you were going to die."

"How'd the devil did you get in here?" He slumped left.

Anna pulled him upright. "Aurora borrowed one of the guards; I acted like his one night stand."

He let gravity pull him to the right. "Why do you have her eyes?"

Anna blinked. "What?"

"You've the same look Allison did. Am I seeing things again?"

"You've said that to me before, Aaron. You've gone loopy. It's the blood loss."

"Do you love him?"

"Of course." She looked away. "He's a good man. He pulled me out of the gutters of London. He gave me my life back."

"Why can't you look at me?"

"Garden variety contempt for a wanker who roots for Arsenal."

"You're still not looking at me."

"That's it; I'm calling for a MedVan."

A wave of fear, partially of getting cyberware, but mostly of being arrested, surged from within. He lunged, rather lurched, into an aimed fall at her hand before she could dial—but wound up tasting carpet.

26

MINOR DETOUR

"Wait on that van," called Aurora from the back.

"In there?" asked a child's voice.

Aaron grunted, coughing up a glob of blood as he raised his head to look down the interior hallway. A shadow stretched along the carpet from the bathroom door. A bare child-sized foot stepped out into view, followed by the blurry shape of a naked tween. The girl let off a yelp and flew back out of sight.

Aaron blinked a few times, trying to get his vision to clear.

"Where do you think you're going?" said Aurora, giggling. "Take this."

"But, you said he was going to die!" said the child in a raised, pleading voice.

Anna's eyes went wide; the NetMini slipped from her hand and hit the rug with a plop.

A girl, perhaps eleven, with waist-length blonde hair and luminescent blue eyes hurried out of the bathroom. She clutched a plum colored towel to her chest, which covered her from armpit to knee. Aurora followed, wrapped in a similar towel, though on her it stopped an inch away from indecent. The girl stepped with care around the debris, hesitant and making faces as though she put her feet down on some alien substance rather than carpet. As soon as she caught sight of Aaron, all hesitation left her and she rushed to him with such urgency she lost her towel. The girl fell to her knees amid the blood, and tore Aaron's shirt open enough to get both hands on his bare chest.

Anna hadn't moved so much as an eyelash since the child appeared; her hand curled as though she still held the NetMini.

Aaron looked into the most innocent face he'd ever seen, fascinated by the blue light shining out of the child's eyes. Her hands pressed warm against his skin; a sensation of numbness spread out from where she touched until he felt nothing at all. Pain from stab wounds in his back became noticeable by its absence. He let his weight pull him to the floor, certain the loss of sensation was the first step into the next world. The sight of Aurora wrapping the towel around the little girl lingered on his retinas, melting to a ghostly image and then a smear of color.

I see many hurts. The child's voice sounded earnest in his thoughts. *Do not have the worry.*

Fog overtook his mind. The next thing he knew, he stood alone in the center of a frictionless stadium, in his Arsenal uniform. Intense lights bathed him from all sides. A hovering stone sat on the border of a goal, pentagonal panels opening and closing as it spun about, compensating for the drift with such speed it looked as though the sphere rotated atop a single set of metal studs rather than an ever-changing array of thrusters.

He glanced at the stands where one person jumped and cheered without sound. Backlit by the floodlights, the indistinct figure could've been Allison or Anna. He smiled and nudged the stone an inch forward with a telekinetic poke to score. Aaron squinted at the woman, trying to see past the glare and recognize a face. Lights grew brighter, swallowing her. His hand shielded his eyes, but the whiteness built to blinding.

Aaron snapped out of his dream with the urge to take a huge breath. The child sat back on her heels nearby, engaged in a staring contest with Anna who had moved to take a proper seat on the sectional. One bloody hand clutched the towel at her chest. Aaron straightened, gazing at his blood-covered hands, confounded by his lack of agony. He squeezed his thigh, finding it intact. Awestruck, he gawked at the child.

Her little body looked frightfully thin and shook with a faint tremble likely caused by the air conditioning. Something about her pitiful stare and not-quite-closed mouth made him want to squeeze her in a fatherly hug. It took him a second to realize she emanated a mild 'please don't hurt me' telempathic radiation. Aaron's heart skipped a beat, expecting all hell to break loose when his brain came unhinged, but her emotional projection appeared to be more of a hint than a command.

The child offered him a genuine smile. "You should eat."

As soon as she said it, his stomach growled. He rubbed his gut while Aurora puttered around in the back. She soon emerged in a scarlet silk bathrobe that went all the way to the floor, and sashayed to the kitchenette where she helped herself to the food assembler. Anna flinched first, looking away from the strange child with a guilty, apologetic stare at the floor.

"Anna?" Aaron gestured at the girl. He couldn't figure out what disturbed him the most: his wounds had vanished, this child knelt in gore without caring, or that she had come out of nowhere with no clothing other than a bath towel—and didn't seem the least bit embarrassed, even perturbed that Aurora had 'wasted' time attempting to cover her. "What is a little girl doing here? Why isn't she dressed?" He glanced at her, at last processing the intense blue light shining out of her eyes. "Her eyes... They're *glowing*."

Aurora stepped over the still-twitching Rakshasi and sat on the sectional close to Aaron. She offered the girl a cup of hot cocoa, but she didn't react.

"Althea," said Aurora in a soothing tone. "I made a promise to you, and I intend to keep it."

The girl looked at Aaron as if judging him.

Aurora nudged her in the shoulder with the cup. "You won't regret helping him."

"She doesn't regret helping anyone," muttered Anna. "She even saved James."

"Aurora said my dress can't go in the magic door." The girl smeared her bloody fingers down her legs in a futile effort to clean herself. "It maybe is better. I won't get blood on it."

Althea accepted the cocoa and took a sip, giving herself a chocolate moustache. She sent an urgent look at Aurora, forced a weak smile at Aaron, and gazed into her lap. The towel slipped down an inch or so, though she didn't seem concerned whatsoever at it. Aurora leaned down to fix it back in place.

"Ironic," muttered Anna.

Aaron couldn't look away from the angel-faced tween clutching a cup of hot chocolate in two bloody hands. She had to be somewhere between nine and eleven, seemed half-starved, and exhausted.

"Dead material won't cross over," said Aurora. "We didn't have a lot of time to get here."

Anna looked up. "Wait, you mean to tell me you could've pinched the sprog at any time?" She turned red in the face. "All that running around... the tramps... that clawed monstrosity... You—"

"No." Aurora ran her fingers through the girl's hair in a repetitive soothing motion. "She would have had to be *willing* to go with me. I can't force people. I could bring her across, but if she didn't want to go with me, she'd just pop right back out."

Althea looked up at Aurora, with a guarded smile. She seemed to adore the affectionate contact.

"Willing?" Anna froze in place. "You mean she agreed to come with you now?"

"Not to stay," said Aurora. "I promised I'd take her right back once she'd helped Aaron."

Althea exchanged stares with Anna for a moment.

"Uhh." Anna shied away, stood, and wandered into the kitchen. "I'm not really all that nice."

The girl gave Aurora an earnest stare. "She won't see her heart. She has the lies, and believes."

"In time," whispered Aurora. "In time."

"Father always says that." The child grinned. *"Tomará tiempo."*

Aaron slid his feet in close, resting his arms over his knees. *Why do you look so frightened?*

After a slurp of cocoa, she offered a timid glance. *Archon tried to take me. He wants me to do bad things. I got away. I...* She sent a sheepish smile to Aurora before burying her face in the cup again.

You're worried Aurora wanted to kidnap you? Why did you agree to come here then?

"She asked nice," whispered Althea. She pointed at Rakshasi. "I want to help that woman, too."

Aurora stifled a laugh. "I'd say she's not worth the bother, but I know you won't listen. She's the one who hurt Aaron. She's not a nice person, kills people for money."

"This is her home?" Althea set the cocoa on the rug and stood, keeping one hand against her chest to retain her towel. "She was defending herself."

"Not entirely," said Aaron, with a weak chuckle. "I was trying to leave."

Althea tiptoed over to the convulsing figure, earning a disbelieving shake of the head from Anna. She knelt at the woman's side and slid a hand into the neck of her bathrobe. Rakshasi's twitching ceased. Soon, she put both hands on the woman's chest and lapsed into a meditative trance. The towel slipped down, gathering around her like a skirt.

Aaron fought his way upright. He found his telekinesis back to normal and used it to hold Rakshasi down. He did *not* want to witness the effect of a blind-panic Nano claw attack on an innocent girl.

He glanced at Anna. "That woman might be able to help me find Talis."

"It's all right." Aurora held a hand up to delay a lightning bolt. "I know where Talis is already, plus this Tí-zhèn was just a pawn."

"What?" Aaron spun on her. "You know where Talis is?" He almost fainted from anger and surprise.

"Hello…" She leaned toward him, tapping herself on the head. "Clairvoyant with ghosty powers. Talis has quite a welcoming party waiting for her on the other side."

Aaron frothed at the mouth; a glop went flying as he spoke. "You could've found her all this time? You…" He pointed at Rakshasi.

"You asked me to find that techie girl." Aurora winked. "You were rather focused."

"Gaaaah!" He babbled. "Why didn't you tell me you could just find Talis and skip this whole mess?"

"That wouldn't have been nearly as much fun." Aurora examined her fingernails.

Aaron grasped two handfuls of his hair, ready to tear it out. His eyes felt about to pop from their sockets. Anna gave him a 'see what we have to deal with?' smirk.

"Ngh… Why can't I move?" whimpered an accented voice.

"Shit," muttered Aaron, realizing he'd let go of Rakshasi.

Althea brushed hair off Rakshasi's face. "You have many hurts. I will fix them. I told your body not to move because they said you were not nice and might attack me. Do you want me to take the metal poison out?"

"What?" asked Rakshasi.

"Cyberware," said Aurora. "Leave the metal bits, mite. I think she wants to keep them."

"Okay." Althea leaned over the woman, hovering nose to nose. "I'm going to wake up your muscle shapes. Please don't hurt me."

Rakshasi didn't react, but Althea smiled.

A minute later, the weary child stood out of the towel and walked back to retrieve her cocoa. She stopped after three steps, looked down at herself, and went back for the towel. Fatigue kept her eyes half-lidded, but she still seemed afraid. After gathering the towel around her like a dress, she trudged over and took a seat on the floor by her cocoa.

You have the hate. It is a monster at the door love cannot sneak by. Althea sipped cocoa, staring at Aaron. *If you don't make the hate go away, you cannot find the happy.* She raised the cup to her mouth again, and gave Anna a sideways glance, smiling.

Aaron couldn't bear the innocence in her eyes in contrast to the sight of a little girl covered in blood, and looked away. "Yeah... yeah."

Rakshasi sat up, rubbing her chest over a burn hole in her robe.

"You twitch wrong, and your ass is going back down." Anna threw a spark from hand to hand.

"I don't understand what you people are, but you roasted my interface. Everything's offline." The once-imperious Aparna Devi sounded meek. "I'm no threat. I..." She sat up and regarded Aaron with a weary, defeated stare. "I remember feeling great love for Talis. It is gone."

"Someone left a bad inside her head," said Althea. "I fixted it."

"Fixed," said Aurora. "Aren't they giving you an education out there?"

Althea stood, and stared at the floor. "I wanna go home." She gathered the towel tight, shivering. "This place has much cold." Her teeth chattered. *"He's* not here, is he? I don't want to see him."

Anna fidgeted.

Aparna dragged herself upright and staggered to the kitchenette, her limbs barely flexing. She moved with the speed and grace of a centenarian. A brief glare at Aaron, the only man in the room, still carried distaste—as though he tainted her living space by merely existing in it. Compared to earlier, her expression held only a fraction of the vitriol.

She got us both.

The woman jumped at the invasion of his voice in her mind. He read no intent to cause further harm, only pain wracking her body and difficulty moving, as though her limbs were made of stiff wire. A body used to cybernetic augmentation had grown dependent on the electronics. Since the control wiring had fried, the Myofiber synthetic muscles slowed her down as much as they had accelerated before.

I'm sure Preston will cover your repairs. Aaron winked before he gave her a sympathetic frown. *Ehh, sorry about the mess. I only wanted to talk. No hard feelings?*

She wanted him out of her home, wanted the lot of them gone as soon as possible—except the child, who she thought creepy as hell, but not as frightening as everyone else. Aparna made another cup of tea and limped to take a seat at a small table.

Althea looked up with a gasp at the sound of someone moving in the outside hallway. She took a step back and gave Aurora a pleading stare.

"Wait a minute," said Aaron. "You're that special project they've set up out in the Badlands... The field base."

The fear and sadness in Althea's mute expression tore at Aaron's heart.

"How...?" Aaron rounded on Aurora, pointing. "How did you get her here so fast?"

"I'm not a project," whispered Althea.

He cringed. "Sorry, mite. Not what I meant. The project is Zero being out there..."

"The city police bring the bad to Querq," muttered Althea.

"What?" asked Aaron.

"Technology." Aurora winked. "She had a rather negative experience last time she visited West City, so anything modern she feels is evil."

"Oh." Aaron stared at the snow-white woman. It hit him at that moment that her lips hadn't moved. He couldn't recall them ever moving. "What's with the telepathic voice?"

She laughed. "Part of my oddities. The usual way never quite worked for me. Radiant telepathic communication. Can't help it."

Althea finished off the cocoa and tossed the cup over her shoulder.

"Hey..." Aaron caught the mug with a telekinetic hand, guiding it to a table.

The child looked at him, confused.

He decided not to bother. The kid lived in the Badlands, and he didn't have the energy to waste on an explanation of trash cans she wouldn't understand. "Never mind."

"How did you get her here so fast?" asked Anna.

Aurora bounced from the couch, nose in the air, one hand on her hip, the other up as if holding a pipe. She lowered her voice as deep as it could get. "A little thing I like to call being the most powerful astral traveler in the world."

Althea's nervousness broke up into giggles.

Anna rolled her eyes. "Honestly, Lauren?"

"Spirit doors. Distance doesn't work quite the same way on the other side." Aurora held both arms out to the girl. "Come on, mite. Your lips are turning blue. Let's get you home."

Air-conditioning induced shivers ceased. Althea's face lit up as she took both of Aurora's hands.

"Might want to get him cleaned up a bit, Anna." Aurora blew an air kiss.

Aurora and Althea held hands for a moment, toe to toe. Aurora closed her eyes and leaned her head back. A momentary expression of surprise manifested on the child's face an instant before they both dissipated in a glowing silver fog, which swirled into a tiny point. A plum-colored towel and a red silk robe fell empty to the rug.

"Well, shit," said Aaron. "Now there's something you don't see every day."

"Come on, then. Into the shower with you." Anna grabbed his suit jacket as if leading a wayward schoolboy and gave him a light shove toward an interior hall. She glanced around the apartment and offered an apologetic smile at Rakshasi. "Sorry about the flat."

"It can wait. Wouldn't want to taint her facilities with man cooties."

"She won't mind." Anna shot the other woman a dire stare.

Aparna cringed, refusing to look away from her tea. She made no effort to hide the fear on her face. Aaron almost felt insulted at not inspiring the same sort of dread that the tiny woman next to him did.

"Bother. I'd just as soon be away from here." He pulled his destroyed jacket off on his way to the exit.

Anna followed at an unenthused meander, a somber stare fixed at the floor with an added trace of a pout on her lips. He stopped short at the door, making her bump into him and look up.

"For what it's worth..." He took her hand. "I don't think you're a freak. I think that little one's right about you. There's another Anna in there somewhere, hiding."

"It's not going to work," she muttered, close to tears. "My knickers aren't going to fly off because you're all of a sudden charming and sensitive after almost dying."

"I'm not trying to get you in the sack." He squeezed her hand before backing into the outer hallway. "I'm trying to say thank you."

SOME DESERVE TO DIE

A aron replayed the events of the past two hours in his head while the relaxing spray of hot water hit him from all sides. Shimmer had given him all the data on Rakshasi, every cyber part, address, even the technical schematics of her apartment—which he'd glossed over. He wondered if the file contained any information about the lockdown routine or the disorienting gas mechanism.

He closed his eyes amid the spatter of spray soap, astounded to have walked out of Rakshasi's flat with no greater problem than deep hunger. The only remnant of his near-death experience manifested as a dull ache centered in the core of both thighs… and another ruined suit. However, considering the major bones in his legs had been salami-sliced not too long ago, he couldn't complain.

His growing urge for food kept him from running another shower cycle. The hotel room had felt stuffy and uncomfortable on the way in, but he stepped out from the steamy autoshower into air that qualified as downright frigid. He swiped a towel from the wall and ran it over his head where the too-short dry cycle hadn't quite finished on his hair. Red lettering stitched into the end caught his eye:

Towel will ignite if removed from the hotel property. Do not steal.

"Self-immolating towels. Ahh, the wonders of modern technology." He wrapped it around his waist, entertaining momentary second thoughts about having something capable of spontaneous combustion that close to his tender portions, but he wasn't planning on going outside. "Note to self, keep this bloody thing far away when Anna's watching frictionless."

"Very funny," said Anna.

She waited for him in the bedroom, sitting at the end of one of the twin Comforgel beds with her chin in her hands. Her expression held a mixture of sad and awkward, and she didn't look up. Unable to resist, he peeked at the tip of her brain, finding her attempting to stifle guilt and shame for an unexpected sense of attraction to him. He spun on his heel as though forgetting something in the bathroom.

I still got it. The enormous shit-eating grin mirror-Aaron flashed back at him faded with the memory of the look she'd given him as they left Rakshasi's place. Surface skimming wasn't necessary to tell how she felt about her powers. She'd told him she'd accidentally killed a man when she'd been twelve, a defensive reaction in the middle of being beaten. How long had she believed she'd murdered her father and not some CSB tosser? An event of that magnitude could make a psionic ashamed of their powers. He'd seen similar cases when he'd been with Division 0. A traumatic enough event associated with their gifts could make them afraid to use them ever again. He tapped the sink for a moment, trying to sort out his thoughts, and wandered back to where she had arranged a clean suit on the unoccupied bed. *She had to have sensed that peek. Great, I just made it more awkward.* Aaron picked at the suit, straightening it.

"I know you're spoken for."

Anna still didn't move.

He slid on a pair of boxers under the towel and let the damp cloth fall. "I'm sorry about your parents."

Anna deflated with an outward breath. Her voice came a hair above a whisper. "Sorry about your wife."

"Thanks." He took an undershirt from the stack and sat on the end of the bed. "Are you hungry at all? I'm famished."

"It's from the girl." Anna's face lit up from her NetMini's terminal screen. "I'll order us something."

She remained quiet while he dressed, not moving except to retrieve food from the delivery bot when it buzzed the door. The unmistakable fragrance of fish and chips swam into the room.

"Cute. You're taking after Darwin now."

"What's that supposed to mean?" She sounded halfway between sad and bored.

"Oh, nothing." He plopped down at the tiny table by the front window, attacking his portion.

"Look, Aaron. I know what you're thinking. He's forty-five, I'm twenty-eight, he's stuffy..."

Aaron held a hand up until he finished chewing. "No, nothing to feel bad about. I understand. I'm not trying to get in your knickers. The whole time I played for Arsenal, I had girls throwing themselves at me." His tone conveyed more annoyance than bragging. "All they wanted was their fifteen seconds and as much of my money as they could get. Shallow. Insincere. You probably don't believe me, but I never touched one of them." He stuffed his mouth, chewed twice, and forced it down. "When I got here, things were different. Allison had no idea who I was. I... owe it to her to make that bitch pay."

"James thinks this is a giant waste of time. He understands, though. He knows how you're feeling. I'd love to get my hands on the bastard that shot my mother."

"I'm sorry." Aaron's appetite faded for all of a second. "That had to be hard."

"I was two. I don't even remember her, just the bastard posing as my father."

"Still not easy." He dumped so much pepper on the chips Anna sneezed.

"I killed him. I was twelve." She fell into a chair, picking at her food. "I didn't know he wasn't my dad then. He got so worked up when I'd get emotional and something would blow up. Ironic, I think. He was worried I'd accidentally kill him in a fit of teenaged angst, so he drank himself to the point he became someone else. One night he was hitting—"

Aaron grabbed her hand. "You don't have to go back there."

"It's all right. He wasn't my father, just some CSB agent." She clenched her fists.

"Would it be easier to live with if he was really your dad?"

Overhead lights faltered but didn't explode. "No. I would rather it though. If he was my real father, that'd mean I had a family even if it was a ballsed-up one. Better a painful truth than a pleasant lie." She scratched at the table for a moment. "A lie won't last forever; something'll eventually come along and ruin all the defense I build to weather it, and it'd hurt all over again—likely worse. Truth will always be right in front of you. No surprises." She sniffled into a laugh. "Look at me, all wallowing in self-pity." Wet sapphire eyes locked on his. She reached across the table to hold his hand. "I can't imagine… It was beyond cruel to make you shoot her."

Aaron's appetite went down for a three-count. "I don't know what to do with myself anymore. Without her, I can't find meaning in anything."

She squeezed his hand. "I'll help you kill Talis if it's what you want. It's the least I can do."

He let off an uninspired chuckle and jammed a third of a piece of reassembled cod in his mouth. Anna slid back to her side of the table and tested her chips. She looked as unimpressed with them as Aaron felt.

"Seems we've got to cross the pond to get a decent meal," said Anna.

"I'm starting to doubt I can beat her. Everything's going to sod."

"You're Awakened now, Aaron. She's merely a psionic. She won't know what hit her."

"Rakshasi wasn't even psionic and look where I wound up." He stabbed chips with a fork, four at a time, cramming them into his mouth. "Mrff, mmmf mmm."

"She had the advantage… of you being pig-headed and trying to do everything alone."

"I thought you didn't like killing."

"I don't." Anna frowned at her lap. "A little girl once told me some people deserve to die. I think she's right."

Aaron whined at his empty carton and dropped it. "Althea?"

"Yeah."

"Why was she afraid of you?"

A cloak of guilt fell all over her again. "I thought we were helping. Her whole life, people had kidnapped her to exploit her abilities. Archon wanted to protect her from that. I thought she'd become addled and mistook some bandits for being family. You know, the Stockholm thing. She's a hard one to read. I've never seen a person so… innocent." Anna dropped her fork. "We all thought the little primitive was so afraid of the modern city she craved the familiar world she left behind, even if it meant being someone's pet. She ran off and I… hurt one of her friends when he tried to kill me." Anna rubbed her throat. "Word of advice, don't piss her off. She looks all sorts of harmless, but…"

Aaron scrunched his eyebrows together. "I doubt that girl would swat a mosquito."

"Depends on who that mosquito bit." She stared down.

His NetMini rang.

When he pulled it from his pocket, the name Mikhail Kovalev popped into being over a nav pin.

"Who is it?" Anna nibbled on a bit of fish.

He stared at the device until the holo display timed out and went dark. A slow exhale let all the air from his lungs. "Someone I probably ought to talk to."

STOLEN ANGEL

Anna's hand lay on the seat between them, though her attention focused away from him out the window. Aaron pondered putting his hand atop hers, but contented himself with smiling at it. For once, he'd take the high road. His gaze traced lines around the contour of every knuckle, daydreaming about what it would feel like to touch her. The mutual awkwardness forming between them could blow up at any moment, in different directions. He could hope Archon did something stupid, so it wouldn't look as bad on him if he made a move, or he could wait and see where fate went. Or, he could accept Anna was not his dead wife, and stop feeling like an idiot.

He leaned his head back and closed his eyes, letting the rocking PubTran taxi relax him. What if he had glimpsed an image of Allison through the veil that separates worlds? She'd asked him what he was doing. Could she have meant his near-suicidal quest for revenge? That would be something Allison would say. She wouldn't want him to get hurt because of what happened to her. She'd never let him hear the end of it in the afterlife if he did.

"This place looks risky," said Anna, breaking him out of his pleasant trance.

"Aye." He sat up.

Fog rolled by in clouds, gliding down abandoned sidewalks. Half the cars parked at the sides of the road looked like they'd been there for decades. Most had bullet holes and broken windows. Distant dogs barked and fought, brash music from some far off squat apartment throbbed. The car's ventilation system sucked in the fragrance of charring meat and barbeque sauce. He blinked at such a pleasant aroma existing in a place like this.

The front end of the cabin turned bright blue with the appearance of a holographic cartoon car about the size of a housecat. Shapes formed by the headlights and bumper made it seem to smile.

"Arrival at your selected destination is imminent," said an electronic voice at some midpoint between boy and man. "Please note the sector you are entering is considered dangerous. PubTran Corporation reserves the right to charge for any damage or loss of this vehicle occurring from an unscheduled violence event."

"Are they routinely scheduled?" asked Aaron.

"I do not understand your question," chirped the car.

"You said *unscheduled* violence event. That implies that if we planned one ahead of time your disclaimer wouldn't apply."

The car remained silent for a moment. "Thank you for submitting feedback to PubTran Corporation. I have passed along your comments to our marketing and legal departments for review. Thank you for choosing PubTran."

Aaron grunted as the vehicle jammed to a halt. Whirring vibrated in the frame for two seconds before the car slid sideways, nestling up to the curb between two behemoth vans. The side door opened, flooding the cab with the recognizable briny putrescence of the southern wharf district. The eastern edge of Sector 1562 left him about five miles from the black zone and about ten from the ocean. He didn't think anything in this area would be much of a threat to him, especially not with Anna along for the ride.

"Wait in the car." He started to push the door down.

"Hey!" she yelled, putting her arms up to catch it. "I'm not some helpless little flower."

"I know." He transferred his grip on the door to clasping both her hands. "I'm not worried about you being hurt. I'm worried about you being seen. The man I'm meeting with is from Division 0."

"Have you completely lost your marbles?" She tried pulling him back into the car.

"Thank you for choosing PubTran for your transportation needs. Please exit the vehicle to reduce liability."

"Need you to wait here," said Aaron.

Anna tugged at him. "What the devil are you doing? Come on, let's get out of here."

"Wait fee for Sector 1562 is two hundred fifty credits per five minutes. PubTran Corporation regrets any inconvenience this fee causes. However, due to the danger present in Sector 1562, we must—"

"Yes, yes," yelled Aaron. "I agree. Keep the meter going, I won't be long."

"Aaron…" Anna whined.

"Trust me." He gave her a telekinetic lift back into the car and closed the door.

Aaron walked away from the PubTran car. A gust of warm wind, thick with humidity and the stink of low tide blasted out from between two buildings, nearly pushing him off the sidewalk. He held his breath for a few steps until it died down, and hurried about two blocks before reaching a playground that hadn't seen a child since before he was born. Near a rusting set of monkey bars stood a man in a long, black coat. He'd opened the front, letting traces of a Division 0 dress uniform peek out. At Aaron's approach, he raised his head with a paternal smile. He looked in his later forties, perhaps early fifties, with darkish skin and short, neat hair.

"I wasn't sure if you'd agree to meet me here," said Mikhail.

Aaron accepted the outstretched hand and shook it. "If there's anyone inside I still trust, it's you."

Mikhail waved him off with a bashful chuckle. "You're too kind." His mood darkened. "I'm so sorry about Allie."

"Thanks." Aaron looked down. "Sorry about the tracer. Hope he didn't hurt himself too badly."

"He'll be fine." Mikhail stuffed his hand back in his coat pocket. "I want you to know I believe you about the compulsion. The investigations board feels it's a lie since suggestion is so unlikely to work in that situation. I've gained some traction with the command council regarding my opinion that this woman you described might be an unusual case."

"Like Althea?"

Mikhail coughed. "How did—"

"Classified?" Aaron smiled. "I met her a few hours ago." The mirth bled out of his expression. "She's the reason I'm not dead."

Mikhail leaned into a cautioning glare. "You should come in. These chances you're taking…"

"I know... I know. Without an assurance of Talis being made a priority, I have to do this."

"You know I can't pull the kind of strings Burckhardt does. Do you think this Talis person may be like the girl? Something we haven't seen yet? Perhaps she's a military project, which could explain why the brass almost seems to want to let her get away with it."

"C-Branch likes to keep tabs on the suggestives, don't they?" Aaron grumbled. "Cull the herd when they get too strong. Maybe they missed this one."

"Or she's one of theirs." Mikhail squinted at the smog overhead. "Something stinks about this whole thing, Aaron. Ravindra is convinced you killed Allison on purpose because no one with true love could do that."

Aaron hung his head, shaking it. "Oh, for all the cliché..."

Mikhail's breath stuttered as though he meant to laugh, but the weight of the topic held it down to a weak smile. "I think we can sort this out, but I need you to come in. Running around out here just makes you look guilty. I believe you were compelled, and Carter is almost ready to consider the... incident that occurred in the infirmary an accident."

Headlights lit up on the van in front of the PubTran car. A few seconds later, it drove away.

Aaron fidgeted. He glanced out of the corner of his eye at the spot of white hair hovering inside the PubTran he'd left two-ish blocks away. "I've had some insight on that. I... Did any of them survive?"

Mikhail pursed his lips, nodding. "Only those within a close radius died. Lieutenant Garber, Officers Rios and Frost, as well as Dr. Korran were killed instantly. Chase and Dean made it, though Dean had to get a metal leg. She's not too happy. She's applied to have her tissue regrown, but due to the expense of that... it's taking a while to process the approval."

"Send her out to that Badlands post. The kid can probably..." Aaron got distracted by a low-flying delivery bot. *What the hell am I in the middle of?*

"You know." Mikhail wagged a finger. "I think that might be a good idea. They'd adore the data from such a procedure."

"Something happened when Talis forced that command into my psyche." He brought Mikhail up to speed on what Archon told him. "Invasive psionics trigger a violent, involuntary reaction. I... think you can read without setting it off. It's only when a psionic attempts to change or influence things, but maybe going too deep would set it off too." He squinted. "Garber wasn't trying to do an *implant* was he?"

"May I?" asked Mikhail.

"Aye, one moment." Aaron took a deep breath, calling to mind as much as he could remember from the medical evaluation they performed the day Allison died.

He relaxed, letting Mikhail's consciousness filter into his. Mikhail's probing felt careful, going only where Aaron opened the way, and not trying to force a read from an unready thought. Scenes replayed in a series of speed-up, slow-down bursts. The event lacked the depth of immersion that occurred when Archon did his telepathic dive, making the experience akin to watching a holo-vid as opposed to reliving it.

Aaron saw himself in the center of a white room, surrounded by people in medical uniforms poking and prodding while a doctor hovered over him. Lieutenant Garber, a telepath from I-Ops walked in, officially to read his mind for verification of his claim of coercion. After a brief 'are you ready' look from Garber, he stared at Aaron with intent. Seconds later, Garber shot straight up into the ceiling, bursting like a man-shaped water balloon while the doctor, equipment, and technicians went flying in all directions.

Mikhail pulled away, looking ill. "That presents certain problems."

"I hope it's not the sniper-rifle-from-two-thousand-meters sort of problem."

"No." Mikhail put a hand on Aaron's shoulder and squeezed. "You suffered a psionic assault while on duty. Assuming everything clears, they're going to put you back out there. What happens the next time someone pokes your brain and you go off like a psionic bomb?"

Aaron deflated. In the span of a breath, he'd entertained hope of getting his old life back and had it pulled out from under him. "Oh." He glanced at the taxi again. "It might not be permanent. This bloke said he might be able to correct it, but it could take away being Awakened."

Mikhail perked up. "What did you say?"

"It might not be permanent."

"No, that other word."

"Awakened?" Aaron cocked an eyebrow.

"Where did you hear that from?"

"The man calls himself Archon. He had a peek under the hood and said he thought it possibly impermanent. Didn't want to go messing around since he seems to want me all jacked up powerful."

Mikhail narrowed his eyes, rubbing his chin. "I thought I understood what was going on with you, Pryce, but you throw me a spiral screamer."

"A what?"

"Oh, right... You're not keen on Gee-ball." Mikhail chuckled. "You're making a mistake associating with those people. They've managed to steal a classified military battlecruiser. That little girl you met escaped from them. Still not entirely sure how an eleven-year-old managed that. We got quite an earful about that Archon fellow from her." He rolled his eyes. "If you ask me, she should've let him die... would have saved a lot of people a lot of pain, but I suppose she's just not wired that way."

"Aye. You're right on that point." He explained what had happened at Rakshasi's apartment, including how the girl insisted on healing her too. "Where the devil would they hide an entire battlecruiser? There's only so much ocean."

Mikhail smirked. "Starship, Aaron, Starship. No one uses battle*ships* anymore."

"Archon nicked a military spacecraft?" Aaron blinked. "They don't seem anywhere near organized enough to—"

"It's true. CENTCOM isn't sharing much with us, since they don't understand the nature of what they're dealing with. They still think there's only a handful of psionics in the world, and the ones who aren't with us are nothing to worry about. Half of what we know as fact, they consider horseshit. The Senate is eating itself alive calling for this man's head on a post."

"They know who Archon is?"

"In a vague sense. They know there *is* a man out there calling himself Archon, but little else." Mikhail sighed out his nose. "You may be the only one on our side of the fence who's seen him in person aside from the girl and remembers it. Solomon got a look at him, but only briefly. He tried to take over her mind when she hesitated."

"Solomon?" Aaron cocked an eyebrow.

"It's classified." Mikhail faced sideways. "I hope you're still on *our* side of the fence."

"Well, f'you ask me, he's not planning on doing anything dangerous. He claims to want to flee persecution on Earth. You know what it's like for us in most ACC territories, and even some independent nations. Is that so wrong, to want to be able to live without fear?"

"There are easier ways to do it than stealing a prototype battlecruiser."

Mikhail shook his head. "Those fools all think his plan is to bombard the Senatorial chambers on the moon."

"Of course, their first thought is a direct attack. Sounds like guilty consciences."

Mikhail gave him a long, pointed stare. "I know you're not a killer. I trust you, and I want you to come back to us. You might have just stumbled into a way to do just that." He gripped Aaron's shoulder again, squeezing. "If you can find that ship, maybe even figure out some way to neutralize Archon, you'd get a hero's welcome."

Aaron stared at the old playground wheel, rusty and creaking in the wind. Mikhail let his arm drop to his side.

"I'm hardly a hero." His voice faltered. "I failed my wife. She died by my hand."

"Nothing you do is going to bring Allison back, but she wouldn't want you throwing your life away, either. There aren't words enough to express how sorry I feel about what happened to her. One person is to blame for her death, and it's the suggestive."

"Talis Lir." Aaron tempered his sadness with anger so he didn't lose the ability to speak. "Has there been any progress hunting for her?"

Mikhail glanced down the street.

"They're not even looking, are they? Everyone thinks it was me. So, how long do I have?"

"Have?" asked Mikhail.

"Before C-Branch puts one in my brain that I don't see coming."

"You have not yet been elevated to that level of threat." Mikhail rocked back on his heels. "In no small part due to my influence."

"I can't come back in until I get Talis. I can't let Allison's death go unpunished. If I have to rely on someone like Archon to do that, so be it."

"Perhaps you can convince him we are not his enemy. If what you say is true, and all he wants is protection and rights for psionics, why is there a conflict? We want the same thing."

Aaron looked at his hand. "I'm not sure if I should salute you. Am I active or a fugitive?"

Mikhail smiled. "That depends on if you want the official or unofficial answer."

"That depends on how much is classified." Aaron winked.

"Solomon's a pyrokinetic. C-Branch tried to clone and amp one as a weapon, but she got away. Little hard to handle. Archon made a play for her, but she balked at the last minute. C-Branch stuck their dicks in it, and the whole thing turned into a giant mess. When she had second thoughts about Archon, she says he tried to modify her thoughts. Your… situation might just be the only way we have to get inside his group without being detected. He'll hesitate before trying to do anything to your brain."

"I'm not sure anymore." Aaron started back toward the PubTran car. "I'll need time to think about it."

"I know who you are, Aaron. Allison knew too." A note of whimsy entered Mikhail's voice. "I'm pretty sure that young lady staring at you knows too."

Aaron stopped walking. *If he only knew who she was.*

Grit scratched as Mikhail moved to walk away. "Take care of yourself, Sergeant. Hopefully, you'll figure out who you are soon."

A BIT OF SWEET

The PubTran car's hatch door squeaked open. Anna let go of it, scooting back to give him room. Aaron paused with one foot in, glancing over his shoulder at the playground. Mikhail was nowhere in sight. Except for the baleful rusty cry of the metal wheel with rainbow-painted handrails, nothing stirred. He ducked the drab grey and blue flap and fell into the hard plastic seat, wondering why they even bothered with a layer of thin cloth.

"Wait fee is currently one thousand two hundred fifty credits. Would you like to continue waiting?"

"No," said Aaron.

Anna leaned forward. "Sector 13628."

"Destination fee, four hundred and six credits. Do you accept?"

"Yes," said Aaron.

The car lurched into the road, pulling a one-eighty with squealing tires and racing off to the north. Aaron couldn't help but notice her nervous shivering; the unforgiving plastic seat transferred it from ass to ass. Quiet lasted all of two minutes.

"Who was that?"

"One of my former superiors."

"Your captain?"

"No."

"Lieutenant?"

"No."

She looked at him. "Aaron."

"That was Mikhail Kovalev, Division 0 Regional Commander, West City."

A sound like a drop-kicked rat came out of her. She clamped her hands over her mouth.

"He's a friend. I was high profile when I came over from London, and he took me under his wing. I had some anger management issues to work on. Being forced into police work wasn't my idea, but it did sort of grow on me eventually. Would you believe I was once a bit of a prima donna?"

"You?" She blinked. "No."

"Now *that* sounds like sarcasm. So where are we going?"

"The facility. You should meet the others."

"Guess the little one doesn't want to play with the Awakened?" He shifted, searching for a way to sit that didn't transmit every bump to his tailbone.

"No, she's a little cheesed off at us. Archon in particular."

"She's awakened though, right? Accelerated Healing is a documented talent, though aside from her, it's not known to be able to work on anyone other than the person using it."

"Aye. She is."

"So what'd your old man do to get her angry?"

"Oh, nothing much… influenced some mercenaries to dart her in the ass, stuffed her in a box for a six-hour ride away from her family, and kept her locked in a room in a big, scary abandoned nuclear power station. She also got rather cross with me for ruining this pitiful skirt she had made of scraps. Bloody thing fell to bits when I tried to clean it. Gave 'er a clean, new dress, but you'd have thought I strangled her puppy." Anna waved her hand around. "The man couldn't see her as a person capable of making decisions. Treated her like a helpless little child that needed daddy to come in and save her from the cold, cruel world."

Aaron didn't say it, but the look in his eyes did.

Anna went florid crimson and glared at the window away from him. "It wasn't like that at all. He didn't force me to do anything. You know what it's like in London, for people like us. Not everyone's a bloody celebrity. I fell, Aaron. I fell hard." She sniffled. "I don't fancy talking about it."

"Yeah. Look, I'm sorry. I didn't mean to insinuate anything."

Anna softened.

"He certainly seems to be the trusting sort."

"Are you being sarcastic?" She squinted.

"No." He smiled. "Just wondering how territorial he gets since we've been spending a rather lot of time together without adult supervision."

"He's quite busy. Besides, he knows nothing could happen between me and an Arsenal wanker." She folded her arms. "I'm not a cheat."

"Wanker? I thought I'd been promoted to twat."

She jabbed him in the side with a finger.

"Ouch." He laughed for a tick, before giving her a serious stare. "I'm not sure I quite trust him. I wasn't a cop for all that long, but something seems off about the man. Whenever I mention him, you get that far off look in your eyes."

She leaned into him as the car pulled a hard right and plunged into a PubTran-only access tube with a loud *whoompf*. Rumbling shook the roof as the tiny top wheels made contact with plastic. He grunted at the near vertical ascent to The Highway and smiled at her lack of effort to avoid contact. Acceleration pinned them to the seat like a fighter aircraft in a hard climb. Two hundred feet of sealed tube blurred by with an eerie pneumatic whirring noise. Eight seconds later, the car reached the end. Speed imparted a few inches of air when ramp became flat road. Sparks flew as it settled into the half-width exclusive lane, barely big enough for the automatic taxi.

"Bugger." Aaron rubbed his backside. "For what they charge for these blasted things, you'd think they could afford cushions."

"Supplemental comfort enhancers are optional for an additional twenty credits," said an electronic voice.

"James is driven to save psionics from ignorant fools. He sometimes loses himself in his work and can come off a bit impolite."

"Aye. Abducting children *is* rather rude, isn't it, and there you go again with the doe-eyed stare."

She punched him in the arm. "Come off it."

"I'm not getting the same sort of feeling from you, Anna." He waved his NetMini at the center console, paying for the 'supplemental comfort enhancer.'

"Please stand a moment," said the electronic voice.

As soon as they got up, an eruption of thick, beige foam sprayed from nozzles on both sides, covering the seat with a glistening gelatinous mass. The glop hissed and bubbled, flooding the cabin with eye-watering fumes; dullness spread from the edges toward the center, and it puffed up.

"Please sit," chirped the cab.

Anna gave him a 'you first' look. Aaron eased his weight down, finding the not-quite-sticky surface neither as nasty as he expected nor as comfortable as he hoped. Still, the mystery substance had formed enough padding to make the ride bearable. The lingering chemical odor, he could've done without. Anna sat at the edge, as if afraid to let her entire body touch the 'cushion.' Her expression reminded him of someone with an unpleasant task ahead of them they couldn't avoid and didn't want to do.

"Something wrong?"

She picked at her nails. "No. You just got me thinking about Althea. When we had her, it was the one time I remember really disagreeing with James. He focused entirely on what he wanted to accomplish, and that little girl was so pathetic and sad. I… I didn't want to be mean to her. I tried to be nice, but she hated us." Anna wrapped her arms around herself and leaned forward. "I felt like such an ogre. She reminded me of someone I knew back in London."

"Younger sister?"

"Something like that."

Aaron considered taking her hand, but decided against it. "Archon seems like a block of sour coated in a bit of sweet."

She flashed a wistful smile. "Perhaps."

An earnest smile spread across his lips. "You, I think, are the reverse."

FOLLOWING THE LIGHT

Anna refused to look at him for ten minutes. He pressed his fingers into the wonderful butt-preserving ooze between him and the infernal plastic bench. The ghost of his touch faded away as the foam eased back to its prior shape within seconds of his letting go. He pressed down again and watched the indentations fade. Amid the awkwardness in the taxi, it provided a welcome mindless distraction. Sway imparted to the little wheeled box from private cars blurring past at more than double their speed had gone from scary to relaxing.

"Aaron?" she whispered.

"Hmm?"

"I've been wondering something."

He leaned closer, feeling a bit of a rush. "What's that?"

"When you went after that assassin"—he slouched, disappointed—"you had that girl shadowing you on the 'net, right?"

"Aye. She'd gotten me through the locks, masked the security feeds. We're clean."

Anna looked at him. "Why didn't she disable the sleep gas or turn the lights back on?"

He gawked at her as though she'd slapped him.

"I—" Aaron took out his NetMini and tried to call Shimmer. It rang to vid mail. He ended the call and tried twice more. "Bollocks."

"Think she sold you out?"

"I don't think so…" He eyed the device in his hand, unable to shake a building sense of worry.

Seconds before he tried to call her again, the NetMini chirped. The icon for a text message floated above it, a blue coin emblazoned with the image of an envelope. He gestured as if to grab it and the messaging terminal panel unfolded in midair. A bright green square contained a ‹1› in the top left corner by the word ‹new›. When he poked it, a black window appeared with green text.

‹Help. They found me. This is an automatic message sent via deadman program.›

"What the devil…?" Anna leaned in.

Aaron's eyes roamed in circles. "Deadman switch… usually cuts off a machine if you let go of it. Program? Shit, she must've set up a distress call to send itself automatically if she didn't hit a button every so often."

"Who? She?"

Aaron didn't have time to wonder if an almost-undertone of jealousy in her voice came from her or merely his hope. He looked at his NetMini, noting the time. "PubTran, change course. Go to Sector 10302, Happy Panda Noodle Bar."

"Course change to closer destination results in new, lesser trip fee of two hundred thirty-two credits. Do you accept?"

"Yes, yes. Bloody fuck, yes. An extra hundred credits if you get there fast."

"PubTran Corporation does not authorize unlawful operation of—"

"Five hundred."

The car shut up and managed to get up to a hundred and sixty. Rattles and taps emanated from everywhere, even parts of the roof that had nothing apparently to rattle or tap. Cars streaking by along the inside lanes had become distinct vehicles rather than blurs of color.

Anna closed her eyes. "Shit, shit shit shit. What crazy bollocksed up thing are you doing now?"

"The Syndicate's got Shimmer. They're going to kill her." He punched the seat. "I… I've gotta do this. Stay with the cab, and go somewhere safe."

"The hell I will. Aaron, the last time you ran off on your own you got turned into Arsenal wanker sushi."

"How much do you care if a cop sees your face?"

She lost what little color she had in her cheeks. "I…"

"It's fine. Stay with the PubTran."

Anna picked at the fabric of her leggings where it bunched at her knees.

"Archon wouldn't want you getting seen. This is my mess. Sons of bitches must have somehow followed me there."

"Aurora found her for you. It's our mess too." She put a hand on his arm. "I'm going with you."

Six minutes later, the little PubTran car slammed on its brakes amid a busy street full of cars and pedestrians. The architecture on both sides resembled thousand-year-ago-China carved out of a stage set and pasted to the lower four floors of skyscrapers. Above that, the usual plain silver high-rises continued. Wires strung across the road at the level of the second story held dangling round paper lanterns decorated with pictograms. Some pedestrians dove to the ground as a reflex to the sound of hard braking. Two corporate-looking men in long coats pulled pistols, aiming at the PubTran.

Aaron and Anna wound up on all fours, barely avoiding a face-first meeting with the dashboard. The door popped open.

"Thank you for using PubTran. Travel time: four minutes thirty-two seconds."

"Aye." *Bloody murderous machine.* He crawled out and stood on wobbly legs.

Anna followed.

The two men lowered their weapons and walked off.

"Last chance," said Aaron.

She gave him a stern look.

He pointed. In front of a building faced with an orange and brown recreation of ancient pagoda construction, beneath the glow of a twelve-foot-tall dancing holographic panda, sat a Division 0 patrol craft. Half its armored bulk intruded upon the sidewalk, bottlenecking pedestrian traffic down to two bodies' width. A middle-aged man in a panda costume stood with a sign at the street corner. Despite the smile molded into his panda-head hat, his real face had a 'someone shoot me' expression. He offered the pair an unenthused wave.

"Every day around now, Ridge is here having dinner. He's addicted to whatever they put in their ramen."

"Can you trust him?"

"Probably. Are you sure you're okay with this?"

"Probably."

He wasted no more thought on it. A minute's delay could kill a nineteen-year-old girl. Tactical Officer Vernon Ridge nearly choked on his food when Aaron tapped on the opaque armored panel where a window should be. On the inside, electronics made it a window. Aaron waved at the tiny hole containing a lens. The inch-thick armored panel motored its way into the door, letting the smell of hot soup waft out.

"Fuck me…" Noodles hung off the bottom lip of a man who could stand to lose about ten pounds. "Pryce?"

"No thanks, mate. I need a favor."

"Are you fucking nuts?" He slurped the danglers in and swallowed. "Half the goddamn city is trying to find your ass. You come walkin' right up to me? You shouldn't be able to walk with balls that big."

"Ridge, there's a girl's life at risk. I don't have time to explain. You know me, Vern. You know it was compulsion." He grasped the door in both hands, summoning his most convincing, pleading stare. "Oi, where's your charming partner?"

"Nuñez is flying a desk. Somethin' about needing time to deal with whatever your little girlfriend did to her."

Anna folded her arms, smirking.

"Not now, mate. I wouldn't be asking if it wasn't important."

"Man…" Ridge stabbed his chopsticks into the bowl. "If I get busted down to TO1 for this, I'm gonna kick your ass. Whadda ya got?"

"Nineteen-year-old, Lily Braddon."

"I know I'm psychic, but I need more than that. You got a picture for a Citycam sweep? PID? Address, anything?"

Aaron paced, growling. "Dammit, no. Just an anonymous text, which I'm sure she bounced around a million relays."

Ridge slurped two mouthfuls of noodles while Aaron stewed in circles. "Hey, sorry man. You know how it is. Justice is only for the wealthy."

Aaron whirled on his ex-partner fast enough to make the man spray broth on the dashboard and reach for a sidearm. "Wealthy."

"I'm clean, bastard. I ain't gonna take no bri—"

"No. She was wealthy. Her father was an executive for Chrysalis Corporation. She's gotta have a chip. Run Lily Braddon through the system."

Ridge slurped broth from the bowl balanced in his left hand while poking his way around the KidTrak database. "Yeah, you're right. Good instinct. She got tagged sixteen years ago. Got a signal on it too, looks like Sector 10192, right by the wall."

"I need another fav—"

"No fuckin' way man. Just talkin' to you without trying to bring you in could get my ass fired, or charged."

"Ridge, please trust me."

"Aaron, you know I—"

"I could 'steal' your car.'"

Officer Ridge whined. "That's such an assload of reports to fill out."

"I could really steal it."

Ridge gave him the sort of look the wimpy kid gives the bully before the beating: faint hope that maybe today they'd get a pass.

"Come on, Ridge. They're going to kill her."

"Fine." He shoveled great mouthfuls of noodles, broth, and shrimp into his face.

Aaron ran around to the passenger side and hopped in. Anna slipped into the back.

Ridge brought the car's drive system online. "So, who's the girl?"

"You'll live longer not knowing," said Aaron, deadpan.

Ridge turned white.

"I'm kidding. Go!"

The patrol craft leapt straight up, knocking at least twenty people to the ground amid sparking tendrils of ionic downblast. Anna slid across the bench seat in back and smacked into the window as Ridge pulled a stiff turn to face east. Within seconds, he'd gotten up past three hundred miles per hour.

"No lights or sirens. They see that coming, they'll kill her if she isn't already dead."

Ridge nodded to the terminal pane. "Vitals are still showing from the KidTrak."

"Those things transmit vitals?" Aaron looked at it. All it displayed was body temperature, which had a green icon by it. "Body temp. Doesn't mean she's still alive."

"Hey." Ridge let go of the sticks long enough to shrug. "I'm just trying to be an optimist here."

Within three minutes, the eastern edge of the city came into view. The massive wall that dominated most of its length towered over the buildings in its shadow. Dusty brown scrubland stretched as far as they could see into the desert of what used to be called Nevada. Ridge steered a few blocks south and came in low. The desert vanished behind the wall as ground wheels extended with a low mechanical whirr, locking out with a heavy *clunk* that jolted the frame. The instant rubber touched plastisteel, Aaron shoved the gull wing door up and jumped out.

"That one there." Ridge pointed at a five-story cube of a building that appeared ready to collapse from wind force alone.

"I owe you." Aaron patted the roof twice.

Ridge glared at him, shook his head, and pulled off into the sky. Aaron jogged up to the corner of the building, slowing to a creep as soon as he got close against the wall.

No guards outside?

Anna's voice in his mind almost made him yell. He spun around to make eye contact. *That would attract attention.*

He snuck to a twisted mass of aluminum that used to be the front door of some kind of professional building. Debris of walls, furniture, and forty-year-old medical equipment littered the otherwise empty hallway. Aaron stepped past the smashed entryway, buoyed on by the echo of voices from deeper inside. Anna followed, taking a little longer to get around the scrap metal in the foyer.

"Was great doin' business with ya, man." Darwin's voice echoed over the room.

Aaron's heart stopped for a moment. Anger and anxiety built in his hands, making them twitch. He lost some care, moving at a normal walk to where light leaked out of a rotting pair of wooden doors. Whoever used to own this office had money, the wood was real—and moldy. He stopped breathing to tolerate having his face against it and peered through an old shotgun hole.

The room inside had been long-ago gutted, reduced to naked wall spurs and steel I-beams along the ceiling. A fat man with medium-dark skin stood behind a banged-up metal desk, wearing a black suit that oozed Syndicate. He shook hands with Darwin who grinned at something small in his grasp, no doubt a cred stick with more money on it than the man had ever seen in one place.

Shimmer, still in her tank top and white/grey camo fatigue pants, lay face down on the floor. Her powder blue hair darkened in spots from what could only be blood. Six other men stood around her as if appraising their work, brandishing scraps of rebar, pipe, or boards.

"I gotta ask ya," said the man behind the desk. "Not that we don't appreciate the gesture, but why'd you give her up?"

Darwin held up a three-inch black plastic device, pinched between his thumb and middle finger. "The price was right."

Desk Man grinned.

"Anytime." Darwin snapped his fingers, tossing credstick up and catching it in a closed fist. "Let me know if you need anything else. A pleasure workin' with yas."

He spun to walk out, heading right for the door where Aaron hid. He had only known the man for a few months, but the sense of betrayal left him stupefied. Darwin made it three steps before his chest exploded with the sound of a gunshot. He blinked and looked down at the crimson seep. A second shot tore a hole in his gut, and he went down. He dragged himself forward a few more inches and went limp, lifeless eyes focused at the credstick.

Desk Man shook his head as he lowered a giant handgun. "I ain't got no tolerance for betrayers." He held his arms to the side, looking for affirmation from his cohorts. "They're like feedin' fuckin' pigeons. Do it once, they'll do it all the time. No principles."

Aaron's rage bubbled over, summoning a telekinetic wave that smashed both wooden doors into an explosion of splinters and chunks. He tore the pistol out of Desk Man's grasp, launching it across the room and through a cinderblock wall.

After the initial shock wore off, Desk Man raised a hand in a gesture of greeting. "You're too late, my friend. Our business with Miss Braddon is completed."

Aaron looked down at Darwin, who wasn't moving. Blood crept outward along the pale cement slab where he'd fallen. "The girl wanted revenge for her murdered brother. You Syndicate tossers do the same thing. Someone kills one of yours, you kill one of theirs."

"Not exactly," said Desk Man. "We usually kill two or three to get the point across, and that little bitch wasn't Syndicate. Pity she was so good with electronics. We could'a used her, but there was no trust there. She didn't want to work anything out."

Aaron stepped over Darwin. "You've got two seconds to leave, or you're all dead men."

Desk Man gestured at Aaron. "Kill him too."

The six men raised their bludgeons. Aaron disregarded them for the moment, seizing Desk Man with a telekinetic hold and sending his screaming bulk to the far right of the room. Anna walked up alongside on Aaron's left.

"This hardly seems fair," she muttered. "There's only seven of them."

He blamed himself for Shimmer, in the same way he wore the mantle of guilt for Allison. He reached the point of cracking, screaming random, incoherent obscenities. Desk Man's pleading morphed into an unintelligible warble as a vengeful burst of telekinetic force sent him into the left wall, creating a hole not quite big enough for him. Fragments of cinderblock and gore spattered all over the adjacent room.

Anna gestured at the largest man in the pack, launching him off his feet with an electrical discharge as big around as her arm. The smoking body hit the ground six feet away, still. The other five went from advancing to backing away.

Aaron grabbed them all, snarling, and glided them to the same launch point from where Desk Man took his final flight. All five wailed and begged like children. Two wet themselves.

Anna grabbed his arm. "Aaron, must you?"

"Do you want to deal with their retaliation?"

Three of them swore not to say a word.

Little Anna stood up on tiptoe to get her face in his field of view. "Do you want to deal with murdering them?"

He shuddered with rage. "They beat a defenseless girl to death and enjoyed doing it. This isn't murder; it's a summary execution for what they did to an innocent. If there's any cop left in me…"

"You'll have them arrested."

Aaron couldn't help but see Allison in her eyes. He stared down, feeling defeated for a moment. Two breaths later, he pointed at Shimmer. "Look at her. They're Syndicate; they'll be out in a few months."

"I suppose." Anna bundled her coat and turned away from them, and Aaron.

He flung them into wall, floor, and ceiling, breaking holes in plaster, cinderblock, and studs. One by one, the Syndicate men went from flailing panic to limp weight. Aaron dropped them in a heap.

"They're not dead. I just gave them a light thrashing. What about 'im then?"

Anna exhaled, seeming relieved. "He's just napping. That wasn't a killing shock."

"A block of sweet coated in a bit of sour." He sniffled.

By the time he trudged to Shimmer's body, the tears came unbidden. Grief hit him as heavy as if he watched himself kill Allison all over again.

A LITTLE LATE

Aaron dropped to his knees at Shimmer's side. Her sinewy figure lay in an ungainly face down sprawl, arms and legs spread. Gentle telekinetic force lifted her, rotated her over onto her back, and set her down in a serene pose. If not for the bruises on her face, she'd have looked asleep.

Anna walked up behind him. "Are you all right?"

He snuffled and wiped his eyes. "I'm becoming quite sick of stumbling over women people've taken advantage of."

"Not to sound too cruel, but… hello pot."

"That's different." He gestured at the girl on the floor in front of him. "Those were women, this is just a girl… The ones I…" Faces flashed by in his memory, dozens of women he'd known for one night. Who knows how many of them had been hurt when he never came back.

Anna squatted behind him, resting a hand on his shoulder.

"I found a tom in a motel room, and another girl these tossers used as bait. I should've done more for this one. I shouldn't have left her there alone." He launched the desk through the ceiling, shouting "fuck" loud enough to redden his face.

The primal sound echoed into silence. She squeezed his shoulder.

"Do you think Allison kept leading me to these kids, hoping I'd remember who I was?"

"I dunno. That's more a question for Aurora. I don't really do the ghost thing. I just electrocute stuff."

Darwin let out a wheezing gurgle of a cough. His roommate and former friend curled on his side, one hand over the bullet hole in his chest. Anger overtook Aaron. He leapt to his feet and pounced on top of him.

"You bastard!" Aaron pulled Darwin up by a fistful of his shirt collar and punched him in the nose. "How the fuck did you find her?"

"Stone."

Aaron throttled him. "What?"

"Frictionless... orb... recorder." Darwin gurgled. "Saw you reading the maps."

Not only had his friend betrayed him, he'd used a frictionless game orb, a supposed gift, to do it. All the energy seeped out of Aaron's voice. "Why?"

"Heh." Darwin gurgled again. "I dunno. Just wanted to. Couldn't stop thinking about it."

"Aaron, do you make a habit of being rash?" asked Anna.

"Seems, aye." He gazed at the blood seeping out of Darwin's chest. "I shouldn't have involved her in this."

Darwin closed his eyes. "You just gonna watch me die?"

"Aye," said Aaron. "Something like that."

He leaned back and gurgled, waiting for death. Anna swiped at the back of Aaron's head. When he looked up at her, she tapped her temple. Aaron's heart stopped for the second time in ten minutes.

He seized Darwin by the shirt, two fists bunching up at the man's throat as he leaned over him. Lightheadedness crept over his head from an opening telepathic link. Deep within the man's brain lurked the telltale trace of a suggestive compulsion. The psionic adjustment looked recent, but Darwin had no memory of anyone who seemed a likely candidate for the implant. Aaron forced an image of Talis into Darwin's consciousness as bait, but it triggered nothing.

She must've wiped the memory. He shook with rage. Random bits of debris rattled in the distance.

Aaron lowered his fist. "Darwin, you were compelled. It wasn't you."

"Son of a bitch." He laughed up some blood. "I get it now. Why you drink so damn much."

"Hang on, mate." Aaron patted himself down, searching every corner of his suit until he found a single stimpak in the jacket's right pocket, clinking against Allison's nameplate. He held it up. "Here we are."

A soft whine escaped Shimmer.

"Aaron. She's still got surface thoughts. She's not dead." Anna gave him a light slap in the back of the head again. "I was talking about her. Didn't you think to look in her head before assuming she'd kicked it?"

The small, red autoinjector slipped out of his hand. Darwin's body shook as he forced one arm up and curled his fingers around the stimpak on his stomach. Aaron twisted on his knees to peer at the girl. Sure enough, she had weak surface thoughts; amid a fog of pain and lack of any desire to move, she believed she heard a faint male voice repeating her name. Real or imagined, her brother calling her was a bad sign.

"I've summoned a MedVan," muttered Anna.

Aaron didn't care a trauma team would come with police. Private citizens reporting gunshot wounds always triggered a Division 1 escort. He doubted Anna had a corporate gold or platinum service plan with Ancora Medical. They stopped asking questions at gold and would even help finish off your problem at platinum, if the risk wasn't too great.

Aaron grasped Darwin's hand, squeezing it into the stimpak. One thumb flicked the yellow safety cap off the metal end as he twisted it over to point at his friend's chest, and hesitated. Two rounds from a Class 5 handgun had left gaping wounds in his torso. A single stimpak seemed like putting a bandage on a missing arm. Still, it might buy time for the MedVan crew to save him.

He listened to Shimmer's brain again. Cory's beckoning voice had grown louder. Lost in a dream, she pictured foggy hedgerows full of flowers in the shape of a maze. She imagined herself twelve again, playing hide-and-seek with her brother.

Aaron stood. Darwin's hands slipped off his, and the stimpak.

"It's okay, man…" Darwin wheezed. "I'll hang on 'til the van gets here. Don't let the kid die. She's half my age."

Aaron hesitated. "Bullshit man, you've been shot. She took a beating."

"Yeah, been shot. Go on, man." Darwin coughed. "You're always savin' the girls."

"Aye, that's been working out *so* well for me." He snarled, looking back and forth between them for a second.

Shimmer convulsed.

"Do it," whispered Darwin.

"Fuck." Aaron rushed to her side, skidding to a halt on his knees and stabbing the autoinjector into her chest. He pushed down on it until the faint hiss ceased. After it fell silent, he dropped it and gathered her hand in his. "Come on, Lily…"

He trembled, though he couldn't tell if it came from the sight of Shimmer looking so dead or how close this felt to losing Allison. Once again, he found himself on his knees with a lifeless woman's hand in his own. Even if he didn't fire a gun that ended this girl's life, exposing her hiding place was just as lethal. Aaron looked up at Anna, a wordless ask of 'are they here yet?'

Out of the corner of his eye, he caught motion. Darwin's arm slid lifeless from his chest and flopped to the ground at his side.

"No." Aaron squeezed Shimmer's hand, gripped by the dread he'd wasted the stimpak. Finger-mark bruises covered her forearm.

Anna's boots clicked as she paced to the door, away from him.

"Come on, Lily!" he shouted before trying telepathy. *Lily! Come on out of that maze.*

Her surface thoughts had gone blank and dark. Darwin didn't appear to be breathing. He stroked the back of her hand.

"Anna, you should go. Don't be here when the police arrive."

She shot him a worried look. "I don't like that tone. You're not giving up?"

"I—"

A loud *crack* made him jump. The smell of ozone hung in the air, and one of the Syndicate thugs moaned.

Anna held up a sparking hand. "You dogsbodies stay right there. Next one won't tickle."

Strength filled the girl's hand; she squeezed his fingers and whispered, "Took you long enough."

"What?" He leaned over her, forcing her eyes open with his thumbs. "Did you just say something?"

Her breathing forced blood out of the corners of her mouth. "I said it took you long enough to find me. Next time, get here *before* I get my ass kicked."

A distant siren lofted apart from the din of advert jingles and hovercar traffic.

"I'm going to tell them you're psionic."

She forced a frown. "Please don't. I don't wanna get the process. Damn police are as corporate as everything else in this piece of shit city."

"Gee, thanks. I used to be one of those cops."

She rolled her eyes. "Okay, maybe there's some exceptions."

"It's this POS city or spears and loincloths in the Badlands." He patted her hand. "I think you like tech too much, but you'd look cute dressed as a tribal."

"Ow. Don't make me laugh."

A rush of dust blasted off the front wall and swirled in the door. Intense light flooded the lobby area backed by the roar of high-output ion thrusters. Shimmer's hand tightened around Aaron's. She trembled.

"Am I dead? Is... that... heaven?"

Dark figures moved in the blue-white light, creating long, creeping shadows in the floating dust. Two men and a woman in immaculate white armor bearing the logo of Ancora Medical entered behind a pair of Division 1 patrol officers. A deep woman's voice outside barked orders about perimeters and security. Aaron raised an eyebrow at the small laser pistols on the medic's belts, Starpoint Pulsar 2s. One step down from an E-86, but still more than a match for anything a medical response team might run into.

"No," said Aaron. "But they're as close to angels as you'll ever meet."

Five Division 1 officers approached; the outer edges of their deep blue armor tinted white in the glare from behind. The medics moved around the police officers. The woman paused by Darwin for all of four seconds before joining the other medic at Shimmer's side.

"You called me Lily," she whispered. "No one's called me that since..."

"Don't talk, hon." The medic pulled an amber visor down over his eyes, which lit up with a green grid and a horizontal outline of a body in various shades of red and blue. "Give us a little room, please."

Aaron backed up. *Lily, those Syndicate wankers might not stop. They'll think twice about comin' after you if you're with Zero. Organized criminals aren't the only ones who take revenge to the next level.*

"I... suppose they pay well," she whispered, right before passing out.

A blue armored glove settled on his shoulder, drawing his gaze up a beefy arm to a full-face helmet. Two square spots darkened in the mirrored silver, on either side of Aaron's warped reflection. No doubt the man inside ran his face through the system. The scanners would confirm he had no weapons or cybernetic implants.

"Give 'em some space, and let the medics work. What happened here?"

Aaron let the officer pull him upright and away. They swarmed on Shimmer, attaching tubes and wires connected to portable kits. The shorter man jogged out to retrieve a stretcher. More Division 1 officers came in, apparently summoned by his partner when he saw the pile of Syndicate thugs.

One of the cops looked around as if lost. "Gene, did you see someone behind me? I swore I just bumped into a person."

"Nothin' there man," said a woman to his left.

The cop escorting Aaron went rigid; armored gloves creaked around his compact rifle.

"Yes," said Aaron, sounding exasperated. *I'm Division 0. On an undercover mission. The whole fugitive thing is a cover.* He flashed the same smile that got him in bed with three women a few nights earlier. Whether or not Mikhail could make good on his offer, it couldn't hurt to run with it.

"Psionic," muttered the cop. "How—"

Aaron glanced at the man's nameplate. *Officer Diaz... Do you know I'm not making you think things? Easy. I'm not a suggestive. Check my file; I'm telekinetic with a dash of telepathy. If I was gaming you, I'd have left already. Of course, you understand why I can't talk about this aloud. It's a clandestine operation. Don't breathe a word of it to anyone. The brass would be happier if you leave me entirely out of your report. You blokes can take all the credit for saving this girl from the Syndicate.* He leaned to the right as they loaded Shimmer onto a floating stretcher. "Is she going to be all right?"

The lead medic stood almost a head taller than Aaron. Sympathetic brown eyes set in dark brown skin softened. His appearance seemed incomplete without belt-long dreads, but that probably defied Ancora's dress code. "Yeah. She'll be sore for a few days but no permanent damage. There's still some internal bleeding, but the stim shot slowed it down quite a bit."

Aaron smiled; the sudden lack of worry left him feeling tired.

Diaz poked the rifle into his side. "Give me one reason why I should believe that."

Aaron's used-hovercar-salesman smile felt mile-weary. *Verify it if you like with Regional Commander Kovalev. The operation was authorized right from his desk, over three layers of command. Oh, and, please make sure the girl meets with someone from Div 0. She's a psionic as well. I'd do it, but I'm tits deep in this undercover.*

"Uhh." The officer looked around, lowering his weapon. "Okay... so, what is this mess?"

Shimmer and her hover-gurney glided by, flanked on either side by the medics.

"Syndicate." Aaron gestured at the pile. "The girl's brother was one of you guys, Div 1. Officer Cory Braddon. He died a couple years ago when his cover was compromised. She's been giving 'em the business via the GlobeNet since."

"How's this related to your uhh..."

"I needed someone found. She's a deck jockey. Complete accident all this happened while she was helping me."

"What about him?" The cop nodded to Darwin.

"He's... Some poor fringer sod who got stuck in the wrong place at the wrong time. Whatever deal he had with these Syndicate chaps went sour. I got here right as they shot him in the back." Aaron stared at his former friend. His assessment wasn't an overt lie, but it felt like one.

Glimmering bands of light danced in the dust. The thrum of idling ion drives built into a roar before rushing away and up. Aaron continued staring at Darwin as the MedVan's engine noise faded to silence and took the brilliant light with it.

"Are you sure that's it?"

"Informant," whispered Aaron. "Syndicate killed him for leading me here. I feel bad for the guy."

"Yeah. Poor bastard. Come on."

The officer walked him to a row of idling blue and white Division 1 patrol craft. He paused, seemed to think for a few seconds, and turned back toward him. "I sure hope you're not fuckin' with me."

Aaron lacked the motivation to smile or crack wise. He stared through a blast hole in the wall, at about where Darwin's body lay under a sheet of white plastic. After a momentary pause, he shook his head in a faint gesture of 'no.'

"Best of luck." The cop patted him on the shoulder and trudged back inside.

Aaron squinted into the wind, trying to pick out the departing MedVan from the thousand spots of light in the sky over the shadowed city, drifting like embers above a black fire.

RECKONING

C ircuit fragments littered the floor between Aaron's feet. The optics Darwin had planted in the battered frictionless orb would send no more secrets out of the room. He'd found them tucked into one of the vectored thrust portals, almost in plain sight had he studied the orb with any care. Rats had made a nest of the gouge in the wall where the 'stone' had hit. His angry telekinetic lash-out should have destroyed the camera or at least knocked it loose.

It wasn't in there then. He tilted the tiny lens between thumb and index finger. *How did Talis know to target Darwin?*

He looked up at the dark blue curtains separating Darwin's sanctum from the rest of the apartment. He still hadn't gone inside. Staring at it for another hour wouldn't make the cloth part to reveal Darwin's half-awake smile. He smiled at the memory of a sleepy roommate stumbling in his boxers, scratching his ass on the way to the bathroom. Whatever the man had been, he didn't deserve the kind of end fate gave him.

Aaron loathed Talis.

The thought of her clenched his fists and made his arms shake. The hatred he felt for her had bled over to women in general. To him, all of them had been various degrees of Talis, sucking the life out of anything and everything they could for their own personal gain. Not Allison. She wasn't one of *them.* He slouched forward, cradling his head in both hands. Oppressive silence reinforced the truth of Darwin's lack of being. As annoying as he'd found the man so often, he'd become something of a best friend. Another month or two, and he'd have probably thought of the man more like a brother.

He'd expected the worst from Strawberry, but she wasn't one of *them* either. That poor girl only wanted to survive. Neither was Andrea. Like Darwin, she'd been a victim of circumstance. A convenient piece of bait victimized so the Syndicate could get to him. Another girl he'd gotten hurt. Shimmer... No, that wasn't his fault. She'd done that to herself clashing virtual sabers with organized crime ever since her brother died.

Aaron stomped on the camera bits, yelling random obscenities as he hopped about, plucking chips and bits of plastic from his bare foot.

Maybe the Syndicate's want to kill her wasn't his doing, but he had led them to her. Shimmer wasn't one of *them*. Nor was Anna. He pulled Allison's nameplate out of his pocket and held it up.

"Is this you? Have you been trying to tell me something?" He touched his forehead to the cold metal. "One horrible bint, not all of 'em."

He sat up, scowling at the cloth door. "Damn it all, Darwin. Why'd you have to choose *this* flat?"

"Are you seeing ghosts now too?" Anna's voice echoed in the outer hall.

Aaron twitched with the urge to hide the mood on his face, but wound up not bothering. She stepped over the wreckage of a former shelf cabinet he'd smashed hours ago upon waking.

"Rough morning?" She looked at it. "You got drunk last night?"

"No, that's the problem." He managed a weak smile, but her affect seemed cold.

"Aurora's got an idea where your bogie woman is. Archon wants this dealt with soon and you to stop mucking about."

"Right." He stood. "S'pose then I'll either be done with it or dead by tonight."

Anna's eyes hardened. "Don't do anything stupid. We need you."

"Did I do something wrong?" He reached for his suit. Boxers wouldn't be a great outfit to wear to a murder, but it would make for a good clip on the NewsNet. "You're a bit frigid today."

"We're wasting too much time with this." She faced away from him. "Hurry up."

"I got too close, didn't I?" He shrugged into his jacket. "You're right. You're Archon's girl. Sorry, luv. I can't turn it off."

"You conceited bastard." She whirled about, pointing. The soft smile on his face seemed to leech the vitriol from her glare. "It's... complicated."

He took the E-90 out of the drawer, shrugged into its shoulder harness, and positioned the weapon under his left arm. "I understand. I was trying to see Allison in you, and... it was wrong of me to step over that line."

Anna poked her boot at some debris. "You're different than James. You're both right arrogant bastards, but you don't take yourself quite as seriously. He's always busy."

"Well, you should tell him to get unbusy then." Aaron buttoned his jacket up as he walked over. "You're certainly worth it. Half the world's psionics can wait a tick."

She cut off a laugh. "We'll be late. Come on."

SECTOR 156 WAS SOUTH OF THE APPROXIMATE END OF FORMER CALIFORNIA. The great wall stopped a few miles away, leaving the rolling nothingness of the Badlands in plain sight, seventy-five meters below. To the south, the city plates ended in an uneven row, as though the builders decided one day to walk off the job and never return. One of the two ramps down gleamed in the sun, visible from where they stood at the edge, leading to the continuation of civilization at ground level. Few people wanted to live on the edge of the plates, especially without the protection of the wall. Ten miles of private airport as well as cheap storage space occupied a strip along the precipice.

Aaron felt nothing as he stared out over individual houses in the distance. Separate properties in the scrub brush stayed in the price range of the middle class due to the horrible heat, bugs, and inflated rumors of what crawled out from under the city after dark. His gaze settled on a large sprawling field of junk, arranged in six towering rows behind a one-story ranch house. A man in a red flannel shirt, jeans, and a cowboy hat carried a box to the bed of a large black pickup truck. Behind him, a young teenaged girl (also in a flannel shirt and jeans) with long brown hair repacked tools into a case. The pair seemed happy, even if they did work with junk.

Cold air swept over him. He took a step away from the edge, shivering from an unexpected patch of freezing air. Silvery fog billowed out of nowhere and coalesced into Aurora. When the sight of her nude figure did nothing for him, Aaron figured he'd reached the point of not giving fuck all about what happened to him. She seemed disappointed her bouncing boobs barely got a sideways glance.

"Lauren!" whisper-yelled Anna. "You're out in the street."

"I'm aware of that." Unconcerned, she winked at Aaron. "Your friend has got a compound set up out in the southeast. Far enough away to count as Badlands. No police. Seems like it used to be some kind of heavy factory. From the half-built hulls, I'd say they made Mars transport shuttles or some such thing there."

Anna took her shin-length coat off and draped it over Aurora from behind. "Even if you don't care, you'll attract attention."

"That is kind of the point, dear." Aurora didn't resist being covered. "She's got a handful of mercenaries, but they don't appear to be expecting trouble… at least not from the direction of the city. All their heavy weapons are set up facing east."

"Talis is there now?" asked Aaron.

Aurora peeled the coat off and handed it back to Anna. "Yes. Don't worry about me, hon. I'll find someone to wear once we get there."

She dissipated into fog, which swirled around Anna and seeped into her.

"Keep my hands to myself," said Anna.

"I wouldn't dream of doing anything naughty," said Anna.

Aaron rubbed the bridge of his nose. "I don't want to know."

THREE MILES FROM THE CITY, ANNA BROUGHT THEIR STOLEN COMPACT CAR to a halt. Its tiny, ten-inch tires coupled with the packed earth road had made the PubTran taxi's seats seem like paradise, even without the extra 'comfort enhancer.' A blast of hot, dry air rushed in as both side doors swung up and open, right angle flaps touched above the centerline. His first breath of rust-flavored dust made him cough. Anna took off her coat, wadded it up, and threw it into the car. Not a full minute outside, and already, her forehead glistened with sweat. Aaron ditched his suit jacket as well and pulled the first three buttons of his cobalt blue shirt open.

"I think we overdressed for this party."

"If you think I'm going starkers like Miss Freak, you're mistaken."

Aaron pushed the car door closed. "That was a neat trick with the car."

"Power switch is just an electric circuit. Little juice in the right place and it doesn't matter if it senses the right 'mini inside."

Aaron shielded his eyes with a hand, gazing at where a vast abandoned structure turned the near horizon from dirt brown to metallic. Swaths of darkness shifted behind the blur of heat haze, flecked with the occasional harsh glint of sun. Incomplete outlines of colony shuttles loomed over the place, tattered fragments of tarp and wire drifted from exposed frame struts. Hulking shapes creaked in the occasional breeze, sitting like a row of dinosaurs come to a tar pit to die. Rusting superstructure studded with long-broken construction arms surrounded their bloated forms. Aurora had misinterpreted their size; these ships would have carried people three thousand at a time to new homes on other planets.

"There." Anna pointed. "There's an old tram shaft that'll lead right into the place."

"I don't see it," said Anna.

"How can you not?" Her left arm waved until her right hand caught it by the wrist and forced it down. "It's right bloody there."

Aaron, whistling innocently, walked in the general direction indicated.

"Fine then," said Anna. "I'll go on ahead."

Frigid vapor seeped out of her, coalesced into a directional mass, and washed over him. Not an unpleasant sensation given the 106-degree heat. Alas, it didn't last long. Anna jogged to catch up, looking angry.

"Aurora kept rambling. This place's been shut down for at least three decades. Company got taken over, something about money."

Aaron surveyed the spread of decaying industry. "Isn't it always?"

"Cheaper to build in zero g."

They walked in silence for about fifteen minutes before a dancing, waving, and quite naked Aurora caught their eye up ahead. She stood on a patch of metal grate, near a circular tunnel large enough for a monorail. Tumbleweeds had built up in the opening, which moaned as the wind crossed it. As soon as they saw her, she dissipated into mist once more.

"She enjoys that entirely too much." Aaron stuffed shaking hands into his pockets. "I should've had a beer or six."

"Withdrawal?"

"Either that or nerves."

"Cats and dogs," muttered Anna.

Aaron laughed. "Random."

They picked their way among a mass of windblown debris, weeds, branches, trash, and a few wire bundles. Enough holes marred the ceiling to allow sunlight into the shaft, though it didn't do much for Aaron's concerns of a cave in. A two-foot wide rail ran down the centerline, dividing the walkable floor into two separate channels. Old grate panels set into concrete provided a flat surface above a rat's nest of wires and components. At least out of direct sunlight, the tunnel offered a cooler environment. Beetles as big as potatoes scurried out of their way.

Anna walked up ahead, voice echoing despite her whisper. "Cats and dogs living together. Total anarchy."

"You've been spending too much time around Aurora. You're starting to go loopy."

"Wembley 2411. All-star match. Do you remember Geer and Ainsley?"

"We're back to this again?" Aaron chuckled. "Geer did outscore him. You should be happy."

"Aye, but their team lost. Your man Ainsley spent more time interfering with Geer than playing."

"Why is it every time Manchester does poorly, we did something? Is it that unfathomable to consider the prospect that Manchester—or a Manchester player—is fully capable of playing like shite sometimes?"

Anna slowed enough for Aaron to catch up and walk in step on the other side of the rail. He peered up past some hanging vines, also dead, at the underside of a starship's nose end. Closer, it looked even more ruined. Rust had eaten its way out from the seams in its skin, more vines and weeds clung to pockets packed by windblown sand. A baritone laugh echoed off the metal plating, scaring away a few dark birds from superstructure far overhead.

Forty some odd yards later, Anna broke the uncomfortable silence. "Their team might've won if Ainsley wasn't cocking about. A Manchester player and an Arsenal player on the same side, and all he could do was interfere with him."

"Are you trying to say you expect me to cause problems?" He winked. "Besides, Ainsley wasn't interfering with Geer, he was just showboating."

"Speaking of showboating." Anna pointed forward.

Aaron peeled his gaze away from her, albeit reluctantly. The tunnel opened up about thirty yards ahead where a debris field outlined the former presence of a train platform. Not far from the end stood an armored six-wheeled A3V painted in military green. Next to it, a gleaming full-conversion cyborg. Aaron figured him for a Class 3. He was only seven feet tall, and the body attempted to follow the basic contours of an over-muscled human man rendered in gleaming chrome. Shrouds on both arms hinted at the presence of large sword-style blades, as if the giant assault rifle in its right hand wasn't deadly enough.

Two heads stuck out of the armored assault vehicle, one behind a twin 30mm cannon at the center point, the other emerged to the shoulders from a hatch by the front left corner. All three of them seemed focused on something occurring deeper in the compound.

"I suppose this is where we abandon stealth."

Anna stretched her arms and swiveled her head around. "Indeed. Please don't do something stupid."

"You don't have to come with me." The presence of the E-90 under his left arm filled him with dread. "I don't want to…"

"You won't." Anna glanced at him, ice in her eyes. "I'll put you on your ass before you shoot me."

Aaron grinned. "Manchester always does go for the injury play. You want the borg or the truck?"

"That's just something you wankers say when you lose." She advanced. "Borg."

BREAKING AND ENTERING

The A3V, officially known as the Agile Armored Assault Vehicle, was a semi-amphibious six-wheeled troop carrier weighing about sixteen tons or thereabout, depending on configuration. Prior to the advent of plastisteel, such a vehicle could've been thirty or more. This one lacked add-on modules such as anti-aircraft batteries, missile racks, or high-energy particle cannons. Despite everything he had seen in recent history, Aaron's confidence at being able to lift such a machine fell square in the realm of 'yeah right' as he took a wide stance. Two weeks before Allison died, he'd lost a bet in the squad room when he failed to hold a desk aloft for ten minutes. Sure, other telekinetics could shove cars around, but none of them could *type* with their power or fasten their boots—all five snaps at once. Subtlety had been the major reason he'd gotten away with his frictionless 'tweaking' so long. A scoundrel's grin formed.

None of them could open a bra from thirty meters away either.

He focused on the military truck's mass. The strain showed on his face right away. Six individual suspensions groaned as wheels went from supporting the thing to dangling from it. Aaron grunted, adding the useless gesture of lifting his arms as if they bore great weight. Foot by foot, the A3V glided upward at a pace suggesting it emerged from the muck of a bog. Shouting men inside spun about looking for some way to explain their flying, wheeled, brick.

As the bottom of the tires passed the nine-foot mark, the cyborg mercenary spotted him. Darkness in the tunnel couldn't conceal him or Anna from thermal scanners. The borg raised his rifle. Anna reached forward, clenched her fist, and drew her arm back toward her chest.

Headlights exploded in a shower of sparks. Lightning crackled and hissed, connecting the tip end of the A3V to the cyborg's back for less than a full second. His scream started human before it melted into digital scraps that sounded like high speed rotary saws grinding together. The distorted roar pitch-shifted down and stopped seconds later. The chrome body went rigid, shaking and convulsing on his feet.

Aaron coughed at the reek of burned electronics and pushed the vehicle higher while creeping forward out of the tunnel to keep it in view. Sparks crawled up and down the chrome figure; tiny threads of blue light buzzed and lapped at the ground. Anna jolted him again, this time with a smaller streamer of lightning from her outstretched hand.

The cyborg fell over backward, stiff as a statue.

On the A3V, the turret gunner opened up with the 30mm. Considering the elevation and the turret's inability to shoot down at such a harsh angle, the man's only motivation had to be making noise to summon aid.

With a heavy grunt, Aaron rolled the A3V over, upside down. Shouts came from the distance, but against the blasts from the heavy cannon, sounded indecipherable. One man slipped out of the center hatch, dangling and kicking. Distant clanks and tiny explosions rang out from wherever 30mm slugs struck one of the incomplete starship hulks. A great, groaning creak of metal preceded a heavy crash and a massive plume of dust off to the west.

Once he'd lifted the A3V some thirty feet off the ground, Aaron let go. After a hasty breath, all the strength he'd used to raise it shifted to downward force. Sixteen some odd tons of armored vehicle smashed into the ground, cutting off the endless machine-gunning with a deafening hollow *boom*. A wall of silt and concussion knocked Aaron and Anna on their backs and coated them with a thick layer of light brown. He found the dirt comfortable in the post-exertive euphoria that came with releasing such a burden from his mind.

"Well, that's subtle." Anna coughed. "Did you intend to drop that thing on the borg, or was that luck?"

He reached up and wiped clean smears in the dirt over his eyes. "Luv, I made a career out of putting metal things exactly where I wanted them to go."

She appeared to be in no hurry to stand either. "You realize you drove two goaltenders into the bottle, one to the looney bin, and one quit, believing himself incompetent."

Aaron sat up. "He played for Man U. He *was* incompetent."

A tiny spark hit him in the left ear, about as hard as a finger flick.

"Ow! Cripes, woman."

She zapped him again. "Don't call me 'woman.'"

"Right, bitch." He rubbed his ear.

Her hard face lasted only seconds before she cracked up laughing. "Not very fancy, is it?"

"I'm telekinetic. I pick things up and put them down."

Clouds of dust billowed off to the left in the breeze, revealing the blown-out shell of the upside-down A3V. Wobbling walls gave it the impression of a stepped-on synthbeer canister where the ends had popped off. Metal creaked. Anna sat up. Another metallic screech came from the hull, echoing out of what had become a huge resonance chamber. Aaron cringed at the sound.

"Aaron…" Anna scrambled to her feet. "So do cyborgs."

The nose-end of the smashed transport groaned upward. A pair of mauled corpses slid out the back, tumbling to a halt in the dirt mounding by the rear door. Aaron stared in disbelief at the roaring ruin that had once been a gleaming chrome cyborg. Skeletal plastisteel struts peeked out from split Myofiber bundles. Armor plates dangled on loose wires. Both of its eyes glowed red-orange, brighter with the lack of a faceplate. Human teeth rendered in metal lent it a menace that would linger in Aaron's nightmares for months to come. It heaved and groaned, shuddering as it struggled to lift the A3V off the ground. Whatever it attempted to say came out as a series of digitized warbles and white noise. Already damaged synthetic muscles frayed and snapped.

Anna stared at the A3V. Electrical arcs swarmed the outer hull, crawling toward the front and down the cyborg's arms. Aaron yanked its legs out from under it with a telekinetic pull at the same instant an intense white arc peeled away from the wreck, nailing it in the chest. The cyborg slapped into the ground on its back and burst into flames a split second before the A3V fell on it for the second time.

"That boy had to be a Manchester fan. Keeps trying even though he knows it's futile."

Anna drew in a breath to fire back, but wound up just giving him a sad look.

Aaron's mirth drained. He glanced to the right, in the direction of distant shouting. "Aye. I suppose that makes me a Man U fan after all. Come on, then. Let's get this over with."

He trudged down a huge road formed by clear space between rows of colossal construction stations. If enormous lumbering starships had wheels, they could've driven the route without touching the stacks of machinery and debris on either side. Aurora's information placed Talis in the command and control building at the southeast corner of the facility. Metal hulks groaned in the wind all around him. Anna looked up every few paces as if to say something, but changed her mind each time. After a hundred yards, the road ended at an empty berth. Spanning struts crisscrossed the upper reaches of the cavernous trench, bedecked with rotting automatic welders and lifters. Crude totemic fetishes hung by rope and wire in places, twice the size of a man, twisting in the wind.

A smaller walkway, only as wide as a two-lane highway, continued left from there, past a forest of pipes as thick as his torso connecting a globe-shaped tank to the metal ground. He ducked among them for cover from the source of several voices up ahead.

Nine figures, five men and four women, wearing piecemeal armor and modern clothing, stood in the open with vacant stares. All gaped at the sky as if the act of breathing had become the most fascinating thing in their world. Aaron levitated a rifle away from one of the women and brought it close enough to grab. She didn't react.

One by one, he disarmed the others, sending their weapons floating up to a catwalk ringing the top of the globe tank, well out of reach. After a moment's hesitation, he emerged from his hiding place and jogged past them. None paid him any mind.

Twenty meters and a right turn later, he glanced at Anna. "That was... eerie. What do you think she did to them?"

Anna looked away from him, studying the old machinery. "I'm not sure what she did to them. I'm not a suggestive. I've no idea how it works or what it's capable of."

"What about your boy, Archon?"

"Yes, he's quite skilled."

"How skilled?"

"Enough to make a snobby bitch of a doctor 'waste' her time on a povvy piece of street trash." She kicked a golf-ball sized hex nut rolling.

"Bitch didn't think I was worth her time since I was on the dole. He made her detox me and enjoy doing it."

"I see." Aaron stared at the back of her head for a moment, wondering how else Archon might've tinkered. What Mikhail said about the pyro repeated in his thoughts. His mind stalled with momentary paralysis at a conflict between seeking vengeance for a dead woman and rescuing a live one.

Someone fired at them from overhead, snapping him out of his mental quandary. Rifles protruded from the windows of an elevated walkway, forty feet up, spanning between two control stations of adjacent build-berths. At least six mercenaries angled to get shots. Two more popped up from behind a mass of scrap metal on the ground, one raised a pistol while the other clutched a small remote control in his hand.

Aaron's first instinct sent him running to the right for the nearest cover. He dove and slid on his side, skidding to a halt behind more pipes. Sparks and bell-like rings filled the air as Talis's personal army unloaded on him. Fortunately, the industrial construction consisted of plastisteel at least an inch thick. Incoming rounds pierced one side, but not the second; eerie whizzing spirals buzzed as the pipe trapped slugs.

He tucked himself up against the fattest one, fumbling with his purloined assault rifle, not used to a weapon that large, heavy, or ballistic. Anna seemed to have frozen in panic, standing out in the open without moving. By some miracle, not one of the mercenaries fired at her.

"Anna, get down!" he yelled.

She ignored him.

Screaming her name again, he dragged her off her feet and sent her flying into him. Without realizing it, he put an arm around her and rolled on top to shield her.

"Gah!" she yelled. "What the hell was that for?"

He hefted the rifle. "You were just standing out in—"

When the assault rifle fired, it knocked him flat on his back and into the open. He held on for dear life, triggering at the crosswalk without bothering to aim for a specific person. His 'fish in a barrel' technique caused the incoming attack to stall. Anna flipped over and crawled under a low, horizontal pipe. She propped herself up on one knee, releasing a series of lightning bolts at the two men on the ground.

The one with the pistol howled, but weathered the attack. His return fire made her dive, chest flat to the dirt.

"I was forcing them not to see me, twit."

Aaron shifted aim, still on his back, firing twice at the man shooting at her. He missed, but came close enough to make the guy duck. Amid a temporary reprieve from incoming bullets, he scrambled around to his knees and scurried up against the nearest protective metal tube.

"Damn, this suit is ruined." He clicked off another shot or two into the floor of the overhead walkway.

That time, someone screamed.

"Telepathic invisibility," she said. "I was fine."

"Oh." Aaron snapped off a shot at a moving shadow by the ground-level junk pile. "Maybe I just wanted to hold you then."

She laughed, sounding unaware of the truth in what he'd said. Aaron caught himself feeling drawn to her, and forced the emotion away. Fate had decided to be cruel all over again. Why bother trying to fool himself?

Too soon. Too dangerous. Too spoken for.

A *clank* rang off a nearby pipe right before Anna shrieked. Blood ran down the left side of her head. She hit the ground in a ball, shouting obscenities. Aaron leapt up, holding down the trigger at the guy she had electrocuted. The massive rifle overpowered him and bucked around wild until he used a little telekinesis to help hold it steady. At least three rounds hit the man in the chest, spraying the struts and narrow pipes behind him red. Blood seeped out of his mouth, and he slumped forward over the debris.

"Anna!" yelled Aaron.

"I'm fine." She pressed one hand into her head, in front of her left ear, pointing with her right at a gouge in the pipe. "Shrapnel graze. Shallow, but it hurts like a bastard."

He grabbed her arm and hauled her upright, eyeing the now-abandoned walkway. "Come on, we're clear."

"Where'd they go?" She muttered.

"No bloody idea." He knocked a few grimy windows out with brief telekinetic jabs to get a better view inside. "No one's in that tunnel now."

They moved out from the nest of pipes in the direction of the control house. Anna snarled and swung her arm out. Aaron looked toward her as a lightning arc connected her hand to a man hiding behind a mass of scrap metal on the opposite side, holding a little boxy device. Her left cheek glistened red from an inch-long cut between her ear and eye.

"Sons of bitches," shrieked Anna, as she added more power to the bolt.

Coppery ozone settled on Aaron's tongue as the aura of energy surrounding her intensified. Aaron cringed a step away and winced at the sight of the man at the wrong end of her lightning. Froth bubbled out of the man's mouth, his eyes burst into a spray of liquid, and the small device in his hand erupted in a shower of sparks.

No sooner did that happen than a series of eight tiny explosions went off overhead, rippling from one end of the walkway to the other. Aaron looked up as shrapnel and fire blew out from both ends of the crumbling observation platform. Stressed metal groaned in protest for a second; it came loose with an ear-splitting wail of rending plastisteel and fell straight toward them.

Anna stared at it like a deer in the face of oncoming traffic.

He screamed and gathered a telekinetic surge before slamming it into the oncoming mass. The falling corridor buckled and twisted; debris fell from both ends. Effort sent him to one knee. Plummeting slowed to gliding, then to hovering. The forty-meter long span stalled about twelve feet off the ground over them.

"Holy shit." Anna gasped, backing up. "Aaron..."

Six mercenaries, some bloody, some limping, came out of a concealed stairway among the machinery a short distance ahead and to the right. They jockeyed around pipes, rifles and pistols aimed. The sight of the flying wreckage stalled them in their tracks. Aaron's face burned. Blood thrummed within the veins in his forehead; spittle seeped from his lips. Blur crept into the periphery of his vision, darkening to black. The tunnel narrowed. *I gotta ditch this bastarding thing before it falls on us. I can't hold it... much... longer.*

Aaron snarled, shoving his arms forward as he launched the massive length of scrap, halfheartedly aiming for the mercenaries. The groaning mass smashed into the tangle of struts and pipes, shredding plastisteel like paper. Dust and fragments flew everywhere. If any of the mercs screamed, no one could have heard it over the horrid screeching of metal.

He sagged to his knees and went forward onto all fours, panting, dizzy.

"Aaron..." Anna patted him on the back. "Are you okay?"

"Touch of a migraine, luv."

She squatted, rubbing his back. "I... I don't think Archon could've even caught that thing."

Aaron laughed out a tendril of blood and spittle. "Didn't he say he 'dabbled' at TK?"

"He's got a right odd definition of 'dabble.'"

"Anna?" He sat back on his heels. Any hope of preserving his suit was long gone. "Do me a favor?"

She nodded.

"If we see another man with a detonator, please don't throw lightning at him."

Her eyebrows scrunched together. "Sorry... startle reaction. Didn't rightly think."

He pulled his pink silk handkerchief out of his breast pocket and dabbed at her wound. "We should've brought a couple of stimpaks, shouldn't we?"

"I wasn't expecting this chaff to be much of an issue." She cringed each time he touched her cut.

"I've saved your life twice."

She narrowed her eyes. "Still not getting into my knickers. Call it even for ruining my life while you cheated. So many miserable afternoons."

"Hey, lookie what I found," said a baritone voice behind them.

They whirled. The deep pitch sounded nothing like what anyone would have expected from the figure standing there. A scrawny man with a thick black beard and a green military soft cap bearing silver captain's bars held a shiny white rifle up to them, sideways as if to show it off. Under a loose, open camouflage shirt, a black tee bore an image of Mars with a middle finger over it. Fatigue pants and boots said ex-military, though his utter lack of muscle tone proved otherwise.

"This was the best I could find," said the man, with a trace of a British accent. "I've never played with a laser rifle before. Starpoint too, someone's got credits to burn. Should be fun."

Anna and Aaron exchanged glances.

"Aurora." They spoke simultaneously.

"See, now you're getting good at this," chirped the man before adding a giggle that made Aaron's skin crawl. "Oh, here, luv." He tossed Anna a stimpak from a belt case.

Aurora, wearing the mercenary, took point, leading the way to the edge of a deep pit used to test the hull integrity of new ship chassis with water. Only the last ten of the sixty-meter deep hole still held liquid. Whatever substance lined the bottom of the chamber could no longer be termed water in any sense of the word. Its color varied from seaweed to loam and clusters of trash and possible biological matter drifted about. The dead snakes and rats didn't do much for the fragrance. Even from fifty meters above, it stank.

Aurora fired over it at a few straggling mercenaries rushing along grated walkways, sending bright green streaks across the chasm. In the waning daylight, they lingered for a few seconds as retina burn. Molten plastisteel sprayed out of her misses, glowing orange beads sizzled on the sand. Of course, the stark visibility of her weapon drew return fire like moths to a candle. The Captain took a ricochet to the shin and fell. He, rather she, laughed as though playing with a laser rifle was the highlight of the decade.

"That way," he said. "Go past the tank and round to the right through the engine test vent. It leads right to the observation deck of the control house."

"Just leave you here?" asked Aaron.

"Oh, I'll be fine. I haven't been killed in a couple of weeks." Her next shot caught a running man in the chin, splitting his head in half and lighting it on fire. He dropped without screaming. "Now I've got the hang of this thing… don't have to lead targets. It goes wherever I point."

"You need help," muttered Anna.

"No, I think I can hold them back." She fired again, the laser slicing a pipe with only a mild delay in penetration. An armored, muscular woman hit the ground screaming with half an arm and a face full of molten metal.

"Not that kind of help." Anna pulled on Aaron. "Come on."

⟡ ⚔ ⊞ ◔ ☯

AARON STEPPED OFF THE NARROW LADDER ONTO A RUSTY METAL SURFACE, and reached for Anna, though she ignored his offer of assistance. They had climbed down into an engine test bed, a two-hundred-meter-long trench, ten deep, that ended with a curve intended to direct exhaust forces into the sky. Down here, they had protection from crossfire. An elevated observation bay overlooked the pad at the far end where the ship undergoing testing would've been. All of the windows were broken, creating a strip of twinkling glass on an overhang. Aaron thought it resembled the head of a giant robot embedded in the ground.

Small lizards scurried out of their way as they moved at a jog along the trench. Scorch marks on the metal walls varied from blue to purple in bands, progressively blackening as they got closer. At the approximate halfway point of their journey, a dark-skinned woman with straw-blonde dreadlocks appeared in the window. She raised a long, scoped rifle in their direction. Aaron stared at her, shaking. She had the bearing of African royalty, high cheekbones and an imperious set to her brow. Distance muddled her features, but Aaron didn't need to see her up close to know the shape of every pore on her too-perfect face.

Talis.

If not for every fiber of his being yearning to grind her into salsa, he would have regarded her as gorgeous. Too pretty; she probably spent a lot of time in Reinventions. She flashed a mocking smile and yelled something, which from a hundred meters away sounded like a simple bark. From a ground-level door, a small army of security bots emerged: five on treads, two orbs, and three walkers.

Aaron didn't bother looking for cover, since the metal trench offered none until the ship pad at least ninety meters away. A telekinetic yank ripped the rifle out of Talis's grip. Aaron frowned, disappointed the gun-turned-missile hadn't torn anything off her. For a brief second, the whites of her eyes appeared distinct, and she dove below the level of the windows. She knew he had to see her to pull her out of the window. A rush of anger dulled his wit; he felt stupid for targeting only her rifle. That error twisted around and became her fault too.

He slowed the sniper rifle enough to catch and took aim at the advancing robots.

"A gun, Aaron? That's rather pedestrian."

His first shot detonated the head of one of the walkers. A shower of orange sparks spewed like a sparkler from the neck as the rigid body fell over.

"It's effective, isn't it?" He shot the second walker in the chest, staggering it. It and the third walker both opened fire with assault rifles. Clicks and pings echoed all around them. A second round from the sniper rifle blasted it apart. "I'm saving my energy for the bitch."

Anna ducked the whisper of bullets passing overhead. "I'll get the orbs; you'll never hit them without cheating."

He let out a dark chuckle.

Tracked bots whined as they pushed themselves up to full speed, about twenty miles per hour. Anna waited for the much faster hovering orbs to get closer. Their size limited them to using pistol-sized weapons, which gave them a close engagement range. Orb bots relied on extreme maneuverability as well as their smallness for survival. Gangbangers and even most seasoned soldiers often ran from them rather than waste ammo trying to hit such a tiny, evasive target.

Anna smiled. To her, they were metal wrapped around power cores. What she had up her sleeve for them couldn't miss.

Aaron sighted on the third walker, lining up the space between its optical sensors before pulling the trigger. Despite his inexperience, a scoped rifle at a mere hundred meters made accuracy trivial. Fortunately, the automatic targeting system adjusted itself to compensate for range, so Aaron's lack of knowledge regarding windage and bullet arc meant nothing.

The walker's head unit bent backward, crushed as if sledgehammered. It dropped its rifle and flailed about.

Flickering light flared in the dim trench. A brilliant electrical arc lapped from orb to orb. Azure flames belched from the gun port of the one on the left as its magazine went off. It exploded, causing a legion of dust scuffs on ground and wall where bullets and bits of shrapnel ricocheted. Its companion fell with a resonant *clang*. The inert ball of metal rolled past them, still moving about forty miles per hour.

Aaron's final two bullets hit the front end of the leading tank bot, appearing to do little more than make it stop driving. However, when it remained still, he wrote it off as destroyed without fanfare.

One by one, Aaron seized the remaining four tracked bots with telekinesis and heaved them up and out of the trench. Two opened fire; bright blue muzzle flare spinning about, setting off a fusillade of pings and clanks overhead and spraying him with a few stinging pieces of micro-shrapnel before it tumbled out of sight.

Anna squinted at the sky, looking down after the last distant smash. "Well, I think you broke her toys."

Aaron stormed forward, focused only on the knowledge *the bitch* was in the building up ahead. Anna had to jog to keep up with his stride.

"Don't do anything rash," she said.

He walked on.

"I mean it, Aaron. Please don't do anything stupid."

Enough gap between the engine mounting pad and the trench bottom existed for him to walk under it without ducking. A grid pattern of light bathed the area from the lattice overhead. He coughed, his nose balking at the overwhelming reek of chemicals. Nothing appeared wet. The metal itself exuded the stench of fuels that had been tested here. It couldn't have been healthy to inhale; he imagined a year off his life with each breath.

Aaron didn't care.

He stopped in the shadow of the observation deck by a plain metal door decorated with bands of rust. The knob refused to turn, and the control panel beside it had likely been dark for years. Aaron backed up two steps, glaring at the shattered windows. The deformed walker bot clattered into the wall a few meters behind him and fell over. Anna finished it off with an electrical discharge, which passed over it, spider-crawling up the metal tunnel wall.

Aaron faced Anna; his murderous glare softened to a feeling of protectiveness. He looked again to the broken windows and latched a telekinetic feeler onto the ledge.

After giving her a brief, concerned look, a trivial effort launched him airborne and through the window, leaving her outside by a locked door.

CAT AND MOUSE

Aaron didn't expect Talis to be in the observation room, but he still spent a minute throwing desks around while ignoring Anna calling him a reckless bastard from outside. Workstations sat in two rows, facing the window. Panels of test equipment lined the side and rear wall, except for where two enormous holo-panel projectors were mounted. From the size of the room, he imagined at least a crew of twenty involved in testing the engines. Aside from the smashed windows, the room had three doors. The one in the left corner went to a bathroom, the right corner to a break room. An access panel by the remaining exit, a sliding set of double armored doors, looked to have been shot out.

He laughed at a pair of rifle magazines, loaded with twelve rounds each, lying abandoned on a desk. *Hope that bitch was pissed she didn't get to use them on me.* Aaron squinted. *How did she know to set up here?*

Anna's angry screams grew faint as he made his way into the corridor. Datapads and old coffee cups littered the floor amid tipped carts laden with tech parts. His shoes crunched with silica grit, buildup from years of open windows swallowing sand. The place sounded, and felt, deserted. He bypassed meeting rooms, labs, and offices, trying to estimate the most open path a fleeing psychopathic bitch would have taken wherever the floor had no dirt with footprints.

His route led him to a non-working elevator. A woman's handprint broke the dust on the stairwell door to its left. One kick opened it, and he quickened his pace on the way down. Four stories of switchback steps brought him to ground level and into a room resembling the waiting area of a starport. Three banks of chairs faced a physical display screen as big as a billboard. Were it not cracked, it might've been worth money as a historical relic.

Mercenaries lay scattered about, eight women and two men. All had the same vacant stare as the ones outside. None reacted to his presence. Aaron stepped over them, collecting three handguns, which he tucked into his belt, and another assault rifle.

A door to his right flew open. He swiveled and squeezed the trigger, but the weapon buzzed, safety on.

"Sweet shit!" screamed Anna; she looked ready to kill him.

"Go outside." He pushed the door closed with telekinesis.

"I'm not leaving you alone in here." She slammed herself against the stuck door twice, popping it open again. "What if she influences you all over again?"

He was grateful for the anger in her heart at that moment. Worry, or something else, would've made her eyes look too much like Allison's. "That's exactly what I'm afraid of."

She trotted over, rage fading to concerned hesitance. "Oh, Aaron... You think she'll..."

"Go outside." He pulled away from her, stomping in the direction of a large hospital-white hallway. "She's going to try. She can't command me to do anything now... I think." He stopped, looking at her. "But if she tries, I won't be able to control what happens."

"What about telempathic influence? She could make you calm and placid. Will changing your emotions set you off?"

He stiff-armed a flapping door out of his way. Debris jammed the corridor on the other side; broken lights spat the occasional spark or weak flickering element where a scrap of LED remained intact. Unseen rats scurried and scratched. A scrap of black fabric on a protruding metal chair leg spurred him onward.

"I don't know. I missed my second appointment with the medics for an evaluation."

"Don't be a twat." She followed. "I'm serious."

"I think she's mind wiping her former servants so the department can't mine them for intelligence."

Anna gulped. "You never said she was a mind blaster."

"I only skimmed her resume."

"Twat." She slapped him on the shoulder.

A surprise flange from a twisted shelf stabbed him in the thigh when he walked into it. He yelped and jumped back, hand clamped on the cut. In a fit of rage, he sent a wave of telekinetic force down the hallway, crushing the junk into, and sometimes through, the wall.

With a growl, he seized a desk less than thirty feet away and launched it straight up. Talis looked up from where she had been hiding behind it, exposed without cover in a patch of sunlight from the hole he'd made in the roof two stories above. Her cockiness had gone out to lunch. She looked like the victim of a slasher vid come face to face with the supernatural creature hunting her.

Before she could get on her feet, Aaron wrapped telekinetic force around her, crushing.

"*No!*" She yelled. "*Put me down!*"

The psionic suggestion smashed into his forebrain with the weight of a load of bricks. Reality melted away to a chaotic swirl of energy. Psionic force tore at his mind, a sensation like hands pulling at a jelly mold. When awareness returned, he gazed at parting clouds of mist. An attempt to take a breath resulted in coughing. He moaned, putting a hand on his face. *Something's wrong. I shouldn't be conscious this soon. I don't feel hung—ouch.*

His back burned. A line of pain crossed from the base of his left ribcage to his right shoulder, as though someone had whipped him with a red-hot steel cable.

"Oh, that's mildly unpleasant."

The ceiling wobbled. When it happened a second time, he realized Anna stood over him, kicking him in the side. Her lip appeared somewhat swollen and blood trickled out of her nose.

"Did you just kick me?"

She did it again.

"What's that for?"

"You flung me into the bloody wall." She fumed for a moment, but calmed. "I know it wasn't on purpose, but I tend to react to pain with violence."

"You zapped me, didn't you?" Aaron's scabbing back peeled away from the metal ground as he sat up. Whatever other witticism he intended to bestow upon her emerged as a piteous squeal.

"Stopped your rampage, didn't it?" She pushed a stimpak into his shoulder. "A brain's all electrical energy dancing around... Guess I hit the reset button."

Agony became mild pain for a second before turning into maddening itches. A mental image of tiny crab-like nanobots crawling all over his back didn't help.

"Got a few extras from Aurora. You did slam Talis into the wall, but she got up."

Aaron snarled and scrambled to his feet before stomping forward. Anna's pleas for him to slow down echoed off walls pockmarked by debris. His brief eruption leveled most of the hallway, opening paths into numerous conference rooms and a section that looked like a cafeteria. Thick, white dust hung in the air like fog, glowing in halos around flickering LED light tubes dangling from wires amid mangled frames. The haze obscured vision much past about fifteen feet.

He followed the corridor to the right at an L, surprising a muscular Asian man in body armor. Aaron had the drop on him, though Talis watched around the corner at the end of the stretch of hall. As soon as she saw Aaron, she darted out of sight.

The man stared at Aaron's rifle, raising his hands. "I ain't got no idea what the hell I'm even doing here, chief."

Aaron disregarded him, intent on pursuing Talis, leaving the mercenary to figure things out on his own. He sprinted toward the sound of a slamming door, running away from Anna's yelling.

"Stop! I don't trust it. She's leading you."

Through a small window in a pair of red free-swinging doors, he caught a glimpse of a wave of thin, hay-colored dreadlocks. This close, nothing would stop him short of Allison herself stepping out from beyond the veil.

"Talis!" he screamed, slamming the doors open and leaving his arms outstretched to either side as they flapped closed behind him.

His shout echoed over itself into infinity, coming back to him from the walls of a cavernous space. Large metal constructs, long, cylindrical, and shrouded in an intricate tangle of pipes and wires, hung in a massive chamber with a three-story ceiling. Suspended in a grid, the enormous machines formed a forest of abandoned technology with thousands of hiding places. Chemical seep oozed from between panels and from ruptured hoses. Flared cones near the bottom suggested they might be starship engines. Regardless, they sat here too long to be of any use, dangling like colossal pigs in a slaughterhouse. Echoing footsteps called to him from the other end, splashing. He advanced among the engine carcasses, using them for cover like trees, a soldier stalking his prey across a manmade jungle.

Anna crept along behind him, staying two pillars back. Talis whimpered somewhere up ahead.

"I'm not buying it, bitch," said Aaron, surprising himself by not shouting. "You're not the weepy type."

He moved to the next engine, swinging his rifle back and forth. Nothing. His next rush put his back against a hanging titan hard enough to make it sway a little. At a *creak*, Aaron glanced up past the jumbled mass of pipes and wires along thirty feet of rotting engine. He couldn't see the immense chains holding it aloft, and hoped they didn't pick that moment to give out after however many decades they'd been abandoned here. He aimed down all possible paths, finding each one empty. Wind howled from overhead vents, throwing the room into a disorienting clamor of shifting machinery and clanging metal.

I don't like this. Anna's voice pierced the din, straight into his mind.

Banging from ahead sounded like a fist on a disobedient door. The desperate pounding of a helpless woman running away from a monster. *Too helpless.* Aaron's doubt popped like a soap bubble. This wasn't a trap; she'd seen the start of what would happen if she tried to invade his mind. Anna had saved her life. Aaron had become the monster of Talis' worst nightmare—an off-the-chart telekinetic immune to her best ability.

She's not acting. Anna reacted to people being terrified of her with shame. For Aaron, Talis being terrified of him caused a flood of vindication. He reveled in it.

I am a monster, you bitch, and I'm coming for you.

He threw caution to the wind and lunged out from behind the chemical-bleeding machinery into a 'corridor' formed by rows of swaying engines. Frantic banging echoed in the distance, rhythmic, and mesmerizing, each hit echoed back once in the cavernous room. Aaron moved up to a jog, ducking the occasional damaged component or windblown sway. Fluorescent green liquid splashed underfoot where numerous collected puddles merged into a toxic lake. Fluid reached less than an inch deep, but meant the loss of another pair of shoes. Aaron didn't care if he had to pull an Aurora. He'd walk naked through the entirety of West City to have this moment.

The end of the corridor led to an open space between the last row and a dingy concrete wall covered with a layer of blackening over three quarters of its height. Stains ended at the approximate level of the curved nacelles atop each engine. Imagining the amount of liquid necessary to fill this chamber enough to dip starship engines in made him feel small on an atomic level.

Talis flailed at a door in the periphery of his vision, a blur of motion that made him smile. He opened his coat as casually as if going for a Nicohaler, and took out his E-90. He studied his face in the mirror-like surface of the department-issued energy pistol and wiped a dark smudge from his cheek.

Aaron pivoted on his heel and walked closer to the pathetic figure cowering against a twenty-foot square blast door. She gave up slapping on the access panel and stared at him, flattening her back against the wall.

The E-90 beeped when his fingertip touched the trigger, indicating it accepted his fingerprint.

He smiled. "Hello, Talis. I've been looking all over for you."

A SUGGESTION OF DOUBT

Aaron held the pistol tilted forward, using the round portion of the ring-dot sight to frame Talis's wide-eyed face. It bothered him how timid she acted; he'd spent months tracking a haughty, arrogant, soulless bitch. With each passing week, the enigma that was Talis grew from a woman to a creature from the deepest Abyss. A demon in female form. Unstoppable, fearsome, inhuman, and cruel. The person cowering in front of him seemed none of those. Perhaps she knew he had once been a softie and hoped to exploit him yet again.

Alas for her, she had killed that Aaron.

"Wait. We can talk about this," she whispered, raising a hand as if it would stop his laser.

'Just-joined-the-force' Aaron would've looked for any option to avoid hurting a woman. That man would've personally driven Strawberry to a shelter. His former self would have dragged Andrea to a social services office kicking and screaming. Pre-Talis Aaron would've worried and pestered Shimmer until she agreed to come to the dorms.

Aaron lifted the pistol to aim. The glowing blue dot on the front post sight rose into the ring, covering her face.

"The last time you talked, I killed my wife."

Anna emerged from the hanging maze; echoes of her boots on the metal floor clicked back across the cavernous chamber as she ran up alongside him. She gave him a wary look and glanced at Talis.

"I had no idea she was your wife," yelled Talis. "I swear. I just saw two cops."

"This is the same weapon that took Allie." Aaron shifted his focus; the gun blurred, Talis became clear. "Goodbye."

A deep resonant thud came from the blast door, and it rumbled downward into the floor. Talis made no move to go for it, pinned to the wall by fear of the laser pistol aimed at her face. Telekinetic force pushed Aaron's hand aside an instant before he fired. A streak of azure light traced a glowing squiggle in the wall inches from her head, hazed by a puff of smoke.

"Aaron, one moment, please," said Archon, as he stepped over the top of the descending door.

Wind from behind lofted his shoulder-length chestnut hair and set his white and blue ascot aflutter. He had the same tweed coat as he wore last time they'd met.

Talis shifted, grinning at Archon like long lost family.

"One moment?" yelled Aaron. "This bitch killed Allison!"

He screamed with rage, flinging Talis into the air before launching her across the room. Her shriek became an unladylike belch as he accelerated her into a blur. Opposing force slammed into Aaron's mind. She went from a streak of color to a hanging body in the blink of an eye and retched. Aaron growled and reversed the direction of his push, lining it up with the opposing energy so they combined. Again, Talis streaked into a backward blur, leaving a trail of vomit in the air. Archon broke out in a copious sweat, the red of exertion shone clear on his face.

Opposing forces equalized. Rather than explode like a water balloon on impact, Talis slowed enough to suffer only a sprained arm when she struck the thermacrete wall.

"Aaron, you must calm down." Archon raised a hand, keeping it up until the telekinetic war ceased. "My word, you are powerful. Then again"—he offered a wan smile—"I am but a mere dabbler at telekinetics."

"Why the fuck are you protecting her?" Spittle flew from Aaron's teeth as he panted.

Archon raised both eyebrows. "You have your revenge now, my boy. There is no need to slay the woman."

"Oh, there is every need to." Aaron raised the E-90 again, triggering another telekinetic back and forth.

Talis screamed and slid to the floor, ducking the random laser blasts hitting the wall on all sides of her.

"Anna, would you please de-charge that thing?" said Archon, sounding beleaguered.

Anna looked at Aaron. Red faced, he stared, daring her to do it. She looked down.

"She's Awakened," said Anna. "How else do you think she was able to force you to kill your wife past your emotional bond?"

Aaron coughed as though he'd been kicked in the stomach. "W-what? You're trying to recruit the bitch that killed Allison?"

"Listen to reason, Aaron." Archon gestured toward him. "If you kill her, your little 'revenge quest' is done and at an end. You would have little left but a hollow shell of a past life forever to lament." He sauntered closer. "Look at how she's cowering, weeping, begging... Do you think Allison would approve of slaying a helpless girl?"

"I'm pretty sure I'd feel rather happy for a few days at least." Aaron locked eyes with Talis. At the first sign of any manner of an 'I win' look, all bets would be off.

Archon held his hand out, beckoning Talis into a one-armed hug. He patted her on the shoulder. "I've made a few adjustments to our friend here."

Aaron glared; for once, he didn't mind his little 'backlash' problem.

A nervous smile danced across Archon's lips, twitching his goatee. "Would not you find it more fitting for her to remain alive as a loyal underling? She is one of us, Aaron. She is *Awakened*."

"I'm going to put her to sleep." He raised the gun.

Archon's eyebrows flared, his glance shot to Anna.

Anna put a hand on Aaron's arm. "Listen to him, please."

He met her pleading stare. Was she making her eyes look like Allison's on purpose, or did he only imagine it? Anna tugged his arm down. Her smile at least seemed genuine. *Fear. She's afraid of Archon... or is she afraid of me?*

Aaron lowered his arm.

"Surely, you can see the benefit her talents can bring to our organization. The Awakened are too rare to squander the life of one, even if she did cause you great suffering. Think about how she was, Aaron." He turned a dour frown on Talis. "How do you imagine she feels now?"

"Like she's getting away with murder." Aaron snarled.

"On the contrary. People like her cannot stand not being in control. They adore having power and using that power over others." He pulled a finger across her jawline. "Is that not right, dear?"

Talis gazed at the floor with a demure posture.

Aaron grumbled. "She's going to betray you as soon as she can."

"I rather doubt that." A sweet smile pursed Archon's lips as he caressed her cheek. "Since you did force the man to kill his dear wife, I do think you should apologize."

"I…" Talis shook where she stood and dropped to her knees. A second later, she burst into tears, wailing as though she had been the one forced to kill someone dear to them. "I'm so sorry, Aaron." She sobbed. "I had no idea your partner was your wife. I just saw two cops."

Talis continued blubbering and wailing, begging Aaron to forgive him as she crawled forward and clasped her arms around his legs.

Anna couldn't watch.

Aaron let his finger off the E-90's trigger. *This isn't right. Even Talis would have preferred I kill her to this.*

Archon gestured at Talis. Her wailing faded to sniffling and post-crying staccato breath that made her sound like a little girl with a skinned knee. Aaron couldn't reconcile the proud, arrogant creature he'd so despised for months with the sad wretch in front of him now. He still wanted to kill her, but couldn't escape the thought even Allison would ask him not to.

"She did not seek to harm you personally," said Archon. "She saw two police officers. Departmental policy is not to allow close relatives to serve together, is it not? How could she have known?"

Aaron scowled. Guilt shifted from Talis to himself for insisting—no, begging—Captain Torres to allow them to ride together. If he had obeyed the rules, Allison would still be alive. He would have killed some other poor slob, and who knows what would have happened to his career, but it wouldn't be as bad as now. The emotional scar wouldn't have been anywhere near as deep; he wouldn't have awakened, and he wouldn't be caught up in *this* mess.

He slouched. Anna squeezed his arm. Defeat saturated his very being, though she looked closer to tears than he felt.

"Now that this unpleasantness has abated, shall we call it an evening?" Archon's placating smile still held a trace of unease when he looked at Aaron. "We have much to accomplish. Are you ready?"

Aaron's glare bored into Talis, who knelt before him like a conquered peasant, the embodiment of meekness. No trace of victory lurked in her face.

"I'll need a moment to think about it."

MISPLACED

T he sudden presence of electronic music made Anna jump. Archon rolled his eyes and let off a belabored sigh. He raised a delaying finger and paced a few meters off to the left with his NetMini held to the side of his head in sound-only mode. Talis crawled away from Aaron and got to her feet, staring at the ground.

Aaron put a hand on top of Anna's. "What was that look before?"

She gazed into the rippling green puddle around her boots. "They didn't believe you because they couldn't look into your mind. I'm sorry, Aaron." Her expression became brittle. "I know what it's like to have friends turn on you."

"Missing? What do you mean missing?" Archon raised his voice. "The bloody thing is over a mile long."

Aaron squinted at him. "Oh?"

Anna fidgeted. "Some of my friends thought me dangerous. Didn't want me around, thinkin' I'd bring the CSB down on them. I'd told them I was psionic weeks before, and it didn't bother them."

He glanced at Talis, still with her hands clasped in front of her and eyes downcast. She had the posture of a scolded schoolgirl. *Aye, funny thing that.*

"You do not just 'misplace' corporate samurai or enormous military starships!" yelled Archon. A moment of angry shuddering ended with fingertips pressed to his temples. "Tell Lauren to find him."

Anna's longing glare peeled away from his. She walked over to Archon and placed a comforting hand on his shoulder. He mumbled into the NetMini a moment longer. When he snapped his arm down, he turned toward her with a basic smile and they shared a dispassionate kiss. Her eyes brimmed with worry and sadness.

Archon kissed her again, with no more intensity than the first time, and patted her on the back. "Come on, luv. There's been a complication. Mamoru's gone missing."

He strode into the hallway beyond the blast door, with Talis following. Her demureness had faded; she strutted at his side as though she owned the world. Aaron narrowed his eyes. *There you are. Some of you's still alive in there.*

Anna's sad face lessened when she made eye contact with Aaron. "Coming?"

"Anna…" Aaron trotted up to her, lowering his voice to a whisper. "I'm starting to get a bit worried about you."

"Me? You're worried about *me*? I'm not the one with suicidal visions of revenge." Her tone came off accusatory, though her grin took the sting from it.

"You said you've had friends turn on you. Do you think they might've been influenced?"

"Influenced?" She blinked. "Who would bother?"

Aaron nodded in the direction of Archon. "He completely reprogrammed that bitch. This isn't the same woman I've been after. I don't even recognize her."

"You…" Anna's face flushed. "You're saying he's…"

He leaned close enough to kiss her cheek, whispering, "I saw that kiss. He looked like an irritated executive making nice with a wife he's cheating on."

She fumed, though her eyes welled with tears. "He's busy, Aaron. That's what it is. He's busy, and he's gotten bad news. Someone's stolen the Angel."

"The little girl?" Aaron raised an eyebrow.

"No, twat. Not a metaphorical angel, a starship *named* Angel." She jabbed him in the chest with her finger. "James found me in the gutters of London and saved my life. I've no reason whatsoever to believe he's done anything to me other than help, and I'll not tolerate another word to the contrary. Besides, what would it have accomplished?"

Rage simmered in her sapphire eyes, tempered with doubt. At any second, she looked as if she could burst into sobs or go off on a lightning-tossing bender. He suppressed the urge to reach up and caress her cheek. Forty some yards away, Talis waved to them from the side of a sleek, luxury hovercar, beckoning them to follow.

He narrowed his eyes at Archon's back. "What could he have done, indeed."

Anna gave him a light shove in the gut. "You're turning into a paranoid bastard, Aaron. James is on our side. I owe him everything I have, and I *do* love him… even if he is a bit of a twit sometimes."

"Are you sure you're all right? You've got such a sad look."

Anna looked down. "Not you too."

"Me too?"

"Althea said the same thing; said I was 'sad inside.'" She clenched her fists.

"The girl is an empath, no?" Aaron tried to summon a smile but couldn't find it. "She would know."

"I had a shitty childhood. Of course I'm not well adjusted."

She walked off toward the car, boots echoing in the hollow space like the ticking of some great clock counting down.

Aaron thumbed Allison's nameplate. *Still cold.*

"Are you with us?" she asked, without looking back.

With us or against us, aye? Aaron thought back to his meeting with Mikhail. Anna paused halfway to the car to smirk at him. A momentary glance flitted between her and Talis, settling on Archon as he climbed into the driver's seat. Anna looked angry, wounded, and pleading all at once. A feeling he had not let in for months clutched his heart. The dread glimmering at the edges of her eyes lessened as he moved toward her.

Aaron jogged up to her side. "You're right. Division Zero can't be trusted. When they figure out they can't contain me, I'll either wind up dead or in a plain white box. I'm on board. Where do I sign?"

She let out a breath she'd been holding, allowing a flimsy smile. "We've got all the paperwork at the old plant. Health plan's a bit wonky, though. The doctor we wanted didn't take the job."

"I'll try not to get dead then." He winked.

Anna exhaled a chuckle tinted with sadness, and headed for the car.

Aaron let the cold nametag slip from his fingers into his pocket and grasped the door handle. Talis peered over the front seat with a demure smile for a second before facing forward. He bowed his head and let a long, silent sigh out his nostrils. It would only take a second to rip the E-

90 out of his jacket and end Talis. Archon couldn't possibly react in time to stop him. Anna needed him. He couldn't put a finger on why he believed that, but the gnawing feeling wouldn't leave him alone. That little girl saw the same things he had in her: sorrow, resignation, vulnerability, a person forced to be someone they weren't. If he killed Talis, he might be killing Anna too. He couldn't leave her with Archon.

Something wrong? asked Anna in his mind. *Are you coming?*

He pulled the car door open and got in. "Yeah."

Worry glimmered in her sapphire eyes. "I'm not sure I like that look."

Aaron bowed his head and tried to let go of vengeance, for her sake. Even if she didn't know it. Even if he couldn't have her. "I'm just peachy. This thing wif Talis ain't exactly the kinda thing I kin just drop."

Talis shrank in on herself.

Anna put a hand on his leg. "Archon knows what he's doing. He will protect us all."

Will he? Aaron glanced at her and put his hand on hers. "Aye. Let's go."

The car rose into the air and steered north. Going with 'The Awakened' could end wrong in a thousand different ways, but at least he felt as though he might do some good for Anna. He didn't trust Archon whatsoever, something about the man struck him as off. Mikhail's words rattled around Aaron's head. Could he trust his old mentor to get Division Zero back on his side? Aaron closed his eyes and let out an inaudible sigh.

Nothing for it but to try. Oy, Allie, could really use a hint about now.

fin

ACKNOWLEDGMENTS

Thanks for reading book five of The Awakened series!

I'd like to thank Mark Woodring – for being the editor every writer is overjoyed to work with.

Additional thanks to Jackson Tjota for the cover illustration, Ricky Gunawan for the interior art, and Alexandra Thompson for the cover layout.

ABOUT THE AUTHOR

Originally from South Amboy NJ, Matthew has been creating science fiction and fantasy worlds for most of his reasoning life. Since 1996, he has developed the "Divergent Fates" world, in which *Division Zero, Virtual Immortality, The Awakened Series, The Harmony Paradox, and the Daughter of Mars series* take place. Along with being an editor at Curiosity Quills press, he has worked in IT and technical support.

Matthew is an avid gamer, a recovered WoW addict, Gamemaster for two custom RPG systems, and a fan of anime, British humour, and intellectual science fiction that questions the nature of reality, life, and what happens after it.

He is also fond of cats.

Visit me online at:
    Facebook: https://www.facebook.com/MatthewSCoxAuthor
    Amazon: https://www.amazon.com/author/mscox
    Pinterest: https://www.pinterest.com/matthewcox10420/
    Goodreads: https://www.goodreads.com/author/show/7712730.Matthew_S_Cox
    Email: mcox2112@gmail.com

OTHER BOOKS BY MATTHEW S. COX

Divergent Fates Universe Novels

Division Zero series

- Division Zero
- Lex De Mortuis
- Thrall
- Guardian
- Harbinger

The Awakened series

- Prophet of the Badlands
- Archon's Queen
- Grey Ronin
- Daughter of Ash
- Zero Rogue
- Angel Descended

Daughter of Mars series

- The Hand of Raziel
- Araphel
- Ghost Black

Virtual Immortality series

- Virtual Immortality
- The Harmony Paradox

Prophet of the Badlands Series

- Prophet's Journey

Divergent Fates Anthology

(Fiction Novels - Adult)

The Roadhouse Chronicles Series

- One More Run
- The Redeemed
- Dead Man's Number

Faded Skies series

- Heir Ascendant
- Ascendant Unrest
- Ascendant Revolution

Temporal Armistice Series

- Nascent Shadow
- The Shadow Collector
- The Gate to Oblivion
- The Queen of Discord

Vampire Innocent series

- A Nighttime of Forever
- A Beginner's Guide to Fangs
- The Artist of Ruin
- The Last Family Road Trip
- The Phantom Oracle
- How Not to Summon Demons
- Ordinary Problems of a College Vampire
- A Vampire's Guide to Surviving Holidays
- An Introduction to Paranormal Diplomacy

Standalones

- Wayfarer: AV494
- Axillon99
- Chiaroscuro: The Mouse and the Candle

- The Spirits of Six Minstrel Run
- Sophie's Light
- The Far Side of Promise anthology
- Operation: Chimera (with Tony Healey)
- The Dysfunctional Conspiracy (with Christopher Veltmann)
- Of Myth and Shadow
- The Girl Who Found the Sun

Winter Solstice series (with J.R. Rain)

- Convergence
- Containment
- Catalyst

Alexis Silver series (with J.R. Rain)

- Silver Light
- Deep Silver
- Silver Quarrel

Samantha Moon Origins series (with J.R. Rain)

- New Moon Rising
- Moon Mourning

Vampire For Hire series (with J.R. Rain)

- Moon Master
- Dead Moon
- Lost Moon

Maddy Wimsey series (with J.R. Rain)

- The Devil's Eye
- The Drifting Gloom
- Dark Mercy

Samantha Moon Case Files series (with J.R. Rain)

- Blood Moon

Immortal Operative series (with J.R. Rain)

- Broken Ice

Four Elements series (with J.R. Rain)

- The Elementalist
- The Black Rose
- The Wakefield Curse

Young Adult Novels

The Eldritch Heart Series

- The Eldritch Heart
- The Cursed Crown

Evergreen Series

- Evergreen
- The World That Remains
- The Lucky Ones
- Nuclear Summer

Standalones

- Caller 107
- The Summer the World Ended
- Nine Candles of Deepest Black
- The Forest Beyond the Earth
- Out of Sight

Middle Grade Novels

The Adventures of Ubergirl series

- My Dad is a Mad Scientist
- Aliens Ate My Homework
- The End of all Halloweens

Tales of Widowswood series

- Emma and the Banderwigh
- Emma and the Silk Thieves
- Emma and the Silverbell Faeries
- Emma and the Elixir of Madness
- Emma and the Weeping Spirit

Standalones

- Citadel: The Concordant Sequence
- The Cursed Codex
- The Menagerie of Jenkins Bailey

www.ingramcontent.com/pod-product-compliance
Lightning Source LLC
Chambersburg PA
CBHW031119210626
46816CB00016B/1724